The Bloodvein Wand

Brimstone Chorus
Elizabeth J. Brown

Kobold Books

Contents

Kobold Books Limited
71-75 Shelton Street, Covent Garden
London, WC2H 9JQ
koboldbooks.com

Paperback ISBN: 978-1-0683978-1-3
Hardcover ISBN: 978-1-0683978-2-0
E-book ISBN: 978-1-0683978-0-6

Cover design by Ben Baldwin: www.benbaldwin.co.uk
Editing by Kate Gallagher: nerdgirledits.com

To my readers: without you, my writing would be nothing more than words on a page. You bring my stories to life.

Thank you.

Prologue

As the door to Banning Lawrence's safehouse swung shut behind him, Archibald Morgan rubbed his temples and sighed. The spell he'd used to stave off the poisons infecting the boy's mind had consumed a considerable amount of energy. But it was the emotional toll that had truly drained him. In ten years Banning would die, and it was Archibald who had sealed his fate.

He'd known from the outset that the boy was troubled, understandably so. To have his loved ones ripped away by a demon, to watch them in the throes of agony before drawing their final breath—it would break even the most resilient of minds. And with the essence of that same demon still festering inside Banning, threatening to overwhelm him every time his emotions had gotten the better of him, it was no surprise the boy's judgement had been clouded.

But never in a month of Sundays could Archibald have predicted how spectacularly Banning's inability to follow the most rudimentary of instructions had blown up in his face. Not only was Kar'roc's Maw inaccessible—ensconced within the belly of a hellhound... a hellhound in the custody of the Order of the Iron Seal no less—but Mundy Wilcoxson had been incarcerated, too.

The black-market cryptid trafficker had been tasked with securing an artefact for him. A very expensive one that had eluded Archibald for decades: the Bloodvein Wand. And just when it was within his reach, Banning had ruined everything. Two of the three remaining fragments of Solomon's stone—embedded within the dagger and wand respectively—had been snatched from his grasp. It was maddening.

Archibald was determined to find out whether the Bloodvein Wand was in the hands of O.O.T.I.S. After centuries of searching, centuries of planning, he wasn't about to leave anything else to chance. Not anymore.

Archibald headed towards the car. No sooner had he approached than his driver, Oliver, got out and opened the back door for him.

With a nod, Archibald climbed in. A dull *thunk* followed; the car dipped slightly as Oliver returned to the driver's seat and started the engine.

'Home, please, Oliver,' he said.

'Very good, sir.'

The soft rumble of the tyres faded into the background of Archibald's thoughts and the world outside his window became an inky-black blur.

'If I may say, sir,' Oliver said, meeting his eyes in the rear-view mirror, 'I believe Banning truly thought he was helping you.'

Archibald straightened up and held the man's gaze, the leather creaking lightly beneath him. 'I daresay you're right. Still, what's done is done.'

Oliver said nothing more, his focus returning to the road.

Exhaling deeply, Archibald dropped his head back and closed his eyes. He was exhausted. Two-hundred-and-sixty-eight years on this Earth. Today, he felt each and every one of them.

Absently, he rubbed at his neck, the raised black veins there meeting the brush of his fingertips. They were a reminder that, no matter how his time on Earth appeared to eat away at his very soul, each day was a blessing. A lesser man would have succumbed to the demon rot a lifetime ago. But he was no lesser man. His kind were born of dark energy from the realm of fire and shadow—gifted with the ability to harness it, to will it, to shape it. A rare and glorious poison permitted only to those strong enough to drink from its lethal chalice.

Of course, to do so too often was folly. His master, Black Barrow, had taught him that much. And yet... life always had a way of stacking the deck, turning what seemed like a winning hand into a series of unfortunate draws.

Archibald was running out of cards. No matter how strong he was or how skilled, he would also fall foul of the toxins corroding his body and mind. In fact, he'd convinced himself long ago that the only reason he still had control of his faculties was due to his sheer stubbornness. He had a goal, and he would realise it at any cost.

Time was a funny thing. He'd forgotten so many details over the centuries—the colour of his wife's eyes, the soft touch of her skin, the melody of her voice—yet, Archibald could still remember her gut-wrenching screams as they tore from her throat. Still remember the terror that contorted her beautiful face as the demon tried to rip their unborn child from her womb. And what had he done as his beloved had shrieked his name, begging for his help?

He'd frozen.

In spite of all his power, in spite of all his training, he'd been rendered useless, leaving himself open to the demon's assault. But Barrow? Barrow had hurled Archibald out of harm's way and saved his life. His master had been dragged through the split in reality, into the demon realm, in Archibald's stead.

Barrow had been like a father to him, sacrificing himself as if Archibald were his own blood. And it was the gravest mistake he could have made. Because of that single choice, that one act of pure emotion, the world was now coming apart at the seams.

The Brimstone Chorus—the end of days—was already in motion, and Barrow had been the catalyst. There was a cruel irony to it. From a young age, his master had instilled in Archibald that demons were not to be reckoned with. Treating with beings beyond the veil was to tempt fate itself. Even lesser demons posed a threat in their ability to breach the veil, given the right conditions. But they could be contained, banished, dealt with.

It was the stronger creatures, those whose raw power the veil actively repelled, that were the true danger. As a youth, Archibald had questioned the logic of it, but had never found an answer to fully satisfy his curiosity. Yet Barrow's warnings had stayed with him: 'There is always something waiting in the shadows to fill a void.'

A pang of shame twisted in his chest. How disappointed his master would be to look upon him now. The man he'd become was far removed from the apprentice the doctor had left behind. He had gone against Barrow's teachings, bartered with demons, made poor choices, done unspeakable things. And all the while, his master suffered in his place.

Black Barrow was an unyielding force, but the strength of the archdemon claiming dominion over him was immeasurable. It was only a matter of time before it eroded the last remnants of his master's soul. And when that day came, it would seize full control of his body, a body that, despite the veil's ancient protections, would rend reality apart and bring humanity to its knees.

It would be the end of civilisation. The end of everything.

It was inevitable.

And yet, if Archibald could locate the last remaining fragments of Solomon's stone and make it whole once more, there might still be hope. With the stone restored to its full strength, he'd have a chance of exerting control over the archdemon. A chance to save his master. The world. *His* world.

But time was running out.

His pursuit of Kar'roc's Maw could wait. For now, it was safe enough within the Order's headquarters. What he needed more was to locate the Bloodvein Wand. Banning's blunder had thrown a spanner in the works, especially with Mundy Wilcoxson now detained, but the wand had to be within reach. Few would recognise the artefact for what it truly was, let alone understand its immense potential.

Yes, all he needed to do was find it. Simple enough.

After all, it was probably just stowed in a box somewhere.

Chapter 1

Five Weeks Later

AT SOME POINT THE screams had stopped. Seconds ago? Minutes? He couldn't be sure. In the end, it didn't matter.

With a triumphant grin, Eric Pearson lifted the slippery organ up, sending warm rivulets of blood to trickle down his wrists and soak into the cuffs of his red ceremonial robes. He was so close. It was going to work this time; he could feel it.

And to think that before he'd found the book, he'd known nothing of other realms, of demons, of magic. *The Grimoire of Unholy Contracts and Spirits*. His discovery had changed everything. But the book alone wasn't enough. Not yet.

'Brothers,' Eric said, his icy breath fogging in the flickering candlelight. 'The time is nearly upon us.' He raised his voice to carry over the pitiful whimpers of the two caged women remaining.

A murmur of excitement rippled through the gathered men. They were his chosen few, oathbound to stand by his side as he cast off the shackles of mortal existence to ascend to greatness. In return, Eric would elevate them to heights they could only dream of, giving purpose to their, until now, unremarkable lives. One by one, they took their places around the ritualistic circle carved into the concrete cellar floor.

Stepping around the butchered corpse of the woman at his feet, Eric strode towards his Brothers, careful to maintain his grip on the slick liver. The heavy weight had surprised him the first time, but he was used to it now. He just hoped he hadn't damaged it too badly when he'd cut it loose. This had to work. He *needed* it to work. Each failed attempt only increased the risk of getting caught, and he wasn't going to let that happen. Not when everything he wanted was within reach.

The familiar whispers stirred inside his head. They were faint, barely a breath, but unmistakable. Like the quiet rasp of stone grinding against stone just beneath his consciousness.

The voices were pleased.

Crouching, Eric placed the organ at the centre of the designated arcane symbol. It had taken him hours to gouge that shape alone, chipping away at the concrete until it resembled what was inked in the pages of the book. The circle in its entirety had cost him days; the fruits of his labour so pitiful at first that he'd almost given up. But there was no mistaking the pattern now. Every line, every painstaking notch, had been charred into the floor—a reminder of his very first summoning and a promise of what was yet to come.

He straightened, wiping his gore-stained hands on his robes, and stepped back to join his Brothers at the circle's perimeter. His gaze swept over the intricate sigils one last time, to ensure all of the other symbolic artefacts—the bird skull, the feather, the shard of mirror and the copper key—were still perfectly aligned. Satisfied, he nodded.

'Brothers, are we ready?'

Not a word was spoken. Instead, each of them bowed their heads in turn, faces obscured by the shadows cast by their cowls.

'Then let us begin.'

The chanting started as it always did, softly at first then rising until his Brothers' voices and his became a single, rhythmic droning sound.

Heat bloomed at his collarbone where the blackened veins throbbed, carving intricate patterns beneath the pale landscape of his flesh. They were a "gift" from the demon. A permanent reminder that he must fulfil his end of the bargain.

Within minutes the first symbol blazed, flooding the cellar with an ethereal blue light. The stench of scorched meat filled his nostrils. He glanced down as the sizzling organ blackened and shrivelled, the strength of his voice unwavering.

This was it. It was happening!

The second symbol flared into life, followed immediately by the third, fourth, and fifth, until each one of them pulsed with radiant magic. An unseen force surged upward with a sound like a thousand blades being drawn, enclosing the circle in a rippling barrier that warped the air within. Eric could feel its power—a quivering pressure that skipped across his skin and made the hairs on his body bristle.

A grin split his face.

Eric reached into the inner pocket of his robes, closed his fist around the crystal wand and pulled it free. The sight of it exhilarated him, as much now as it had the day he'd first laid eyes upon it. The wand was crude in design: a shaft of frayed copper wire wound down a translucent length of partially exposed quartz. But what it lacked in aesthetics it made up for in value. He examined the ruby-red gemstone set into the knots of burnished metal. The *pièces de résistance*—a fragment of Solomon's stone.

Specks of crimson light refracted through its facetted surface, eager flashes of recognition that danced across his hand. Eric shifted his grip slightly, scarcely registering the pinpricks of pain as the splayed ends of copper sank deep into his flesh.

He didn't need to see his Brothers' faces to know they were watching him. Their voices became louder, rising in fervour with every repetition.

The air within the circle groaned, a cavernous judder that resonated through the building. The shockwave scattered fragments of plaster and brick dust across the floor. Something shimmered before Eric's eyes, distorting the space around it.

And then it happened. The fabric of reality ruptured. Torrents of choking black smog flooded the space inside the barrier, whirling and eddying against the invisible walls of its confines.

Yes! Yes!

The whispers surged forward, no longer content to remain in the periphery of his mind. Like a tempest, they raged inside his skull. Urging him to continue. Demanding success.

Eric thrust the wand at the barrier. The stench of sulphur became overwhelming, clinging to the back of his throat and bringing tears to his eyes, but still he repeated the words of the incantation.

'Vamonthir, warden of secrets, heed my call. Vamonthir, guardian of forbidden knowledge, I summon thee. Vamonthir, keeper of hidden truths, I beseech thee: appear!'

The wand quivered in his grip. He'd scarcely felt the wire carving bloody channels into his flesh before, but he could feel it now. His palm was becoming slick, with blood seeping between his fingers and dribbling down his hand. The wand drank its fill. The ruby gemstone was ablaze, a vibrant beacon against the backdrop of putrid miasma spewing from the void inside the barrier. But it was the crystal beyond the copper binding that transfixed Eric. Crimson threads, drawn from his own sacrifice, snaked through the quartz, pulsing in time with the beat of his heart, like exposed veins.

It was working. It was really working! He was going to change his fate. Become something more. Something worthy. Something powerful. Never again would he be forced to cower under the fists of another. Never again would he bow to the whims of the weak, the petty, the undeserving. No more fear, no more submission—only power, absolute and eternal.

Without warning, the red light of the gemstone winked out. At the heart of the crystal, the scarlet tendrils of his blood began to fade, retreating from its core until they paled to become nothing more than sorry pink streaks.

He snapped his gaze to the circle. His eyes widened.

No!

The rift contracted in on itself, atrophying until all that remained was a purling black haze. The blue glow of the symbols guttered out, the wall of energy collapsing. Clouds of dust billowed out across the concrete floor, extinguishing the candles and plunging the room into darkness.

The rustling of robes was quickly followed by the bloom of light from an LED lantern.

'No…' Eric lunged forward, grasping wildly at the empty space where the tear in the veil between realities had been. '*No!*' White-hot rage enveloped him. He let out a bellow, hurling the wand against the concrete. It clattered across the floor, sliding to a stop at the feet of one of his Brothers.

Striding forward, Eric rounded on the man. His breathing was ragged, his chest heaving. He bunched his fists into the rough fabric of his Brother's robes, jerking him forward violently. 'What happened? What fucking happened?'

'I—I don't know,' the man stammered, his cowl falling back to expose his shock. He bowed his head to stare at the floor.

Eric whirled, the vein in his neck throbbing as he took in each of his Brothers' faces. Not one of them met his eyes.

Cowards.

'Well? Is someone going to tell me what the fuck happened?'

The shuffling of robes was his only answer.

Rolling his neck, Eric took a deep, shuddering breath, and released it through clenched teeth.

'We were so close,' he muttered. Taking another breath, he shook his head and bent to retrieve the wand. He winced when he noticed the small chip in the crystal. He'd let his temper get the better of him. *Again*. At least the gemstone was unscathed. According to the book, that was the true source of the wand's power anyway.

Straightening, he returned the item to his pocket and surveyed the mess. The room was coated in a layer of grime. The discarded beer kegs, the empty plastic crates, the stacks of metal-framed chairs—all of it covered. Even the whitewashed brickwork had been turned dingy grey.

He scowled at the two imprisoned women. They recoiled, edging back as far as the cages would allow.

'Again,' Eric said.

When no one responded, he turned around. His Brothers shifted uneasily on the spot, scatterings of dust falling from their robes.

'I *said* again.' He pointed to the cage on the left, his action eliciting a muffled sob from the woman cowering inside.

The men exchanged nervous glances, something unsaid passing between them, until one dared to step forward. Ben Cunningham, tall and lanky, stooped slightly as he did. His mouth hung open in that aggravating way that made him look perpetually clueless.

Ben said, 'Please Brother, it's getting late.'

'Late?' Eric replied.

The whispers rustled in his mind, like dry leaves caught in a breeze. They were disappointed.

Ben continued, nervously smoothing his unruly, mousy-blond hair. 'It's just my wife will be wondering—'

'Your wife, Brother Cunningham?' Eric marched across the circle, the hem of his robes snagging on a few still-smoking candles. It sent them scattering across the concrete. Ben flinched as Eric stopped just in front of him. He held his thumb and index finger inches apart. 'We're this close to gaining untold power. This close to being granted abilities that will set us apart from the rest of mankind. And you're worried about your *wife*?'

'You don't understand, she get's really mad when—'

Eric backhanded Ben across the face.

The man staggered back, eyes bulging in disbelief. He brought his fingers to his bloodied mouth, the colour draining from his face. His lips remained parted in that slack-jawed look of confusion that made Eric's teeth itch.

That dumbfounded expression ignited a fresh fire inside Eric's chest. Before his next thought could fully form, Eric was on him, raining blow after frenzied blow until the other men pulled him away.

'Please, Brother, I think there's another way,' one said.

Eric shook free of their grip and turned to glare at the speaker. 'Another way?' he spat, forcing the words through gasping breaths. 'Brother Bains, have you been keeping things from me *yet again?*'

'There's a gatekeeper—'

'A *gatekeeper?* And you're only telling me this *now?*'

His Brother's mouth gaped briefly as he considered his response. At least he had the decency to look sufficiently chastised. He'd always presented as intelligent, tactical, but how much of that had been a show for Eric's benefit? Cruelty Eric understood. Of the four Brothers before him, he trusted Tommo, the cruellest of them all. Even Sean's depravity and the spineless Ben's simple-mindedness had become reliable tools. But when the lines between being pragmatic and calculating blurred so easily, that's when things became dangerous.

After a moment, his Brother knocked his hood back from his head and gave a small shrug. 'I thought this would work.'

'So, then we find the gatekeeper.'

'There's one problem.'

'Which is?'

'The gatekeeper's being held inside O.O.T.I.S headquarters.'

The Order of the Iron Seal.

A collective gasp broke out around him, followed immediately by several hushed comments. He shot his Brothers a look, commanding their silence.

A gatekeeper?

Throwing a gatekeeper into the mix would change everything. No more ritualistic circles. No more human sacrifice. No more clandestine meetings in the cellar of a derelict pub. A gatekeeper would guarantee their success. Would guarantee that he'd be awarded the gifts promised to him by the book.

He'd be respected. Feared. Worshipped. He'd be a god.

Yes, everything was falling into place. Just one more hurdle and the world would be his.

Stroking his jaw, Eric smiled and turned to Ben, who was clutching at his face and making gurgled, wheezing noises.

'Brother Cunningham, tell your wife you're tied up for the next few hours. We have plans to make.'

He'd come this far; he wasn't going to let a little thing like O.O.T.I.S get in his way.

Chapter 2

KILL HER.

Charlie flinched as Chekonost's strident voice scraped inside his skull, like fingernails down a blackboard.

I told you to shut up.

He smoothed his face into a neutral expression and glanced around the open-plan office, to make sure that no one was watching him. The last thing he needed was another person asking if he was okay. They'd think he was losing it. Except, it was closer to the truth than he cared to admit.

AND I TOLD YOU TO KILL HER.

Charlie regarded his colleague. For years she'd sat at the desk beside his, her acrylic nails *tap, tap, tapping* against the keyboard—a sound that had grated on his nerves at first. Over time, though, he'd grown accustomed to it, until it blended seamlessly into the backdrop of his working days. She'd become a fixture: a constant presence in the predictable rhythm of his routine. And if there was one thing Charlie valued above all else, it was routine. The fact that she was one of the few team members who could make a decent cup of coffee didn't hurt, either.

She'd even been there the day Jacqueline Fletcher—sole survivor of the Wilcott Road cemetery murders—had made him realise that Stephen was the Caravan Cannibal. It had turned his world upside down, and everything that followed had led to this moment. The day was shaping up to be yet another low point in the unrelenting shit show his life had become, since the demon that had once possessed his now-dead friend became trapped inside his head.

Of course, he had no one to blame but himself. Using the incantation stolen from *Ritualistic Sacrifice in Ancient Magical Practices* to banish the demonic essence back into Kar'roc's Maw had been *his* idea. Becoming the dagger's master had been *his* idea. If he had not done that, Banning Lawrence wouldn't have kidnapped his family to extort the Maw from him. And he wouldn't have become host to the very essence he despised. If he'd known then what he knew now, would he still have made the same choice?

I'm not killing Rosie.

SHE IS EATING YOUR CAKE.

As if on cue, Rosie brought a generous slice of vanilla sponge to her mouth and took a bite, pale crumbs clinging to her lips before she licked them clean. She wasn't the only one; several others milled around, paper plates in hand, chatting as they helped themselves. Over the past few hours, the table had become a chaotic spread of scattered crumbs, discarded napkins, and half-empty cups. Charlie had already tried tidying it up once, his OCD begging he restore some order, but he'd been shooed away with a laugh and a dismissive wave.

It's not my *cake.*

He tugged absently at the polished black ring on his little finger—a gift from Auntie that, in the weeks since he'd put it on, refused to come off. Christ, as if becoming master of the Maw hadn't been bad enough, now he was stuck with this eyesore. What it did he had no bloody clue, but according to the letter left to him by the elderly, blind soul keeper, he'd know when the time came.

IT HAS YOUR NAME ON IT.

Charlie's gaze dropped to the hand-piped, blue frosted lettering that spelt out his name. His forehead creased.

SEE? IT LITERALLY HAS YOUR NAME ON IT.

It's for everyone.

Truth be told, he hadn't even tasted it. Just the sight made his stomach turn. Not because he didn't enjoy cake—what kind of monster didn't enjoy cake?—but because of what it represented.

There's no way I could eat an entire cake by myself.

NOT WITH THAT ATTITUDE.

Sighing, Charlie resisted the urge to shake his head. He checked his watch. It wouldn't be long before this gathering was over.

'I don't think I've ever seen so many people in here at once.'

Charlie looked up at the sound of DI Clarke's voice. He'd been so distracted by the demon's constant stream of complaints and petulant remarks that he hadn't even noticed his supervisor approach.

'I was wondering whether you were going to leave your office today,' Charlie said.

The DI shook his hand with a chuckle. 'I wouldn't have missed this for the world. Honestly, I never thought I'd see the day—the great Charlie Haynes retiring.'

The words landed like a punch to the gut, but he forced a smile. 'Technically, this is my second retirement.'

Clarke nodded amiably. 'Are you absolutely sure there's nothing we can do to tempt you to stay?'

'I wish there was. But it's time I put my feet up, spend a bit more time with my family, and watch my granddaughter grow up.' His delivery was flawless, the lines so well-rehearsed, he didn't miss a beat.

'Can't say I blame you. We're going to miss you around here.' Clarke positioned himself next to Charlie, taking in the office's occupants, and cleared his throat.

Oh shit...

Charlie felt his mouth go dry. Before he could voice his protests, Clarke raised his hands, motioning for silence.

The conversations died down. Within an instant, all eyes were on Charlie. Warmth flushed his cheeks.

WHAT IS HAPPENING? WHY HAS YOUR HEART RATE INCREASED?

He shifted uncomfortably, ignoring Chekonost's question.

'I'll keep this brief—unlike Charlie's career with the police.' That drew a few laughs. Clarke gave him a wink. 'Most of you know Charlie through his work in the unsolved crimes unit. But some of you—those old enough to remember *The Thin Blue Line* when it first aired—will remember him as a detective. If it wasn't for this man,'—he gripped Charlie's shoulder like a proud father, which, given his DI had to be at least twenty years his junior, only deepened Charlie's embarrassment—'there'd be some seriously nasty people still at large today.'

Murmurs of agreement rang around the office, and more than one cheer.

'The Greenhithe Ripper, the Butcher of Medway, the Carter Twins, the Cathedral Strangler.' The DI released Charlie, counting on his fingers as he reeled off the monikers. 'And let's not forget his most recent triumph, the Caravan Cannibal.'

TRIUMPH. The demon scoffed. DUMB LUCK. IF IT WEREN'T FOR YOUR PREDECESSOR'S CRIPPLED BODY, I WOULD HAVE GUTTED YOU LIKE A FISH. IT IS JUST MY LUCK THAT BOTH MY HOSTS HAVE BEEN SUBPAR SPECIMENS OF HUMAN VERMIN.

Charlie stiffened.

DI Clarke stepped forward to grab a glass of orange juice off the food-laden desk. He raised it in the air, allowing enough time for everyone else to follow suit, then said, 'To Charlie!'

A chorus of 'To Charlie!' rang throughout the crowd.

When the din subsided, the DI gestured to Rosie, who waddled forward clutching a gift bag. She handed it to Charlie, beaming as he accepted it.

'Just a little something from all of us,' she said.

'Uh, thank you.' Under the collective stare of his colleagues—*former* colleagues—Charlie opened it. Inside was a rough, hessian bottle bag. He pulled it out, a smile spreading across his face as he read the word *Lagavulin* printed on the fabric. 'Thank you, this—'

'Open it properly,' Rosie interrupted, her voice hitched with excitement.

Carefully, Charlie pulled the bottle free. His jaw dropped. This was no ordinary bottle of Lagavulin; this was a Fèis Île 2016. It must have cost them a few hundred quid.

He traced his thumb over the raised lettering on the brown glass, his eyes scanning the label. A few flabbergasted seconds passed before he remembered to feign a squint. It was easy to forget that, just months ago, he'd needed reading glasses. That was before he'd become master of that damned dagger. Now, his vision was sharp, every detail in crisp focus, no matter the distance.

'I...' Swallowing past the lump lodged in his throat, he glanced up. 'I don't know what to say. Thank you. This is incredible. Working with you all has been one of the highlights of my life. Kent Police has been a second home to me, and you a second family. I'll miss seeing you all around the station. Granted, I won't miss how the aircon always seems to be stuck on arctic blast, or whatever it is Lee insists on microwaving for lunch every day.' He pointed at the man; laughter erupted at Lee's spluttered protests and feigned offence. 'But I really will miss working with everybody.' Charlie's voice broke. He cleared his throat, his heart heavy with sadness. 'Thank you.'

THIS IS YOUR OWN DOING.

Charlie's smile faltered. He slid the bottle of Lagavulin back inside the hessian bag, using the movement to mask his unease at the wave of applause.

I HAVE ALREADY TOLD YOU, ALL YOU NEED TO DO IS FIND THE GATEKEEPER. THEN, ONCE MY ESSENCE IS RETURNED TO MY BODY, YOU WOULD BE FREE TO LIVE OUT THE REMAINDER OF YOUR PATHETIC LITTLE LIFE AS YOU SEE FIT.

Be quiet.

He was sick to the back teeth of hearing about the damned gatekeeper. Ever since they'd laid eyes on the young, blond man inside O.O.T.I.S headquarters, the demon had been relentless—demanding on a daily basis that Charlie drop everything and find a way to reach him. Christ, they'd only seen the lad for a few seconds. That was over a month ago. Granted, Charlie still remembered the vivid green of the boy's eyes, and the way the sigil had reacted to his presence. Even if he'd wanted to get to him, there was no way Charlie would make it past the black suits guarding him.

Clenching his left hand into a fist, Charlie tried to ignore the phantom throb from the three raised dots to the left of the convex line scarring the flesh between his thumb and index finger.

IT BENEFITS US BOTH.

Shut. Up.

The demon fell silent, its frustration seeping through their mental connection.

The DI placed his empty glass down on the table. 'Well, I'm afraid I'm going to have to love you and leave you, Charlie. Some of us still have work to do.'

No coaster, condensation already pooling against the laminate. Charlie's eye twitched at the sight of it. He clenched his jaw, forcing himself to ignore it.

'I suppose you'll be stopping for a pint at the Cricketers with a few of the others after you're done here?' Clarke asked.

'No, no.' Charlie waved away the suggestion. 'It's my daughter's birthday today. I'm under strict instructions to pick up a few bits before I head over to hers. Evie, my granddaughter, wants us to pull out all the stops. It'll be my last weekend there before I move back into my own place.'

In truth, the repairs had been finished weeks ago—each brief visit to tend to his fish showing the steady progress—but Evie had begged him to stay until the party. While Charlie had cherished the extra time with his daughter and granddaughter, he knew that wasn't the real reason he had delayed his return home.

The demon had destroyed more than just the physical structure of his house; it had severed every emotional tie he'd once had to the place. He'd been beaten within an inch of his life there. He'd become bound to Kar'roc's Maw there. But worse than anything else, he'd watched Stephen die there.

By the end, Stephen had begged Charlie to end his suffering—a broken, desperate, and utterly defeated man. It had shattered Charlie's pained heart to see him like that. The thought of returning, of sleeping mere feet from where his best friend had taken his final, agonised breath, filled him with a dread so visceral, it made him feel physically sick.

Clarke chuckled. 'Two parties in one day? The perks of retirement, eh?'

Suppressing a wince, Charlie motioned at the gathered crowd. 'Thank you. I really appreciate all this.'

'Don't thank me, it was Rosie who organised everything. But seriously, if you ever change your mind, the door's always open.' With a final good-natured clap on the back, DI Clarke eased his way through the throng of people to his office, exchanging a few pleasantries along the way.

Charlie glanced across the room to where Rosie had returned to her slice of cake. He met her eyes and waggled the gift bag, mouthing *thank you*. She nodded in return, before popping the last chunk of sponge into her mouth and turning back towards the table of food.

'How're you holding up?'

Jasmin Khatri appeared beside him. She flashed him a grin, knowing full well that being the centre of attention was his idea of hell.

'Honestly? I was ready to leave hours ago.'

'Don't be such a grouch. All these people are here for you. It's nice. Shows how much everyone thinks of you around here.' She nodded at the gift bag, dark eyebrow arched, blue eyes sparkling mischievously. 'Just in case it wasn't obvious from that bottle clutched in your hands.'

He grunted a reply.

Jasmin tsked. 'Don't give me that scowl, I see right through you.'

His lips quirked into a smile.

Nudging her sleeve up, Jasmin checked her watch. 'Look, give me half an hour or so to sort a few things out, then I'll help you take your stuff down to the car. Okay?'

'Sure.' Charlie watched her leave, her gait thrown off by her limp. It was much better than it had been just weeks ago. At least now she could walk without having to stop every few yards, or her face contorting with pain. Even so, it was a reminder of how he'd nearly lost her, nearly lost his family. Nearly lost everything. From what he'd been told, Banning Lawrence's body was never recovered, meaning he was most likely still out there somewhere. Just the thought of it made his blood boil.

His jaw clenched. Instinctively, he reached for the ring on his finger, tracing the outline of the diamond set into the polished black band.

The presence within his mind stirred. It always seemed to react to his emotions—anger especially—riling him up, egging him on, like it wanted to see just how far it could push him before he snapped. It was becoming harder and harder to control, a constant distraction that impaired his ability to focus. And the demon knew it.

It was deliberate. A game. And so far, it was winning. It was trying to take everything from him. First his career, then what—his sanity? His life?

THIS IS OUTRAGEOUS!

Charlie relaxed the tense muscles in his face and blinked.

What?

ARE YOU BLIND? LOOK.

Knowing that Chekonost could only see what was in his line of sight, Charlie scanned the area in front of him with a frown. Nothing appeared to be out of the ordinary.

As if feeling his gaze, Rosie turned, plate in hand, and gave him a small wave. He waved back, still none the wiser about the demon's outburst.

I don't see anything.

THAT IS HER SECOND SLICE OF CAKE.

Christ.

Ignoring the continued complaints, Charlie returned his attention to his desk, and the two cardboard boxes that contained the last physical reminders of his presence within the station.

Two boxes.

A lifetime with the police and this was all he had to show for it.

He slid his finger along the edges of the perfectly aligned stack of notebooks, then paused. His hand hovered above his business cards. Removing one from the box, he scanned the familiar text with a sigh.

This wasn't what he wanted. None of it was. But how in the hell could he rid himself of the demon without O.O.T.I.S finding out? He had no chance of getting anywhere near the gatekeeper, not while it was secured within their headquarters. And even if he did manage it, Charlie didn't fancy his odds against the black suits. He damned sure wasn't about to risk getting thrown in a cell for God knows how long. It was bad enough they still insisted he have regular check-ups to monitor the effects of the dagger. Never mind the fact they still had him under surveillance.

No, he'd have to find another way. There had to be a book. A spell or something...

Tucking the business cards into his trouser pocket, he made a mental note to bring it up with Diane. As long as he kept his wits about him and didn't expose his secret, maybe he could coax the information out of her.

Not that it would be easy.

Things between him and Diane had been awkward ever since he'd turned down her offer of a dinner date. He'd wanted to accept, *God*, had he wanted to... But with the demon that murdered her husband taking up residence inside his brain, there was no way that could happen. It's not like he could avoid her—she was still his handler after all—and truth be told he didn't want to. He enjoyed her company, and it was obvious that she felt the same way. But between every flirtatious glance and lingering touch was Chekonost.

The demon despised her. Despised him. Despised the whole human race. And with the constant stream of vile rhetoric resounding inside his skull, just holding a simple conversation with Diane was hard enough. He didn't want to lose her, but until he could rid himself of the entity permanently, he had nothing to offer her.

Still, that didn't mean he couldn't ask her a couple of questions. And, if he found the answers he was looking for, the first thing he'd do once Chekonost was gone was whisk her away for a lavish meal.

All he had to do was not fuck it up.

Chapter 3

'PLEASE, JOSH, YOU HAVE to get me out of here...'

Joshua glanced back at the stairs. The dim glow of the LED lantern cast wavering light across the damp, crumbling brick walls of the derelict pub's cellar. Shuffling forward on his knees, his red robes trailing through the dust-coated concrete, he edged closer to the cage and pressed his palms against the bars. Sophie's grime-caked fingers clasped his hands through the gaps. The chill of her skin made him flinch.

'I c-c-can't, Soph. I... I just can't.' He bowed his head, tears pricking at the corners of his eyes. There was nothing he could do. He knew it. Sophie knew it. He was useless. He'd always been useless. Letting his sister down time after time, ever since they were kids.

'You can! Please, Josh, he's going to kill me.'

'No.' He shook his head emphatically. 'Eric's our brother. He would never hurt you.'

'He's not our brother—'

'H-he is!'

'*You're* my brother, Josh. Eric locked me in a fucking cage. Eric butchered those other women.'

The empty cages hadn't escaped his attention, but until this very second, Josh hadn't allowed himself to contemplate what that meant. They had begun with five women. Now, it was just Sophie and one other, who had curled in on herself and was sobbing quietly.

'He won't hurt you, Sophie. H-h-he won't. He won't.' He repeated the words as though it were a mantra bolstering his conviction.

'Look at me. Josh. *Look* at me!' Sophie's breath fogged in the chill, a sour-white cloud that dissipated in the mildew-filled air.

Swallowing, he did.

His sister's brown eyes were red-rimmed; the dirt on her cheeks had pale, glistening tears running through it. Her hair, once a lustrous chestnut colour, now hung lank and greasy around her face. Her clothes were filthy, and somehow she'd managed to rip her jumper. That wasn't good. Not when it was so cold down here. Within the shadows of the tattered fabric, where the contours of her ribs protruded, he could see goose bumps on her exposed skin. He felt the quiver of her fingers as they clung to his. He heard the chatter of her teeth behind cracked lips that were so blue, they looked bruised. She was freezing.

He'd given her a coat the last time. Eric must've taken it away. It was what their mother used to do to them as children, when she'd been upset—take away their coats, their shoes. Oftentimes, she would make them stand outside in the bitter cold until they lost all feeling in their fingers and toes.

That was a lifetime ago. That was when he and Sophie had shared almost everything: the same dark hair, dark eyes and scrawny builds. They'd always been small for their age. Sophie, two years younger, had been especially tiny. But that made sense, given there had never been enough food. Sophie had filled out in her teens, her limbs becoming proportional to the rest of her. Josh had carried on growing, all elbows and knees, always looking half-starved even into adulthood—not that he felt much like an adult at twenty-three.

He'd be lying if he said Sophie's good looks hadn't made him a little jealous. But to see her now with sunken hollows for cheeks and the sharp angles of her collarbones, it was heartbreaking.

He choked back a sob.

Eric *had* to have a reason for treating their sister like this. Josh didn't fully understand it, but there had to be one. Eric had always looked out for them, always protected them. He'd been the one to root through the bins for scraps when their stomachs were empty; he'd been the one to take the beatings whenever their mother's temper flared. All he'd ever done was keep them safe. Whatever this was—whatever Eric was doing—it had to be his way of protecting Sophie. Of protecting *them*.

Sophie gripped his hand tighter. 'Josh, you have to listen to me. Eric's going to kill me. Something's wrong with him. Ever since he found that book, he's changed.'

Josh winced. It was *his* fault Eric had found the book in the first place. It was just supposed to be a little courier job, a way to make ends meet. How could he have known it would lead to this?

She continued, 'You have to get me out of here before it's too late. I don't want to die here, Josh. Please, I don't want to die.' Sophie began to weep, her body convulsing in the confined space of her prison.

'H-h-he wouldn't. He wouldn't.'

Sophie cried out in frustration, ripping her hands free from his to slam them against the bars. Josh flinched back. The clatter caused the other woman to jerk upright with a startled yelp.

'Soph, stop! They'll hear you.' He glanced back at the stairs again.

The colour drained from the other woman's face as she took in Josh. She scrabbled back, her feet kicking wildly. But there was nowhere for her to go. The cages were little more than heavy-duty dog crates. They were not intended for anything larger than a Great Dane.

He wanted to reassure her, to let her know he wasn't a threat, but the words wouldn't come. Josh knew what she saw when she looked at him. A captor. A tyrant. But he wasn't either of those things. Just because he wore the robes, just because he had the same face as his twin brother, it didn't mean he was one of them. He hadn't meant for any of this to happen. If he'd known then what he knew now, he'd have destroyed that book the first time he laid eyes on it. But it was too late. Eric had found it. He'd never been able to hide anything from Eric.

'Josh, I can't stay here anymore. I can't stay here with him and his loser friends. You *need* to get me out. Please,

Josh. Before he comes back. *Please*. He's going to kill me.' There was an edge to Sophie's voice now, a flush in her cheeks that betrayed her anger. 'Do you understand that, Josh? He's going to kill me. I'm going to die. And it'll be *your* fault.'

He clapped his hands over his ears. Josh shook his head, flinching back from the cage. 'N-n-no. No. That's not... I'm not...'

Sophie's eyes bulged, her expression morphing into shock, then realisation, then fear.

'I'm sorry, Josh. I'm *sorry*. I didn't mean it.'

He squeezed his eyes shut, pulled his knees in against his chest, and rocked where he sat. 'No. No, no, no.'

'Josh, I didn't mean it. I just got angry. I'm sorry.'

Focusing on the sound of his heartbeat calmed him. Josh sucked down a breath. He held it there for a count of ten, then released it, exhaling loudly through his mouth. After a few repetitions, his pulse slowed. He opened his eyes.

Sophie was staring at him, her body tense. 'Josh?'

'I'm sorry, Soph.'

She visibly relaxed, slumping back against the cage. It shuddered against her weight, stirring up a puff of dirt that drifted lazily across the plastic tray beneath her.

Only the sounds of worried breathing broke the silence.

Finally, Josh sighed; with it his body sagged. Maybe Sophie was right. Maybe Eric really was too far gone.

'What can I do? Even if I d-did help you, he knows where to find you. You'd have to leave. Your home, your job, everything. You'd have to start all over again. You'd have to l-l-leave me.' He swiped at his eyes with the cuff of his sleeve, then recoiled when he noticed the dark stains discolouring the fabric.

Shuddering, he refocused on his sister. 'I tried to keep you safe, Soph. I really did. All I've ever wanted is to keep you safe.'

'I know.' Her reply was barely a whisper. She reached for him again, her bottom lip trembling. 'I don't want to leave you, but you didn't see what he did to the others. He's lost it. Completely lost it. He's not the same anymore. He's not the Eric we grew up with.'

'Okay. Okay, I'll think of a way to h-h-help you. Maybe if—'

A floorboard creaked overhead, followed by heavy footsteps. They were headed for the cellar.

Josh pushed himself to his feet, rapidly brushing the grey streaks of dust from his robes, and stepped away from the cages. Unsure of what to do with himself, he scurried towards one of the metal-framed chairs set apart from the rest of the stack and perched on its edge.

The door swung open, allowing a wave of artificial light to stream in. The figure—Tommo judging by the height and broad shoulders—entered with a mumbled curse. He trudged down the first few steps. The glow of the lantern in his hands harried the shadows, causing them to warp and stretch away from him. Tommo sniffed, nose wrinkling in disgust, and glanced at the captive women. Muttering, he scanned the room, his blue eyes falling on the dark corner where Josh sat.

'Eric, is that you?'

He shone the light in his direction. Josh didn't reply. Then Tommo took another step forward, causing Josh to flinch.

Tommo huffed and shook his head. 'Joshua. What are you doing down here?'

'I... I... N-n-nothing.'

Tommo's ginger eyebrows drew together. He surveyed the cellar again, as if searching for evidence of wrongdoing, before turning his attention to Sophie. Glaring, he stomped towards her cage and gave it a quick once over—yanking on the padlocks and giving the bars a cursory shake. Satisfied that it was still secure, he addressed Josh again.

'Joshua,' he said, closing the distance between them. 'Come back upstairs. I need to talk to Eric about tomorrow.'

'I, uh... I don't—' Tommo's fingers clamping around his arm cut off his reply. He hauled Josh to his feet.

'Now.' Tommo released him with a scowl and stalked back up the creaking stairs, leaving him with little choice but to follow.

Rubbing at his bruised flesh, Josh glanced back at Sophie. She shook her head, fresh tears spilling down her cheeks.

He felt her eyes on him until the moment the cellar door swung shut behind him.

He'd let her down. *Again.*

Chapter 4

IT WAS A STRANGE feeling, walking through the station for what would be the very last time.

Charlie slowed his pace, memorising the sterile white walls, the sharp lines, the wide open-plan spaces that had always felt cold and unwelcoming. He'd hated how corporate this building was, a far cry from the rustic charm of the smaller police stations where he'd begun his career. Yet now, as finality pressed down on him, he would miss the damned place—LED lights and all.

IT DIDN'T HAVE TO BE THIS WAY.

Jolting out of his reverie, Charlie adjusted the cardboard box in his hands, tightening his grip on it.

YOU BROUGHT THIS ON YOURSELF.

His jaw tightened. No matter how hard he tried, there was no ignoring the discordant voice that tore through his thoughts day in, day out. The demon was relentless, twisting the knife every chance it got. His second retirement hadn't been a choice; with his wretched passenger spewing its poison inside his skull, there was no way in hell he could have kept working.

FIND THE GATEKEEPER, AND YOU WON'T HAVE TO LIVE LIKE THIS ANYMORE. YOU OWE ME.

Owe you?

I SAVED YOUR DAUGHTER AND GRANDDAUGHTER. THIS IS THE LEAST YOU CAN DO.

Charlie took a breath. He *really* didn't need this right now.

You only did that because I used the dagger to force you to.

BUT I DID IT.

I owe you nothing. You murdered people. You tried to murder me!

THAT WAS MONTHS AGO.

The sound of teeth grinding filled Charlie's ears. He relaxed the muscles in his face and exhaled. There was no point trying to reason with the entity, it was unhinged. How Stephen had managed to cling on to any shred of humanity after over three decades of listening to its toxic drivel, he had no idea.

STEPHEN?

A familiar feeling of contempt rolled through him.

I GAVE STEPHEN EVERYTHING HE WANTED. REVENGE. RETRIBUTION. JUSTICE.

No. You turned him into a monster. Used him to slaughter scores of innocent people.

INNOCENT? Sardonic laughter pervaded Charlie's mind, growing with intensity until the demon spoke again. I HELPED HIM HUNT DOWN THE PEOPLE WHO MURDERED HIS FAMILY. THAT'S MORE THAN I CAN SAY FOR YOU. WHAT DID YOU DO TO HELP YOUR SO-CALLED FRIEND? NOTHING!

Dull pain radiated through Charlie's fingers. He looked down to see he'd crushed the edges of the cardboard box.

STEPHEN WANTED THEM TO DIE. TO SUFFER. HE ENJOYED IT.

No.

YES. AND YOU WILL, TOO. YOU'LL END UP JUST LIKE HIM. A *MONSTER*. WITH EVERY PASSING SECOND THE DAGGER'S HOLD ON YOU STRENGTHENS. YOU CAN FEEL IT HAPPENING, I KNOW YOU CAN. YOU SHALL BECOME NOTHING MORE THAN A SLAVE TO KAR'ROC'S WILL. A THREAT TO ALL THOSE AROUND YOU. MEGHAN. EVELYN.

Enough!

Charlie staggered towards the door, his mind reeling. He didn't want to think about the Maw, how it was changing him—physically, mentally, emotionally. The Order's records were extensive, but they focused on the dagger's usage, not its connection to its master. According to them, nothing had been documented about the toll it took on those who wielded it. But the changes were undeniable. The dagger had enhanced his eyesight. His hearing. Christ, it had even altered his blood. And that was before he'd decided to play host to the demon inside it.

What was it Auntie had said? That if he didn't strengthen his soul, his connection to the demon realm would eat away at his mind, piece by piece, until he was little more than a puppet.

How the hell was he supposed to strengthen his soul? Was it already too late? Jesus—what was going to happen to him?

The rapid beat of his heart hammered inside his skull. He gulped down a breath, then another.

It wasn't enough.

He needed to get outside.

Fumbling with the box, he slammed into the exit door, groping for the handle with a clammy hand. It swung open. He lurched through it, just about keeping his balance as the sounds of the outside world enveloped him.

'Whoa, you alright, fella?'

Charlie's head whipped up at the sound of the voice. A uniformed officer approached, unlit cigarette in hand.

Righting himself, Charlie nodded. 'Yeah, I'm fine. Just... tripped. Couldn't see where my feet were going.' He jiggled the box to illustrate his point, hoping he didn't look as rattled as he felt.

The PC scanned its contents with interest, then looked him up and down. 'Last day?'

Charlie nodded again. 'Retiring.'

A low whistle escaped the man's lips. 'Nice. I—'

'Oi, Jonesy, you coming back with that lighter or what?' a male voice called out.

Jonesy opened his fist revealing a cheap, plastic disposable lighter. 'Oops.' Lifting the cigarette to his mouth he sparked up. 'Suppose I'd better let you get on. Enjoy your retirement.'

'Cheers.'

As the PC moved away, Charlie caught sight of the other man. Dressed in a navy-check suit, he was propped up against the railings that separated the grounds of the station from the public walkway. He looked vaguely familiar. And then it hit him. He was one of the detectives—Matt... or was it Mark?—from the Area Crime team where Nick worked.

A knot tightened in his gut.

Five weeks ago, Detective Constable Nicholas Stacey had admitted himself to Alnus House, the mental health treatment hospital. Charlie still hadn't seen him. The man had lost his husband. His dog, Lily. His sanity. And he'd done it all for Charlie—to help find Meghan and Evie when Banning Lawrence had abducted them.

He'd tried a couple of times to drop in, but Nick had refused all visitors, and every voicemail he'd left for him had gone unanswered. Charlie had convinced himself Nick would reach out when he was ready. But deep down, it was a pathetic excuse. The truth was, after everything that had happened, he wasn't sure he could face Nick. Instead of growing a pair, Charlie had visited Lily instead, using the Rottweiler—the *hellhound*—as a way to ease his guilt.

'Charlie, is that you?' The detective—Matt, it was definitely Matt—pushed himself off the railings and joined them, stopping Jonesy in his tracks. He nodded at the box. 'Shit, don't tell me you're leaving?'

'Afraid so.'

'Lucky bastard's retiring,' Jonesy chimed in, passing the lighter to Matt.

'Blimey, I thought you'd be here forever.' Rummaging in his trouser pocket, Matt pulled out a pack of Embassy Gold and offered one to Charlie, who nodded.

'Me too,' he said, keeping his tone light. 'Me too.'

'Here, let me take that for you.' Cigarette between his lips, Jonesy took the box from Charlie and placed it on the ground. 'Jesus, that's heavy. You taking the whole office with you?'

With a snort of amusement, Charlie selected a cigarette, took the lighter, and lit up.

Only the hum of traffic from the adjacent A-road permeated the silence that followed.

'So,' Matt said, 'What have you got planned for your free time?'

FINDING THE GATEKEEPER.

Charlie winced and took another drag, taking a second to compose himself. Smoke filled his lungs; he found the dull burn oddly comforting. He held it there, enjoying the brief moment of familiarity, then exhaled. Some of the tension in his body released with it.

'The usual,' he said. 'Gardening. Maybe a bit of clay shooting. Enjoying a glass or two of whisky.'

The other men chuckled, not picking up on the edge to his tone.

'That sounds—'

'Charlie?' Jasmin's sharp voice caused them to turn as one. 'Are you *smoking*?'

She held the rest of his belongings, staring at his hand in wide-eyed shock.

He looked down at the cigarette between his fingers, his brow furrowing as if only noticing it for the first time. *Christ*, he hadn't given it a second thought. It had been over thirty years since his last smoke and now here he was, sucking on an Embassy like it was still the '80s. The taste in his mouth became suddenly bitter.

'Jesus, Khatri,' Matt said, 'It's his last day. Let him celebrate.'

Jasmin's mouth twisted with irritation. 'HR would have a field day if they caught you lot here.'

Matt scoffed. 'Nobody cares. It's not like it's the public entrance. Anyway, I've never actually heard of anyone being written up for smoking outside the building.'

She lifted her chin, staring him down. 'There's always a first time.'

Blowing a thin line of blue smoke out the side of his mouth, Matt flicked his cigarette onto the concrete and crushed it under his shoe before kicking the butt away. 'I need to get back to the office anyway. Have a good one, Charlie.'

Jonesy followed suit. 'Yeah, uh, me too.' He gave Charlie a nod, before shooting Jasmin a nervous glance, and followed Matt back inside the station.

She watched them skulk away, then, fixing her gaze on Charlie, broke into a mischievous grin. 'Meghan's going to kill you.' She practically sang the words.

Charlie groaned.

She was right. He'd made a point throughout his daughter's childhood and teen years to warn her about the dangers of smoking, that it was a disgusting habit. If Jasmin told Meghan, he'd never hear the end of it.

'Give me that.' Jasmin manoeuvred the box she carried to her hip and snatched the cigarette from Charlie. She took a quick puff, then ground it out against the wall and tossed it into a nearby hedge.

His mouth fell open. 'Jasmin!'

'Oh, don't be a hypocrite. Mutually assured destruction.' She gave him a wink. 'Come on, let's get these bits to your car. If you don't get your arse into gear you're not going to get to the bakery in time.'

As he picked up the last remnants of his career with the police, Charlie tried to ignore the pit in his stomach. Whether it was the smoke still clinging to his lungs, or the surge of raw emotion twisting at his insides, it made him feel nauseous. He'd never been good with change, and in the last few months it seemed like his whole world had been turned upside down.

A sharp stab against his thigh stopped him in place. He shifted the box to one hand and rooted inside his pocket for the culprit. His unsolved crimes business cards—he'd forgotten he'd even put them there. He shoved them in his jacket pocket. What the hell he would do with them now, he had no idea.

With a final glance back at the behemoth of a building, he hoisted up his belongings and walked away from the only constant throughout his adult life.

Chapter 5

DOCTOR SACHIKO NAKAMURA WAITED for the automatic lock on the heavy-duty steel door to whir into place behind her before heading for the nearest coffee machine.

It had been a long day. In a few hours she'd be back at her flat, glass of red wine in hand, watching repeats of *The Great British Bake Off* with her leftover carbonara. The thought brought a smile to her lips. As much as she loved her work, her parents were right, she'd been spending far too much time at the lab.

The soft *clack* of her low-heeled shoes against the marbled floor mingled with the general buzz of activity as she walked. Exchanging nods and mouthing the occasional *hello* to a few of the familiar faces, she made a mental tally of everything she had to prepare for tomorrow.

All the usual admin. Some overdue bloodwork analysis. A couple of physicals. Plus, her weekly assessment of Charles Haynes.

Her mouth pressed into a thin line at the thought.

When she'd first been assigned as Charles' medical specialist, Sachiko had assumed it was a matter of logistics rather than design. Just another patient added to her caseload. But as the months of check-ups rolled by, it became clear that she'd been chosen for a reason. Charles was, putting it mildly, a challenging patient. Blunt, disagreeable, and as stubborn as they came; he had a knack for testing patience. His aversion to needles turned simple procedures into battles. And although he tried to mask his OCD, his obsessive tendencies added another layer of complexity to the most routine tasks. Combined with his years as a detective—which had left him both cynical and deeply mistrustful of O.O.T.I.S—he was the kind of patient most doctors would have found impossible. But somehow, she managed. Whether it was her persistence or sheer unwillingness to let him off the hook, Sachiko could always get him to do what was needed.

Regardless, she liked Charles. He reminded her of her dear old *ojiichan*; just like her grandfather, beneath Charles' gruff exterior lay a kind soul. Plus, he made her laugh—not intentionally, of course, but there was something about his constant complaining that brought a smile to her lips.

But Charles was hiding something. She was sure of it.

When she'd voiced her concerns to her superiors five weeks ago, following the events at the dockyard, they'd been quick to implement safeguarding procedures. Covert surveillance followed, enforcement of mandatory scheduled appointments ensued, and even Diane continued in her role as Charles' handler.

But without knowing his secret, Sachiko's suspicions gradually lost credence with her employers.

It hadn't helped her case that Charles had been happy to comply with the appointments. Maybe happy wasn't the correct word—he always found something to grump about—but he'd been respectful and polite during their time together. And somehow, he'd managed to pass every test she'd laid out for him, making her doubts seem more and more unfounded. So, with no evidence to the contrary—and Charles unable to summon Kar'roc's Maw—the Order no longer considered him to be a credible threat.

Still, she couldn't shake the gut feeling that something had happened to him during the battle with Banning Lawrence. Something involving the dagger. For someone Charles' age to come out of that fight virtually unscathed—even with the physical advantages of being the dagger's master—it didn't add up. But all the eye-witness reports had been unanimous. Banning Lawrence had possession of the dagger right up until the moment Lily ripped off his hand and swallowed both.

Sachiko wanted to believe she was mistaken about Charles—it seemed to be the general consensus—but her intuition nagged at her, telling her she was right.

Rounding the corner, coffee machine in sight, Sachiko fished a handful of coins from the pocket of her lab coat. What she wouldn't give for a proper latte from Déjà Brew, the coffee shop across the road, but if she didn't finish what she was working on, she'd end up staying late again. Plus, she never came out with *just* a coffee. Sachiko prodded at her stomach and frowned.

Feeding the coins into the machine, she heaved out a sigh and selected a drink.

'Flagging?'

Startled, Sachiko jerked her head towards the voice.

Damanjeet stood there, fixing her with his deep-brown eyes before quickly averting his gaze. He towered over her, slim and wiry, his hands buried in his pockets. They usually were; it was like he never knew what to do with them. He was socially awkward in a way that belied his genius. Initially brought in as a software engineer, he now oversaw the whole development team. His systems had been implemented throughout every branch of O.O.T.I.S, making him an invaluable asset. And yet, he could barely maintain eye contact during conversation, often fidgeting with his sleeve or tapping his fingers against his leg. It was almost endearing how someone so brilliant struggled with even the most basic of social cues.

'Damanjeet...' She paused as she caught the slight tick in his jaw, visible even beneath his neatly trimmed beard. For some reason, he bristled at being called by his full name. 'Daman, you made me jump.'

'Oh, sorry. I seem to have that effect on people. Probably my height.' He pulled his hands out of his pockets, waving them frantically. 'Not that I'm saying you're short.' Damanjeet's cheeks flushed. 'I just, uh... didn't mean to scare you.'

'It's fine, really.' Sachiko offered a small smile and picked up her drink, careful not to squeeze the flimsy plastic cup too hard. It might not be the best coffee in the world, but it was definitely hot. 'Well, I'd better get back.'

Damanjeet took a clumsy step closer, as though unsure of how to close the distance between them. 'Actually, I'm glad I bumped into you.'

'You are?'

'Yeah.' His gaze flicked to the ground for a moment before meeting hers. 'I want to get your advice on something.'

'Advice?' Sachiko blinked. She was no IT expert.

He leant past her, forcing her back a step, thumbed a pound into the coin slot and selected a beverage. The machine hummed, dropping the plastic cup into place. A stream of hot liquid *whooshed* into it, splattering and frothing to the brim before tapering off in faltering drips.

'It'll make more sense if I show you,' he said, lifting his cup. 'It'll only take a minute.' When she hesitated, he added, 'I promise.'

'Okay, sure.' A minute or two wouldn't hurt, and she was intrigued. Damanjeet, the tech mastermind, wanted *her* advice. Perhaps this was his way of trying to get their working relationship back on track. Since drunkenly blurting out at the Christmas party that he loved her smile then asking her out—she'd refused—he'd become shyer around her. It would be nice if things could get back to normal between them.

As they walked, Sachiko took a sip of her coffee, trying to imagine what he wanted to show her. The bitter tasting liquid scalded her tongue and she gasped.

'*Kuso.*' She glared at the contents, like it had betrayed her.

Damanjeet raised an eyebrow. 'Did you just swear?'

'Sorry. It's *really* hot.'

'Hot coffee. Who would've guessed?'

She shot him a look, unsure if he was being sardonic. But when he cracked a grin, the tension in her body dissolved and she returned his smile.

When they reached his department, Damanjeet increased his stride and opened the door for her. One or two heads looked up from their dual monitors, but other than that, their arrival went largely unnoticed.

The banks of desks had been clustered in the centre of the expansive room. It always struck her as odd how the developers huddled together yet barely interacted. In place of conversation, the soft hum of computer fans and the rhythmic clicking of fingers on keys filled the air, punctuated by the occasional quiet cough and the scuff of feet. Unlike the sterile, whitewashed interior of her lab, here, the pale terracotta brickwork showed through, a character visible throughout so much of the Order's headquarters. It lent the space a warmer feel. Freestanding black display cases lined the walls on the far side, showcasing a variety of vinyl figurines under glaring LED lights. She was fairly confident the figurines were gaming-related. Aside from one *Jujutsu Kaisen* character, she didn't recognise any of them.

Across one of the clusters, she caught sight of Michelle and gave her a small, friendly wave. No doubt they'd be texting later. Michelle never missed an opportunity to gush over Paul Hollywood to a fellow *Bake Off* fan.

Damanjeet cleared his throat, pulling Sachiko's attention away from the other woman, and gestured to one of the two glass-panelled meeting rooms. They were recent additions to the room, each brightly lit and with a large central desk surrounded by plush, grey-leather office chairs.

'Go ahead. I'll just grab my laptop,' he said and half-jogged to his desk.

Sachiko entered the indicated room and took a seat, a small thrill of anticipation running through her. It felt good to have her opinion valued. She placed her coffee on the desk and brushed a stray piece of thread from the arm of her lab coat. Her attention drifted to the plant in front of her, its plastic leaves thick with dust. Somehow, she wasn't surprised it was fake. She made a mental note to water her own plants when she got home.

The sigh of the glass door announced Damanjeet's arrival. He sat beside her and opened his laptop, his fingers flying across the keyboard as he searched for whatever it was he needed.

'Here,' he said, positioning the laptop for her to see.

Sachiko slanted forward, nudging her glasses up the bridge of her nose, and studied the screen in front of her. Her forehead creased. 'A restaurant menu?'

'So,' Damanjeet said, seemingly oblivious to her confusion. 'I'm thinking of trying a new place for dinner. But I can't decide between this one, or—' he tapped a couple of keys with his left hand, '—this one? What do you think?'

Sachiko blinked, her interest deflating like a punctured balloon. She'd been ready to dive into a problem, offer her hard-earned knowledge as a respected peer. Instead, she was being asked about dinner options.

Damanjeet mistook her silence for contemplation and flicked the keys again. A row of tiny windows flashed across the screen for a split second. Sachiko squinted at one of the images—an artefact. Something about it tugged at her memory, vaguely familiar. She'd almost forgotten that Damanjeet's department worked alongside the Artefact Protection Division to assess threats and ensure proper containment. Just as she was about to ask what she was looking at, Damanjeet's fingers worked the keys again, and the thumbnails vanished.

She pointed at the screen, a question forming on her lips. Damanjeet locked his hand around her wrist, surprising her. She gaped at him.

He released his grip, immediately pulling his hand back. 'Sorry, it's just... fingerprints,' Damanjeet said, the apology a rushed mumble.

Sachiko returned her attention to the laptop. The menu stared back. Mocking her.

'I thought this would be work related,' she said.

Surprise flickered across his face. 'Work related? No... I just wanted to know which restaurant you preferred the look of.'

She could feel heat rising in her cheeks. This wasn't just a complete waste of her time, it was insulting. Did he really consider her work so trivial, she could drop everything just to help him choose between wood-fired pizza or pan-fried bream? She'd dedicated years to her career—years of medical school, foundation training, speciality training—and worked tirelessly to establish herself as an expert in her field, to become an indispensable member of the Order and make a difference in the world. It meant everything to her. And now, to be so blatantly disrespected? It was too much.

'Daman...' Sachiko took a breath, to regulate her tone. She was just tired. This was all an innocent misunderstanding. Damanjeet didn't have a malicious bone in his body. After all, she'd made the assumptions here, not him. And it's not as if she knew anything about code. He'd asked for advice, not help. *I'm such an idiot.* 'Is this really all you wanted my advice on?' She gestured to his employees. 'You could have asked anyone about this.'

He cleared his throat and looked away.

Sachiko crossed her arms, eyes narrowing. 'Daman?'

'Okay, okay.' He rubbed at the back of his neck, clearly searching for the right words. 'I was... kind of hoping that you'd join me?'

'But—'

'Look, I know I blew it at the Christmas party. Had one too many. Made things weird between us. But it's been a few weeks since then, I thought maybe—'

'You thought maybe that after I turned you down the first time, a better way to go about things would be to trick me?' The words came out harsher than she'd intended.

Damanjeet shifted on his seat, the soft leather creaking beneath his weight.

'I wasn't trying to trick you,' he said miserably. 'This all sounded so much better in my head. I'd been waiting to bump into you. I just thought...' He trailed off in a helpless shrug.

Exhaling loudly, Sachiko said, 'Daman, we've talked about this.'

He gave her an imploring look. 'I know, it's just—'

'I've told you I'm not looking for a relationship right now. And I really don't appreciate you dragging me down here under false pretences.' After pushing herself out of the chair, she yanked her coffee off the desk. The cup buckled in her grip, sloshing black liquid across the light-grey lacquered wood.

'Look, I—' Damanjeet began.

'Thank you, but I've got things to do.' She whirled on her heel and strode out of the glass room.

Unlike her arrival, her exit drew quite a bit of attention, especially when Damanjeet called out after her. She ignored him. Ignored them all.

That puppy-dog expression... She'd hurt his feelings, but she'd been perfectly clear at the Christmas party.

Better he understood now than fixate on something that was never going to happen. Still, she hadn't intended to embarrass him in front of his team like that.

Letting the tension drop from her shoulders, Sachiko resisted the urge to look back. Sure, she could have handled things better... Okay, a *lot* better. But she had more pressing issues right now, like finalising the details of her latest test for Charles.

Chapter 6

Sᴏᴘʜɪᴇ'ꜱ ᴍᴜꜰꜰʟᴇᴅ ꜱᴄʀᴇᴀᴍꜱ ꜰʀᴏᴍ below set Eric's teeth on edge. He stopped in his tracks, scowling down at the floorboards, and stamped his foot until the racket subsided.

'She's been doing that off and on ever since I caught Josh down there with her,' Tommo said, dragging a hand through his unkempt ginger hair.

'Josh.' Eric's fists clenched. 'What was he doing?'

'Just talking to her, I think.'

'You *think?*'

Tommo held up his hands in defence. 'I checked the locks on the cage.'

Eric made a frustrated noise. 'Keep an eye on him. I don't want the two of them alone again.'

His Brother nodded in understanding.

The screams started again.

Eric kneaded the bridge of his nose in an effort to dull the throbbing in his head. God, he hated that sound. Funny really, given that those shrieks of terror were among his first memories of his sister. Those memories had followed him throughout their childhood, each one seared into his brain, forcing him to relive the past whenever his mind wandered. They were horrific, traumatising, but also proof of his worth, of his ability to fulfil his role and keep her safe.

Then one day, those screams changed. Became sharper. Desperate. He could still see Sophie on the bed in the room they shared, trapped beneath their mother's latest boyfriend. The man had both her wrists pinned above her head with one hand, while the other yanked at her jeans. Eric knew he'd been no match in strength for the bastard, but he didn't need to be strong. He just needed a weapon. Eric had crept to the top drawer of the dresser, grabbed the penknife there, and pulled out the blade. Then, without a sound, he'd rushed the man and stabbed him in the side. Pulled the knife out and stabbed again. Once, twice. Two solid strikes rewarded him with a bloom of red that soaked through the guy's shirt. Then the bastard hit him across the face, knocking him down. But Eric had held onto the knife, clutching it like a lifeline. When the man had come barrelling off the bed, Eric had screamed for Sophie to run, to hide. He'd swiped at the guy again, catching his arm and spraying blood across the walls before the arsehole had laid into him. It had been one of the worst beatings of his life. When he'd come to, the man was gone. He hadn't been able to get out of bed for three days, but Sophie was safe. That was the day he'd realised he'd kill to protect her.

It was exactly the same now. She just couldn't see it.

Fuck. The summoning wasn't meant to have taken this long. Wasn't supposed to have been this hard.

It had seemed so simple when he'd first found the book—the one that idiot Josh had tried to hide from him. Of course, he hadn't known what it was initially—neither of them had. The fact that it was written in Latin hadn't helped matters much. Thank fuck for Google Translate. But over time he'd pieced it together, realised that *The Grimoire of Unholy Contracts and Spirits* was no mere book, but a compendium of demons and how to summon them.

And that was when the fun had started.

It hadn't worked at first. The thought of all those hours spent painstakingly carving symbols into the concrete—the blistered skin, the bleeding fingers—still made his hands cramp with phantom pain. Even when he'd completed the circle, his attempts had failed time and time again. The frustration, the disappointment had been almost too much to bear. And his Brothers... He could see their faith in him, their faith in the book, wane day by day. He'd come within an inch of tearing the thing to shreds. But then it happened.

He still remembered the sheer elation he'd felt as the writhing mass of shadow dissolved within the confines of the circle to reveal Vamonthir, warden of secrets.

Vamonthir had been terrible to look upon. Even the hand-drawn sketch on the book's fragile pages hadn't prepared him for what stared down at him from inside the circle. Its form was... wrong, twisted—almost human, but grotesquely elongated, with limbs too long and angular and teeth too pointy. Cracks across its scorched skin glowed faintly, as though embers smouldered just beneath the surface. Its eyes pierced him, two points of burning light filled with a dark malevolence that seeped into his bones. And as Vamonthir shifted, the shadows surrounding him seemed to also bend, as if the darkness itself was recoiling from the warden's presence. It hadn't moved beyond the circle, but Eric felt it encroach on him, pressing against the air, suffocating him with its sheer existence.

Eric had staggered back, his legs nearly giving way, a scream tearing from his throat. It still haunted him to this day. In that moment of weakness, he'd shown himself to be unworthy. The book was very specific about each step of the summoning ritual, but whether it was due to the shock of success or the demon itself, Eric had forgotten everything and given it the upper hand.

So, instead of exerting control over the creature, like he'd practiced time and time again in his waking moments, Eric had struck a deal, a blood oath—the demon's promise now etched into his skin and throbbing in his veins. He would open a gateway between the human and demon realms and in return, Vamonthir would give Eric the ability to harness the energy from the realm of fire and shadow. Magic. Power. Control.

Except Eric had not managed to make good on his end of the agreement. No matter what he tried, he could not breach the veil between worlds. Yet the demon's mark remained, inching slowly across his flesh, calling to him.

Relentless whispers teased him with a power he could never quite reach. Mocking his failure.

And then, in a stroke of good luck, the wand had come into his possession. He'd recognised it from the book immediately. The Bloodvein Wand, so named because of the sacrifice it demanded of its wielder. A small price to pay given that it had the power to command demons.

But Josh had thrown a spanner in the works.

Trying to make ends meet after his courier side-hustle fell through, the idiot had listed it on eBay. eBay! Eric had removed it from sale as soon as he'd realised—not that it'd gotten more than a couple of watchers. But, during the few hours of listing, it had caught the attention of O.O.T.I.S. If Brother Bains hadn't given him the heads-up, he'd still have been inside the flat when it was overrun with agents.

Bloody Josh.

With that one braindead decision he'd almost ruined everything. Now Eric was forced to live in a derelict pub, surviving on the charity of his Brothers. He'd been advised to leave his phone, his wallet, everything behind when he'd fled. His only belongings were now the book, the wand, and the handful of clothes and snacks he'd managed to cram hastily into a backpack.

In Eric's desperation, he'd had to adapt his plans. With the Bloodvein Wand in his possession, perhaps he didn't need to open a gateway after all. He could simply call upon the demon and compel it to bestow its gifts upon him. Except that hadn't worked, either.

He'd managed to summon Vamonthir once, but no matter how hard he tried—no matter how many women he sacrificed, no matter how much of his own blood he gave—he couldn't repeat the feat.

But with a gatekeeper, Eric could finally fulfil his end of the bargain. Power would be his. No longer would he have to cower and scrape to eke out a pathetic existence. He'd finally have the strength to protect himself. To protect his sister. Sophie might hate him now, but soon she'd realise he was doing this for them. For her.

And if all the ramblings he'd heard about the Brimstone Chorus, or whatever it was called were true, Sophie would need all the protection Eric could give.

He rolled his neck, aware that Tommo was watching him with a guarded expression. The skin on his collarbone itched. He scratched at the web of black veins that threaded his flesh.

The other woman joined in with Sophie's yells from the cellar beneath them. Eric's lips pressed together, the throb behind his eyes becoming more urgent.

He stamped on the floor again, harder this time, the rotten boards flexing dangerously beneath every *thump*.

'Shut up! Now! I mean it!'

The noise died down. How long it would last he had no idea, but he couldn't stomach another outburst right now. He needed some space to breathe. To regroup.

Tommo remained quiet, his eyes never leaving Eric's face.

Eric turned to him. 'Brother Thompson, I think you and I need to have a little chat about what to do if Josh tries to throw a spanner in the works tomorrow. How about we take a walk?'

Tommo's shoulders relaxed. 'Yeah, sounds good.'

In a few hours, the rest of his Brothers would return. It would be their last meeting before they put their plans into action. Tomorrow would be the first day of the rest of Eric's life.

Chapter 7

ANOTHER SPEEDBUMP JOLTED CHARLIE from his thoughts. He cast a glance at the white cake box secured on the passenger seat, and flicked the indicator up to make a right. He'd made it to the bakery just in time, after stopping off at a petrol station for a packet of mints to mask the stale taste of cigarettes. The smell of smoke still clung to his clothes. He'd lost count of how many times he'd longed for an Embassy since kicking the habit, but he'd never given in. Not once. Not until today.

What's happening to me?

I TOLD YOU. THE DAGGER'S HOLD ON YOU IS BECOMING STRONGER.

Chekonost was a liar. A manipulator. But even so, Charlie couldn't deny there was some truth to the demon's words. All the more reason to speak to Diane—carefully.

Gripping the steering wheel tighter, he slowed the Audi A4 Avant to a stop a few houses down from his daughter's. His usual spot outside the yellow-bricked terrace had been taken by a metallic-blue MINI hatchback.

Recognising the car, he groaned.

Debbie.

It wasn't unusual for his ex-wife to be at social gatherings for either their daughter or granddaughter. Sure, it'd been hard seeing her at first, but he and Debbie had managed to keep the peace over the years. But right now, with the demon harassing his every thought, this was the last thing he needed.

He couldn't recall Meghan mentioning that Debbie would be here today. Knowing his ex, she'd likely decided to drop by unannounced.

Killing the engine, Charlie mentally braced himself. All he had to do was smile and nod. He could do that. He wasn't about to let Debbie ruin his last weekend staying with Meggy and Evie.

Come on, suck it up, Charlie. What's the worst that could happen?

Laughter scraped through his skull.

Stay quiet.

The laughter faded but the malice remained, seeping through his being until every hair on the back of his neck stood on end.

Clenching and unclenching his fists, Charlie took a sharp breath in and released it slowly.

It was just a party. He'd already gotten through one today, he could get through another.

Charlie grabbed the cakebox and got out of the car. As he bumped the door closed with his hip, he remembered the gift bag on the rear seat. It'd be just his luck if someone saw it and smashed the window to help themselves. No way was he letting his bottle of Lagavulin get nicked, especially not when it was a Fèis Île 2016.

Decision made, Charlie balanced the cakebox against his chest, grabbed his gift from the Audi, and locked up before heading for the house. He looked forward to cracking open the bottle later that evening. Drowning his sorrows. Not that alcohol did much for him anymore, not since he'd become master of Kar'roc's Maw. Just one of the many "benefits" of his bond with that damned dagger.

His phone chirruped in his jacket pocket. For a moment, he considered checking it, but quickly came to his senses. He wouldn't hear the end of it if he dropped Meghan's cake. And the whisky? Virtually irreplaceable.

The floral scent of perfume hit him as he reached the front door. He knew that smell...

A splitting pain cleaved through his head, stopping him in his tracks. He gasped as a lightning storm of fragmented memories flashed behind his eyes.

That same flowery scent. The obscured, glass panels of his old front door as he pushed it open. Yellow roses scattered across the hallway floor in a spray of shattered blue glass and water.

No. It was his house, but these weren't his memories... They were Stephen's.

Using the wall for support, Charlie tried to force the images from his mind. He took a step forward, the whisky almost slipping from his grasp.

Stop it!

He could feel tightness in his chest; pain in his damaged leg as he hauled himself up the stairs; the agony of his bruised and battered body... of *Stephen's* body, step after excruciating step.

And then he was staring at his bedroom door, listening to the muffled grunt of a man inside.

All too late, he realised what the demon was showing him—and who he would see on the other side of that door, locked in the throes of passion with another man.

I said stop! Now! Chekonost, I command you to stop!

The sigil on his hand pulsed and the memories winked out. A trickle of sweat ran down Charlie's spine. His gut roiled. He swallowed and tried to calm his breathing.

In all the weeks that Chekonost had been inside his head, never had it resisted Charlie's will like this. Was it getting stronger? Without access to the Maw, was it only a matter of time before the demon took control completely?

No. He was the dagger's master for Christ's sake. That had to mean something... right?

A sense of amusement rippled through him.

Rolling the tension from his neck, Charlie manoeuvred the gift bag and dabbed his brow with the back of his sleeve. He opened the front door.

A waft of heat hit him, as well as the sounds of voices coming from the living room.

'Grandad!'

Evelyn sprang from the kitchen, her slippers slapping against the tiles. She stopped directly in front of him, adjusting the sling that secured the blue cast around her fractured arm. Her pale-green eyes zeroed in on the cakebox, and a wide grin spread across her face.

'Is that Mum's cake?' she asked, flicking her raven-black hair over her shoulder and reaching for the box.

Charlie lifted it higher, chuckling at her resulting pout. 'Yes, it's your mum's cake.'

'Can I have a look?'

'How about you let me inside first?'

Evie stepped back, giving him space.

'What's in the bag? Is that for Mum, too? I thought you already gave her a present this morning?'

Charlie kicked off his shoes and nudged them against the wall, putting them in their usual spot. 'What is this, twenty questions?'

'I'm curious.'

'Hi Curious, I'm Grandad.'

Evelyn sighed and rolled her eyes. 'Please can I see the cake?'

'In the kitchen. I don't want to drop it.'

He walked into the modest kitchen and, with Evie practically on his heels, set the cakebox down on the worktop. No sooner had it left his hands than his granddaughter had it open.

A soft gasp escaped her lips; she beamed up at him. 'Oh my God, Mum's going to love it.' She leant over the cake, her nose inches from the chocolate buttercream swirls piped around its top edge. A crease appeared between her eyebrows as a couple of brightly-coloured sprinkles dislodged from one of the swirls. 'It *is* vegan though, right?'

It was Charlie's turn to roll his eyes. 'It better be. It bloody well cost enough.' He placed the gift bag down beside it, wincing as it *clunked* against the granite effect laminate, and fished out his phone, checking it.

'It's a text from Jasmin,' he said, more to himself than to his granddaughter. Evie made a *hmm* of acknowledgement that confirmed she wasn't really listening anyway. 'She got caught in traffic.'

Between all the congratulatory messages about his retirement and the reminders about Meghan's party, the battery was on its last legs. Charlie set the mobile down to charge. He slid the phone to the back of the worktop, aligning it flush against the edge of the tiles. The small act of neatness soothed him, bringing a brief moment of calm to the chaotic swirl of his thoughts.

Evie replaced the lid on the cake box and turned her attention to his gift. 'What's in the bag?'

'Whisky.'

Her nose screwed up. 'Oh... Yuck.'

Charlie scoffed. 'It's the good stuff I'll have you know. It's my retirement present.' He lifted it partway out, exposing the yellow Lagavulin label on the brown glass bottle.

'Expensive yuck,' Evie teased.

Familiar laughter set Charlie's teeth on edge; he attempted to ignore it. 'Has your grandmother been here long?'

Evie shrugged. 'No. She said she was just dropping in to say happy birthday.'

'Right. How about you give me a couple of minutes to get my coat off, use the loo, and I'll come join you all?'

'Okay.' Giving the cakebox another appreciative glance, Evie ducked out of the kitchen, leaving Charlie alone.

He listened as her voice joined the chatter in the living room. He could really do without this right now. Kneading his temples, he blew out a breath. Whatever the demon had done when it had taunted him with Stephen's memories now left a dull ache behind his eyes.

YOU KNOW, ALL YOU HAVE TO DO IS TAKE ME TO THE GATEKEEPER—

No. We're not having this conversation again.

Charlie slipped out of his brown waxed jacket, hung it in its usual spot, and entered the downstairs toilet. All he needed was a minute to himself—time to regain his composure before facing his ex. But his thoughts drifted, unbidden, back to Stephen's memories.

Christ, it's not as if he hadn't known Debbie had been unfaithful. Meghan wasn't his, not by blood. It had shattered something inside him. That final, childlike, unquestioning part of his soul that he'd so desperately clung to since the day his mother had walked away, leaving him to endure the drunken fists of his father. He'd been left with nothing but broken pieces, trying to force them back into place, as if they still fit. The truth had been there for years, festering, but the idea of seeing it through Stephen's eyes—as if Charlie had been standing there himself—was something he couldn't stomach.

He clenched his fists, frustration coiling hot and tight in his chest. He wasn't sure who he was angrier at: Debbie, for betraying his trust, or himself for still carrying the weight of it all.

Squeeze, release. Squeeze, release. Squeeze, release.

The rhythm steadied him bit by bit, loosening the tension in his muscles.

With a deep breath, he turned on the tap and splashed cold water on his face; the chill cut through the haze. He looked at his reflection. Tired hazel eyes stared back at him, framed by lines etched deeper with every passing day.

'Come on, Charlie,' he muttered. 'In the past few months, you've faced off against murderers, demons, monsters. I'm sure you can handle a couple of hours with your ex-wife.'

His reflection didn't appear convinced.

Tightening his resolve, he squared his shoulders and joined the others in the living room.

'Dad, we were starting to get worried,' Meghan said. 'It's not like you to be late.'

Before Charlie could respond, a low growl cut through the room. He looked around, searching for the source. The growl came again, followed by a sharp yip, and he finally spotted the Chihuahua peeking out from the folds of Debbie's oversized handbag.

It bared its teeth at him.

Charlie blinked, perplexed.

'Sorry, Meggy. Just had to stop off and get a few bits first.' He gave his ex a curt nod. 'Debbie.'

The dog barked again, the sound high-pitched and grating. The noise stabbed through his skull, amplifying the dull throb behind his temples. He winced, feeling his shoulders creep upward with every piercing yap.

Debbie didn't bother to calm the creature, which only added to his irritation. Instead, her lips quirked in faint amusement. 'I hear you retired today. Congratulations.'

'Thanks,' he replied evenly, keeping his expression neutral. Trust Debbie to go straight for the jugular.

The relentless barking only grew louder. Caught between disbelief and irritation, Charlie glanced at the tiny dog. How could something so small make such a racket?

He shifted his attention to his daughter. Meghan's shoulders were stiff, her smile tight and brittle. He recognised that expression all too well; she'd worn it often as a child, caught in the crossfire of their marital problems.

The barking morphed from noise into something physical, cutting through his skull and carving into his brain.

'Shush now,' Debbie cooed, her words too gentle to tame the furious little beast.

Charlie raised his voice over the disruption. 'Jasmin will be here soon.'

Debbie's flinch didn't go unnoticed. Jasmin and Meghan were a couple. By all accounts, she still hadn't adjusted to their daughter's new relationship.

SHE IS NOT YOUR DAUGHTER.

Fresh pain exploded behind Charlie's eyes. Stephen's memories surged, crashing over him like a tidal wave.

A feral cry ripped from his... from *Stephen's* throat as he burst through the bedroom door.

Stop!

Debbie's face flushed and panicked, her blonde hair dishevelled, as she clambered off the man she'd been straddling.

I said stop!

Her cry of shock as she scrambled naked off the bed—*their* bed—while the stranger gawked at him, wide-eyed, before fumbling to yank the duvet over his wilting prick.

Stop! Stop! Fucking stop!

The sigil on his hand flared and the recollections cut off abruptly, replaced by the demon's shrill giggle.

Blood thrashed in his ears and muscles strained against his skin, as Charlie stared at his ex-wife.

Chapter 8

Debbie's forehead wrinkled in response to Charlie's glare.

The dog continued to bark.

He forced himself to stay put, to keep his voice even. 'Can you shut that thing up?'

Debbie blinked at him, as if surprised by the intensity of his tone. 'What? Max? He's just saying hello. Aren't you, baby boy?' She reached into her bag, scooping up the snarling Chihuahua and cradling it against her chest. The creature settled slightly but continued to growl low in its throat, its beady eyes locked on Charlie as if it knew something the others didn't.

He exhaled sharply, pinching the bridge of his nose.

'Dad, are you okay? You look a little flushed.' Meghan's voice just about registered over the sound of his hammering pulse.

'I'm fine. I just... need a drink.' He forced the words through his teeth, turned on his heel, and stalked out of the room.

With the kitchen door closed, Charlie braced himself against the worktop and sucked in a breath.

What the fuck was that?

MY KNOWLEDGE OF YOUR SPECIES' MATING PRACTICES IS LIMITED, BUT IF YOU NEED ME TO TRY AND EXPLAIN—

Why? Why are you doing this to me?

YOU KNOW WHY.

The laminate flexed beneath his grip; Charlie eased his fingers up from the worktop. He clenched and unclenched his fists in an effort to gain control.

Squeeze, release. Squeeze, release. Squeeze, release.

It was no good. The images of his ex-wife's infidelity were seared into his mind's eye. He needed something. A cigarette. A shot. Anything to take the edge off.

His gaze fell upon his retirement gift.

Charlie ripped the Lagavulin bottle free from its hessian bag, and poured himself a generous measure. No sooner had he downed it than he was pouring himself another. Familiar heat hit the back of his throat; he hissed and emptied the glass again. Rich flavours of smoke and sweet citrus lingered on his tongue, but he got no enjoyment from them. The fire inside his chest consumed his every sense.

How could she? How could Debbie do that to him? In their home, their bed?

The demon's laughter gouged at his brain.

YOU DID THIS TO YOURSELF.

He closed his fist around the bottle. His jaw clenched.

'Grandad?'

YOU ARE THE ONE WHO IMPRISONED ME IN THE DAGGER. YOU SHOULD HAVE LET ME KILL

THE BOSWELL WOMAN. SHOULD HAVE LET ME RETURN TO MY OWN REALM.

Shut up.

'Grandad?'

INSTEAD, YOU FORCED ME INSIDE YOUR DECREPIT BODY. USED MY STRENGTH TO SAVE THE SPAWN OF ANOTHER MAN. AND FOR WHAT?

His body went rigid. *Shut up!*

'Grandad, are you listening to me?'

YOU ARE AS MUCH A SLAVE TO THE DAGGER AS I AM. IT WILL BLACKEN YOUR HEART. CORRUPT YOUR SOUL. YOU WILL BECOME EVERYTHING YOU DESPISE. DESTROY EVERYTHING YOU LOVE. YOUR FRIENDS. YOUR FAMILY. YOU WILL BECOME A MONSTER.

'Shut up!' Charlie launched the bottle across the kitchen. It hit the wall in an explosion of glass and whisky. His body shook. His lungs fought to gain air from his sharp, shallow pants.

And that's when he heard it: a quiver of breath. So quiet, so fragile that he knew even before turning who it belonged to.

His granddaughter stared back at him, fear in her pale-green eyes, the colour drained from her face. Christ, how long had she been standing there?

'Evie, sweetheart, I...'

She recoiled from him. Her lower lip trembled, tears spilling down her cheeks. 'I'm s-sorry, I didn't mean to make you m-mad,' she whimpered. Choking back a sob, she fled from the kitchen.

'Evie, please...' Charlie let her go, a lump in his throat. His shoulders sagged under the crushing shame. How had he let this happen?

Harried footsteps quickly followed. Meghan rounded the corner with Debbie on her heels.

'Dad! What's going on?'

The two women gaped at the state of the kitchen. It was then that Charlie noticed the full extent of the damage. Where the bottle had struck, there was now a gaping hole in the wall; layers of plaster and grout had been reduced to dust on exposed brick. The neighbouring tiles were cracked, or missing great chunks, and were coated in a spray of amber liquid that pooled on the worktops and floor below.

Over the stunned silence, the small dog continued its incessant yapping.

'Meghan, I—'

'What the hell did you do?'

'I... I'm sorry.'

'*Sorry?*' she spat, her porcelain skin flushed red. 'Jesus, Dad, look at what you've done! I think you need to leave.'

'Meggy, please, I'm sorry. I didn't mean to...' He trailed off. What could he say? There was no explanation he could give her that would make sense. 'At least let me get this cleaned up first.'

'No. I just want you to go.'

'I—'

'Just. Go.'

He gave a single nod, unable to look his daughter in the eye. Meghan and Debbie stepped back, allowing him to pass, their respective anger and shock radiating off them in waves. The Chihuahua snarled, gnashing its teeth at his back. Swallowing hard, Charlie stuffed his feet into his shoes and grabbed his jacket. Not a word was said as he opened the front door and stepped out into the chill of the late afternoon.

The *bang* from Meghan slamming the door behind him startled a few nearby pigeons into flight.

Charlie made his way back to his car. He'd never felt so shitty in his life. The look of fear on Evie's face would haunt him forever.

He increased his stride to the car, blinking rapidly against the prick of tears. What was happening to him? Was this how things had started for Stephen? How long before it was *him* murdering people in the street and gouging out their eyeballs?

No.

There wasn't a chance in hell he'd let Chekonost turn him into the monster Stephen had become.

DO NOT BLAME ME. IT IS KAR'ROC'S WILL THAT BENDS YOU, NOT MINE. DAY BY DAY HIS GRASP GROWS TIGHTER. BY BINDING MY ESSENCE TO YOURS, YOU HAVE ONLY STRENGTHENED YOUR CONNECTION TO THE DEMON REALM. STRENGTHENED YOUR LINK TO KAR'ROC. YOU WILL NOT WIN. WHEN WILL YOU ACCEPT THAT YOUR ONLY CHANCE OF SALVATION LIES WITH FINDING THE GATEKEEPER?

Charlie glanced back at Meghan's house. The dull ache in his chest had spread throughout his body, making him feel numb. He scrubbed a hand down his face and continued walking.

HOW FAR MUST YOU FALL BEFORE YOU UNDERSTAND THE TRUTH OF WHAT I AM SAYING?

Truth? Charlie scoffed. *You're a demon. What the hell would you know about truth?*

The demon bristled, its contempt palpable.

IF YOU DO NOT WANT TO BECOME THE MONSTER YOU SO DESPERATELY FEAR, THEN FINDING THE GATEKEEPER IS YOUR ONLY OPTION. MY BODY IS ROTTING IN THE REALM OF FIRE AND SHADOW, ONCE IT PERISHES, YOU WILL HAVE NO OPTION BUT TO REMAIN MY HOST UNTIL THE DAY YOU DIE. YOU NEED TO CHOOSE: DO YOU WANT TO RISK EVERYTHING JUST TO SPITE ME, OR DO YOU WANT YOUR LIFE BACK?

Chapter 9

MUTTERING TO HIMSELF, JOSH slumped down on the bed. The battered metal frame screeched in protest beneath his weight. He shifted, feeling each and every crossbar through the thin, lumpy mattress.

Right now, he'd have done anything to be back in his flat. The poky one-bed might've been a little rough around the edges—with a constant draft, and a tap that never quite stopped dripping—but at least the bed had been comfortable.

He missed electricity. He missed hot, running water. But most of all, he missed being able to come and go as he pleased.

A thin rectangle of pale moonlight bled past the edges of the plywood sheet boarding the window. For a while he stared at it, watching motes of dust drift in and out of view, imagining the kiss of the breeze against his skin. What he wouldn't give for some fresh air. The air in every room in the derelict pub was thick with the dank smell of mildew; it seemed to be seeping from the walls. The once-white paint was mottled with black, bloated and blistered from the damp, like a festering wound left untreated. Every breath he inhaled had a taste to it, like the rot was creeping into his lungs. Josh pulled the robes tighter around himself and shivered.

With his eyes squeezed shut, he rubbed briskly at his arms and tuned in to the sounds of the abandoned building. The groan of old pipes, the creaks and pops of wood settling, the skitter of rats beneath the floorboards; he'd become used to them now.

He hadn't meant for any of this to happen.

'It was just a job,' he whispered. 'Just a job.'

He buried his head in his hands.

He'd been a courier. Driving around in a beaten-up Vauxhall Corsa, delivering packages for pennies a piece, barely scraping enough together to make rent each month. So, when someone had offered him cash-in-hand to transport one little box, of course he'd jumped at the chance.

Mundy Wilcoxson. The bloke had been intimidating, for sure. In fact, he'd reminded Josh of those biker gang members he'd seen on TV: thick with muscle, tattoos covering almost every inch of visible skin, and with the skinhead and beard to boot. At first, he'd hesitated, but Mundy had offered him the money there and then, and there was no way Josh was about to turn down a wad of twenty-pound notes. Anyway, he'd seemed friendly enough, and how scary could someone who had a front lawn full of garden gnomes really be?

Everything had been great. At first.

He and Mundy had come to an agreement. Alongside his regular job, Josh would pick up and deliver the extra packages, no questions asked. In return he would be rewarded handsomely. Josh had even joked that he should upgrade his Corsa for a white transit van, but Mundy had dismissed the idea, saying that the old banger was perfect.

'Inconspicuous', that was the word he'd used.

That had made Josh laugh at the time, considering that the bloke's car was anything but. Though, if he was being honest, he'd have given his right arm to own a car like the burnt-orange 2013 Mustang GT 5.0. Imported, obviously.

Josh had always been a car enthusiast; it was one of the few interests he shared with Eric, apparently. He'd even enrolled in a mechanic apprenticeship, and it had gone okay for the first few weeks. The ribbing he'd gotten for his stutter hadn't bothered him—it was part of the banter. And when his colleagues had hidden his tools, he'd known it was just because he was the newbie. But Eric... Eric didn't take too kindly to that kind of thing. Before he knew what had hit him, Josh was out on his arse, apprenticeship done for. After that, he'd decided to find work where he wasn't around other people. Delivering packages just made sense, and after he'd met Mundy, all those long, lonely hours driving around by himself suddenly became worth it.

In the first few weeks alone, Josh had made enough to splurge on a new laptop, get himself a decent TV with a sound system, and even afford a finance plan to upgrade the furniture in his flat. For the first time in his life, he was comfortable.

But then a package went missing.

Mundy had been incensed, screaming and swearing down the phone. He'd even rooted through the back of Josh's Corsa, chucking parcels here, there, and everywhere. It had landed Josh right in the shit with his company when multiple customers phoned up to complain about their damaged goods.

The missing package hadn't been there. Or at least that's what Josh had thought at the time. When he got back to the flat, still a little shaken, he'd found the thing wedged under the front passenger seat. He'd briefly considered returning it, but Mundy's temper had made him think better of it.

Instead, he'd taken the neatly bound parcel inside his flat and hidden it under his bed, never to see the light of day again. Why he hadn't just binned the thing, he still didn't know. Maybe, because he'd convinced himself that one day he'd return it, even though deep down, he was too afraid of Mundy to actually do it. But as far as Wilcoxson was concerned, Josh had never received it in the first place. Life carried on as usual. The package was never mentioned again.

Until the day Eric found it.

Josh could still remember waking up and finding the book beside his pillow; the confusion that followed as he rubbed at his bleary eyes; the faint crinkle of paper as he sat up. When he'd turned the book over in his hands, recognition hit like a punch to the gut. It was the parcel he'd hidden away, the one he'd tried so hard to forget.

Eric had left it there. Whether to make Josh aware that he'd found it or simply a careless gesture, Josh didn't know. Either way, he wanted nothing to do with it. He couldn't even think about Mundy without his stomach clenching. If he found out Josh still had the book... well, he didn't dare imagine what would happen to him.

The book was heavy, bound in cracked brown leather. Gold lettering on the spine had faded to almost nothing and its brittle, yellowed pages gave off the faint aroma of coffee and almonds. It was old—Josh could tell that much—and decorated in beautiful, spidery script. In places the ink had aged to brown, and the intricate diagrams of circles covering the parchment made his head spin. It wasn't English. Latin, maybe? He couldn't say.

Eric had become obsessed after that. He'd clearly shown his friends, because soon it was all they could talk about. Whenever Josh entered the room, the other men, giddy at first, would quickly clam up when they realised he was not Eric. But he'd snatched enough of the conversations to piece together some of what was going on.

Josh never saw the book again. Eric had hidden it from him.

He'd thought Eric was doing him a favour.

He'd thought wrong.

Eric had always been their protector, the one who kept him and Sophie safe. He was the one constant Josh could depend on. But after the book entered their lives, something changed in Eric. Sophie kept telling him so. He just didn't want to believe it. He couldn't.

Even after all the bad Eric had done, Josh wanted to believe the protector still existed, buried deep inside. Because if Eric wasn't Eric anymore, then who—or what—was he?

Maybe if Josh had just returned the book to Mundy, none of this would be happening. Sophie wouldn't be trapped in a cage in a dank cellar in the middle of nowhere, he wouldn't be hostage to Eric's friends, and those women... they wouldn't be dead right now.

Josh's stomach clenched. Their blood staining the concrete, the metallic, tangy stench of it mingled with mildew and rot, made him nauseous. He hadn't been there to see them die, *thank God*. Eric hadn't allowed it. He didn't want Josh involved in whatever he was doing, and didn't want him near Sophie anymore. But Josh still found ways to see her. He still witnessed the aftermath, still heard every grim detail from his sister as she sobbed hysterically behind the bars of her cage.

This was all his fault.

If he'd just returned the book. If he wasn't such a bloody coward...

A sharp knock jolted Josh upright on the bed. He licked his lips, shrinking in on himself, as another, more urgent, knock rattled the door in its frame.

'Eric?' It was Tommo.

Josh didn't answer.

'Eric, are you in there?'

The door swung inwards, raining flecks of paint across the floor as Tommo slammed into the frame. Josh shielded his eyes against the explosion. A flashlight reached him. He shuffled back until the wall pressed against his spine.

'Eric?' He swept the room with the light, coming to a stop on the bed. Tommo's mouth twisted in a sneer. 'Joshua. The others are starting to arrive. Come back downstairs.'

Josh flinched, but otherwise didn't move.

'Come down, before I drag you down,' Tommo said, his words clipped.

'I don't w-want to.'

'I don't w-want to,' Tommo mocked. 'You think I give a shit what you want? This is your last chance, Joshua. Either you come down willingly or I'll lock you in one of those cages.'

'You wouldn't. Eric wouldn't be happy if you d-did that.'

'I'm sure he'd understand.'

The silence stretched between them, a line of tension so thin, it threatened to snap at any moment.

Tommo took a deliberate step forward, his boot thudding on the floorboards.

'Okay,' Josh said hurriedly, scrambling off the bed. 'I'll come downstairs.'

Tommo made a sound caught halfway between disgust and amusement, then withdrew from the room letting darkness take his place.

Josh wrung his hands and tried to keep up with Tommo's long strides. He knew that locking him up was a bluff. There's no way he would risk Eric's wrath by locking him in one of those dog crates, not when it would mean leaving him alone with Sophie. Tommo was scared of Eric, they all were.

But bluff or not, Josh couldn't refuse. Sophie was a prisoner too, and the last thing he wanted was her getting hurt because of him. Even without Eric there, he'd learnt how to take a beating as a child, learnt how to ignore the insults and constant threats from their abusive mother, learnt how to mask his pain and sorrow because the slightest thing could set her off. But the one thing he'd never learnt was how to stop being afraid for his sister.

Chapter 10

SACHIKO CLOSED HER LAPTOP, rolled the tension from her neck, and stretched. Her stomach growled, a sharp reminder she'd eaten too little. She poked at a piece of wilted lettuce between two slightly hardened, room-temperature slices of bread on the burnished silver worktop. That had been her lunch—she checked her watch—over *six* hours ago.

Too often, her work had a way of consuming her. She could grab something now, before they stopped serving hot food for the late shift, but it would turn into an excuse to stay even later. Sachiko had promised her parents—especially her *okaasan*—she'd try to stop putting her career ahead of everything else.

But, honestly, what else did she have? Her family was in Japan. She'd known when she'd chosen this path that she'd be leaving them behind. Although... maybe it had been the other way around. Her sister had been born with the gifts of their bloodline, able to wield magic as every generation had before them. For centuries her ancestors had honed their abilities. They'd been revered for their magic—after all, it was an honour to become an instrument of the Order of the Iron Seal. Yet, Sachiko's own blood had betrayed her.

Charles had once asked her if she was a witch and she'd told him no. It was true. She wasn't a witch, but given her genes, she should have been.

Charles.

Her gaze settled on the small, white, octagonal dish just inside the door, the salt at its centre piled into a gentle, sloping cone. *Morishio*. Back home, it was widely believed that *morishio* could repel malevolent forces, with folklore even claiming that the salt would be disturbed in the presence of evil. But this dish had been warded to unleash a far more violent reaction, turning ancient superstition into something palpably real. It was her latest attempt to confirm her suspicions about Charles and yet another reminder that, compared to the rest of her family, she was sorely lacking. She felt that familiar pang of resentment—one she'd spent a lifetime trying to bury. If she'd had access to the latent magic woven into her bloodline, maybe she wouldn't have to rely on charms and wards.

Even so, part of her wished she had thought of using *morishio* sooner. Her eyes flicked from the salt pile to the vent just above the louvered steel door. She swallowed hard, the memory of the naeshin attack dredging up images of the demon's yellow eyes and undulating silver-plated body from her subconscious. A shudder rippled down her spine. If not for Charles' intervention that day, she would be dead.

With a soft shake of her head, she tossed the sandwich into the bin and began tidying her desk, in preparation for her assessment with him in the morning. She'd have straightened everything up anyway, but a tidy space made him feel more at ease. He'd made his opinions of O.O.T.I.S quite clear on day one, plus it was obvious that the clinical space put him on edge. Yes, Charles certainly had trust issues. The chances of him opening up about what had really happened at the dockyard were slim to none, but she would try. And one way or another, *morishio* would give her the answer she was looking for.

A soft, metallic rapping on the door pulled her from her thoughts.

'Just a second...'

She returned a beaker to its place on the shelf before hurrying to answer.

Damanjeet stood on the other side, wearing his coat, a coffee in each hand. She glanced at the logo printed on the side of one cup. Déjà Brew.

'I come bearing gifts,' he said with an apologetic smile.

She raised an eyebrow.

'A peace offering,' he added, holding one cup out to her.

Sachiko knew she should refuse out of principle, but she couldn't deny the skip of excitement at the prospect of decent coffee.

She accepted the drink with a slight nod, indicating he could come in. The fact that he'd gone to the effort of getting it from Déjà Brew instead of the vending machine had earnt him a few moments of her time.

Damanjeet entered, shrugging off his coat, fumbling slightly as he tried to balance his coffee. His heel caught on the edge of the doorframe, throwing him off balance.

There was a sharp crack as his weight landed on the octagonal dish. He followed with a startled curse.

The *morishio*! Sachiko's stomach dropped.

Damanjeet lifted his foot. Grains of white salt scattered from the sole of his shoe. He shot a puzzled look at the ruined dish. 'What the hell did I step on?'

Quickly setting down her coffee, Sachiko rushed forward to pluck up the two pieces of broken ceramic.

'It's *morishio*,' she said quietly, eyeing the white grains now spread across the floor tiles.

'It's what?'

'Salt. It protects against evil spirits and negative energy.'

His sceptical frown came as no surprise. 'Negative energy?'

Running her thumb along the rough edge of one of the fractured pieces of the dish, Sachiko sighed. Without it, the *morishio's* reaction to Charles' presence might be too subtle to discern.

'How does it work?' Damanjeet asked.

'In Japan, salt is used to purify. You place it at a room's entrance to keep evil out. Usually, it's on the other side of the door, but I didn't want anyone to step on it.'

'Oh.' He let out a nervous laugh, his gaze darting away. 'Guess I messed that up.'

Sachiko tried to move the conversation along without sounding rude. 'If the salt scatters, it means there's a threat.'

'But the door opening could scatter it, right? And it's just salt—would you even notice if anything happened to it? A few scattered grains of salt aren't much of an alarm system.'

She pressed the pieces of the broken dish back together. 'It's got a little extra oomph.'

His eyebrows lifted. 'It's warded. Clever. What—does it explode or something?'

'Something like that. The end results wouldn't be too dissimilar to this.' She waved a hand at the mess. 'I'll have to ask APD to make me another one.'

Luckily, she still had a few more favours she could call in with the Artefact Protection Division, otherwise she'd be forced to wait the mandatory six weeks that all low-priority items were issued. She wanted to test a theory and with Charles due in tomorrow, she couldn't afford to wait.

'Shit.' Damanjeet palmed his forehead. 'I'm sorry. Let me help you clear this up.'

'It's fine, really.'

'Honestly, I insist.'

Conceding, Sachiko pointed to the cabinet with the dustpan and brush. Discarding the broken shards in the bin, she frowned. *What a waste.*

Once the last of the salt had been swept up, Damanjeet tugged at his sleeve nervously.

'Look,' he said, taking a breath, 'about earlier, I just wanted to apologise. What I did, calling you to my office, it was out of order. I shouldn't have lied to you. It was unprofessional, and I know I crossed a line. I'm sorry.'

'Thank you, Daman. I appreciate that.'

Sachiko brought the coffee to her lips and took a sip, savouring the mellow taste. Her stomach grumbled in earnest.

'Did you forget to eat again?' Daman asked.

'Not *forget* exactly,' she replied, a hint of defensiveness creeping into her tone. 'I had a lot to catch up on.'

'Manage to get everything done?'

'Near enough,' she said quickly, glancing at a rack of test tubes. 'I was just putting everything away before I go home.'

Damanjeet nodded, apparently not picking up on the hint to leave. He let his gaze wander around the room. The gentle hum of the air-conditioning unit settled between them as his eyes drifted over monitors, microscopes, and racks of neatly labelled bottles and beakers, meticulously arranged against the spotless, whitewashed walls. After a moment, he returned his focus to her.

'Well, thank you for the coffee,' she prompted.

'So... we're good?'

Sachiko smiled. 'We're good.'

The tension in Damanjeet's shoulders visibly eased. A grin spread across his face. He lifted his coffee cup in a cheers gesture before taking what she could only assume was a victory sip.

'I suppose I'd better let you get finished up then,' he said. 'Unless you want me to stay and help? That way I can walk you to your car... if you want?'

There was an almost childlike innocence in the way he asked, one hand rubbing the back of his neck as he waited for her response.

Sachiko's insides twisted. She'd known about his interest long before the Christmas party, which was why she'd made it clear their relationship would never go beyond friendship. It's not that Damanjeet wasn't her type, she had no room in her life for romance right now. The Order came first. Letting anyone in risked her focus, her goals, her future. That was a price she couldn't afford to pay.

'No, it's fine, you don't have to do that.' She waved the offer away, then quickly added, 'I need to stop at pathology first, anyhow.'

His disappointment seemed to deflate his body a little. He flashed a smile and shrugged. 'No problem. Well, I won't keep you.'

When it became clear that she wasn't changing her mind, he backed up to the door. His foot skidded a little in the salt, the sound of grains grinding between his shoe and the tile.

'Oops, I guess we missed some.'

'That's okay, I'll get it before I leave.' Before he could say anything else, she added, 'See you tomorrow, Daman.'

'Oh, erm, yeah. See you tomorrow.'

He gave her a small, hesitant wave, then grabbed his coat and let the door click shut after him.

Sachiko pressed her fingertips to her forehead and groaned. Obviously, she was going to have to be a little more direct with him from now on. Still, that was a problem for her future self.

Her attention drifted back to where the thin dusting of salt glinted on the tiled floor. Her eyebrows knitted together.

If the *morishio* worked as intended tomorrow, she'd have bigger issues than a little spilled salt.

Chapter 11

THE DRONE OF CONVERSATION drifted through the damp-mottled walls. Eric arched his back, wincing as the tension cracked through his spine. He did his best to ignore the persistent itch that radiated across his collarbone. The dark veins, like rivers of poison, whispered of his inadequacies as they mapped each day's failure across his chest. Still, he would fulfil his end of the bargain soon and the demon would give him what was rightfully his.

Filling his lungs with musty air and releasing it, Eric turned the Bloodvein Wand over in his hands. The frayed strands of copper snagged on his scabbed palms. He trailed his finger across the chip in the quartz, cringing inwardly. The memory of him launching the wand across the cellar in anger turned his stomach. The artefact was his future. Without it he'd continue to be a nobody. A nothing.

Worse than a nothing, he'd be a loser. Just like *mummy dearest* always said he was.

Their mother had not been a kind woman. Bitter was probably the best word for her. Well, maybe not the best, but definitely fitting. She'd never wanted children.

She'd made that clear to them. Kids were a burden. More mouths to feed. Ungrateful. Selfish.

Talk about the irony.

She had no issues pocketing the child welfare payments for them, though. Not that the money ever stretched beyond her next fix. Eric could still recall the sharp, acidic smell of the milky-white liquid clinging to the insides of the syringes littering the living room floor. Vinegary almost. Whatever hadn't made it into her veins left a permanent stain wherever it landed. That was why his mother always wore T-shirts, even in the dead of winter. Unless, of course, she had company. Apparently, it was fine for her children to see the track marks lining her arms, but not the men she brought into her bed—at least, not until they stuck around for more than a few days.

She was a toxhead. Eric understood that much now. But even as a child, he'd learnt to despise the sight of those waxed paper sachets she brought home, each stamped with the silhouette of a little black dragon.

Dragon Scale. A single baggie barely lasted a week. Sometimes they'd watch her, wide-eyed, as she tipped the powder onto a spoon with shaky hands, then dissolved it in water over the flame of her lighter. The way it clouded when the first bubbles broke mesmerised him, becoming almost pearlescent in appearance. The way it shimmered as it caught the light looked like something out of a storybook. Like some magical potion. Beautiful. Or at least Sophie had thought so.

She'd tried once to make a potion of her own. Where she'd found the packet, he hadn't the foggiest, but she'd dumped the whole thing into a little plastic bowl filled with water. Except, when she'd tried to heat it, the bottom of the bowl had blackened and warped, causing molten plastic to drip and scorch her fingers. How she'd howled. Josh had been no help; he never was in a crisis. He just disappeared. As always. So, it had fallen to Eric to try and help her.

He'd done his best, scooping her up as she writhed and wailed; barrelled into the bathroom with her; shoved her hand under cold water. But that was where his ten-year-old medical expertise ended. They'd needed an adult. It meant trying to wake their mother.

After becoming lucid enough to realise what had happened, she'd gone ballistic. Eric had taken the blame of course; it had been his job to protect his sister. Even now, he felt the vice-like grip of his mother's fingers around his throat. The feel of her choking him, his struggle for breath, his vision narrowing and the blood pounding in his head as he'd tried to break free. And the sound—*God*, the sound—of Sophie's terrified screams as she begged their mother to stop.

Eventually, she'd released her grip, letting him collapse to the floor in a blubbering heap, but it was just a momentary pause in the onslaught.

He'd barely managed a few ragged breaths before the kicks started—sharp, unrelenting blows that sent pain lancing through his trembling body. The first crack of his ribs had been agonising, a white-hot burst of pain that tore a bellow of anguish from his lungs. Before he could even process it, she'd delivered a brutal kick to his mouth that had split his lip wide open and sent a spray of crimson across the floor. In that moment, he'd wanted it to end, to let the pain swallow him whole. But Sophie—who would protect her if he gave up?

Somehow, through the haze of pain, Eric had found the strength to scream at Sophie, telling her to run. To get as far away as she could.

Then he'd blacked out.

That was the last time he saw their mother.

When Eric had regained consciousness, he found himself in a hospital bed. Over the next few days, he'd been visited by countless strangers. Doctors, nurses, police officers, social services. And although he'd hoped that things would improve, that he and Sophie would finally be free to have a normal childhood filled with happiness and love, instead of fear and abuse, it just wasn't meant to be. They were bounced around the foster system, too troubled to ever fit in, too broken to ever be whole. But he'd maintained his role as her protector. Made sure he did everything in his power to keep her safe.

Even now, though Sophie didn't believe it, he was still looking out for her. Admittedly, keeping her in a cage was far from ideal, but it was the only way to make sure that Josh wouldn't ruin everything. He had a way of doing that.

Josh. Eric sneered.

Pathetic, spineless Josh. Always the first to run when things got hard, leaving Eric to face the fallout. Every threat, every beating, every messy consequence—Eric bore it all while Josh cowered in the shadows. The very thought of him festered like rot in Eric's mind. And Sophie? She idolised Josh, hung on his every word.

As if Josh had ever done anything but fail her. It was infuriating.

If not for the risk of alienating Sophie forever, Eric would've rid himself of Josh years ago. But she'd never forgive him if she found out. And the idea of Sophie—the only person in this godforsaken world he actually gave two shits about—wanting nothing to do with him? That didn't bear thinking about.

So, Josh stayed. For now.

Sophie might hate him at the moment, but in time, she'd understand. Everything he was doing—everything he'd ever done—was for her. The world was a dark, brutal place, growing crueller by the day, but once he summoned Vamonthir, once he claimed the demon's promised power, all of that would change. He'd create a reality where Sophie would thrive, where no one could ever harm her again. She would finally see Eric for what he truly was: her protector, her saviour, her brother.

'Brother Bains is here.' Tommo broke him from his musing.

Eric turned and nodded. 'Thank you, Brother Thompson, I'll be there in a second.'

Tommo watched him for a moment, his eyes flicking to the wand, then, with a dip of his head, he retreated from the room.

He and his Brothers had gone over the details countless times in the past few days. But still, this was the last opportunity they'd have to iron out any wrinkles in their plan. Infiltrating O.O.T.I.S headquarters would be no mean feat, even with their man on the inside. This had to go without a hitch. He'd spent most of his childhood caged in the prison of abuse and neglect, too weak to change his fate, but now Eric had the opportunity to make sure he'd never be at the mercy of anyone else ever again. He wasn't about to let it slip through his fingers.

Eric placed the wand carefully back in its hiding place, dusted off his hands, and made his way through to the bar, where his Brothers were waiting. Without the familiar weight of the copper-bound crystal in his hand, he felt naked. Exposed.

Ben Cunningham eyed him from where he leant against the wooden counter atop the brick-bar front, the bruises on his face still livid from where Eric had attacked him days ago. Although his expression didn't show it, Eric could feel the man's resentment.

The whispers in Eric's head sighed, a rattling breath of dissatisfaction that resonated inside his skull.

Anger flared in Eric's chest. He balled his fists, consumed with thoughts of shattering his Brother's nose, of smashing his face into the empty bottles that littered the bar. It would be the least he deserved. How dare he stand there sulking like an ungrateful brat?

Ungrateful brat. The words stung. Something his mother used to say.

Eric stopped mid-stride, his gaze locking onto Ben. 'Something you want to say to me, Brother Cunningham?'

Ben rolled his eyes; the motion emphasised his slack-jawed expression.

Eric darted forward, grabbing Ben's chin in a vice-like grip. He forced his head down until their eyes met. 'I said, is there something you want to say to me, Brother Cunningham?'

Eric's unyielding grasp mashed his lips together. Ben struggled, his protests coming out in unintelligible garbles.

'How much pressure do you think it would take for me to crush your jaw?' Eric said, his voice almost gentle. Ben's eyes widened and pinpricks of sweat formed on his forehead. A primal instinct stirred inside Eric. The heat in his chest shifted, no longer blazing with fury but smouldering with something darker.

Control. Superiority. Power. *God*, it was intoxicating.

The whispers stirred at the edges of his delight, urging him to squeeze tighter.

With a grunt, Ben wrenched himself free, ruining the moment.

'That's it!' Ben yelled, rubbing at his jaw. The angry red imprint of Eric's fingers stood stark against his skin.

'I'm out. I'm fucking out. You've lost it!' He turned to the others, his voice rising. 'He's fucking lost it.'

They stared back at Ben, their faces impassive. Except for Sean, who smirked openly. Ben gaped at the other men, as though he'd expected them to take his side. He was sorely mistaken.

'Fuck it, I'm gone,' he added.

As Ben turned to leave, Eric grabbed his wrist. Strange how, despite being a good few inches taller, Cunningham seemed so small now. 'Does your wife know about your gamer girlfriend?'

The colour drained from Ben's face. 'How did you...' His eyes snapped to Sean. 'You bastard! You hacked my computer?'

Sean waggled his eyebrows, a shit-eating grin on his round face.

Ben shrank back against the bar as if he were no longer able to support his own weight.

Satisfied, Eric took a seat next to Tommo.

Little tantrum aside, he couldn't help but feel a sense of pride, seeing his Brothers adorned in their ceremonial garb. How far they'd all come since those days of shooting zombies online until the early hours of the morning. How strange to think that a common interest could have ultimately united them in a cause far greater than themselves. They were going to change the world, and Eric was going to lead them into their new utopia. He would be a god and they his disciples.

'Brothers.'

'Brother,' they replied in unison.

Eric made himself comfortable. 'Nice of you to join us, Brother Bains.'

The man grimaced. 'Sorry, I had to push a last-minute update to the production server. I couldn't leave until I was sure it deployed successfully.'

'Problems?'

He waved away Eric's concern. 'No, no. It's all good. Everything's in place for tomorrow. I've got the ID badges too.' He reached past his robes into his trouser pocket and pulled out a handful of plastic identification cards. 'You shouldn't need them,' he continued, handing the cards out. 'I've added your fingerprints into the system. Your bloodwork too, just in case. Not yours though, Sean—'

Eric cleared his throat pointedly.

'Uh... I mean, Brother Adams. You're going to have to wait outside in the van instead of Ben—Brother Cunningham.'

Sean's face screwed up in confusion. 'Why...' He trailed off, beady grey eyes widening as the realisation set in. He raked a hand through his tangle of greasy black curls, and shifted his bulk on the metal chair. 'Oh. Sure. No problem.'

Eric watched the exchange, confused. The fact that they were hiding something from him rankled. He ran his tongue over his teeth, but before he had a chance to ask about it, Ben let out a scoff.

Pushing himself away from the bar, Ben straightened. 'That wasn't the plan. It's my van, I'm not letting Sean drive it. Have you seen the state of his car? It's a biohazard.'

'Sorry, Ben, but Sean...' Bains flicked a nervous glance at Eric. 'I mean, Brother Adams, can't enter the premises.'

'And why's that?' Ben barked, glaring at the two men. 'No. Don't just look at each other. If there's some reason I can't drive my own van, I want to know.'

'Yes, Brother Bains, I'd like to know too,' Eric said, his words clipped.

The man tugged awkwardly at his sleeve, then rubbed the back of his neck. 'He's already in the system.'

Eric jerked upright in his seat. 'He's *what?*'

'Well, technically it's not him who's in the system,' he continued, shooting Sean a wary look, clearly deciding whether or not he should elaborate without the man's say so. 'But his fingerprints and DNA are.'

'And why exactly would that be?' Eric snapped.

'They're related to an unsolved crime.'

All eyes turned to Sean, who smirked and gave a shrug in response.

'Yeah, I bet I can bloody guess what sort of crime too,' Ben muttered. 'Say no, did she?'

Sean scowled. 'Watch it, Cunningham, or you'll get a broken nose to go with that busted lip and black eye.'

'I'd like to see you try, you fat fuck.'

'What did you just say to me? Are you forgetting that I have screenshots—'

'Enough!' Eric stood, thrusting a finger at Sean. 'Sean, shut the hell up. Ben, sit down. Now.'

Ben hesitated, his shoulders taut, as if he was weighing his options. But after seeing the expression on Eric's face, he slumped into his seat without another word.

Breathing sharply through his nose, Eric smoothed the front of his robes and cracked his neck. 'Tomorrow we're going to break the gatekeeper out of O.O.T.I.S headquarters. This is our last chance to go through the plan and make sure we haven't missed anything. Now, I don't know about the rest of you, but I definitely don't want to spend the rest of my life behind bars. So how about you two idiots quit your bitching and listen?' He stared them down, challenging them to argue.

Sean held up his hands in silent submission, Ben folded his arms and averted his gaze.

Good enough.

Lowering himself back into the chair, Eric exhaled. 'Let's go over the details one last time and then everyone can go home and get some rest. Because tomorrow, our lives will change forever.'

Chapter 12

Hot water cascaded down Charlie's body, slowly easing the tightness in his muscles. He scrubbed out the last of the shampoo and let his head fall back beneath the torrent. Fat droplets pelted his face, sending a pleasant tingle through his skin. Enveloped by steam and deaf to the sounds beyond the shower, he allowed the quiet moment to stretch, relishing every second of it. It was his only sanctuary these days.

Still, images of Evie—wide-eyed with confusion and fear, flinching away from him as though he might hurt her—tormented his thoughts. In the hours since he'd been home, he'd drained a bottle of whisky. It might as well have been water. With nothing to take the edge off the guilt and self-loathing, darkness had consumed him.

It had taken him a while to realise, but the demon's presence was less intense near water. He should've remembered this—Diane had told him as much on their first date, right before it had been interrupted. But then she'd also said that an open body of water could sever the demon's hold over its host, driving its essence back into the dagger.

Unable to brave the murk of the River Medway, he'd driven to Brighton and near enough caught pneumonia thrashing about in the English Channel like a complete lunatic. If not for the early-morning crowd of cold-water swimmers passing at that very moment, someone might have thought he was drowning. God only knew what the agents tailing him had thought.

It also hadn't worked.

Whether it was because, as the dagger's master, his connection to Kar'roc's Maw was different than it had been for Stephen, or because the blade was stuck inside Lily's digestive system, he didn't know. But either way, he'd been forced to listen to Chekonost's relentless bitching while he shivered on the one-and-a-half-hour drive back home.

A noise cut through the roar of shower water. He shut it off, standing still to listen. The doorbell rang again. Muttering a curse, he palmed the glass-panel door open and stepped out onto a towel.

'Who in the hell is that at this hour?'

Grabbing another towel off the radiator, he quickly dried off, wrapped it around his waist, and hurried down the stairs. In the few seconds it took for his feet to hit the cold hallway tiles, a million thoughts had already cycled through his head. Was there an emergency? Was someone hurt? But there was no urgency to the ringing, no insistent knock to accompany it.

O.O.T.I.S perhaps? Those inconsiderate bastards had priors for expecting him to drop everything at a moment's notice. Or maybe it was Meghan, here to demand an explanation for what had happened earlier. Guilt twisted in his gut like a knife. No, not Meghan. Not this late. Not past Evie's bedtime.

The bell chimed again as he reached the front door. Through the frosted glass, he made out the shadow of a figure. With a grunt of frustration, he yanked open the door, a surge of frigid air needling into his damp skin.

His jaw dropped.

'Debbie?'

No sooner had he recovered from the sight of his ex-wife standing on his doorstep than the demon's mocking laughter filled his mind. He clenched his jaw, his fist tightening around the door handle.

THE HARLOT RETURNS.

'What are you doing here?' His tone was caustic.

She said nothing, her brown eyes roaming his bare chest where the raised silver scars marked his childhood, before lingering on the curve of his abdominals. She unfastened her oversized handbag, which, mercifully, did not contain a yapping Chihuahua this time, and rummaged inside.

He peered past her at the driveway.

'I parked down the road,' she said simply. 'Thought you might not answer if you saw my car.'

She'd got that much right.

'You left this at Meghan's.' Debbie held his phone out to him.

'Oh. Thank you.' He went to take it, but she held on until he met her gaze.

KILL HER.

'It smells like paint,' she said, looking past him into the hallway.

He gave her an incredulous look.

She continued unperturbed, 'I think we need to talk about what happened today.'

'No. We don't.' Snatching the phone from her grasp, he took a step back. Not only was his damp skin starting to break out in goose bumps, but he was in full view of the neighbours wearing nothing but a towel.

'Charlie, what you did today... poor Evie was beside herself.'

'Thanks for bringing my phone back. Goodbye, Debbie.' He went to push the door shut with a little more force than was necessary. It stopped short, juddering against the flat of her palm.

She yanked her hand back with a hiss, curling her fingers in on themselves. 'I just want to talk.'

NOW SHE INTRUDES UPON YOUR TERRITORY. SHE CHALLENGES YOUR AUTHORITY. KILL HER.

Quiet.

'We've got nothing to talk about.'

'Please, Charlie, something's going on with you. I need to know you're okay.'

'I'm fine.'

'Just give me ten minutes.'

'My life has nothing to do with you anymore.'

'It does when it concerns our granddaughter.'

'*Our* granddaughter?' He spat out the words like acid.

Debbie didn't react. Didn't so much as flinch. But then, after a lifetime of practice, she wore deceit like a second skin.

KILL HER. SHE IS A LIAR. SHE MADE A FOOL OUT OF YOU.

Charlie's body tensed, his pulse quickening.

Just stop.

Mistaking his pause for deliberation, Debbie stepped closer and placed her hand against his chest. 'Ten minutes, then I'll leave. I promise.'

Her perfume filled his senses, the warmth of her palm awakening something raw inside him. He drew back, breaking physical contact, and fixed her with a dark look.

KILL HER. EAT HER EYEBALLS. I CAN'T REMEMBER THE LAST TIME I HAD ANY REAL FOOD.

I'm not killing my ex-wife.

FUCK YOUR EX-WIFE. I WANT TO EAT.

I don't care what you want. I command you to shut the hell up.

The demon's resentment bristled through to his core, but it said nothing else.

Debbie sighed, her posture sagging into something bruised, something vulnerable. 'Charlie, please.'

Against his better judgement, he stepped aside and allowed Debbie to brush past him into the house. He gave the door a firm shove; her scent wafted around him as it shut.

This was a mistake.

He turned to look at her, his fists already balled tight at his sides.

Ten minutes. He could control himself for ten minutes. The sooner this was over, the sooner she would leave. Despite everything she'd done, despite the lies, the heartache, he wasn't going to harm her. He was no animal.

And with the demon unable to take possession of his body without his permission, what was the worst that could happen?

Strident laughter exploded inside his skull.

'The place looks nice,' Debbie said, slipping off her heels and stepping deeper into the hallway. Her gaze surveyed the walls, the fish tank, and finally landed on him.

Charlie's jaw clenched. 'You said you wanted to talk. So, talk.'

Her expression was caught between curiosity and amusement. 'You're different.'

The words hit him like a wave of ice water, momentarily dousing the fire inside and leaving a chill that spread through his bones. *Christ*, did she know? No. That was impossible. There was no way she could know about the demon.

KILL HER ANYWAY, JUST TO BE SURE.

A muscle under his left eye twitched. He forced his face into something neutral.

'Different?' he echoed, keeping his voice low, controlled.

Debbie nodded, stepping closer, her bare feet padding against the tiles. 'Different,' she repeated. 'It's in your eyes. Your posture. The way you're holding yourself.'

'What the hell does that mean?' he spat. 'Look, if you don't want to talk, get out.'

But she didn't leave. Instead, she closed the distance between them, her perfume curling around him. He hated how her floral scent pulled memories to the surface. Of her touch, her warmth—her lies.

'Charlie,' she said softly, using the tone she did when she wanted something. 'I'm worried about you.'

'You don't get to worry about me anymore.' He squeezed his fists tighter, knuckles whitening.

She reached out and grazed his chest with her fingers.

NOW SHE MOCKS YOU. SHE THINKS YOU'RE WEAK. SHE THINKS YOU'RE STILL THE SAME FOOL WHO BELIEVED HER LIES. KILL HER.

The demon's voice echoed in his skull, causing his fingers to curl and uncurl, as if they might wrap around her throat of their own accord.

Debbie's touch lingered, her thumb brushing against him in a way that felt too familiar, too deliberate. Her lips parted slightly. Her gaze pinned his, as if daring him to react.

He did.

In one swift motion, he grabbed her wrist and pressed her against the wall. The movement was controlled but forceful, his larger frame caging her more petite one. Her breath caught. Her pupils dilated.

The demon roared its approval, the sound reverberating through his bones. YES. SNAP HER WRIST. THEN SNAP HER NECK. END HER.

'You don't get to come in here and play concerned,' Charlie said, his voice rough. 'Not after everything you've done.'

Debbie's lips curved into the faintest smirk, her chest rising and falling against him. Her eyes still locked onto his.

'So intense,' she murmured, her voice maddeningly close to amusement.

Charlie tightened his grip. Debbie gasped; the sound spurred on something darker in him. Something primal, something that wasn't entirely his.

He was losing control.

KILL HER.

Charlie released her wrist, his breaths coming hard. She had to leave. Now. Before he did something he would regret.

KILL HER!

'Get out,' he growled, his voice trembling with the effort it took to keep control.

Debbie tilted her head. Then, her smirk faded into something unreadable. 'I'll leave when I'm ready.'

Charlie slammed his palm against the wall next to her head. The sound from the crack he made echoed through the hallway. Plaster dust rained onto her hair, but she didn't flinch.

YES! CRUSH HER SKULL!

Christ, why wasn't she running? Why wasn't she scared?

He could feel it—the twisted part of him driving his every thought, his every emotion. Whether it was the demon screaming in his skull, or the dagger's influence over him, he couldn't say. All he knew was he was coming apart at the seams.

He needed her to leave. Now.

But deep down, Charlie already knew. It was too late.

Chapter 13

Josh blinked, his movements slow and stiff. His gaze went to the men seated in a circle near the bar. He had no idea what they were talking about, or even how long they'd been sitting there. He didn't dare ask. None of them had noticed his arrival anyway, and he wasn't about to announce himself. He needed to focus on what mattered: helping Sophie. But even as his mind rallied, fragments of their discussion vied for his attention.

'The dark web? You bought explosives, from the *dark web*?' Tommo scoffed, his doubt obvious.

Muffled, indistinct shouts from the cellar below drifted up through the floorboards. Squeezing his hands into fists, Josh tried to drown out the noise. Sophie or the other caged woman? He couldn't tell. But the thought of his sister, cold, filthy and terrified, ate him up inside. It brought back memories of their childhood. Memories he'd spent a lifetime trying to block out.

Not one of the men acknowledged the sound.

'*Yes*. The dark web,' Sean said tersely.

God, he hated Sean. He hated them all, but Sean was by far the worst. The things he said were vile. And the way he looked at the caged women, at Sophie, made

Josh's skin crawl. If it weren't for his computer skills, the others probably wouldn't have had anything to do with him.

He was a sicko. No one there could stand him, especially not Ben. The two of them were constantly at each other's throats—maybe because, unlike Sean, Ben had actually found a woman who wanted him.

Sean shifted on the metal chair. It groaned under his bulk. He dragged his stubby fingers through his tangle of greasy, black curls and glowered at Tommo. 'They'll work, alright? I did my homework.'

Tommo scoffed again. 'And if they don't—what then? We'll be royally fucked.'

'They'll work. I checked the reviews.'

'*Reviews*? Are you having a fucking laugh?'

'What would you know about it? Stay in your lane, Tommo. Let me worry about the explosives. You just carry on babysitting Josh.'

With a sour look that could have curdled milk, Tommo gave Sean the finger.

More stifled shouts below permeated the fraught pause in conversation.

'For the love of God, will someone go and see what they want!' Tommo yelled.

Sean repositioned himself again and for one heart-stopping moment, Josh thought he was about to volunteer.

'I'll go,' Ben said, his chair scraping against the scuffed oak flooring. He unfolded his lanky frame and got to his feet.

Josh exhaled quietly, relief washing over him. Keeping his expression neutral, he met Ben's gaze. Purple-black bruises were still livid on his face. He ran his tongue over the scab on his split lip, and returned the look with a flicker of hostility before leaving the room.

His heavy footsteps descended the stairs; the dampened drone of Ben's voice followed. Josh strained to listen, but the response was barely audible. Still, the yelling had stopped, which had to be a good sign.

Within moments Ben was back in the room.

'Sophie,' he said by way of explanation, taking his seat. 'Wanted more water.'

Tommo spoke to Sean again, picking up where he'd left off, 'What if you take out the whole O.O.T.I.S headquarters with us inside?'

'That won't happen,' Sean said.

'How d'you know? Just because you've watched a few online tutorials doesn't make you an expert.'

'And what's the alternative? It's not like I had much notice to get this ready.' Sean scowled and flashed a look at the man sat next to him.

Josh couldn't remember his name. Damien? Something like that. Compared to the others, he seemed to be around the least. Josh had disliked him from the moment they first met. There was something off about him. Maybe it was the way his dark eyes lingered on people when he thought no one was watching. Or maybe it was the beard. Josh didn't trust men with beards. Not since his mother had terrified him with stories about Santa Claus creeping into his room on

Christmas Eve to cut off his fingers and toes for being bad. 'That's why his suit is red,' she'd said. 'From the blood of all the naughty boys and girls.'

The man—whatever his name was—tossed up his hands defensively. 'I told you I thought the book would work. Anyway, I have a backup plan.' He shot Sean a contemptuous sideways glance. 'Just in case.'

Sean rolled his eyes.

'If you fuck it up, we'll be spending the rest of our lives inside a cell. That's all I'm saying.' Tommo shrugged. If he was trying to come off as nonchalant, he was failing. Miserably. He turned his attention to Josh. 'What d'you think?'

As one, the men turned to regard him.

Every muscle in his body tensed. Josh licked his lips, unable to grasp a single coherent thought in the murk of his mind. What did he think? He didn't have a clue...

'I... I think...' Warmth bloomed in his cheeks. 'I...'

Tommo leant forward in his seat, his head tilting slightly. His expression darkened. 'Joshua?'

Josh shrank in on himself.

Tommo huffed out a breath and dragged a hand over his ginger hair. 'For fuck's sake... Great. Just great.'

The men exchanged glances, their expressions ranging from irritation to unease.

'Well, this is bloody brilliant,' Ben said, kneading his forehead. The shadow cast by his arm blended with his bruises. 'What if Eric leaves us with this turd tomorrow?'

'He won't,' Tommo said.

'How can you be so sure? We're putting everything on the line. And this'—Ben gestured wildly at Josh—'idiot keeps showing up without a clue. My wife's already on the warpath after I got *mugged*.' He air quoted the last word. 'Wants to get the police involved.'

'Just divorce the fat bitch,' Sean muttered under his breath.

'Fuck you!'

Tommo held up his hands, putting a stop to their bickering. 'It won't happen tomorrow. He's only here because he heard Sophie, and she's not going to be there.'

'Expert now, are you?' Sean sneered. 'Why don't we just kill her? Eliminate the distraction once and for all, then Eric will finally get rid of Josh.'

The men continued to argue, ignoring Josh's sharp intake of breath. Did Eric really hate him that much? Maybe he should. After all, it was always Eric who'd got the raw end of the deal, taking the beatings meant for him and their sister. But Sophie? He hadn't thought Eric would actually let her come to any real harm. Josh needed to help her escape.

How though? With Tommo always sniffing around, there was no chance.

Tommo barked a humourless laugh. 'Oh yeah, that'd go down really well with Eric. She's technically his sister too, y'know. And besides, she's insurance.' He jerked his head at Josh. 'Against this one deciding to do anything stupid.'

'Wouldn't be a problem if Eric got rid of him, too. He's a waste of space.' Sean sniffed. 'Just look at him—gormless twat. Does my head in that I can't tell them apart.'

Josh hunched his shoulders, trying to make himself smaller. It was true—he and Eric looked the same—but the resemblance was only skin deep. Josh was the weak one. The useless one. He knew Eric's men hated him for it. And maybe they were right.

It wasn't as if he didn't know Eric's patience with him had been wearing thin; they'd made that clear time and time again. But it had never crossed his mind that his brother might want him gone for good. Eric had always kept him safe, always made sure he had food in his belly. That had to mean something. He wouldn't really try and get rid of him... would he?

Tommo huffed. 'Like that's going to happen. Whether you like it or not, they're a package deal.' He spoke as if Josh wasn't sitting just inches away

'I think—'

The sound of barking cut Sean off. With it, the squabbling died. All heads turned in the direction of the noise. With the windows boarded, there was no way for them to judge how close the dog was.

'Fuck,' Sean hissed. 'Turn the lights off.'

For once, everyone was in agreement, quickly switching off the LED camping lanterns and plunging the room into darkness.

Blind to his surroundings, Josh had no choice but to listen with the others. He rubbed nervously at his collarbone, holding his breath.

The barking became louder. Short, sharp little yaps that ricochetted like bullets inside the room. Worse still, they were accompanied by the calls of its owner.

'What do we do?' Ben whispered.

'Just keep quiet,' Tommo replied.

Yells erupted from the basement. Their desperate cries for help were fuelled by such raw, animalistic intensity, they froze the blood in Josh's veins. The screams were interspersed with a frenzied clatter of metal, as he imagined the cages being tested to their limits.

Sean lurched out of his chair. 'Fuck! Grab the lights, we need to find whoever's out there before they call the police.' Light exploded around them. Lantern in hand, he raced out of the room.

The others quickly followed suit. But when Josh went to stand, Tommo gripped his shoulder, forcing him back down.

'Not you,' he said, his fingers digging tighter. 'You stay here. Don't move until we get back. Understand?'

Josh gave a weak nod.

Releasing his grip, Tommo bolted away.

Josh took a shaky breath and counted back from ten before exhaling. Certain that the other men were gone, he snatched up the last remaining light and hurried towards the cellar.

The women's shrieks pierced his skull as he raced down the stairs two at a time.

'Josh?' Sophie croaked, shying away from the light.

'We need to hurry.' Rushing to the cage, he tested the padlock and winced. He'd need to find something strong enough to break it apart.

'Did it work? Did the person with the dog hear us?'

'I don't k-know.' His sister's face dropped. She shared a nervous glance with the woman in the cage beside her. Josh moved the lantern around, casting jerky light over the floor and walls. 'Tommo and the others, they've gone after them. We won't have l-long until they get back.'

A dented stainless-steel keg caught his eye. Placing the light down, he darted over to it and tested its weight. It was heavier than expected considering it was empty—a good ten kilograms at least. Lifting it against his chest, he carried it hastily back to the cage.

'Soph, move.' Waiting until his sister was as far back as humanly possible, he slammed the keg down on the lock.

A loud *clang*, broken only by the startled yelps of the women, reverberated around the cellar. But the padlock remained intact, showing no more damage than a slight notch where the keg had struck.

'Shit!' Hoisting it up, Josh put his full weight behind the next swing.

Again, the women shrieked. Again, the lock remained unbroken.

No, no, no. This couldn't be happening. He needed to break her out. Needed to save his sister before it was too late.

The sound of arguing and a door banging shut froze him to the spot.

'Josh, please! *Please*, you have to get us out of here!' Sophie's voice trembled, rising in pitch with every panicked word.

'I—I...'

Heavy footsteps pounded against the floorboards above, raining fragments of dust and plaster down into his hair.

'Joshua?' a voice rang out, urgent and strained.

Tommo.

Josh staggered back, letting the keg fall with a crash.

'No, Josh! No. Help us. Please, you have to help us,' Sophie pleaded.

'Joshua!' Tommo's shout was louder this time.

The cellar door shrieked on its hinges as it was slammed open. Harsh artificial light flooded in. Heavy footsteps thundered down the stairs, punctuated by Tommo's grumbled curses.

His eyes locked on Josh. 'There you are! I told you not to move.'

'I... I just wanted to...'

'Yeah, yeah. Whatever.' Tommo approached Sophie's cage and gave the lock a firm yank.

Josh held his breath, waiting for him to notice the slight dent. He needn't have worried. Tommo moved his attention to the second cage, giving it a cursory once over.

He turned to face Josh, but whatever he was about to say was interrupted by the sound of laboured grunts and raised voices.

'No, let me go first, fucking knob jockey.' Sean appeared at the top of the stairs, his back to the cellar. In awkward backwards steps he made his way down, struggling with something in his arms.

'Stop pulling!' Ben hissed between pants.

'Just hurry the fuck up, before she comes to and starts thrashing about.'

It was then that Josh saw the woman they were carrying between them. Her boots were caked in mud, her jeans too, as if she'd fallen—or had been pushed. Her head bobbed with each step, a mess of brown hair obscuring her face. Ben's hands were locked around her chest, supporting the bulk of her weight, his expression strained.

When he reached the last step, Sean released his hold.

'What the fuck?' Ben lurched forward, almost losing his footing as he fought to keep his grip on the woman. Half-stumbling, he sloped down the last few steps and managed to right himself at the last second. 'You arsehole!'

Damien followed after, looking decidedly unimpressed as he picked at a muddy stain on his robes.

Ignoring Ben's complaints, Sean stalked towards the caged women.

'That, was really fucking stupid.' He crouched down, thick fingers weaving into the bars of Sophie's cage.

She glared back at him.

Sean added, 'If it were up to me, I'd cave your head in and be done with it. But for some inexplicable reason, Eric wants you alive. You on the other hand...' He shifted his gaze to the other woman, who flinched back. 'You're disposable.' Rising, he wiped his muddy hands down his robes and stood next to Ben. 'I'm going to teach you two a very valuable lesson about behaving yourselves. For your own good.'

He inclined his head, signalling to Ben. Ben stared back at him blankly, still clutching the newcomer.

Sean rolled his eyes. 'Put her down. Jesus Christ.'

Frowning, Ben laid the woman on the concrete and stepped back. She groaned weakly.

Josh released a breath. She wasn't dead.

'Your light.' Sean held out his hand to Tommo.

Tommo squinted in suspicion, but handed it over. 'Just put her in one of the cages and be done with it.'

Sean smiled. 'Cages? Oh no, that won't teach them anything.' The white glow of the lantern skimmed the cellar as he searched. He was taking his time, leering at the caged women before moving onto a new area. Eventually he stopped, the light falling on something dark and metallic discarded on the floor. 'This should do the trick.' He stooped to grab it.

When he rose, Josh saw he gripped the handle of a sledgehammer.

His chest heaved with stilted, uneven breaths that caught painfully in his throat. His pulse roared in his ears, drowning out everything but the metallic scrape of the discoloured weapon dragging against the concrete. He tried to call out, to tell Sean to stop, but his voice betrayed him, locked tight in his throat. Why couldn't he move? Why couldn't he do something? The scene unfolding in agonisingly slow motion.

'Just remember,' Sean said, hefting the sledgehammer over his shoulder with a grunt, 'this is because of you.' In one sharp swing, he brought the weapon down on the dog walker.

Her skull caved with a wet, meaty crunch, the impact shattering bone and rupturing flesh in a spray of crimson. Shards of her teeth scattered across the floor, a dark pool spreading beneath her twitching body.

The cellar exploded in a cacophony of hysterical screams, cries of outrage and mutters of disbelief.

Josh dropped to his knees and retched.

'Quiet!' Sean's voice echoed through the clamour, demanding immediate attention. There was a squelch as he pulled the sledgehammer free from the deformed mess of the woman's face, strings of bloody tissue and pulp clinging to the block of gore-splattered steel. He lowered his voice, addressing Sophie directly, '*You* did this. Remember that the next time you decide to do something stupid.'

Josh wheezed, clawing at the front of his robes, at his neck. The air was too thick, too heavy to fill his lungs.

What if it was Sophie next time? What if his sister died because of him? He wasn't strong enough to save her. He needed help. Oh God, he needed help!

Arms trembling and cold sweat pricking across his skin, Josh fought for breath. Darkness twisted around him, filling his vision. He reached out, grasping blindly for Sophie, for his sister, but he hit the concrete before he could. The pounding thump of his own heartbeat was the last thing he heard as he succumbed to the inevitable.

Chapter 14

He'd lost control.

Simple as that. Fucked up big time.

Charlie winced against the morning sunlight and released the blind with a hiss before pacing his living room. He could still smell Debbie's floral perfume, a lingering reminder of the madness that had taken hold of him.

Christ. What had he done?

What the hell am I going to do?

He raked a hand down his face.

What am I going to tell Meghan?

No. He could never tell Meghan. He could never tell *anyone*. If they ever found out what he'd done...

'Shit.'

He glanced at the carpet, then at the hallway, his gaze drawn to the glaring crack in the plaster there and the blood staining the wall. The evidence was everywhere. His guilt laid bare for all to see. He couldn't bring himself to do anything about it right now. Just the sight of it made his stomach roil.

And her car. Where did Debbie say she'd parked it? What if someone had seen her entering his house?

Entering but not leaving. There might be witnesses. Loose ends.

He swore again.

Memories of the previous evening replayed in his mind. He shook his head in an effort to force them out.

He'd been so riled up. He shouldn't have let her in, damn it. It was a mistake. He'd known it at the time. But it was too late now. The damage was done. All he could do was cover his tracks and hope for the best.

The whisper of tyres outside brought Charlie up short. He rushed to the window and tugged the blind open just a fraction. *Jasmin.* With a curse, he ducked out of sight.

'Double shit.'

Squeezing his eyes shut, he attempted to formulate a plan.

The ring of the doorbell followed by a swift knock obliterated his thoughts. Not moving an inch, Charlie held his breath. Maybe if he didn't answer, Jasmin would leave.

Another knock followed, harder this time.

'Charlie, open up!'

He remained perfectly still.

'Look, I know you're in there. I literally just saw you looking out. Don't be a dick, open up.'

Cursing himself, he trudged into the hallway.

Smoothing his features, he opened the door a few inches. 'Jasmin, what a pleasant surprise.'

She arched a dark eyebrow in response, clearly waiting for an explanation. When it became apparent that none was forthcoming, she crossed her arms and gave him a withering look. 'Really? This is how you want to play it?'

'I... uh...'

'Are you going to leave me out here until I freeze?' Her breath fogged in the frigid air.

Charlie stared at her, words dying on his tongue, as his mind fumbled for an excuse.

She leant in, one gloved hand pressing against the door.

He tightened his grip, holding it firmly in place.

Jasmin frowned. 'Charlie, what's going on? Why can't I come in? You're acting like you've got a body hidden in there.'

He swallowed hard, forcing himself not to look back at the cracked plaster.

Her blue eyes sparkled with sudden mischief.

'Charlie?' she said, her voice dropping to a conspiratorial whisper. 'Have you got company? Is it Diane?' A sly grin spread across her face.

He shook his head, words still eluding him.

'Come on, Charlie,' she teased, 'Your secret's safe with me. I'm just impressed you finally made a move.'

Panic clawed at his insides. He opened his mouth to protest, but only managed a strangled croak.

'Charlie?' Debbie's voice drifted from upstairs.

The change in Jasmin's expression was instant, all humour gone. Her eyes narrowed, darting from Charlie to the space behind him. 'Tell me that's not who I think it is. Charlie, please tell me that's not your ex-wife.'

His shoulders sagged beneath the weight of his shame.

'Charlie?' Debbie called again, her footsteps creaking on the floor above. 'Who's at the door?'

Jasmin took a step back, her expression hardening into a mask of disgust. 'Seriously?'

'It's none of your business,' Charlie snapped. He flicked a look at the stairs and lowered his voice. 'Just drop it.'

'The hell I will. Debbie? Your ex-wife Debbie? The one who—' She shook her head in disbelief. 'Jesus, Charlie. After everything she put you through? After what she did? And now you're back together?'

'We're not back together!'

'When Megs finds out—'

'No! Please, Jasmin, she can't know about this. Please, don't say anything.'

'You think I'm an idiot? Of course *I'm* not going to say anything, but Debbie...' She left the sentence hanging.

Charlie groaned and pinched the bridge of his nose.

'What the hell were you thinking?' Jasmin added.

'I wasn't—'

'Clearly. But *Debbie?*'

'It was a mistake.'

'I thought you were into Diane?'

Charlie flinched.

'Jesus, Charlie,' Jasmin continued, 'what's going on with you lately? That outburst in front of Evie yesterday—yes, Megs filled me in. She's still fuming by the way.' The look on her face told him that she intended to have a whole other conversation about that.

'Retirement—and honestly, I never thought I'd see the day—then I catch you smoking, now this? I just don't get it.'

'You don't *get it*?' he said flatly, rubbing at his left hand, at the sigil.

Her expression softened. 'Look, Charlie, I know you've been through a lot. Between Stephen, O.O.T.I.S, and what happened at the dockyard... it's been hard for you. I get it. But with the way you've been behaving lately, I'm worried you're losing it.'

'Losing it? Of course I'm losing it!' Hearing the creak of another floorboard above him, he lowered his voice again. 'My best friend turned out to be possessed by an eyeball eating monster. I find out demons and witches are real. I get bullied by the supernatural fucking secret service. Then my family gets kidnapped by a psychopath with magical powers and I—' He snapped his jaw shut. *Christ*, he'd almost let the cat out of the bag.

'And you what?'

'And I can't say a damned thing about it to anyone. Evie and Meghan don't remember a thing. I haven't seen Nick since he admitted himself to Alnus House. And all Sachiko ever wants to do is stick me with a needle like I'm some sort of pin cushion.' He shook his head and sighed. 'Even with the medication the nightmares have started again.'

'You can talk to me, Charlie.'

'I know. I know I can, it's just...'

'You still don't trust me after finding out I work for O.O.T.I.S?'

'No, it's not that.' He shrugged. 'It's just been a lot to process.'

A breeze stirred at Jasmin's ponytail. She smoothed it back into place.

'Is Evie okay?' Charlie asked, avoiding her gaze.

'Yeah, she's fine. You know how resilient kids are.'

Her tight smile told him there was more to it than that, but he didn't push it.

Soft footsteps padding down the stairs made him turn. Debbie's mouth curled into a smile. Oblivious to the way his every muscle tensed, she sauntered into the living room and returned a second later with a black-lace bra in her hands.

Christ, of course she'd make a performance out of it. Why couldn't she just put the damned thing back on like a normal person? Debbie never missed an opportunity to twist the knife, and this was no different.

PLEASE, NO. I BEG YOU! I WOULD RATHER PIT INFERNALS REND THE INNARDS FROM MY BODY AND FEAST UPON MY FLESH THAN BE SUBJECTED TO SUCH VILE ACTS OF DEPRAVITY AGAIN.

Jasmin cleared her throat.

Cheeks burning, Charlie gave her an imploring look.

'You're an idiot,' she muttered.

AND THE SOUNDS. I CAN STILL HEAR THE SOUNDS OF YOUR FLESHY BODIES MASHING TOGETHER.

Please, stop.

THAT IS WHAT I SAID, BUT YOU DID NOT LISTEN. I CAN NEVER UNSEE SUCH HORRORS. MY MIND IS FOREVER SOILED.

Stop.

SOILED!

Sensing his ex-wife behind him, Charlie opened the front door wider in the hopes that she would get the hint.

Debbie ran her finger over the cracked plaster, where spots of his blood smeared the white wall.

'Looks like you cut yourself when you punched it,' she mused, turning to the door and shamelessly tucking her bra into her handbag. 'Jasmin, I didn't expect to see you here.'

'I could say the same.' Jasmin's eyes never left Charlie as she spoke. She was enjoying watching him squirm.

'Jesus, could this get any worse,' he breathed.

A familiar car pulled up outside the drive. Charlie's jaw dropped. 'Oh, shit.'

Jasmin followed his gaze. 'Oh shit is right.'

Charlie could only look on in horror as Diane climbed out of her car, pausing briefly to grab something from inside.

His appointment with O.O.T.I.S! As his handler, it was Diane's job to ensure he attended his routine check-ups. How could he have forgotten? She was always like clockwork.

He turned to Debbie. 'You need to leave.'

She huffed. 'Well, that's rude.'

Every click of Diane's heels as she made her way up the driveway was like a nail in the coffin of his impending doom.

'Do something,' he hissed at Jasmin.

She held up her hands. 'Nuh uh, you made your bed.'

The knot in his gut pulled tighter.

Diane, clutching a drink carrier with two cups, flashed him a smile. As she drew closer, her brow creased. Her loose golden-blonde curls stirred in the breeze as her amber eyes flicked from Charlie to his ex-wife and back again.

'It seems you're popular today,' Debbie purred.

'Charlie, Jasmin,' Diane said with a nod, before returning her focus to Debbie. 'I'm sorry, I don't believe we've met?'

'Deborah. I'm Charlie's wife.'

'Ex-wife,' he blurted.

Diane's gaze lowered to Debbie's handbag, where the bra was still on show. Her lips pressed together. 'I see.' She turned her attention back to Charlie. 'Well, I came to give you a lift to your appointment, but I can see now that you're otherwise engaged. I'll leave you to it.' She swivelled on her heel and strode back the way she'd come.

'Diane, wait, please!' Charlie dashed after her, ignoring the frigid chill of the slabs as his bare feet slapped against them.

Catching up with her, he placed a gentle hand on her shoulder.

She stopped abruptly. And seeing the warning written across her face, he let his arm drop.

'Dee...' Her eyes became slits. He corrected, 'Diane, please, it isn't what you think.'

'Isn't what I think?' Each word balanced on a knife's edge.

'I can explain. It was a—'

'An accident? Are you seriously going to stand there and tell me that you *accidently* slept with your ex-wife?'

'No, that's not... It was a mistake.'

The heat of her glare seared into his soul as she looked him over. 'It certainly was. I should probably thank you. At least now I know where I stand.'

'Please, let me explain.'

'You don't owe me an explanation, Charlie. You don't owe me anything. It's not like we're a couple. You said you needed space and I gave it to you. However you choose to *fill* that space is up to you. I'm sure you can find your own way to headquarters by now.'

'Diane...'

Without another word, she walked away from him.

It was over. Before it had even begun.

THIS IS MY FAULT. I SHOULD HAVE MADE IT CLEAR THAT WHEN I TOLD YOU TO FUCK YOUR EX-WIFE, I WAS NOT BEING LITERAL.

Everything was falling apart. His career was over. His relationship with his daughter and granddaughter was hanging by a thread. And now he'd ruined any chance he'd ever had with Diane, all because of his connection to that damned dagger.

THERE IS A SOLUTION...

Charlie hung his head. He was hollowed out, scraped raw.

Diane's engine roared. He watched, rooted to the spot, as her car peeled away from the kerb, putting all the distance in the world between them.

Fine. Let's find your damned gatekeeper.

Chapter 15

SACHIKO GAVE THE NEW *morishio* dish another glance. Getting APD to make one on such short notice had cost her the last of her favours—she didn't want it to go to waste.

With a frown, she checked her watch again. Charles was never late. She'd give him another ten minutes, then, if she hadn't heard anything, she'd check in with Diane. It was ultimately Diane's responsibility to ensure that he presented at O.O.T.I.S headquarters whenever the need arose. But then Diane was rarely ever late either...

Had something happened to them? Perhaps they were just caught in traffic.

It was too soon to assume the worst, but her impatience was getting the better of her. She needed Charles here—to test her theory. If the *morishio* reacted to his presence, it would confirm what she'd suspected all along. The demon's essence wasn't confined to Kar'roc's Maw anymore—it had taken root inside him.

She pulled her mobile from her pocket. No missed calls. No text messages. With her mind made up, she opened the door.

A dark shape blocked her path.

She leapt back with a startled yelp, her heel catching the edge of the *morishio* dish. Salt scattered across the floor, leaving a sorry-looking mound in place of the cone shape she'd moulded.

Great, she'd disturbed the warding. No harm done. It would still work when Charles arrived.

'Sorry, didn't mean to scare you.' Damanjeet gave a nervous chuckle. 'I was about to knock, but y'know...' He held up the two coffees and gave a half-shrug.

'Damanjeet...' His smile wavered for a split second. She corrected, 'Sorry... Daman. I was just on my way to find Diane.'

'I wouldn't if I were you.' He glanced back, as if checking to see if anyone was in earshot. 'She's on the warpath this morning.'

'Was Charles Haynes with her?'

'Who?'

'He's... Never mind. Do you know if she's been here long?'

'No idea. I bumped into her on the way here and she near enough bit my head off just for saying hello.' He eyed the salt spread across the tiles. 'Shit. Is that my fault?'

Sachiko sighed. 'It's fine. I think perhaps I need to rethink where I put it.'

He held one of the drinks out to her. 'At least it didn't break this time. I guess me and mori...'

'*Morishio*,' she said, eyeing the paper cup hesitantly. Hopefully he wasn't going to make a habit out of this.

The mystic eye of the Déjà Brew logo stared back at her. Relenting, she accepted the coffee with a nod of thanks.

'I guess me and *morishio* don't mix.' Damanjeet stifled a yawn with the back of his hand. 'Excuse me, late night.'

Sachiko noticed the dark circles under his eyes and the scruff of his usually well-groomed beard. His posture seemed a little more rigid than usual, and there was a faint tremor in the hand holding his cup. Just how much caffeine had he had?

'Are you feeling okay, Daman?'

He snatched another look back, then made a quick check of his watch before answering. 'Me? Yeah, I'm good. Nothing an early night won't cure. Plus, it's not like I'll be doing anything more strenuous than sitting at my desk today. How about you? They keeping you locked up in here all day?'

'I was supposed to be doing a health check, but I think my appointment is going to be a no show.'

Someone cleared their throat; it caught them both off-guard. Sachiko peered past Damanjeet to see an agent walking towards them with Charles in tow.

'Excuse me Doctor, but your patient is here,' the agent said, giving her a nod then stationing himself outside the door.

Damanjeet shot a glance at the newcomer before stepping aside.

'I'll leave you to it,' he said, not waiting for Sachiko's response. He hurried down the hallway.

Sachiko let out a breath, glad he was gone. She still hadn't reestablished the boundaries between them, to make it clear that a romantic relationship was off the cards. But Charles was the more pressing issue right now. Damanjeet would have to wait.

Arching an eyebrow at the stuffed pink duck clutched in Charles' grip, Sachiko motioned for him to enter. Her gaze snapped to the *morishio* as he crossed the threshold, anticipating the salt's reaction.

Nothing happened.

She didn't know whether to be relieved or disappointed. On the one hand, Charles clearly wasn't a demonic threat. On the other, that meant that her suspicions of him were completely unjustified. She felt a twinge of guilt as their eyes met.

He inclined his head in greeting. 'Doctor.'

The door clicked shut behind him, the lock automatically sliding into place.

'Good morning, Charles.'

As usual, his eyes flicked to each of the security cameras in turn before he removed his jacket and sat on one of the padded, grey swivel chairs. He scowled briefly at the treadmill stationed next to the examination table, and placed the duck down by his feet. A small squeak sounded from it.

Sachiko gestured at it. 'Another gift for Lily?'

Charles nodded. 'She seems to like them.'

'You're really making good on your promise to Nick.'

'Yeah, well, it's the least I can do, given everything that happened.' The touch of bitterness in his tone didn't escape her attention.

She decided to drop it. From what she understood, his relationship with Nick had become strained over recent weeks, and, given his apparent mood, it was probably best not to pry. 'Anything to report since our last appointment?'

His mouth twitched slightly before he answered, 'No.'

Sachiko placed her coffee down and smoothed her hands down her lab coat. As she did, her fingers grazed the vial of sedative concealed within the lining.

'What's with the salt?' Charles asked.

She felt her cheeks flush. 'Sorry, I didn't have time to clean it up before you arrived. If it bothers you, I can do it now?'

His hazel eyes studied her face. 'No. It's fine.'

'In that case, shall we get the blood test over with first?'

'Sure.' His gaze shifted to the phlebotomy tray, his body stiffening almost imperceptibly. 'Actually, there is something.'

She paused, curiosity piqued.

'The medication you gave me, to help me sleep, it's not working anymore. Are you able to up the dosage at all?'

When he'd first become master of Kar'roc's Maw, Charles had been less than forthcoming about the nightmares that plagued him. He didn't trust O.O.T.I.S. Didn't agree with their methods. Any information he gave was like getting blood from a stone. It wasn't until his stress levels had become so high and he'd inadvertently summoned the dagger in his sleep that he was forced to admit the truth. Sachiko had offered him medication, but he'd refused, just as she knew he would. After the battle with Banning Lawrence, however, he'd finally relented. By then, Lily had ingested the dagger, so summoning it by accident was no longer a concern for Charles or for O.O.T.I.S.

Still, Sachiko had hoped it was a sign of progress—that he was starting to trust them. To trust her. But as her suspicions over the demon's essence grew, she began to wonder if his acceptance had been nothing more than a ruse to lower her guard and throw her off the scent.

Regardless, given how difficult it had been to get Charles to accept any form of medication in the first place, for him to ask now meant things must be bad.

Keeping her expression neutral, she said, 'When did it stop working?'

'A couple of weeks ago maybe.'

Sachiko frowned, her attention flicking to the *morishio*. She pushed her suspicions aside. If Charles was a threat, she would know it already. 'Could you tell me more about the nightmares?'

He tensed, averting his gaze. For a moment she thought he wouldn't answer—when it came to anything even remotely personal, he became guarded—but then he said, 'They're always the same. I'm alone, in a barren wasteland. The ground is uneven, cracked and dry, with jagged rocks and dust everywhere, like something out of a sci-fi film. Mountains in the distance. Thick, black clouds in the sky. And this red glow, like the world's on fire. I walk, but get nowhere. Then everything starts to shake, the earth tearing itself apart beneath my feet. I hear...' He paused, as if trying to decide how to phrase his next sentence, worrying at the black ring on his little finger. It was a new quirk, a way to channel his anxiety that had seemingly replaced his old habit of rubbing at his bare ring finger.

'What do you hear?' she prompted.

'There's something trying to break free, something clawing its way out of the ground in front of me. Something huge. I can feel its hatred, its hunger. And then, just as its talons breach the void, I wake up.'

Sachiko sensed there was more to it than that, something he was leaving out. But she'd learnt that if she pushed Charles too hard, he'd close off completely.

'Do you think it's related to my connection to the dagger?' he said, his eyes drifting to the spot where the reinforced glass cabinet that once held Kar'roc's Maw used to stand.

'It's possible. Are these the same nightmares you were having before your encounter with Banning Lawrence at the dockyard?'

Charles' expression changed. Just the slightest hint of suspicion flickering in his eyes.

'Yes.'

'Through your bond with the dagger you have a direct connection to the demon realm. Perhaps what you're experiencing is a sort of residual feedback. A glimpse into the other side as it were.'

The colour drained from his face. He shifted on the seat, his fists clenching and unclenching in a steady rhythm. 'Christ.' He swallowed and stilled his hands. 'Has this sort of thing happened before?'

'To be honest, I've no idea. Your best bet would be to speak with Diane. She's the expert on Kar'roc's Maw. If there's any documented evidence of something similar, she'd know about it.'

For a few seconds he said nothing, then he released a breath, visibly deflating. 'She's not speaking to me at the moment.'

'Why not? What did you do?'

He stared down at his shoes. 'I don't want to talk about it.'

Sachiko hummed in amusement. Someone was in the dog house.

'That bad, eh? Whatever you did, I'm sure she'll come around. Diane can be hot-headed at times, but she's usually quick to forgive.'

He pulled a face that told her he wasn't so sure.

Making a mental note to update his files regarding the nightmares, Sachiko picked up the tourniquet. She waited for Charles to unbutton his cuff and roll up his sleeve, then stepped forward.

Sachiko added, 'She likes sunflowers.'

Charles tilted his head. 'Sorry?'

'Diane. She likes sunflowers.'

'Oh. Right. Thanks.'

The conversation was clearly going nowhere, but since Charles hated needles, she liked to keep him distracted.

'How was your retirement party?' she asked, tightening the band around his upper arm with a firm tug and prodding lightly at the crook of his elbow.

His posture went rigid. He followed her movements as she pulled on a pair of latex gloves. 'Fine.'

'Did they get you anything nice?' She indicated that he should make a fist. Then, with a practiced motion, she inserted the needle into his vein and secured it in place. Blood flowed immediately, filling the light-blue-topped citrate collection tube in seconds.

'Whisky.' Not giving her the chance to ask any follow-up questions, he said, 'Who was that you were talking to?'

She swapped out the filled tube for the next, her forehead creasing. 'Talking to?'

'When I arrived.'

'Oh! Damanjeet.' Seeing the amused quirk of his lips, she added, 'He's just a colleague.'

'He seemed a bit flustered. Jittery.'

'Did he?'

Charles didn't reply.

He sniffed and, not for the first time, his fingers twitched against the padding of the seat. Could he smell the sedative she was concealing? Sachiko glanced down at him, but he quickly masked his expression. No, of course he couldn't. Her gaze drifted back to the *morishio*, a stark reminder of her unfounded suspicions. Guilt knotted in her stomach.

With the last of the samples secured, Sachiko removed the tourniquet, gently withdrew the needle, and pressed a cotton ball against the blood beading on Charles' pierced flesh.

He tracked her every move, watching her like she might try something. What, she couldn't guess. At five feet two, a little out of shape, and no magical ability whatsoever, there was no way she could overpower him if it came to that. They both knew it. That was why she'd created the sedative—a potent blend of valerian root, propofol, and lindwurm venom. Lethal to most, but for Charles, whose connection to the dagger imbued his body with the ability to neutralise ordinary compounds and toxins, it was the perfect mix to render him unconscious if necessary.

It wasn't personal. She took the same precaution with all her patients. Agents often arrived under the influence of something—parasites, venoms, spells—and could become a danger to themselves and everyone around them. The sedative was a failsafe, nothing more. A tool to balance the scales. Knowing she had it reassured her. Despite her lack of combat training, she could still protect herself if things went wrong.

Even so, Sachiko couldn't deny the relief she felt knowing she wouldn't need to use it on him. Her earlier suspicions about Charles had genuinely terrified her. The thought of having to subdue him—or worse—was something she'd rather not think about. Because despite all his griping, she liked him.

But duty came first. If the demon had been inside him, she'd have done what was necessary.

She hadn't been entirely honest with him earlier. There were a few scattered records about previous masters of Kar'roc's Maw, though they were scarce. And while it was true that Diane was the expert, Sachiko had come across one story, an incident so shrouded in uncertainty, it bordered on myth. Centuries ago, a warlord prince had supposedly become both the dagger's master and the host to its demonic essence. His mind, warped by Kar'roc's influence, had unravelled completely. He'd turned on all those around him, slaughtering vassals, allies, even his own family, in a relentless attempt to breach the veil that lasted weeks, before finally being killed.

She shuddered at the thought of Charles meeting the same fate. In recent history, only Stephen Anderson had succumbed to the dagger's temptation, and he had proven difficult enough to neutralise without being its master as well. But Charles... If her suspicions had been right and he'd been left unchecked, there would have been nothing she or anyone else could have done to stop the past repeating itself.

Whether the tale was true or just a cautionary fable to warn against meddling with forbidden artefacts, she couldn't say. But she was glad it no longer mattered.

Chapter 16

ERIC STEPPED OUT OF the coffee shop, drink in hand, and tugged on the hem of his tailored, black suit jacket. It was too short. At five feet eleven, he was by no means a giant, but the jacket was at least an inch or two smaller in the body than it should have been. Apparently, it was the best that could be found on such short notice. There wasn't much he could do about it now. At least the trousers fit.

Aware of Tommo by his side, he took a sip of coffee and glanced across the road. A swell of excitement rose in his belly. So, this was O.O.T.I.S headquarters?

The building was colossal. Pale terracotta brickwork stretched as far as the eye could see, punctuated by tall, narrow windows that glinted in the sunlight. A wide, sweeping archway carved into the façade encompassed the main entrance, flanked by looming towers crowned with spires that looked as if they'd been plucked straight from some gothic fairytale.

Men wearing black suits that matched his own filtered in and out, mingling with the pedestrian traffic. To the untrained eye, they looked like any other business professionals—bankers, politicians, lawyers. The sort of corporate bloodsuckers who'd be right at home in such a grandiose structure.

Yet, as he stared, he felt his attention begin to drift, and the building slip into the back of his mind. A spell. It was one of the Order's many defence mechanisms, a phenomenon that apparently its agents took months to acclimatise to. He'd been told elaborate spellwork imbued its foundations, intricate threads of magic woven through every inch of the structure to guard against any and every supernatural threat.

But therein lay the weakness. So much care and attention had been given to repel otherworldly threats that they'd overlooked the most obvious: humans. Ordinary men with ordinary weapons.

And he was ordinary. For now.

Eric drained his cup, letting the last of the flat white warm his insides. It'd been weeks since he'd enjoyed a decent coffee—trapped inside the crumbling walls of that godforsaken pub—and he wasn't about to let the pleasure go to waste. He closed his eyes, savouring the last velvety mouthful on his tongue, the rich balance of bitter and sweet filling his senses. With a final appreciative glance, he crushed the cup in his fist and tossed it into the nearby bin.

If all was going to plan, the cameras covering the rear of the building should already be looping on a timed override. Risky, but it was the only way to guarantee they wouldn't catch Sean and Ben planting the charges.

The location was ideal: no public access, no through-routes, minimal footfall. By now the pair should be in position. Each charge had been disguised as something mundane—rat traps, old paint cans—rubbish no one would bother looking at twice.

The explosives weren't for breaching walls necessarily; they were for buying time. When the chaos started, Eric and his remaining Brothers would already be on their way out, the gatekeeper secured in tow, and Sean ready and waiting for them in the van. Timing was everything.

Squeezing his hands into fists, Eric let the sharp pain from his scabbed palms ground him. The simple memory of the copper strands piercing his skin as the crystal drank its fill was enough to refocus his thoughts. What he wouldn't give to have the Bloodvein Wand with him right now. He'd very nearly stashed it in the inner pocket of his suit jacket, but even through the dense material, it would've been obvious that he was concealing something. Plus, it had been made clear to him that any magical artefacts would trigger the building's defensive wards before he'd even stepped inside.

Every detail of the plan had been meticulously thrashed out in the days since he'd learnt of the gatekeeper's existence. He'd grilled his Brothers on every nuance, bombarding them with endless what ifs, until he was sure they were as prepared as they could possibly be. Still, the thought of relying solely on earpieces made him uneasy. But the building operated its own internal network, allowing only authorised devices to connect. Signal jammers and spellwork rendered all external phones useless, and apparently setting up new devices would have meant taking an unnecessary risk. It was probably for the best. Josh couldn't be trusted within an inch of a mobile anyway. He was a liability, one that Eric would hopefully be rid of after today.

The whispers threaded their delicate web through his consciousness, reminding him of what needed to be done.

Giving Tommo a nod, Eric crossed the road.

Up close, O.O.T.I.S headquarters was even more imposing. The sheer number of agents even more nerve-wracking.

Eric glanced at Tommo, who dabbed his brow with the cuff of his suit jacket, his tongue darting out to wet his lips for what seemed like the hundredth time. His throat bobbed as he swallowed. Tommo was clearly on edge and for him, that was bad. Maybe coffee hadn't been the best idea.

Eric shot him a sharp look. 'Stop fidgeting, for God's sake. You're supposed to look like you belong here.'

Tommo mumbled an apology, fingers twitching at his sides.

The plan was simple. Keep your mouth shut. Don't get caught. Yet, Tommo looked ready to bolt—or puke—and Eric had neither the time nor the patience to deal with either scenario.

'Breathe through your nose, not your mouth,' Eric added sharply. 'You sound like a bloody asthma case.'

His disdain grew with every nervous glance Tommo threw around. The man's stiff shoulders, jerky movements, and ashen complexion practically screamed *I don't belong here.* Eric could almost hear his internal monologue: *Do they know? Can they tell?*

Pathetic.

Still, he held his tongue. The last thing he needed was to push Tommo over the edge and make an already shaky performance worse.

It was now or never.

Breath caught in his lungs as Eric stepped through the threshold of the heavy wooden doors.

Not one alarm sounded. Not one agent turned to look at them.

He exhaled slowly and counted the row of metal detectors.

'Third from the right.'

Eric startled at the voice in his ear. Composing himself, he touched the communication device. The fit wasn't great, a spare from a former agent that had yet to be disposed of. Usually, the earpieces were custom moulded to the individual, but as that wasn't an option for their heist. They'd just have to make do and hope the bulky things didn't fall out.

'The security guy's relatively new,' the voice continued. *'Not been here long enough to memorise the faces of all the people who come and go. Don't do anything to draw attention to yourselves and the others won't notice you.'*

The agent looked up from behind the monitor as they approached.

Eric indicated for Tommo to go ahead of him, smiling stiffly as the agent handed his Brother a plastic tray.

Tommo removed his watch, and also put his keys and wallet in it. Without missing a beat, he pressed his thumb against the biometric fingerprint scanner set into the side panel of the metal detector, just as they'd been instructed to do. When the agent gave him the go-ahead, Tommo stepped through and collected his belongings, his shoulders relaxing ever so slightly.

Eric moved forward. His own wallet was still in the flat somewhere. Ben had offered to go buy him a new one. Any excuse to get away from Sean, or so Eric had assumed. Now, as he pulled the pleather wallet with the T-Rex silhouette free from his trouser pocket, he was confident that it was Ben's passive aggressive way of getting payback for the split lip and black eye. He'd regret that soon enough.

The agent's eyebrows drew together briefly as Eric tossed the wallet into the tray. He gestured for Eric to place his thumb on the scanner.

'I love Jurassic Park,' the agent said. 'What did you think of Fallen Kingdom?'

Eric froze. He had no interest in dinosaurs, never had. He forced a smile, silently cursing Ben for putting him on the spot.

'I haven't seen it. My son's the dino buff. He bought it for Father's day.' The lie came easily.

'*No!*' the voice barked in his ear. '*Your file lists you as single with no dependants!*'

Eric felt his every muscle clench. He gave a silent plea to the security camera mounted on the wall above him, where he knew his Brother was watching.

'That's cute,' the agent continued. 'How old is he?'

'He's...' The words stuck in his throat. *Fuck. Four? Eight?* His mind stalled as he tried to calculate a realistic age for his fictional child. He was vaguely aware of the rapid *click clacking* of keys coming from the earpiece.

The agent's smile faltered. Time slowed as his eyes lowered to the monitor.

A shrill bleeping sound made Eric jump. For a heart-stopping second, he thought he was fucked. But when the agent twisted in his seat to look behind him, Eric realised the neighbouring metal detector had been triggered.

'*Six,*' the voice said urgently. '*Say he just turned six.*'

'He's just turned six,' Eric said, forcing himself to relax.

The agent scanned the screen in front of him and nodded thoughtfully. 'That's a great age,' he said, his smile returning. 'Enjoy it. He'll be a teenager in the blink of an eye. Step through.'

Eric willed his feet to move. The adrenaline flooding his body just seconds ago had been replaced by a faint tingling in his muscles, and overwhelming exhaustion.

At the man's signal he reached for the wallet, barely registering what was said to him as he walked forward to where Tommo was waiting.

'Jesus,' Tommo breathed. 'That was a little too close for comfort.'

Eric rubbed absently at the raised ridges on his collarbone. He took a deep breath and released it slowly, scanning the high arches of terracotta that dominated the cavernous interior. The scale of it made his head swim, especially after the claustrophobic confines of the pub. His Brother's description had failed to prepare him for the true spectacle of the Order's headquarters. Everywhere he looked there were immense columns, sweeping staircases and huge, decorative stained-glass windows. It was like standing in the heart of some great museum.

'*What are you two doing? Get moving,*' the voice in his ear hissed.

Pulling his hand away, Eric started walking. Tommo matched his pace. They drew no attention from the men and women in black bustling around them. Nor from the hard-faced agents manning the circular marble desks that they passed in quick succession.

Eric allowed himself a small smile. They were in. They'd done it.

Now for the hard part.

Chapter 17

Buttoning the front of his shirt, Charlie glanced again at the salt spread across the floor. He'd lied when he'd told Sachiko that it didn't bother him. It did. In more ways than one.

The mess he could tolerate. After all, what kind of detective couldn't manage a bit of untidiness? Christ, some of the crime scenes he'd been to had been downright squalid. Sure, those places had sent his anxiety into overdrive, and he'd occasionally needed a moment to wrangle his OCD into submission, but it had never stopped him from doing his job.

But he knew a ward when he saw one. If the pages he'd "borrowed" from *Ritualistic Sacrifice in Ancient Magical Practices* had taught him anything, it was how to recognise magical symbols. And based on Sachiko's peculiar behaviour around him ever since he'd bonded with the demon's essence, he was confident it'd been meant for him.

Except it hadn't reacted to his presence. At all.

HER WARDING WAS FLAWED. SHE DID NOT TAKE INTO ACCOUNT THAT YOUR MEAT BAG

BODY INSULATES MY ESSENCE FROM BASIC SPELLWORK.

That added up. Plus, Jasmin had said that his connection to the dagger caused a magical dead zone around him. It was the reason Diane had been assigned as his handler—to keep an eye on him, since the Order had no way to track him. Aside from Sachiko, nobody suspected a thing. Now that her salt trap had failed, maybe she'd stop watching him so closely. Somehow, he doubted it.

I TOLD YOU SHE KNEW. I TOLD YOU TO KILL HER. YOU NEVER LISTEN.

You tell me to kill everyone.

BECAUSE IT WORKS. HONESTLY, YOU SHOULD TRY IT SOMETIME. IT'S A SOLID STRATEGY. *AND* IT'S FUN.

Charlie suppressed a shudder.

'Right, you're good to go, Charles,' Sachiko said, placing her tablet down. 'Oh, don't forget your duck.'

Nobody called him Charles. He hadn't corrected Sachiko during their initial appointments, mainly because he hadn't expected his visits to become so frequent. By then, it had felt too late to say anything. But now, between her obvious suspicions and the fact that she was an O.O.T.I.S agent through and through, he was glad he'd maintained the barrier between them.

'Thanks.' He retrieved the stuffed toy as Sachiko rapped on the steel door, signalling to the waiting black coat that Charlie was done. 'See you again in a week.'

She offered him a brief, distracted smile as the door swung shut behind him, her attention already elsewhere. The gust of air that followed cleared the faint, acidic tang in the air—something Charlie had only noticed in recent weeks whenever she was nearby. He paused, frowning at the closed door, certain he'd missed something.

Unable to shake the feeling that he'd narrowly dodged a bullet, Charlie nodded to the black suit. The man eyed the neon-pink toy duck in his hands and, without a word, started walking.

Truth be told, Charlie was looking forward to his visit with Lily. She was always so happy to see him, and he genuinely enjoyed her company. They shared a silent bond: both trapped in a situation in which they had no say; both kept under the watchful eye of the Order; both prodded and poked in the name of scientific curiosity. But most of all, they just wanted their old lives back.

Seeing Lily also seemed to dampen the demon's caustic presence inside his mind, offering a temporary respite from the constant spew of toxic vitriol. Now that Charlie had lost the ability to summon Kar'roc's Maw, being near Lily was the closest he could come to the gemstone set within the dagger's pommel. Those few precious minutes with her each week gave him a moment of peace, of control, and of feeling wanted. He'd come to relish them.

Charlie let his mind wander, absently casting an eye over his surroundings.

No matter where he looked, high arches and looming, intricately decorated columns greeted him. And even though the black suits varied his route to Lily as much as possible, he'd come to recognise the figures in the gilt-framed paintings that adorned the walls. Theodore Inman, Francis Moore, Millicent Smith: the founders of the Order of the Iron Seal. All long dead, but more familiar to him than any of the agents tasked with babysitting duties.

Part of him wondered whether he'd cross paths with Diane. The thought filled him with hope and dread in equal measure.

Debbie. His gut clenched.

How could he have been so stupid? It was a huge lapse in judgement.

A LAPSE IN JUDGEMENT? IT WAS AN ABOMINATION! EVEN HELLFIRE COULD NOT PURGE ME OF THIS MEMORY!

Charlie winced as the demon's words slammed through his skull.

YOU GAVE IN TO YOUR BASE DESIRES. IT IS BY DESIGN. THE DAGGER CALLS TO YOU, CORRODING YOUR DEFENCES, UNTIL EVERY LAST PART OF YOUR RESOLVE ROTS AWAY. YOU WILL BECOME A SLAVE TO KAR'ROC'S WILL. HE WILL USE YOU TO OPEN A RIFT BETWEEN REALMS, AND EVERYTHING YOU KNOW AND LOVE WILL BE DESTROYED.

He played with the black ring on his right hand. Auntie had warned him not to do anything that would make his link to the realm of fire and shadow worse. Except after, he'd gone and let a demon enter his mind. He'd barely been holding it together before calling upon Chekonost to save his family. Now, he was losing them.

Before he knew it, he and the agent had descended into the subterranean levels of the building where all the cryptids were housed.

CAGED. YOU MEAN CAGED. THEY ARE PRISONERS HERE. TAKE A GOOD LOOK. THIS IS WHERE YOU WILL SPEND THE REST OF YOUR PITIFUL EXISTENCE WHEN THEY FIND OUT THE TRUTH, SLOWLY DECAYING BEHIND THE WALLS OF A CELL UNTIL ALL THAT IS LEFT IS A WITHERED CORPSE. UNLESS YOU DO SOMETHING ABOUT IT.

Charlie bristled.

I said I'd find the gatekeeper, didn't I? Though, how he'd accomplish it under the watchful eye of the black suit, not to mention all the surveillance cameras, he had no idea.

EXCUSE ME IF I DO NOT PLACE STOCK IN THE WORDS OF A LIAR.

Liar?

ALL YOU DO IS LIE. YOU LIE TO THE ORDER. YOU LIE TO THOSE CLOSEST TO YOU. YOU LIE TO YOURSELF.

To myself?

YOU'RE CHANGING. BECOMING THE THING YOU FEAR MOST: A MONSTER.

He was loath to admit it, but Chekonost was right; he *was* changing. Between the smoking, losing his temper in front of Evie, and then Debbie... it was like he'd lost all inhibitions. And honestly, that scared the shit out of him.

Thoughts of Stephen pervaded his mind. The way he'd begged Charlie to stop him, the desperation and terror in his final pleas—it still sent a shiver down his spine. Was that what he would become?

Shaking the thoughts away, Charlie stared hard at the back of the black suit's head.

The air was cooler down here. The soft drone of the ventilation system filled the space between echoing footsteps as they wound their way into O.O.T.I.S' dark underbelly.

Unlike the upper levels of the building, the heavy-duty steel doors down here looked like those of a police cell. *Similar*, but not the same. He'd made the mistake of peering through one of the observation hatches on his first visit. Even through the tinted polycarbonate, the hateful yellow eyes staring back at him had made him physically recoil. And if that hadn't been incentive enough to drop his curiosity, the biting pain between his thumb and forefinger as the sigil blazed had certainly done the trick.

The black suit escorting him at the time had been less than impressed, roaring at him to never approach the cells without explicit permission. Chekonost had found the whole display endlessly entertaining, its laughter hammering nails into his mind.

THE GATEKEEPER IS CLOSE.

Charlie stumbled, but quickly righted himself before he drew the black suit's attention. He glanced at the cell doors ahead, wondering which of them belonged to the young blond man with bright-green eyes who he'd seen once in passing.

GIVE ME CONTROL OF YOUR BODY AND I WILL LEAD THE WAY.

Fat chance.

I PROMISE I WON'T KILL ANYONE.

Charlie stifled a scoff. *Now who's the liar?*

FINE. I PROMISE I WON'T KILL *EVERYONE*. BETTER?

No. Not better. It's not happening.

A wave of frustration surged through Charlie; the demon's ire became a tangible pressure that raked blades across his brain. Charlie clenched his jaw, forcing his hands to stay steady.

I NEVER THOUGHT I WOULD MISS STEPHEN. AT LEAST HE LET ME HAVE A LITTLE FUN. PLUS, HE ACTUALLY FED ME.

Charlie kept the sigh caged in his throat and focused on keeping pace with the agent in front of him.

YOU ARE A POOR HOST. CHARLIE HAYNES—ZERO OUT OF TEN. WOULD NOT RECOMMEND.

We're not having this conversation again. You don't need to feed. Lily's essence is enough to keep you alive. Unfortunately.

RUDE.

Sachiko had tried to explain it to him once. Because Lily's hellhound form was a manifestation of energy from the veil, when she ingested Kar'roc's Maw, the dagger had become trapped within a bubble of magic. That bubble sustained the energy needed for the demon's essence to exist. Similar to when the Maw had been enclosed within a magical field for Sachiko to study.

Charlie still didn't understand why Lily couldn't pass the dagger. It made no sense. If not as a Rottweiler, then surely as a hellhound? The Order had no intention of letting her transform, though—not that he blamed them. A hellhound, even a hybrid like Lily, was a threat. Containing threats was their job.

If he could get access to Kar'roc's Maw, he could force Chekonost's essence back into the damned thing and finally end this nightmare. But it wasn't as if he could stroll up to the nearest black suit and ask for permission. That would mean admitting the demon was in his head, that he'd been lying to them all this time. He'd practically be begging the Order to lock him up, doomed to spend the rest of his life in a cage, just like Lily. Or worse, to be dissected like a lab rat. No. It was out of the question.

And anyway, there was no guarantee it would work. Chekonost had said the dagger would remain inside Lily indefinitely, unless forcibly removed. Maybe it was something about her physiology or the dagger itself that kept it in place. But the demon also had plenty of reasons to lie. Asking an already suspicious Sachiko would only set off alarm bells. To the Order, the problem was solved. The Maw was contained and there was no risk of Charlie summoning it again.

Diane might have been an option. But he'd fucked that right up. He was on his own.

IT'S NOT THE SAME. I MISS THE PURE RAPTURE OF VITALITY AS I DRAIN THE LIFE FORCE FROM MY VICTIMS. I MISS THE TASTE OF FLESH AS IT SLIDES DOWN MY THROAT IN WARM, WET MEATY CLUMPS.

Charlie's insides roiled. He swallowed down the bitter taste at the back of his throat, glad that he hadn't eaten breakfast.

Stop.

I CAN'T WAIT UNTIL MY ESSENCE IS TRANSFERRED INTO MY OWN BODY. CAN'T WAIT UNTIL I'M RID OF YOU ONCE AND FOR ALL.

On that they could both agree.

The black suit slowed, touching his earpiece as he glanced up at the nearest surveillance camera. After a moment's pause, he dropped his hand. A soft *clunk* sounded, followed by an immediate mechanical *whir* to signal that the door was now unlocked.

Shit.

WHAT?

The door was opened remotely.

MEANING?

Meaning someone somewhere inside the building controls the locks. Even if we find the gatekeeper, there's no way to get to him.

Chapter 18

The demon scoffed inside his head. THERE IS ALWAYS A WAY.

Eyeing the stuffed duck in Charlie's hand again, the black suit pulled open the door and gestured for him to enter. Charlie gave the man a tight smile and stepped into the cell.

The choking tendrils of the demon's presence instantly receded. The loathing, the malice, the bloodlust—once tangled through his every thought—had been cut back at the roots. Though the remnants still clung to the edges of his mind, it was enough to let Charlie breathe again.

He took a moment to savour it. A fleeting second of relative peace before the overwhelming reality of his situation rushed back in.

Unlike with Sachiko's room on the upper levels of the building, the black suit did not wait outside. Instead, he stationed himself behind the control panel in the centre of the room.

That was another issue. How was he supposed to do anything when he was being babysat twenty-four-seven? How in the hell was he going to pull this off?

He was under no illusion that each cell had been specifically strengthened to deal with the threat level of its occupant. And if that was the case, there was no telling what security measures would have been implemented to contain the gatekeeper.

He walked forward, his focus shifting to Lily's enclosure. It was set against the far end of the room—cruel, given that the rest of the cell was large and open—its thick metal frame gleaming weakly under the glaring LEDs. Every inch of the frame was etched with symbols. They pulsed with a pale-blue light, filling the air with a static pressure that thrummed against his skin. The reinforced panels at the front of the enclosure appeared to be made of some sort of glass composite, but the rear was comprised of the same metal as the frame.

It had taken Charlie a few visits to realise that there was a door at the rear; where it led, he had no idea. He liked to think it connected to an outdoor area, somewhere for Lily to burn off a little steam. But in truth, he knew it probably just led to some sort of tunnel network. O.O.T.I.S needed a safe way to transport all its *assets* after all.

The cell itself looked nothing like the rest of the Romanesque building. No trace of terracotta brickwork, no decorative columns or artistry. Just a large metal box. Cold and oppressive. The walls reflected the harsh LED light back in dull streaks, broken only by the storage panels that lined them. No doubt full of weaponry, should the worst-case scenario play out. Not that the black suits wouldn't get fair warning; the security cameras mounted on the ceiling would catch everything, every movement, every breath. There was nowhere to hide. No way to escape.

The black-and-tan Rottweiler lifted her head briefly from her paws as Charlie approached, and gave a single wag of her tail.

'Hey, Lily,' Charlie said, his heart breaking to see her so clearly miserable.

In the few instances he'd been to Nick's house—before everything had gone to shit—she'd been a big ball of energy, barrelling towards him to say hello as Nick tried and failed to rein her in. On one occasion she'd actually managed to knock Charlie to the floor. He'd barely had time to shield his face before she'd covered his hands in wet, doggy kisses. He'd never heard Nick screech so loud, apologising profusely as he dragged her away by her collar. Once Charlie had recovered, he'd seen the funny side.

'I've got a present for you.' Charlie held out the stuffed duck, waving it in front of the glass, in an attempt to get her attention. Lily let out a small huff, her gaze following the toy for a second or two before returning it to the floor.

I TOLD YOU SHE WOULDN'T LIKE IT. A FLUFFY PINK DUCK... FOR A HELLHOUND? RIDICULOUS. INSULTING EVEN. MY IDEA WAS MUCH BETTER.

Breathing hard through his nose, Charlie chose not to engage. Even Solomon's stone in Lily's gut couldn't drown out the demon's voice completely. Maybe if the fragment set into the Maw's pommel were bigger, it would have more of an effect. *Christ*, maybe if the stone were whole, he could shut the demon up for good.

I STILL DON'T SEE THE PROBLEM. THAT CASHIER HAD TWO ARMS. SHE DIDN'T NEED BOTH OF THEM.

Charlie crouched down and tried again. 'Come on girl.'

This time she didn't even look up.

He watched her where she lay, her chest rising and falling beneath her fur, unsure of what to do.

'Look,' he said, putting some enthusiasm into his voice. 'You'll like this.' He pressed the duck's stomach. A shrill squeak filled the cell.

Lily scrabbled to her feet, the warded collar around her neck jangling lightly with the motion, and cocked her head to one side.

MUST YOU DO THAT?

What, you don't like it?

NO. THAT NOISE IS INFURIATING.

With a smirk, Charlie gave the duck another few squeezes in quick succession. The Rottweiler's ears perked up. She play-bowed, front legs extended, paws spread apart, as her tail whipped through the air. Her whole body wiggled with anticipation and she let out a bark.

Charlie smiled. 'See, I told you you'd like it.'

Adjusting his position, he placed the duck on the small platform that fed into the carefully engineered hatch built into the bottom of the enclosure. The interlocking glass panels slid open in a smooth, almost silent way, delivering the item then immediately sealing shut. Faint symbols, etched into the glass, caught the light as the platform returned to its original position. O.O.T.I.S were nothing if not cautious.

Snuffling at the duck appreciatively, Lily gently scooped it up in her mouth and gave it a good shake. Muffled squeaks, interspersed with playful growls, filled the silence—albeit somewhat dampened by the glass separating them.

For a moment, it was just Charlie and Lily. No demons. No O.O.T.I.S. He watched her play with her new stuffed toy like a puppy.

The black suit cleared his throat indicating it was time to leave.

Pushing himself to his feet, Charlie scowled at the man. 'You're joking? I've barely been here a minute.'

'May I remind you, Mr Haynes, that you're here as a courtesy.'

'A *courtesy*? This is the least you can bloody do!'

The black suit's mouth turned down in disapproval.

But Charlie wasn't done yet.

'It's your fault she's here in the first place. You suits spend months following me around, watching my every move, but somehow my family gets kidnapped by some deranged psychopath right under your noses. Then you let the bastard get away.' He barked a laugh. 'In fact, if any of you were capable of doing your jobs, I wouldn't be here either. Really says something about your organisation that a pensioner has cleaned up your mess not once, but twice.'

KILL HIM.

Straightening, the unflinching black suit met Charlie's glare. 'It's time to go.'

KILL HIM!

Quiet!

The sigil on Charlie's hand pulsed in time with the demon's silent indignation, but it said nothing more.

Charlie lifted his chin. 'And what if I disagree?'

A low warning growl rumbled from the enclosure behind him.

'See? Even Lily—' Charlie broke off as he turned to look at the Rottweiler. With hackles raised, ears pinned back and teeth bared, the guttural snarl continued. But it wasn't the black suit she was focused on. Nor was it Charlie. She was fixated on a spot to his left.

Charlie's brow creased. He turned, his confusion mirrored on the agent's face.

Even on the bad days, when Lily seemed down or distracted—like today—she always perked up eventually. But this aggression? This was different. Was there something in one of the other cells? A threat she could sense that he couldn't? His sigil hadn't responded to anything other than Chekonost's sulking, and that definitely wasn't as intense as the pain he'd felt when the naeshin demon had appeared.

But the way she was reacting now... Something was definitely wrong.

A deep, thunderous *boom* erupted from somewhere inside the building, shaking the ground beneath their feet and plunging them into momentary darkness. Charlie tensed, blindly scanning the cell for danger. The sound of Lily's frenzied barking was drowned out by the ear-splitting wail of an alarm. The cell filled with a pulsing red light from the ceiling-mounted beacons.

Red. At least it's not—

His thoughts were severed by a blaring, synthesised female voice.

'Black alert. Black alert.'

Chapter 19

Sachiko yelped as an almighty *bang* shook the building and the lights cut out. Enveloped by absolute darkness, she only had a second to listen to her own panicked breaths before the alarm kicked in with a single piercing screech. Waves of red light flooded the room.

'*Black alert. Black alert.*'

With a hand to her chest, she tried to regain control of her nerves.

A black alert; the building was under attack.

Stay put. She needed to stay put until instructed otherwise. It was the same for all non-combatant personnel.

Piece by piece the practice drills came back to her. She blew out a breath and ran through the steps in her head. First, secure all assets.

'*Breach in Sector Four. Lockdown procedure initiated.*'

Biting on her lip, Sachiko waited until the emergency notification system fell silent. Sector Four. That was to the rear of the building at ground level. But a lockdown? That meant something, or more than one something, had escaped containment, otherwise they'd be evacuating right now. Her thoughts went straight to the naeshin demon. Instinctively, she stared at the vent above the louvred steel door, waiting for smoke to billow out from the gaps between the slats, just as it had done the last time there was a containment breach.

Her eyes flicked to the remaining salt mound on the *morishio* dish. It looked just the same as it had earlier. Silently chastising herself, she refocused on the task at hand. With Kar'roc's Maw no longer contained within the lab, the only items of significance were Charles' blood samples and her research. With a trembling hand, she reached for the biohazard bag containing the vials. The strobing red light did nothing to ease her tension.

She moved swiftly to the other side of the room and punched her code into the keypad. A muted click emanated from the safe set into the wall, its locking mechanism disengaging with a low hum. Sachiko grasped the handle and yanked, cold air hitting her as the door swung open. After tearing the bag apart, she quickly removed Charles' blood samples and deposited them into the specialised compartments of the refrigerated interior, next to an assortment of glass bottles, ampoules and pre-filled syringes. Scanning the room, she confirmed all the biospecimens were accounted for, then closed the safe door. The green LED light blinked on, indicating that it was secure.

Wait! She pressed her hand to her lab coat, finding the outline of the sedative vial. Her eyes flicked up to the vent. Maybe keeping it on her person wouldn't be the worst idea in the world.

That just left her tablet and the desktop PCs. Everything else was considered expendable. All her equipment, her instruments, her specialised microscopes... What if it got destroyed? Her stomach sank at the thought. Hopefully it wouldn't come to that. O.O.T.I.S headquarters was the most secure facility this side of London; any threat should be neutralised in a matter of minutes. Still, the thought had taken root, creeping through her reason until it began to crumble.

No. Follow protocol.

Pulling herself together, she snatched her tablet off the burnished metal worktop.

Without warning the door burst inwards. A sharp crack followed as the *morishio* dish exploded in a spray of salt and ceramic shards.

With a scream Sachiko stumbled back, the device slipping from her grip and clattering against the floor.

Damanjeet stood just inside the threshold. Her momentary relief that he wasn't a naeshin demon was short-lived as she took in the state of him—soaked in blood, his chest heaving.

'Damanjeet?' she managed, her voice tight.

'H-help! I need your help!' His pleas were breathless. Staggering forward, he thrust out his hand against the door for support. His fingers, finding no purchase, left red streaks against the steel.

'What happened? Where are you hurt?'

'Not me.' He sucked down a breath and swiped at his brow, leaving a smear of blood and sweat. 'Please, it's Michelle. We need to hurry!'

Tablet forgotten, Sachiko rushed to retrieve her medical bag and followed Damanjeet as he lurched away. Her shoes slid on the tiles as grains of salt shifted underfoot.

The corridor was chaos. Agents sprinted past under the pulsing red glow, relaying information through their earpieces. A woman in her late thirties slowed when she saw them, opening her mouth to speak. She snapped it shut when she took in Damanjeet's bloody shirt and Sachiko's laboratory coat and bag. Giving a nod, she went on her way.

Sachiko continued forward, shifting the strap higher on her shoulder. There didn't appear to be any structural damage to the surrounding area, but given the state Damanjeet was in, it must have extended beyond Sector Four.

She gasped at the blood dripping from Damanjeet's fingers.

'Your hand...' she said. He opened his fist long enough for her to see the deep gash in his palm, but didn't slow. 'Daman, that looks serious.'

He grunted and shook his head. 'You can patch me up later. Michelle's the one who needs you.'

She felt her stomach knot. Michelle's situation must be dire.

With no choice but to try and keep up, Sachiko adjusted the bag again and tried not to let her imagination get the better of her.

Every second dragged as they negotiated the corridors to Damanjeet's department. As soon as they arrived, he burst into the room; the door bounced back on its hinges. With an *oof*, Sachiko shoved her way inside.

Her heart skipped a beat.

Glass littered the floor. Great shards of it spread from the shattered panels of the nearest meeting room. A chair lay amongst the wreckage.

Sachiko slowed. How could a breach in Sector Four have caused such localised damage? She pushed the thought to the back of her mind and focused. Right now, she had a job to do.

Michelle was slumped against the wall, her chin resting on the scarlet stain that saturated her top. Crystaline fragments, sprayed with crimson, scattered the tiles around her. Something about their placement tugged at Sachiko's attention, but Michelle's critical condition obliterated the thought.

She rushed to the woman's side, dropped to her knees, and placed the medical bag on the floor.

'Michelle? Michelle, can you hear me?'

There was no response.

'Michelle?' Sachiko clasped the woman's arm. The motion caused Michelle's head to bob to the side. Partially clotted blood began to ooze in thick, viscous globs from the gash in her throat, dribbling across her motionless chest.

Sachiko shuddered a breath.

Michelle was dead. Dead before they'd even entered the room.

Her shoulders drooped. She looked up at Damanjeet and shook her head, letting him know it was too late.

'I'm sorry.'

Damanjeet stared down at her, his face blank.

Had he heard what she'd just said? Maybe he was in shock. Not everyone had been exposed to injury and death to the extent she had.

'Do you mind looking at my hand now?' Damanjeet asked.

Her mouth dropped at his request. Her gaze flicked from him to Michelle then back again. Unease fingered down her spine.

'Daman, Michelle is *dead*.'

'I know.' His shoulders lifted in a shrug. 'My hand?'

Her sluggish mind put the pieces together. The shattered meeting room panels. The bloodied splinters of glass next to Michelle's body. The slash on his palm.

'You did this?' she choked.

'I told the team they could come in a few hours late today. A reward for working so hard to push our latest project over the line. Of course, Michelle ignored that. So eager to please. And when the alarms went off and she started running diagnostics... Well, she always was bright.'

Words wouldn't form. Sachiko blinked dumbly at him. 'W-w...'

'Why? Why did I do it?'

'What did you let out of containment?'

'Ah.' He chuckled softly, drumming the fingers of his uninjured hand against his thigh. 'Just a few choice specimens to keep the agents busy for a while.' Inspecting his bleeding palm he tsked. 'S'pose you're not going to patch me up now? That's okay. The important thing is that you're here. With me.'

With him? She shook her head incredulously. All those puppy-dog eye looks, the coffees, the asking her out... This wasn't just some workplace crush. This was obsession!

'I think we'd have been good together, y'know. I could've made you happy. But you always had to be such a stuck-up bitch about it, didn't you? Hiding behind your work like nothing else mattered. Like no one else mattered. Would it have killed you to have a drink with me? Just one?' Damanjeet took a breath, his voice softening, as if willing her to believe him. 'I like you, Sachiko. Can't you understand that? I *really* like you.'

'Damanjeet—'

'It's Daman!' he roared, his face contorting with rage. Sachiko recoiled.

'Jesus! How many times do I have to tell you? Daman. Dam. Hell, I'd even respond to Dan!'

'How could you do this?' Sachiko shuffled back, trying to keep him talking as she mapped an escape route. There was no way she'd make it to the door, not with him blocking her path. Maybe if she could find a weapon of some kind. Or get close enough to use the sedative hidden inside her lab coat...

Damanjeet cocked his head, lifting his hand to his ear. It took her a second to realise that he was listening to someone over an earpiece. His anger ebbed away, replaced by something harder, darker. A slow smile spread across his face.

'I read your file, y'know,' he said flatly. 'Memorised it in fact. Turns out you carry a very rare set of genetic markers. Did you know that?' He smirked, waving the question away. 'Of course you did. How does that feel? Knowing that you were so close to being extraordinary. It's gotta hurt, right? Being a genetic near-miss. Powerless. Helpless. Human.'

'You're human too, Daman. Or have you forgotten?'

He sneered down at her. 'For now.'

'What does that mean?'

'Something's changed, Sachiko. Don't tell me you haven't noticed? The increased breaches. The demonic activity. We're making it worse, y'know.' He took another step towards her, his brown eyes wide, manic. 'I've known it for years. Every time we close off a gateway, we make it worse. Think of it like a dam and the veil is the only thing that separates us from the realm of fire and shadow. All that dark energy, all that pressure, it's building day by day. And what do we do? We go around plugging all the gaps, thinking we're protecting ourselves. But every patch, every seal, it's just aiding the inevitable. I tried to tell them. Presented them with my findings. Showed them the data. But they don't want to listen. That dam's going to burst, and when it does, there'll be hell on Earth. We'll be slaughtered. Mankind wiped out in the blink of an eye.'

Seeing her confusion, Damanjeet shook his head.

'You still don't understand, do you? It's time to choose a side, Sachiko. Come with me, or die with the rest of them.'

'I—I...'

She couldn't process what he was saying. The words sunk into the fog of her mind, distant and muffled. She snatched a breath, the weight on her chest crushing her lungs. The *morishio*. It was all she could think about. Every time Damanjeet had come to her lab, something had happened to it. Like a bad omen, she'd missed all the signs. And now she was trapped. With a madman.

'You're special, Sachiko. I've always known you were special. With your blood... *God*, with your blood, we could finally become what we were destined to be. He won't hurt you. None of them will. I'll make sure none of them lay a finger on you. I promise.' Damanjeet crouched, and brushed her cheek almost sensually.

Sedative forgotten, Sachiko flinched and kicked away from him, her fingers sliding through the blood and glass pooled behind her.

Damanjeet's jaw ticked. He drew his arm back. Slowly. 'I see. What a shame.'

He lunged at her, a blur of motion. His fist struck her temple, delivering a blinding-white surge of agony. Her head slamming against the floor was the last thing Sachiko registered before pain and darkness swallowed her whole.

Chapter 20

LOCKDOWN. THAT WASN'T GOOD.

The black suit loitered by the reinforced, heavy-duty steel door. Stay or leave; the dilemma was written in his frown. His fingers fluttered by his earpiece. He tilted his head slightly before his jaw set. Apparently, the decision had been made for him.

'Mr Haynes, you are to remain here until my return. Do not attempt to leave. Do not touch anything. Do you understand?'

'Sure. Be a good boy. Got it.'

The man's lips thinned. He looked Charlie up and down, shook his head, then yanked the cell door open and stepped out. It closed firmly behind him.

A low growl rumbled from Lily's chest. Charlie watched as she paced back and forth within the enclosure. Whatever was going on, it had her agitated.

'It's okay, Lily. It's okay.' He pressed his palms against the glass. The strobing red light throbbed in his peripheral vision, thrusting the Rottweiler in and out of shadow.

STOP WASTING TIME. THIS IS OUR CHANCE.

Charlie glanced back at the door. The demon was right. Whatever was happening out there had given him an opportunity to get the gatekeeper. But there was an issue. How in the hell was he going to slip past whoever was watching him? The security cameras would track his every move, not to mention the fact that the door to the cell would remain locked until the black suit returned.

IDIOT. ARE YOU BLIND? OR JUST STUPID?

What?

LOOK.

Charlie's gaze snapped to the security camera directly above the door. Even in the strobing light of the alarm, he could see that the lens sat motionless within its domed casing. He took two steps to the side. It didn't move. Frowning, he marched to the far side of the cell. Nothing. The camera hadn't budged.

They weren't on.

WELL DONE. YOU GOT THERE EVENTUALLY.

The explosion had knocked out the power. That meant the emergency generators must be diverted to critical systems—like the cryptid enclosures. If that were the case, then...

Charlie darted to the exit, then stopped, his hand wavering above the handle as he looked back at Lily.

WHAT ARE YOU WAITING FOR?

I can't leave her trapped in this place.

ARE YOU SERIOUS? YOU'RE WASTING TIME!

Lily stared back at him, her deep-brown eyes wide and pleading. A whine escaped her throat.

I'm not leaving her.

Charlie turned back to the enclosure, frustration gnawing at his insides. 'There's got to be a way to get you out of here, girl.'

The demon's irritation prickled across their bond.

Lily let out another soft whine, and continued pacing.

BREAK THE GLASS.

What?

IF YOU WISH TO FREE THE BEAST, THEN FREE HER. BREAK THE GLASS.

Charlie stepped back, eyeing the enclosure sceptically. It had been built to hold a hellhound. His demon-enhanced strength aside, he couldn't possibly break it. Could he?

IT'S DESIGNED TO KEEP THINGS FROM GETTING OUT. NOT IN.

Unsure, Charlie pressed his fingers against the reinforced glass.

DO IT.

Gritting his teeth, he made a fist, drew it back, and swung with all his strength. The sickening crunch of impact registered in his mind before the jolt of blinding agony overtook it. The shockwave travelled through his hand, pain radiating through his shattered knuckles and up his arm in nauseating bursts. Spots flared across his vision.

'Fuck!'

He yanked his mangled hand back with a hiss, cradling it against his chest. Blood dribbled between his fingers where splinters of white bone pierced through flesh. His pulse thudded in his ears, each beat a fresh wave of throbbing torture.

Shrill laughter echoed inside his skull.

MAYBE YOU NEED TO HIT IT HARDER?

'Fuck you!'

TEMPER, TEMPER.

Gradually, the pain dulled as sinew and bone began to mend. His knuckles realigned with an unsettling shift beneath his skin, the fractures knitting together. He flexed his fingers, watching with morbid fascination as the gashes healed right before his eyes.

Aside from a smear of crimson on the glass, the enclosure appeared untouched.

You knew that would happen!

OBVIOUSLY. Satisfaction seeped through the demon's voice. THAT ENCLOSURE WAS BUILT TO HOLD A HELLHOUND.

Charlie growled deep, balling his fists by his sides.

Squeeze, release. Squeeze, release. Squeeze, release.

I hate you.

THEN DO SOMETHING ABOUT IT.

Lily huffed out a half-bark, her ears drooping.

A heavy ache spread through Charlie's chest. 'I'm sorry, girl. I'll try and find another way. I promise.'

She looked up at him, her tail tucking beneath her body before she sunk against the floor of her enclosure.

Heart aching, Charlie walked away from her. He reached for the door handle, bracing himself for what might happen next.

The corridor outside was empty. He eyed the camera—no subtle rotation from it, no faint blinking red light. Definitely off. Nobody could see him. Nobody was tracking him. Nobody would be coming to stop him.

Giving Lily one last sad glance, he slipped outside. Her gaze had fixed on the wall again. The moment the door closed, the pressure in Charlie's skull returned with a vengeance. The demon's presence uncoiled like thorned fronds, snagging and tearing at his consciousness, tainting it with darkness.

I CAN FEEL THE GATEKEEPER. GIVE ME CONTROL OF YOUR BODY AND I WILL LEAD YOU TO HIM.

Not a chance.

A wave of frustration rolled through him. IT WILL BE QUICKER.

I said no.

FINE. JUST KEEP GOING FORWARD.

Charlie set off at a jog, straining to listen for the sound of footsteps. A run-in with a black suit was the last thing he needed. This was his one chance; he wasn't about to blow it.

Behind the cell doors came the chilling sounds of unseen nightmares—scratching, clawing, growling. The sigil on his hand throbbed, a dull ache that quickly intensified into a sharp wasp-like sting. The hairs on the back of his neck stood on end, forcing him to spin around.

From the shadows, yellow eyes watched him. The pulsing red lights only did so much to hide the man's outline. But Charlie recognised him. He'd seen those same eyes staring back at him on his way to Lily. And if he'd thought they were full of malice then, it was nothing compared to the unadulterated hatred glowing in them now.

Charlie blinked, allowing his vision to adjust to the strobing glare. However much it repulsed him, in this very moment he was reliant on the demon's gifts.

The figure looked almost reptilian: sickly yellow scales fanning out from its cheeks ran down the length of its neck and across broad, muscular shoulders. It was humanoid. Disconcertingly so. Or at least that's what Charlie thought until it inched forward to reveal a thick, serpentine tail. Twice the length of its upper body, it uncoiled with an unhurried, fluid, undulating movement. The scales on the tail were larger, more pronounced, its oily sheen glinting under the pulsing red lights.

What is that thing?

URGH. IT IS A NAGA. A PARASITE.

A parasite? I suppose you would know.

Chekonost's low growl reverberated inside his skull.

PAY IT NO ATTENTION. JUST KEEP WALKING.

And if I turn my back on that thing?

IT WILL FIND SOMETHING ELSE TO AMUSE ITSELF WITH.

Bullshit. You're trying to get me killed.

WHY WOULD I DO THAT?

Because you're an evil monster who cares about nothing but itself.

I SUPPOSE YOU WOULD KNOW.

Charlie ignored the self-satisfied tone. *If I turn my back on that thing, it's going to attack me.*

IT WON'T. TRUST ME.

What? Like I trusted you about being able to break through Lily's enclosure?

HA! THAT WAS DIFFERENT.

Charlie adjusted his stance, his eyes locked on the creature before him. *Different how?*

THAT WAS FUNNY. BUT YOU DYING NOW WOULD HELP NEITHER OF US. I WILL NOT ALLOW YOU TO DIE.

Charlie weighed his options. Chekonost was full of shit, but without a host, the demon stood no chance of returning to its own body. At best, its essence would revert to the dagger. At worst... Who knew?

Fine.

Against every instinct, he turned on his heel. A visceral surge of dread electrified his spine, causing the sigil to ignite in searing agony. The creature's talons raked across his back. He cried out as he twisted to the side, barely avoiding their full impact.

With adrenaline flooding his system, he whirled around to confront his attacker.

Chekonost's manic laughter gouged at his brain. I WAS WRONG. THAT WAS ALSO FUNNY.

You spiteful little fuck.

A guttural growl rumbled in the naga's throat, its lips peeling back to reveal a savage grin bristling with needle-sharp teeth. Crimson droplets clung to its talons. With unsettling deliberation, it examined them, then plucked a scrap of his tattered jacket loose and tossed it casually to the ground. The creature raised a gore-slicked digit to its mouth and tasted Charlie's blood with its forked tongue.

Charlie's stomach twisted.

'Are all humans so stupid?' the naga rasped. 'You, a lowly mortal, would turn your back on me? I will enjoy ripping you limb from limb.'

I thought you weren't going to let me die!

STOP WHINGEING. IT WAS JUST A SCRATCH.

You lied to me. Again!

AND YOU IMPRISONED ME IN A DAGGER!

'I don't have time for this,' Charlie spat.

The naga's ridged and scaly brows arched in confusion before pulling down into a fierce scowl. Without another word, it launched itself at Charlie.

Charlie rolled to the side, moving on impulse as the naga's talons swept through the air, narrowly missing his face. It lunged again, its roar of frustration echoing down the corridor. Charlie threw up his arms, stumbling back as razor-sharp claws tore into his flesh. He bit down a curse as blood erupted from the fresh wounds. His carved-up jacket offered little protection against the creature's relentless assault.

Chekonost's strident giggle filled his brain.

You realise that, while you're enjoying yourself, our time is running out.

The wave of amusement cut off abruptly.

FINE.

The pain in Charlie's arm ebbed away, flesh weaving itself back together as the demon healed his wounds.

LET'S GET THIS OVER WITH. GIVE ME CONTROL OF YOUR BODY AND I WILL KILL THE PARASITE.

No.

Chekonost's essence writhed within the confines of his consciousness, probing every dark recess of his psyche, searching for a weakness. Only his link to the dagger as its master had kept the demon from completely overwhelming him, and the thought that one day even that might not be enough sent a creeping chill through his veins.

WITHOUT ME YOU'LL BE GUTTED LIKE A FISH.

'I'll take my chances.'

'Who are you talking to?' the naga hissed. Its slitted yellow eyes flicked up to the security cameras, then narrowed in suspicion. It snarled, lashing its tail across the floor in sharp, agitated arcs. The muscles in its upper torso bunched.

In a blur of scales and rage, the naga was on Charlie again. Its attacks were relentless—talons slicing through the air, tail whipping forward with bone-crushing force. He flung up his arms in a desperate defence, each block sending shockwaves of pain through his battered body. His lungs were on fire. His chest was heaving as he gulped for air between frantic parries.

The naga's claws carved through his flesh with horrifying ease, leaving ribbons of skin and muscle in their wake. He was losing too much blood, each yawning gash deep enough to be fatal on its own.

Only the demon's essence, knitting flesh and sinew with unnatural speed, kept him from succumbing to the onslaught. Even so, he knew he was only moments away from being overwhelmed.

YOU ARE LOSING.

Ignoring Chekonost's warning, Charlie feinted right and drove a punch into the naga's abdomen. It recoiled with a grunt, but its surprise quickly morphed to amusement.

'So, you're not just a human...' The naga shifted its serpentine body slightly, coiling tighter, as it studied him with renewed interest. It remained poised to strike at any moment, its black tongue flickering in the air. With gut-churning revulsion, Charlie realised it was smelling him.

He said nothing and braced for another attack.

The naga snorted, then came at him again. Its arm shot forward, scaled hand tensed, claws aiming straight for Charlie's throat.

Even with demon-enhanced reflexes, Charlie knew there was no dodging this one. If the strike didn't kill him, it'd knock him out cold. By the time he came to, the gatekeeper would be out of reach, and the black suits would close in. If that happened, any hope of getting Chekonost out of his head would be lost. Forever.

Okay! Take control!

The swap was instant. Chekonost burrowed into his muscles, its essence driving into every fibre of his being, forcing him out of his own body and into the distant backdrop of his mind. A powerless observer. Worse still, the demon's glee throbbed inside him, pulsing with dark satisfaction.

Chekonost yanked him to the side, moving Charlie like a puppet. The naga's claws sliced through the space where his throat had just been, missing it by mere millimetres.

'Let's play.' The words came from Charlie's mouth, but they weren't his. His voice sounded off, a bastardised mix of his own and the one that had taken residence inside his mind.

The demon pivoted his body again, pushing Charlie to his limits, testing his speed, his flexibility. He twisted suddenly, bringing Charlie's fist down hard on the back of the creature's neck. His hand made a solid *thunk* sound as it connected, and sent the naga crashing to the ground.

But it wasn't finished. The naga immediately recovered, hatred blazing in its eyes, and dove at him with a feral roar.

Chekonost dodged effortlessly, a laugh bubbling up from Charlie's mouth. Pure, unbridled joy.

Giving no quarter, Chekonost surged forward. Blow after blow, the demon unleashed its pent-up fury on the naga. Black blood dribbled from the serpentine creature's mouth, coating Charlie's knuckles. His skin tore and healed in endless cycles as the demon smashed his fists into the naga's body.

The creature snarled, swiping wildly, but Chekonost was quicker. He ducked low, slipping beneath the naga's sweeping strike, to slam his shoulder into its midsection. The impact sent it reeling back.

'Too slow,' Chekonost taunted.

Before the naga could recover, Chekonost drove Charlie's knee into its chest with enough force to lift it off the ground. It hit the floor hard, its tail thrashing from side to side as it attempted to right itself.

Roars of impotent rage echoed through the corridor. Worthless screams, useless fury. It was nothing but a mindless beast—no, worse, a parasite.

Charlie's mouth twisted into a feral grin, showing the creature his teeth.

Claws flashed towards him, and although the demon jerked his body away automatically, a trail of searing fire raked across his side. He rolled back as the naga's tail ploughed into the floor, sending great chunks of terracotta and shards of debris flying in all directions. The naga roared again, its maw stretched wide, spittle and black ooze spraying in angry clouds. Chekonost saw its movement falter, its exhaustion giving him the opening he needed.

The demon surged Charlie forward, snatching up a jagged chunk of terracotta as it did, and raising it high above his head. With a scream that tore from Charlie's throat, Chekonost brought it down brutally. It cleaved through the naga's skull. Blood sprayed across the walls, the floor, his face. The demon laughed, the sound loud and crazed, as he ripped a hunk of the creature's head free.

The naga toppled backward, its body twitching. It hit the floor, talons curling helplessly before going limp.

Panting, Chekonost discarded the lump of bloodied skull and stood over the corpse. A surge of euphoria, of intoxicating victory, coursed through Charlie's body. If he'd had any control over his muscles he would have shuddered. In that moment, he felt what Stephen must have—the inner turmoil at being swept up in the demon's emotions. It was horrifying.

Enough.

Charlie felt Chekonost's resistance as he attempted to take back control; the dull throb of the sigil pulsed in time with his efforts. For a terrifying moment he was impotent, locked in his own brain like a prisoner. The demon refused to budge.

'I think I'll drive, if it's all the same.' Chekonost's voice dripped with malice.

No. I command you to release my body.

The tingle radiating from the raised markings between his thumb and forefinger amplified, no longer a muted ache but an acute, searing pain.

He felt the anger and resentment build as the dagger's magic forced the demon back into his mind. The struggle was excruciating. Chekonost seemed to take sadistic pleasure in making every neuron scream as it retreated. Charlie bit back a groan, refusing to give the demon satisfaction.

WHAT'S WRONG, CHARLIE-BOY? CAN'T HANDLE A LITTLE HEAD MASSAGE?

Charlie blew out a shaky breath, clenching and unclenching his fists. What if the next time he couldn't regain control? What if the demon worked its way into his body permanently? The damage it could do, the lives it could ruin...

His granddaughter's face flashed before his eyes. Innocent, vulnerable and completely unaware of the danger he posed.

Let's find the gatekeeper.

He could feel the demon's loathing. GLADLY.

Charlie's shoes squelched as he walked through the slick pool of black surrounding the naga's ruined body. The pulsing of the lights bathed the carnage in an intermittent, hellish red glow. He tried not to think about how much of the blood was his, about how close he'd come to death, about how reliant he'd been on the demon. Again.

As he moved down the corridor, Charlie couldn't shake the feeling that things weren't about to get any easier, that he was walking straight into the face of danger. But what choice did he have? The gatekeeper was his only hope now.

Chapter 21

THE GATEKEEPER'S BRIGHT-GREEN EYES watched Eric from within its enclosure. Even with the rhythmic, red pulse casting the room in and out of shadow, those eyes remained locked on him, never straying. Eric wetted his dry lips and absently rubbed at his collarbone.

Whatever he'd been expecting, the young man standing before him wasn't it. Not for the first time he wondered whether there'd been some mistake. The gatekeeper looked no older than nineteen, younger than Eric, with a wiry frame hidden beneath a loose-fitting T-shirt and a pair of worn jeans that hung low on his hips. With his dishevelled blond hair and unassuming posture, there was nothing that separated him from any other teenager out there.

Ordinary. That was the only word Eric could think of to describe him. But those eyes... They were anything but. Cold and calculating, as though they could see into his very soul.

The gatekeeper smirked. His knowing look sent a shiver crawling down Eric's spine. It was like the creature could read his mind.

'Are you sure this is the right cell?' Tommo asked him again.

Eric released a frustrated sigh and turned his back to the creature. 'This is where Brother Bains told us to go.'

'But what if it's a trap?' Tommo's eyes flicked to Ben, as if seeking backup. Ben simply stared with his usual open-mouthed, gormless expression. The pulsing red glow added an almost black sheen to the bruises on his face.

Eric scowled. He'd wanted nothing more than to punch Ben the moment he had stepped into the cell. The timing of the explosions had been off. His instructions had been clear, yet somehow his Brothers had still managed to screw it up. Now, with Daman running late, his carefully laid plans were unravelling, leaving them stuck here like sitting ducks.

'What if Daman's decided to turn us over to the Order?' Tommo said, facing Eric when Ben offered no support.

'Why would he do that?' Eric snapped.

'I don't know... There's that woman doctor he's always talking about, the one he's got a thing for. Maybe he—'

'Brother Bains is the one who got us inside. The one who willingly chose his Brothers over the Order. We know too much about Bains for him to betray us now.'

Tommo opened his mouth to speak.

Holding up a hand, Eric shook his head. 'Just don't. I don't want to hear it.' But now that Tommo had said it aloud, the doubt was beginning to take root. What if Daman was a double agent, feeding them lies all along? He tugged at his shirt collar, brushing the raised black veins beneath his skin. No. Daman wouldn't betray them.

The door flew open, making Eric start. Thoughts of O.O.T.I.S agents armed to the teeth caused adrenaline to spike through his body. Relief washed over him when Daman stepped into the room.

'Brother Bains, you're late,' Eric said, his clipped tone betraying none of his earlier tension.

'Sorry. Had a few things to deal with.'

Eric's jaw tightened as he fought to keep his temper in check. Losing it now would only delay things further. 'How long do we have?'

Daman touched his earpiece, his brow furrowing in concentration. 'There are three assets still out of containment. I may have to release more to keep the agents busy, but I don't want to raise suspicion. The initial explosion covered the first breaches, but after that...'

'We'd better hurry then, hadn't we?' Eric said.

Tommo shifted nervously beside him, his attention darting between Daman and the gatekeeper. 'How are we going to get him—it—out of here?' he asked, anxiety threading through his voice.

'I'll unlock one of the back doors in this sector,' Daman said, placing his laptop down on the console desk at the back of the cell. He flipped it open and started typing. 'The agents are occupied on the other side of the building. It should be a clear route.'

'But how are we going to get this thing out of the cage?' Tommo waved his hand at the enclosure. 'Isn't it dangerous?'

'It's a Level-11 threat,' Daman replied, not bothering to look up.

Ben gulped audibly.

Tommo's eyes bulged. 'Isn't that... *very* dangerous?'

'Yes. But don't worry. The cell is equipped with a neutralisation protocol. I'll show you.'

As Daman continued typing, the gatekeeper frowned. For the first time, his expression shifted into something almost... concerned. Daman finished entering the commands, nodding as he moved his laptop aside and pressed a button on the console.

A hissing sound filled the room, drawing their attention to the enclosure. White gas billowed from concealed vents, swirling as it rapidly filled the space behind the glass. The gatekeeper's green eyes widened before he staggered, thrusting a hand out for support. His face became slack. He swayed in place. Then he collapsed on the floor.

'Give it a moment.' Daman eyed the console intently. 'That stuff would put any of us out in seconds. We just need to give the gas long enough to knock him out fully before I vent it.'

Tommo made a small, nervous noise.

Eric turned to glare at him. 'What now?'

'Nothing,' Tommo muttered, his focus shifting to Daman. 'It's just going to look pretty sus when we haul him out of here, isn't it?'

Daman shrugged. 'Security systems are down. I've diverted power to critical systems—no cameras, no door locks.'

'No door locks?' Tommo's voice raised an octave. 'So those things can just stroll out of their cells?'

'Anything above a Level 3 is contained in a secondary enclosure. Double-layered security. Levels 2 and below are considered minimal threats at best.'

'To agents, maybe.' Panic bled into Tommo's voice. 'We're just people. We're untrained, unarmed... What if we run into a Level 2?'

Daman scoffed, pulling his laptop closer. 'Don't worry,' he said, his fingers flying across the keys, 'There's nothing—' He paused, frowning. 'Oh.'

'Oh? *Oh?* What the fuck is oh?' Eric demanded.

'It seems there's a Level 2 in containment on this floor, but I'm sure it's nothing to worry about.'

Tommo's jaw dropped. He spluttered, looking to Eric.

Eric crossed his arms, sighing. 'Is it likely to come here?'

'I—' Another explosion rocked the building, cutting Daman off. Dust and debris rained down from the ceiling followed by a metal tile crashing to the floor.

Eric cursed, his frustration made worse by the maddening static inside his skull. The whispers crackled and hissed, unintelligible chatter rising in volume and urgency. Gritting his teeth, he rubbed at the base of his throat, fighting to maintain focus.

'Fuck.' Tommo whirled to face Ben. 'I thought Sean said he knew what he was doing with the explosives? That sounded really close.'

Ben's lip curled in a sneer. 'He's a fucking amateur.' His voice was low, barely contained. 'We should have stuck to the original plan. Now look at this mess.'

Eric had to agree. If Sean wasn't careful, the entire building could come down on top of them. He'd been very clear: the explosives were meant to be a distraction, not a demolition.

'I already explained why Sean couldn't enter the premises,' Daman said casting a wary glance at the fallen ceiling tile before returning his attention to the unconscious gatekeeper. 'Anyway, that should be enough.' He pointed to a wall safe. 'Tommo, could you grab the shackles? We'll need to secure him soon after I open the enclosure.'

Tommo nodded, though his hands trembled as he retrieved them. He turned the shackles over, inspecting the symbols engraved into the metal. 'Are they going to be enough?'

Daman nodded. 'They're warded. As long as they remain on, they'll suppress his powers. Ready?'

Tommo frowned. 'Ready for what?'

'When I unlock the enclosure, you're going to put them on him.'

'*Me?*' Tommo spluttered. 'Why me?'

'I'll do it.' Eric snatched the shackles from Tommo, surprised by their weight. The metal felt cool and solid; the symbols hummed faintly beneath his fingertips.

Tommo added, 'But what if Josh—'

Eric rounded on Tommo, grabbing his tie and yanking him close. 'Josh isn't going to be a problem.' His voice dropped to a low, biting snarl.

'I just—'

'Are you going to be a problem, Josh?' Eric shouted, his voice ringing out, sharp and sudden.

The room fell silent, broken only by a faint shuffle from somewhere behind him.

Eric smirked, his eyes still locked on Tommo's. 'See? Not a problem.'

Tommo's gaze flickered uneasily past Eric's shoulder, his Adam's apple bobbing as he swallowed hard.

With a final press of a button, Daman unlocked the enclosure. The gas had mostly dissipated, save for a thin layer clinging to the floor around the gatekeeper's limp body.

Cautiously, Eric pulled open the door, holding his breath as the last wisps of gas coiled around his feet. He dashed forward and clasped the shackles onto the unconscious figure before making a hasty retreat and releasing his breath.

The men stood, staring at the motionless gatekeeper.

Eric broke the silence. 'Shall we?'

Without another word, he and Tommo moved to lift the gatekeeper. Despite his lean frame, he was surprisingly heavy. They fumbled awkwardly to lift his weight, their inexperience becoming increasingly evident as limbs tangled amidst grunts of exertion and irritated huffs.

'Stop!' Eric barked, wiping away the sweat that coated his forehead. 'You get the feet. I'll take the shoulders.'

With more coordination, they shared the gatekeeper's weighty form between them. Eric's muscles burned with the effort, his arms shaking.

'Let's go,' he grunted.

As they approached the exit, the door suddenly swung open. A man in his mid-sixties stood in the doorway, his brown jacket hanging off his arms in tatters. The pulsing red light revealed bloody smears across his face.

They froze. Eric shot Daman a look, the unspoken question of *who the fuck is this* mirrored back at him.

The man's eyes narrowed sharply as they landed on the unconscious gatekeeper.

Before Eric could react, another explosion shook the room. He lost his grip on the gatekeeper, barely managing to keep his balance. Metal ceiling tiles rained down around him, forcing him to protect his head. Tommo staggered back, his panicked screeches piercing the chaos before he launched himself to the ground. Just as Eric thought the worst was over, a deafening groan resonated from beneath them.

He felt it first—the unsettling vibration underfoot. His mind struggled to comprehend what was happening. The floor buckled and cracked, forcing him to scramble backwards towards a cowering Tommo, away from the gatekeeper. Shards of metal snapped upward as a fissure tore across the room, exposing the terracotta beneath. The sounds of straining and popping seemed to be coming from all sides.

Time stalled, his brain catching up a second too late. The ground beneath him gave way. He stumbled back, unable to keep his footing as great chunks of the floor crumbled away.

A scream burst from his throat as Eric plunged into the abyss, his stomach lurching with the sudden drop. The roar of collapsing stone and debris engulphed him, slashing at his skin, bruising his body as he fell. Something solid struck the back of his head, but his unbridled terror numbed the pain.

Darkness closed in as the building devoured him.

Chapter 22

CHARLIE STOOD ALONE, THE cracked red-brown earth beneath his feet as dry as bone. The air reeked of sulphur; he could taste it at the back of his throat, acrid and bitter. A torrid breeze stirred from somewhere, whipping up dust that coated his shoes like rust, staining everything it touched. Old. Decayed. Barren. Everything before him was desolate—a wasteland stretching as far as he could see. In the distance, impossibly large mountains jutted up, and clusters of rocks and caves huddled here and there. But mostly, the land was open. It reminded him of those photos of deserts and canyons. Arid, desolate places where things went to die.

The air clung to him, stifling hot. Sweat drenched his skin. Every breath burned, filling his lungs with thick, choking dust. He shrugged off his slate-grey trench coat and unbuttoned his shirt collar.

'Hello?' His voice was swallowed by the silence.

Charlie started walking, though there was no real destination. No matter how far he went, the inhospitable landscape remained unchanged. The mountains always distant. The caves always out of reach.

The feel of scratchy sandpaper at the back of his throat grew worse. He swallowed; his tongue stuck to the roof of his mouth, dry as ash. *Christ*, it was so damned hot. He needed shade. Anywhere to get out of the scorching heat. His sweat-drenched clothes clung to his skin. His feet ached with every painful step. A dry rasp escaped his cracked lips as he looked up to the sky. The blackened clouds bled red, suffocating the sun beneath them. How could it be this hot?

'Hello?' The word chafed his already sore tongue.

He'd been here before. Done this before. He knew what came next, but still he trudged forward, blinking against the dryness in his eyes.

The ground trembled beneath his feet. Charlie stopped; the muscles in his legs burned now that he wasn't moving. A crack splintered the dry earth suddenly, sending chunks of rock skittering in all directions. The vibrations coursed through him, rattling his bones and squeezing the air from his lungs.

He stumbled back, dazed. Charlie's heel caught on something hard, pitching him on his backside with a jolt.

The ground yawned open with an angry roar, wider and wider until he was staring into a gaping chasm. A blast of heat surged up from the void, scorching his skin. He threw up his arms as the smell of singed hair filled his nostrils.

'Char-lie,' the voice erupted from below, more than just a sound—it was all-consuming. Malevolent.

'Char-lie.'

Panic seized him. He stumbled back, kicking up dust and dirt in his desperation to get away. Every nerve in his body screamed danger. He needed to get up. Needed to run.

'Char-lie,' the voice drawled. It was closer now, louder, surrounding him, sinking into his mind. He felt it in his core. Despite the blistering heat, his blood became ice in his veins.

He clawed at the fractured earth, nails cracking, skin shredding, as he tried to escape the taunt. But his body, sluggish and numb, refused to cooperate. He turned his head only to see the threat of the chasm still looming behind him.

'Chaaar-lie.'

From the deep darkness long, bony fingers emerged, gouging into the sides of the earth in an explosion of dust and fragments of rock. Black talons raked the surface mere feet from where he sat, frozen in horror. He knew what came next.

The creature's horns breached the abyss next, rising slowly. Its face emerged, a hollow, twisted mask of malice with flesh stretched taut over impossibly sharp angles. Its eyes gleamed with hunger. A sneer curled its lips, revealing sharp teeth that glistened in the crimson haze, as if freshly painted with blood.

'Char-lie, it is time.'

'No... no!' His body refused to move, limbs paralysed. His heart thundered in his chest, pounding so violently it threatened to rip him apart from the inside out.

Terror unlike anything he'd ever known grasped him, immobilising him.

As the thing raised its enormous hand, the rancid stench of its breath rolled over him. Shadow swept across Charlie as its talons extended; a malevolent laugh rumbled up from its chest like thunder. Everything seemed to slow as the hand reached towards him, closer and closer...

Charlie's eyes snapped open.

He flailed in the darkness, gasping for air. The weight of the shifting rubble pressed in around him. The pain hit him then, flooding his senses—a raw, searing fire across his body. With his next cry, the fog of unconsciousness gave way to the agony of his injuries.

What the hell just happened?

YOU FELL. THROUGH THE FLOOR.

He flinched at the sound of the demon's voice inside his skull, the slight movement sending a fresh wave of pain coursing through him. Hissing through his teeth, he forced his eyes to adjust to the gloom, vaguely aware of the anaemic artificial light seeping from fixtures on the concrete walls around him.

Fell through the floor... That's right—that last explosion had caused the gatekeeper's cell to partially collapse, taking him and some of the black suits with it.

He was lying on a bed of wreckage, and what was left of the upper floor had been reduced to a pile of rubble beneath him. The level above was not visible due to a heavy barrier of stone and dust. Both sealed him from the cell area he'd just fallen from. Sealed him from the gatekeeper.

He moved to get up. Pain blazed through his arm. With a sharp yelp, Charlie fell back.

BROKEN.

No shit. Fix it.

Something like a huff echoed inside his skull. Grudgingly, Chekonost did as he asked. YOU'RE WELCOME.

Charlie clenched his jaw, refusing to dignify the demon with a response. His mind drifted back to Stephen and the torment he must have endured for all those years. How had he coped?

PERHAPS IF YOU WERE MORE ACCOMMODATING, I WOULD NUMB THE PAIN.

Wait—you can do that? All this time you could have stopped it?

YES.

Then why the hell didn't you?

I DON'T LIKE YOU.

Charlie pushed up amidst the rubble, grimacing. The grating feel of his bones mending, of his muscles stretching and straining as they reformed, was something he'd never get used to. Knowing that the demon could have eased the pain at any moment, but chose not to, pissed him off. He hated that he needed its help. Reliance was a slippery slope, and he almost longed to remember the feel of his stiff knees and creaking joints. Still, like it or not, he was no good to anyone with a broken arm or fractured ribs. His best bet was to find the gatekeeper and reclaim his body.

He took an experimental step forward, debris shifting dangerously beneath his feet. He was in some sort of tunnel. No... the Underground.

The faint smell of oil lingered in the dense air. Tracks stretched out before him, held in place by heavy wooden sleepers, the metal darkened by rust in sections, and polished to a gleam by train wheels in others. Weathered cables snaked along the concrete walls, emitting a low electrical hum that droned just above the sound of settling rubble and the thrash of Charlie's own pulse.

Still in use then. O.O.T.I.S must have needed a way to transport all the monsters in without the public knowing.

Bracing himself against a sheared lump of stone, Charlie clambered down the unstable mound of brick and metal to solid ground. He straightened, his tattered waxed jacket flapping around his arms. Frowning, he tugged at one of the frayed ribbons of fabric, then shrugged the jacket off, letting it fall. The box of business cards tumbled from his pocket, scattering across the gravel ballast in a flurry of white.

I CANNOT SENSE THE GATEKEEPER.

What?

THOSE MEN TOOK HIM.

The black suits?

THEY WERE NOT BLACK SUITS. THEY REEKED OF FEAR. I COULD SMELL THE CORTISOL

PUMPING THROUGH THEIR VEINS. THE SWEAT SOAKING THROUGH THEIR PORES. THEY WERE IMPOSTERS. THIEVES.

You can't know that.

HOW ELSE DO YOU EXPLAIN THE FACT THAT I CAN NO LONGER SENSE THE GATEKEEPER?

Maybe he's dead? The gravity of the thought struck him immediately. If the gatekeeper was dead, he was fucked—stuck with the demon forever, until he became a warped version of himself. A danger to everyone he loved.

THE GATEKEEPER IS NOT DEAD. HE HAS BEEN STOLEN. WE MUST FIND HIM.

Charlie glanced back at the wall of rubble. There was no way out behind them. They were cut off.

The smell of blood hit him. A copper scent that he could almost taste. He looked down at the damp stains of red on his tattered clothes and sniffed.

Not his blood.

He moved along the rubble, past a chunk of wall that was somehow still mostly intact. He saw the fingers first, streaked with grey.

'Shit!' He darted forward and tore into the debris, flinging aside chunks of stone and twisted metal. Dust billowed around him as he uncovered an arm, then a face. A few more frantic tugs and it became obvious—the man in the black suit was dead. Charlie recognised him from the gatekeeper's cell. One side of his skull had been caved in. Blood pooled beneath him, soaking his ginger hair and turning it almost black in the dim light.

Charlie took a step back. There was nothing he could do. It dawned on him then that he'd had been lucky to survive. Was he even capable of dying now?

He shuddered.

Trapped underground, no way out. If the demon was right and those men had taken the gatekeeper, then what? How the hell were they supposed to find him now?

THERE IS ONE WAY.

What?

ASK THE CORPSE.

Charlie let out an exasperated huff and dragged a hand down his face. Whatever game the demon was playing, he wasn't in the mood for its nonsense.

I HAVE THE POWER TO SEE HIS MEMORIES.

Well, what are you waiting for?

IT'S NOT THAT SIMPLE.

Of course not.

YOU WILL NEED TO HELP ME.

Charlie paused. Waiting. Whatever Chekonost was about to suggest, he already knew he wouldn't like it.

YOU NEED TO EAT HIS EYEBALLS.

What? His stomach roiled. *No. No, I'm not doing that.*

IT IS THE ONLY WAY.

No!

IF YOU EAT HIS EYEBALLS, I WILL BE ABLE TO ACCESS HIS MEMORIES AND WE WILL KNOW WHAT HIS PLANS FOR THE GATEKEEPER WERE.

No. I can't.

YOU CAN. IT IS EASY. I WILL INSTRUCT YOU.

No, you don't understand—I can't. Charlie shook his head frantically. His breathing picked up; dust caught in his throat. His hands trembled as cold sweat beaded on the small of his back.

WHAT IS HAPPENING?

I can't. I can't.

He felt lightheaded. His lungs were on fire.

YOU ARE PANICKING.

Of course I'm fucking panicking! You're asking me to eat someone!

NOT ALL OF HIM.

No. No. No. I can't.

THEN SAY GOODBYE TO YOUR FAMILY.

The words hit him like a slap to the face. *What?*

EVERY DAY YOUR LINK TO THE DEMON REALM GROWS STRONGER. EVERY DAY YOUR GRIP ON HUMANITY WEAKENS. SOON, YOU WILL BE A SLAVE TO KAR'ROC'S WILL. YOU WILL HAVE NO INHIBITIONS. NO MORALITY. WHEN YOUR DAUGHTER DISAGREES WITH YOU, WHEN YOUR GRANDDAUGHTER MAKES TOO MUCH MESS, WILL YOU BE ABLE TO CONTROL YOUR ANGER? OR WILL YOU RIP THEM APART?

No! I Would never hurt my family.

JUST LIKE YOU WOULD NEVER LOSE YOUR TEMPER IN FRONT OF EVELYN? JUST LIKE YOU WOULD NEVER FORNICATE WITH YOUR EX-WIFE? YOU HAVE A SEMBLANCE OF CONTROL

NOW, BUT WHAT ABOUT IN A WEEK? A MONTH? YOU WILL BECOME A MONSTER. JUST LIKE STEPHEN. JUST LIKE ME.

No! Charlie staggered back. *No... I...* Christ, was it true? It had happened to Stephen... And he hadn't even been the dagger's master. If this was the only way to protect his family, he had no choice.

The mangled corpse stared up at him accusingly. Charlie shuffled forward, sweat drenching his brow, stomach churning. He'd never handled mess well—his own blood was manageable, but someone else's? It made his skin crawl.

Crouching down, he swallowed past the lump in his throat and touched the man's face before snatching his hand back reflexively.

DO IT.

I... I don't know how.

The demon sighed, irritation seeping through his mind. IT'S SIMPLE. INSERT YOUR THUMB AND FOREFINGER INTO HIS EYE SOCKET AND PULL.

Charlie inhaled as he touched the corpse's cheek with his trembling fingers. It took everything he had not to pull away again. Slowly, he pressed into the eye socket, the flesh warm and slightly pliant. His fingertips met resistance—a nauseating, jelly-like firmness. The eyeball shifted slightly under the pressure, wet and slick.

He gagged, jerking his hand away.

STOP BEING SUCH A COWARD. HE IS DEAD. HE CAN'T FEEL IT. HE IS NOTHING MORE THAN A

SLAB OF MEAT. Something greedy laced those words, a desperate urgency that turned his stomach.

Gathering himself, Charlie tried again. He squeezed his eyes shut, feeling the man's face until he found the sharp contour of his cheekbone. He pressed harder, bile rising in his throat, as his fingers sunk into the socket once more. The corpse's flesh clung to him, sticky and warm. A faint suction pulled him in farther.

Oh God, I can't.

YOU CAN. JUST RIP IT OUT.

His breathing quickened, each gasp more frantic than the last. The air was too thin. He couldn't fill his lungs. His chest constricted painfully. His pulse hammered. Everything felt wrong—the blood on his hands, the gore, the unbearable weight of what he was being forced to do. He opened his eyes—big mistake. Charlie's vision swam. The walls were closing in, the world folding in on itself.

Squeezing his eyes shut again, he gripped the slippery, gelatinous eyeball and yanked. It came free of the socket with a wet pop, but it was caught on something. His stomach churned as he felt the tension of the optic nerve pulling taut, keeping the eye tethered. He gave another sharp tug and the sinewy tissue snapped. Fluid trailed down his hand, causing fresh bile to rise in his throat. The smell, the sound, the warmth of it—it was almost too much. Charlie's stomach twisted violently, causing saliva to flood his mouth.

He swallowed it down, refusing to look at what was in his hand, afraid he might vomit.

THERE. THAT WASN'T SO HARD. NOW EAT IT.

His hand refused to move. Feeling himself sway, Charlie placed his other hand on the ground for support. Focusing on the feel of the cool gravel beneath his fingers, rough and uneven, he tried to slow his breathing. The scrape of the small stones shifting under his touch grounded him as he slowly traced the uneven surface.

WHAT ARE YOU DOING? JUST EAT IT.

Panting, he shook his head.

THIS IS FOR YOUR FAMILY.

His granddaughter's face flashed before him, her pale-green eyes briming with tears, as she stared at him in confusion, in fear. He never wanted to see that look again. Charlie couldn't be the thing that gave her nightmares. If he didn't do this, if he lost the gatekeeper, he may never have another chance to rid himself of Chekonost. How could he forgive himself if he ever hurt them? He'd rather die. And compared to death, was this really so bad? He'd eaten rare steak before.

Just pretend this is the same. Just a piece of meat.

Before he could change his mind, Charlie stuffed the eyeball into his mouth and bit down. The explosion of pulp gushing over his tongue made him gag.

Images flooded his mind.

The dead man, Tommo, sat in a derelict pub surrounded by robed figures. A ritualistic circle. Snippets of conversation. Disjointed flashes of detail—voices overlapping, faces blurring in and out, distorted laughter, a rising chant. Scenes shifted too fast, flickering like static, memories crashing together in a chaotic swirl, too tangled and fragmented to make sense. And then amongst the chaos, the outside of the pub. Charlie recognised it—the White Stag. He'd been there before, with Meghan and Debbie.

Chunks of eyeball rolled around his tongue, the viscous fluid thick in his mouth, slightly salty with a hint of iron and grease. He gagged again.

SWALLOW IT!

It was too much. He retched, spewing the eyeball and a stomach full of bile across the ground.

The memories blinked out.

Charlie heaved, trembling on hands and knees until there was nothing left inside him.

THAT WAS WASTEFUL.

I know where they're taking the gatekeeper.

EVEN SO...

Swiping a hand across his mouth, Charlie pushed himself unsteadily to his feet.

It's a derelict pub just off Chestnut Grove Lane. That's where they're going. We need to find a way out of here.

YOU ARE AWARE THAT I JUST WITNESSED THE SAME THINGS YOU DID? YOU ARE MAKING ASSUMPTIONS. THE ONLY WAY TO BE SURE WOULD BE TO EAT THE OTHER EYEBALL.

Charlie looked down at the mangled skull. The other eye socket was a mess of ruined flesh and bone.

His stomach cramped dangerously. He turned away.

No. We've got what we need. I'm not doing that again. I'm never doing that again.

STEPHEN DID NOT COMPLAIN THIS MUCH.

'I'm not Stephen!' Charlie spat.

It was bad enough he'd just defiled a corpse; he didn't need the demon sullying Stephen's memory, too. He couldn't bear to think of his friend doing such heinous things willingly. Didn't want to imagine the slow, maddening descent into unforgivable depravity. Or the fact that if Charlie didn't act soon, he'd end up the same way.

OH, DID I TOUCH A NERVE?

Ignoring the voice, Charlie surveyed his surroundings. There was only one way out that he could see. He started walking.

A dull *clang* stopped him in his tracks.

WE'RE NOT ALONE.

Chapter 23

Josh blinked away the grit in his eyes, consciousness flooding back in a chaotic rush of terror and confusion. He tried to move, but something heavy pinned him down, pressing so hard he could barely breathe. The weight was everywhere—sharp, cold, digging into his skin. He clawed at it, his hands scraping against jagged edges, but it wouldn't budge.

I'm trapped!

His heart raced, sending adrenaline surging through his veins, as he clawed frantically at his prison. Fingers slipped and scraped across the rough, unyielding surface. Pain sliced through him, his hands slick with blood, but he didn't stop, couldn't stop.

Move! You have to.

With a strangled gasp he dug deeper, managing to toss aside smaller chunks of crumbling stone, ignoring how the sharp edges tore at his skin. Dust coated the back of his throat, each breath a choking haze that weighed heavy in his lungs. He wheezed out a harsh cough; it sent spasms of pain through his chest. It was agony, but it was better than not breathing at all. He needed to fight. For himself. For Sophie.

Each move he made was torturous, the rubble shifting ominously around him, threatening to bury him alive. Then the pressure eased, just a little, and he shoved harder. Suddenly, cool air brushed his face, and with one final heave, he broke free, tumbling out into the dim light.

'Christ!'

Josh blinked up at the person who had just spoken, his mind struggling to process what had happened. A dark figure stood over him, tossing aside a hunk of something heavy that shattered as it struck the ground. Suddenly, it clicked—he hadn't escaped on his own. This stranger had helped dig him free.

It took Josh a moment to focus, his vision swimming. He rubbed at his eyes, but the filth caking his fingers only scraped against his skin. Hissing through a mix of pain and frustration, he got to his knees, coughing again to clear his lungs.

With a wheeze, he gave himself a moment to catch his breath, aware of the stranger watching him. They were in some sort of tunnel... Josh glanced up, noting with a sinking feeling that the mountain of rubble he'd just escaped from had walled them in. What had happened? The last thing he remembered was talking to Tommo...

He shuddered out his next breath. If he could just get his head to stop spinning, could just think...

Josh scanned the ground, his gaze drifting unfocused across the debris until he caught a glint. Something reflecting the dim light. Something... wet? He squinted, following the slick, black trail that led to a soft-looking shape.

Tommo?

Josh froze, his mind refusing to process what he was seeing. Tommo's body was crumpled, half-buried beneath the rubble. Part of his face had been smashed in. And his eye... *Oh God.* Where his left eye should have been was a gaping, bloody hollow.

With a shriek, Josh scrambled upright, his arms flailing, but the moment he put weight on his right foot, a sharp pain shot through his ankle. He stumbled forward, the world tilting.

Strong hands caught him, yanking him back before he face-planted the ground.

'It's okay,' the stranger said.

'He's d-d-dead,' Josh choked.

'He is.'

'What h-happened?'

The stranger hesitated. 'Crushed beneath the rubble.'

'His eye... W-what happened to his eye?'

The man didn't answer. His grip on Josh's arms tightened slightly before he said, 'Can you stand?'

The words barely reached him. Josh's gaze was fixed on Tommo's broken body. He should've felt something—relief, anger, *anything.* Tommo had always hated him, always made his life hell. But seeing him, Josh felt... nothing. Nothing for the man. Just a cold, sick numbness at the sight of death that made his stomach churn.

The man let go of his arms, and Josh staggered back a step.

'You alright? Anything broken?'

Josh tore his eyes from Tommo and blinked at the stranger. 'I... I d-don't think so.' He ran his hands over himself, checking. A few cuts and scrapes, a dull ache at the back of his head, and his ankle. 'Just my ankle... I think. Sprained.'

The man nodded. He was old—mid-sixties at least—with dust and grime streaking his face, and grey hair scattered with chips of stone. His shirt hung in tatters and dark stains smeared the fabric. Blood? The man's eyes narrowed as he looked Josh over, his brow furrowing.

Josh shifted uncomfortably beneath the scrutiny and looked around the space. The walls were curved, concrete, the ceiling low. And tracks on the ground? He focused on that instead of looking back at Tommo.

'Where... where are we?' he asked.

The man's expression darkened. 'My guess? The Underground.'

That made sense. Josh swallowed hard, his throat tight, and nodded. The movement sent a dull throb through the back of his head. He touched it gingerly. There was a lump, but it wasn't bleeding.

'What were you doing up there? Before the floor collapsed?' the man asked.

Josh rubbed at his temples, trying to think. *What if I say the wrong thing? What if he thinks I'm crazy and gets mad?*

'I d-don't know...' His voice wavered.

The man's frown deepened. 'You don't know?'

Josh's chest tightened. 'I... I wasn't... T-they made me come.'

'*Who* made you?'

'The others.' He winced, knowing he was saying all the wrong things.

The man made a frustrated sound. Josh flinched, his gaze dropping to a scattering of white cards half-buried in the gravel next to a pile of brown rags. Slowly, he bent down, battling against the rush of blood to his head.

He picked up one of the cards, angling it towards the dim light. The text was smeared, but he could make out a name.

'Ch-Charlie Haynes.'

The man's eyes snapped to his face.

Josh shuddered under his stare, the intensity of it making him feel like he was being weighed and measured, judged for something he didn't even know he'd done.

'Is t-t-this you?' Josh asked.

Charlie's face didn't change. 'Yes.'

'Unsolved crimes?' A flicker of hope sparked in Josh's chest. Without Tommo or any of the others around, this could be his chance. 'You work for the police?'

'I did. I retired yesterday.' Before Josh could ask his next question, Charlie stepped closer. 'Those men you were with, they took someone. What do they want with him?'

'I d-don't know.' Seeing the older man's sceptical expression, he held up his hands. 'Really. I promise. They don't t-tell me anything. They just keep me around so that they can keep an eye on me. So I can't run.'

'Run?'

Josh chewed on his lip, unsure of how much to say. *What if I tell him everything and he walks away? What if he thinks I'm lying?* The doubt churned in his gut, leaving his words stuck in his throat.

With a frown Charlie turned. His footsteps sounded heavy against the crunching stone as he walked away.

Josh's heart leapt into his throat. *This is it. If he leaves now, Sophie's as good as dead.* Ignoring the sharp pain that lanced through his ankle, he lunged forward and grabbed Charlie by the arm, his grip trembling but firm.

'They have my sister!' he blurted.

Charlie stopped, looking back. 'What?'

'My sister. They have my s-s-sister. S-Sophie. Locked in a c-cage in the cellar of the White Stag. It's an old, abandoned pub. They have another woman, too. You have to help me. If I d-don't go back, they'll kill her. Please! I c-can't leave her there. If anything happened to her... it'll be my fault. It'll be all my fault. Please, you have to h-help her! I don't want her to die!' Tears stung at the corners of his eyes before rolling down his cheeks. He wiped at them, attention locked on Charlie.

The older man exhaled, his expression softening. Then, with a slow sigh, he motioned for Josh to follow.

'You'll help me?'

'Sure, I'll help you.' Charlie paused, eyeing Josh for a moment. 'What's your name?'

'J-Josh.'

'Try to keep up, Josh.'

Relief swelled in his chest, momentarily dulling the pain in his ankle. He stuffed the business card into his trouser pocket and hobbled after Charlie. Sophie needed him. He might have failed to protect her from Eric, but he wasn't about to let her rot in a cage. And with Charlie's help—his experience, his contacts—he might finally have a chance to save her.

'So,' Charlie said, not looking back, 'tell me more about these other guys.'

Josh took a shaky breath. He knew how it would sound, but Charlie *needed* to understand. He needed to know what they were capable of, what they might do to Sophie...

'They're like a c-c-cult,' he said, his voice breaking on the last word.

Charlie stopped dead and turned to stare at him. 'A *cult?*'

'It didn't start that way. I f-found a book.' Josh rubbed absently at his collarbone, avoiding Charlie's eyes. 'It was an accident. I was a courier and it got left in my car. I tried to hide it, but Eric found it—he's their leader. He already had this group of friends. They used to play games together online. But after he found the book, he became d-d-different. Mean. They started wearing robes, having weird meetings. I think they're trying to summon a demon.'

A flicker of something unreadable passed across Charlie's face. 'A demon-summoning cult?'

Josh felt his heart sink. He'd said too much. He sounded crazy. Everyone knew demons didn't exist. 'You'll still try to help my s-sister, right?'

'I'll help you, Josh,' Charlie said. 'How many of them are there?'

'There's Sean, Ben, Damien—no, w-wait.' Josh frowned. 'Not Damien, Daman—and Tommo. Well, not anymore. That was Tommo back there in the rubble.'

At the mention of Tommo's name, Charlie seemed to stiffen. 'And what about this Eric?' His words came a little too fast, like he was trying to steer the conversation away from the dead man.

Josh averted his gaze. 'And Eric.'

'Wait... Did you say Daman? Like Damanjeet?'

'Yes, I t-think so. Why?'

Charlie's jaw tensed. He spat out a curse.

'Is t-that bad?'

'He works for O.O.T.I.S. That means there could be others working with him. It means the Order's been compromised.'

'Oh,' Josh said, unsure of what his reaction was supposed to be. He'd heard the others speak about the Order, but what it was or why Daman working for them was such a problem was lost on him.

'Come on,' Charlie said, motioning ahead. 'We need to get to that pub before they achieve whatever it is they're trying to do.'

Josh nodded, watching Charlie stride off again. How was he still walking? He was soaked in blood, his clothes shredded. If he'd fallen through the floor, too, why hadn't he been injured?

He shook the thoughts away and set off after him in a limping shuffle. This man was going to help Sophie. Nothing else mattered.

'How did you get involved with Eric in the first place?' Charlie asked.

Josh grimaced, trying to think of how best to answer. 'When we were younger, our mum wasn't very nice to us. She used to take these drugs, one with a black d-dragon on the packet.'

Charlie's steps faltered. 'Dragon Scale?'

Josh nodded, then realised Charlie wasn't looking and replied, 'Yes. It made her sleep. But then, when it wore off, s-s-she'd get really mad at us. Lock us outside for hours on end. Or h-hit us.'

'I get it,' Charlie said after a pause. 'Some parents can be arseholes.'

Josh eyed the silver scars on Charlie's exposed arms, understanding.

'I was never strong enough to do anything about it, but Eric would take the beatings for me and S-Sophie. He'd find f-food. Try to keep us safe. He wasn't always the way he is now.'

'Eric's your brother.'

It wasn't a question, so Josh didn't reply. Instead, he eyed the wall where a gaping crack yawned in the concrete, wide enough to swallow him whole.

He tugged nervously at his shirt collar and continued, 'He used to p-protect Sophie, from our mum, from the men she brought home. But now h-he's using her against me. To make s-s-sure I don't run, don't tell anyone what they're doing. I can't leave her there.'

They walked in silence for a while, picking their way through patches of shadow where the wan, yellow glow of the emergency lighting failed to reach. Occasionally, Charlie broke it with more questions: How many people were there in the pub? Where did they work? What did they look like?

Josh answered as best he could, but most of his time had been spent in one dark, dank room or another. When he was around the others, they'd clam up, making it clear he wasn't one of them, wasn't welcome. They tolerated him because of Eric, nothing more.

The tunnel stretched endlessly before them. The farther they walked, the warmer the air seemed to become. More than once, Josh caught his ankle on something unseen, crying out in agony and pleading with Charlie to stop until the pain subsided. They clung to the walls, doing their best to avoid the hidden perils of the tracks. Even so, Josh couldn't block out the intrusive thought about a train suddenly barrelling towards them.

He'd always loathed the Underground. He'd had a brief stint working in London, but hadn't even made it through his probation period before they let him go. He'd hated the crowds. Hated the stifling rush of hot, stale air as he waited behind the yellow line, only to then have to contort into the spaces between elbows and armpits as everyone crushed themselves into the tiny compartment. But now, in the suffocating darkness of the tunnel, the memories didn't seem so bad.

'I always h-h-hated the Tube,' he said.

'You and me both.'

Charlie stopped abruptly, raising his hand for Josh to do the same.

'Wh-what's the matter?'

'Shhh.' Charlie cocked his head.

Josh strained to listen. Then he felt it: a low, echoing growl that scraped through the walls and juddered his bones.

'Shit! Get back.' Charlie pushed Josh back against the wall.

The sharp, echoing *clip-clop* of hooves striking the ground in heavy, deliberate steps filled the tunnel, each impact reverberating around them. From deep within the shadows a faint glow bloomed, steadily intensifying as it approached, casting long, flickering tendrils of orange light ahead of it.

Josh gasped, feeling Charlie flinch beside him. The jarring clashing noise intensified as a large creature stalked around the corner. It resembled a horse, but it was all wrong. Its twisted face showed long, sharp teeth that looked more wolf-like than equine. As it moved its skin glowed, fissures of molten light rippling over the contours of its powerful muscles. It tossed its head from side to side, then raised its muzzle, nostrils flaring as it scented the air.

Josh opened his mouth to scream. Charlie clamped his hand over it, silencing his terror. Charlie shook his head, his eyes wide with urgency, and gestured for him to start moving back the way they'd come.

Josh nodded, heart racing.

The beast hadn't noticed them yet. Its ears swivelled, scanning the tunnel, head shifting slowly side to side.

Josh took a tentative step back. There was nowhere to go, the way behind them blocked, but Charlie hustled him farther into the shadows.

The creature took a step forward, then sniffed again. Slowly, it swung its head in the opposite direction. Its body followed the movement, muscles rippling beneath its glowing hide as it pivoted. Its tail swished once as it started to move off.

It was leaving.

They remained motionless, hardly daring to breathe. After what felt like an eternity, Charlie dropped his arm and caught Josh's eye. With the slightest tilt of his head, he indicated that they should move.

Josh inched backwards. A stone skittered across the ground, dislodged by his heel.

The noise echoed, impossibly loud in the silence. Josh froze, his heart lurching into his throat. *No. No, no, no!* His legs gave way, all strength draining from his muscles.

Charlie grabbed him, hauling him upright with a jerk of surprising strength. Josh bit back a cry, his breath trapped in his chest. His eyes darted to the beast, praying—*begging*—that it hadn't noticed.

The creature stopped mid-step, its ears snapping upright. Its head whipped around as feral eyes fixed on them. For a heartbeat, it stood motionless. Its lips peeled back in a snarl, fangs gleaming like polished daggers in the dim light.

And then it charged them.

Hooves hammered against the tunnel floor like cannon blasts. Deafening and all too fast.

Charlie cursed.

Josh screamed.

Chapter 24

Sachiko peeled open her eyes, blinking against the blur until her vision sharpened. A searing pain knifed through her skull, intensifying with every bump and jolt. She was in a vehicle. A van, judging by the metal walls and cramped space. Swallowing back her nausea, she attempted to lift her head. The motion sent another wave of agony crashing through her. She groaned, giving up, and squinted at the stark-white interior of the van.

She needed to think. Piece together what had happened. But first, she had to sit up. Her hands refused to budge, bound tightly—feet too. Panic flared through her chest. She was stuck. Stuck on her belly with no way to break her bonds.

How had this happened?

Memories trickled back, murky and slow. She'd been at O.O.T.I.S headquarters. The black alert. Michelle... God, poor Michelle! And then Damanjeet...

It was him. He'd done this to her.

The van hit another bump, jolting her head against the hard floor, making her hiss. Despite her best efforts, tears pricked at the corners of her eyes.

He's going to kill me.

She choked back a muffled sob. She couldn't break down. Not yet.

'Hey, you're okay.'

Sachiko startled at the voice, her sudden movement sending fresh pain flaring through her skull. She twisted her neck slowly, trying to locate the speaker. Her vision blurred again, but she caught a glimpse—green eyes and blond, dishevelled hair. He looked familiar.

'Who are you?' she rasped.

'I'm Ash,' he replied, voice smooth and composed.

'Ash?' She squinted, the pulsing in her head making it hard to focus. 'I know you...' She trailed off as the realisation hit. 'You're the gatekeeper.'

He chuckled lightly. 'I prefer Ash, but yes.'

She gasped, trying to writhe away from him, but the thick rope bit into her flesh. The screws in the van's floor scraped against her skin, gouging into her arms and face. And the pain in her head... The endless throb...

'I'm not going to hurt you,' he said, his tone impassive, almost amused. 'Besides, I've still got these on.' He rattled the metal shackles around his wrists. 'You can relax.'

Heat flushed her cheeks. Her reaction had been an instinctive response that even years within the Order hadn't managed to suppress. She was a doctor, for goodness' sake, not some wet-behind-the-ears new recruit. 'I'm sorry.'

'Don't be. It's understandable. I'm a prisoner, after all.'

The steady drone of the van's engine and the hum of passing cars filled the silence that followed.

Sachiko took a breath, forcing calm into her voice. 'What happened?'

'Your colleague and his friends created a distraction and broke me out.'

'Why?'

'To open a gateway, I assume.'

Of course. She pressed her lips together, trying to think past the pounding in her head.

'What did you do?' she asked, surprised by her bluntness.

'What did I do?' Ash echoed with a soft laugh. 'I got tossed into a van.'

'No. What did you do to end up inside a cell?'

His lips curled in a half-smile, as though he'd been expecting the question. 'I saved someone.'

Her brow furrowed. 'You... saved someone?'

'A friend. A human.'

Sachiko blinked, her confusion deepening. 'I don't understand.'

'I saved her from another human.' His voice dropped; his smile faded. 'Didn't go so well for him.'

'Oh.'

'The Order closed my gateway.'

That was standard protocol to contain any threat, to neutralise any points of weakness in the veil.

'It was a mistake,' Ash continued, an edge to his tone.

She stiffened at the words, taking them as a threat.

'The breaches, the gateways, they serve a purpose,' he said quietly. 'They allow lesser demons to return to our realm. But more than that, they serve as an outlet for the energy build-up. Each time a gateway is closed, the build-up loses another point of release. Eventually the veil will rupture.'

'No,' Sachiko muttered. Damanjeet had told her the same thing, but she'd refused to believe it. 'T-that can't be true.'

'I begged the agent not to close it,' Ash said, almost mournful. 'But apparently, protocol overrides reason.'

'Why are you telling me this?'

'Because you need to know. You need to make the Order listen. When you get out of here—'

A nervous laugh bubbled up and out. 'That's optimistic.'

'When you get out of here,' he repeated firmly, 'you need to make them understand. If they keep closing the breaches, your world will be destroyed.'

Sachiko stayed silent. Ash was a demon. A prisoner of the Order. But still... if what he was saying was true, it didn't bear thinking about.

'Okay,' she whispered, 'If I get out of this—'

'*When.*'

'When I get out of this, I'll look into it.'

'Good.'

She shifted, the ropes chafing against her skin. Another violent bump had her biting back a curse.

Muffled voices filtered through the cab, arguing.

'Just drive!'

Damanjeet. She felt her blood boil.

'I don't want to get pulled over,' another voice said.

'That's because you're a pussy,' a third mocked.

She strained to listen as the bickering continued. Three men, including Damanjeet. She didn't recognise the other two, but that didn't matter. All this time she'd been so concerned about Charles, she hadn't seen what was right under her nose. Damanjeet had betrayed her. Betrayed the Order. And for what? She was determined to find out.

Somehow.

'They've been at it on and off for the last hour,' Ash said. 'Apparently things didn't go to plan.'

The voices in the cab grew louder.

'Eric's not fucking here though, is he, Ben?'

'I told you, no names!' Damanjeet snapped.

'Relax. They're out cold. Anyway, what are they gonna do, huh?'

'He's right. Stop being an arsehole,' Ben hissed.

'You'd know all about arseholes, wouldn't you, Ben?'

Ash made an amused sound. 'They're like children. They'll slip up eventually. We'll get out.'

Sachiko wasn't so sure. Damanjeet was intelligent and deliberate. And after what he'd done to Michelle, she'd have to be careful. Very careful. He might be obsessed with her, but even obsession had its limits—and she didn't want to find out what happened when he reached them.

'Who's in charge?' she asked Ash.

'From what I gather, someone called Eric. But they couldn't find him.'

'Find him?'

'One of the explosions collapsed the room my cell was in. Some of them fell through to the level below. Their leader is either trapped or dead. They seem to think he'll make his way back to them. We're being transported to their hideout. They'll hold us until he arrives. Or until they get bored.'

The snide remarks from the cab continued, the voices phasing in and out as the van jerked and bumped towards their final destination.

'Is there anything you can do?' she whispered.

'No. Not with the shackles. I'm not at full power.'

'Your file said you were a malafrax.'

'Yes.'

Malafrax demons were a perfect example of the savagery within the realm of fire and shadow. Once born, malafrax spawn would consume their mother, absorbing her power and strength by ingesting her flesh. They would continue to grow, their strength increasing to epic proportions, until they procreated and the cycle repeated itself.

Sachiko frowned, her mind whirring. 'I thought demons like you got stronger over time?'

Ash cleared his throat. 'Yes. Until we mate.'

From what she remembered, the male would transfer their energy to the female during mating, giving her additional strength to protect herself while incubating her young. Then, like countless insect species, the female would take advantage of the male's weakened state and eat them.

'And if you did mate, you wouldn't survive?'

'Generally, that's the way it works, yes.'

Generally? Sachiko's gaze shifted to Ash, her mind catching on a troubling inconsistency. As far as she was aware, the only thing that could significantly weaken a male malafrax was the act of procreation. But Ash was very much alive. Unless...

Her chest tightened as understanding struck. 'You mated with a human?'

A pause followed. His response, when it came, was quiet. 'Yes.'

Revulsion twisted in her gut.

'That makes you uncomfortable?'

'You're a demon,' she said, as if to explain. 'A malafrax demon.'

'I don't believe you're naive enough to think it doesn't happen. Your realm is rife with hybrids—demon and otherwise.' Ash sighed, a flicker of something like regret crossing his features. 'I can't change what happened. But my power isn't what it used to be, so these shackles will hold until I'm released. You'll have to help me break them.'

'Help you? Why would I help you?'

His piercing-green eyes met hers, unwavering. 'Because if you don't, you're probably going to die.'

'I'm a bit tied up in case you hadn't noticed.' A snorting laugh exploded out of her, releasing all of her frustration, all of her fear, bursting out in that one inappropriate moment of hysterics. She clamped her mouth shut, worried she might be overheard.

'They're disorganised,' Ash continued. 'Scared. All they've done is argue. If we work together, we can escape.'

'Scared people are dangerous people,' Sachiko whispered. She rested her head against the cool floor, the motion of the van rocking her.

Ash said nothing.

How had it come to this? How had she missed the signs? Damanjeet had always been a little awkward, the kind of person who struggled to hold a conversation without getting flustered. But a traitor? A murderer? She couldn't get her head around it. The image of Michelle's corpse flashed in her mind, a brutal reminder that she'd never really known him. She felt the weight of her own fear press heavily on her chest. Warm tears rolled down her cheeks.

The van slowed. Damanjeet and the others had fallen silent. For a moment the vehicle idled, and then the engine cut out.

'Act like you're still unconscious,' Ash whispered. 'It'll buy us some time. Let us get a sense of where we are.'

She nodded faintly, dread knotting in her gut as she heard the front doors open.

Footsteps approached and the van door slid open, sunlight flooding inside.

'Shit. He's awake,' one of the men said. 'Thought you said that gas would put him under for hours?'

'It doesn't matter,' Damanjeet said, though the strain in his voice suggested otherwise.

'I think it does fucking matter,' the man without a name griped.

'As long as he's wearing the shackles, he's powerless. Just get him out of the van.'

Aside from the slight shuffle of feet, no one moved.

'What the fuck did you bring your little girlfriend for anyway?' the man continued.

'She's my backup plan,' Damanjeet said quietly.

'Backup plan?' The man scoffed. 'What, are you going to elope if this all goes south?'

'Shut up. Just get the gatekeeper. We'll put them in the cellar with the others until Eric—' Damanjeet cursed under his breath, catching himself, '—until *he* gets back.'

'*If* he gets back. You saw what happened. I'd be surprised if he's still alive,' Ben muttered.

'He'd better be.' There was an edge to Damanjeet's warning. 'If he's not, we're screwed.'

'Not necessarily. The book's here. The wand, too. We'll figure it out.'

'No,' Damanjeet growled, his voice rough. The suspension creaked and the van dipped, shifting with his weight as he climbed into the back. 'He's the one who summoned the demon. He's the one it marked. We wait for E—*him*.'

'For how long?' Ben asked.

'As long as it takes.'

The van jolted. Sachiko heard the scrape of boots on metal just before rough hands seized her, dragging her forward. She bit back a yelp as they manhandled her out, fingers digging into her arms and legs painfully. Every jostle sent stabs through her body. The pounding in her head sounded like a drumbeat.

Their hold on her was clumsy, their pace erratic. Sachiko felt herself slipping. They had to stop and readjust her weight frequently. The thought that these men might drop her worried her. She wasn't sure she could keep up the unconscious act if they did.

Damanjeet wheezed. 'Get the door.'

'Move, blondie,' a man grunted at Ash.

Sachiko cracked an eyelid open, just enough to glimpse a heavyset man with greasy black curls shoving the gatekeeper through the door of a building. She couldn't get a proper look at it, not without giving herself away, but she saw that the glass panes had been boarded over with plywood.

The air grew heavier as they moved inside, colder even. It carried the sharp stench of ammonia mixed with the rank odour of sweat and mildew. The irregular footfall as they descended a flight of stairs made her stomach lurch. It was dark, almost pitch-black. A basement? A fresh wave of panic rose in her throat, but she swallowed it back down.

'That one,' Damanjeet panted between laboured breaths.

Her feet hit the ground hard, the jarring impact travelling up her legs. Damanjeet's grip tightened to accommodate. The feel of his hands hooked beneath her armpits, grazing her breasts, made her want to crawl out of her skin.

A loud, metallic creak pierced the air before she was dragged a few more feet and dropped unceremoniously onto the concrete. Her skull struck the hard surface with a sharp crack, pain jarring her neck. She clenched her jaw against the cry that threatened to escape, acutely aware of Damanjeet beside her.

A sharp tug at her wrists followed and the bonds slackened. She let her arms fall limply to her sides and remained still, listening intently to Damanjeet's footsteps as he sliced through the rope binding her ankles.

She opened her eyes just enough to see the cage in front of her. Inside another was a young woman with dirt-streaked cheeks and lank, matted-brown hair plastered to her gaunt face. Hollow eyes, rimmed with dark circles and brimming with unshed tears, met Sachiko's. The fear and pity in the woman's gaze twisted something deep inside her. It was the look of someone who'd already given up—a look that screamed this was a place you didn't leave alive.

Abandoning her plan to feign unconsciousness, Sachiko twisted sharply. She scrabbled against the gritty concrete as she kicked out, desperate to stand.

'Uh oh,' a mocking voice sneered from somewhere behind her. 'Sleeping Beauty's awake. Better get a handle on your girlfriend, Daman.'

With her vision swimming, Sachiko staggered to her feet, her limbs sluggish and unsteady. The room seemed to tilt around her. She spotted Ash sprawled on the floor, his face taut with warning, pleading for her to stop.

But fear controlled her now, propelling her forward in a desperate bid for escape. She had to get out, before it was too late.

Footsteps scuffed behind her, accompanied by a weary sigh.

Pain erupted in her knee as something struck it from behind, buckling her legs and sending her crashing forward. Her palms scraped against the unforgiving floor just as her chest slammed into it, knocking the breath from her lungs in one violent rush.

'Now, now, Sachiko,' Damanjeet said. 'Where are your manners? You only just got here.'

He crouched beside her, his hand settling firmly on her shoulder. The weight of his touch sent a fresh wave of revulsion through her. Adrenaline spiked as she jerked and tried to crawl away, but a sharp kick to her ribs stole what little air she had left.

'None of that,' Damanjeet chided. 'You really don't make things easy, do you?' He leant in, his breath hot against her ear, the words a venomous whisper. 'It didn't have to be this way. You'll come around though. I know you will.'

She opened her mouth to scream, but no sound came.

He dragged her backwards. Sachiko thrashed weakly, kicking out in futile defiance, but her strength was already waning. The edges of her vision darkened as her pulse thundered in her ears.

She had to calm down, had to stay conscious. Passing out meant losing whatever slim chance she had left to escape. But the fear sent her mind spiralling out of control.

She barely registered the cold metal bars against her body as she was shoved into a cramped cage. The last of her breath became a pitiful whimper before the darkness swallowed her.

Chapter 25

Josh's screams rang in Charlie's ears.

'Run!' Charlie grabbed the boy's arm and yanked him forward. Josh staggered, his limp making his steps uneven, but despite his obvious pain, he pushed to keep up.

What the hell is that thing?

PIT INFERNAL.

A what?

NASTY. MEAN. AND THAT'S COMING FROM ME.

'Faster!' Charlie urged. The sigil flared, the pain in his hand pulsing with increasing intensity. If that wasn't enough to keep him moving, the thunder of pounding hooves growing louder behind them certainly was.

LEAVE THE HUMAN. HE IS TOO SLOW. LET THE PIT INFERNAL CATCH HIM, IT WILL BUY US SOME TIME.

No. I'm not leaving him to die.

YOU DON'T EVEN KNOW HIM.

The boy's face was pale. His breath hitched as he fought to keep moving.

He's just a kid.

BECAUSE YOU SHARE EMOTIONAL SCARS, YOU THINK YOU'RE KINDRED SPIRITS? DON'T MAKE ME LAUGH. YOUR KIND IS PATHETIC—ALWAYS DEFENDING THE WEAK. HOW YOU CLIMBED TO THE TOP OF THE FOOD CHAIN IS A MYSTERY.

The pit infernal was gaining on them. The molten glow carved into the furrows of its charcoal flesh illuminated the tunnel as it galloped. Its eyes blazed as they met Charlie's. Raw, primal hatred. It opened its maw and unleashed a bark that sounded like stones cracking. The noise reverberated around them. Harsh, sudden, and deafeningly loud.

YOU'RE RUNNING BACK THE WAY YOU CAME. THE PATH IS BLOCKED. THIS IS YOUR CHANCE—SACRIFICE THE SNIVELLING COWARD AND ESCAPE.

Charlie clenched his jaw and focused on Josh, whose breathing had turned ragged. The lad clutched his chest, each step growing heavier. He wouldn't last much longer.

Shit.

Suddenly, Josh veered off to the side. That's when Charlie saw it. A narrow crevice in the tunnel wall. Maybe, just maybe, they could fit inside and find another way out.

'Go!' Charlie shouted, pushing Josh into the crack. The boy squeezed into the fractured concrete with relative ease, contorting his rakish body until he vanished into the shadows. But Charlie, being broader, had to manoeuvre himself into the tight space. Sharp edges scraped against his arms, his chest, and for a moment he thought he might get stuck as the walls pressed in around him. He exhaled, beating back thoughts of being crushed to death.

Light flared behind them, brightening the dark recesses of their hiding place. The pit infernal was right there, its searing form burning in the darkness like a living furnace. The heat radiating off it was suffocating, its every breath sending waves of blistering air into the narrow gap. It wedged its massive head into the crack, snapping viciously. The walls groaned, blackening and rupturing under the relentless strain of the beast's efforts.

'Hurry!' Charlie barked, watching in horror as hunks of concrete began to splinter, falling away in glowing shards around them. The searing heat slammed into him, shrivelling the hairs on his arms and blistering his skin. A sharp, sickening stench hit his nostrils—the unmistakable reek of his own flesh burning.

'I c-c-can't!' Josh's voice rose in pitch.

'Move!' Charlie's hand trembled as he shoved at Josh's shoulder. Another chunk of wall shattered, fiery fragments cascading around him like sparks from a forge. The air scorched his lungs as Charlie dragged in a breath, each inhale a lance of pure agony. 'Josh, move!' he bellowed.

'It d-doesn't go any f-f-further! It's a d-dead end!'

'*What?*'

WELL, I WOULD SAY IT WAS NICE KNOWING YOU, BUT IT REALLY WASN'T.

A second deafening roar shook the tunnel, the force of it vibrating through the ground. The creature's ears cocked towards the sound, just as a low, guttural snarl rumbled through its chest. It yanked its head free from the gap, sending debris and grit tumbling down from above, cutting off its blinding glow and plunging them into near-darkness.

'W-what was that?' Josh said, his voice trembling.

Yes, what was *that?*

Charlie gulped down a breath, the ache in his chest easing, as he blinked away the sweat. The stale air was a welcome reprieve from the blistering heat coming off the creature. His arms itched as the livid burns began to repair themselves.

PIT INFERNAL.

No, the roar. What was that roar?

I TOLD YOU, PIT INFERNAL.

Two of them? There are two *of them?*

BRILLIANT DEDUCTION. I SEE YOUR EDUCATION WASN'T COMPLETELY WASTED.

Charlie inched forward, peeking out of the fissure just in time to see a second pit infernal, larger than the first, bearing down on them.

Oh, fuck.

He balled his fists, feeling the familiar tightness in his chest begin again. If he didn't get control now, his pulse would spiral. The idea of having a panic attack now only made his beat thrum faster.

Not now. Not here. Squeeze, release. Squeeze, release. Squeeze, release.

THIS WOULD BE A LOT EASIER IF YOU LET ME TAKE THE REINS.

He ignored the voice, still clenching and unclenching his fists, but the hammering in his chest only grew louder.

'What's h-h-happening?' Josh said.

Charlie squeezed his eyes shut, exhaling through his clenched teeth. 'There's another one of those things,' he ground out, his voice tight with the effort of keeping it together.

Josh made a strangled noise.

The second pit infernal lunged at the first, sinking its teeth into the smaller demon's hide. The sound of muscle being ripped apart echoed off the walls. Blood sizzled as it hit the floor, instantly evaporating in a hiss of steam. The smaller creature shrieked in agony. It wrenched its body away, turning on the spot to kick out a hind leg at its attacker. The larger demon jerked out of the way, narrowly avoiding a hoof to the face.

'We need to move. Now,' Charlie whispered.

Josh shook his head, eyes bulging, lips quivering. 'W-where? This s-s-side of the tunnel's blocked. There's n-nowhere to g-go.'

'Yes, there is. We need to sneak past them—quietly.'

'I c-can't. I'm s-s-scared.' His entire body quaked.

'You and me both, Josh.' Charlie licked his lips, doing his damnedest to ignore the suffocating tension beneath his ribs. He wiped his slick palms down his trousers. 'Listen to me. You'll be okay. Just follow me. We're going to get out of here.'

Josh huffed out a sob but didn't move.

YOU'RE BOTH GOING TO DIE.

Charlie swore under his breath, then softened his tone. 'Look, Josh, I know you're scared, but we can't stay here. If we do, we're going to die. Trust me, okay? Just follow my lead.'

I CAN HELP YOU.

Yeah, right. And let you try and take over for good? Not a chance.

YOU DON'T SEEM TO HAVE MANY OPTIONS.

I said no.

THEN WE DIE TOGETHER.

Swallowing hard, Charlie edged forward. He made a hand signal for Josh to follow, then, realising that the boy couldn't see it, grabbed his arm and pulled gently.

They inched their way out of the crevice. Flattening their backs against the wall, they edged along the tunnel, letting the shadows swallow them whole. Savage, guttural roars harried them, shaking the air with the raw sounds of battle. The light from the creatures' bodies flickered erratically as they fought nearby, illuminating the space in bursts. One moment Charlie and Josh were cloaked in darkness, the next, exposed. Charlie's breath hitched in his throat, each forward step a gamble.

He could hear Josh beside him, the boy's ragged whimpers verging on choked gasps.

The pit infernals tore into each other, slamming into the walls with earth-shattering force, sending sprays of charred rubble and smouldering dust raining across the ground like hellfire.

Josh froze by Charlie's side, each breath coming faster than the last. The creatures were locked in a vicious battle, their attention fixed on each other, but it would only take one of them noticing for everything to go wrong. Charlie shot Josh a sharp look, silently urging him to keep moving. The closer they got to the creatures, the more paralysed Josh became. If they didn't pick up the pace, they'd be dead.

The larger of the two infernals slammed the smaller one into the wall, its scorching body burning a glowing scar into the concrete before it shattered. A piercing wail erupted from its throat, ricochetting around the enclosed space. Josh gasped, the sound he made all too loud.

Charlie stiffened, his heart thudding painfully in his chest. He waited, eyes locked on the thrashing beasts, sure that one of them would spot them. But neither did.

The smaller pit infernal lunged, gnashing its razor-sharp teeth, sinking them deep into the larger one's flank. The bigger beast reared up, jaws stretching wide in a roar of agony, its lips peeled back in a grotesque snarl. Muscles bunching, it drove its massive head into its opponent's chest, knocking it off its feet with bone-crushing force. The larger infernal towered over its fallen rival, rising onto its hind legs before bringing its hooves down in a brutal stomp. The smaller creature writhed and thrashed beneath the assault, howls of pain devolving into pitiful whimpers. With one final blow, silence fell. The smaller of the demon's body convulsed, twitched, then went still.

Even in the dim glow, Charlie could see the blood pooling from its decimated skull, spreading across the blackened gravel, where it hissed and sizzled, warping the charred tracks beneath it. As the molten glow of its body dimmed, the light tracing down its broken form faded into nothing, and the tunnel filled with the harsh stench of burnt stone and demon blood.

The victor sank its teeth deep into the neck of its defeated opponent. With a violent jerk of its head, the pit infernal tore a chunk of flesh from the loser, tossing it in the air before catching it in its blood-streaked maw. It buried its face in the gaping wound, ripping out sinew and muscle in frenzied bites, devouring the raw meat with unfettered greed. Strings of bloody gore dangled from its jaw, dripping onto the scorched ground with sharp, faint crackles, like water striking hot metal.

Charlie exhaled shakily. 'Holy shit.'

Josh let out a faint whine, seemingly sharing his sentiments. He collapsed back against the wall, sliding to the ground. He shuddered as he curled into a tight ball.

The smell of urine mixed with the stench of sulphur and the reek of death. Charlie glanced down. The boy's trousers were soaked through. But there was another smell, something foul but vaguely familiar. He wrinkled his nose.

CORTISOL. YOU CAN SMELL HIS FEAR.

Charlie wasn't the only one who noticed.

The surviving pit infernal sniffed the air, nostrils flaring. Its burning gaze locked onto them. A growl rumbled deep in its throat as it lowered its head and took a menacing step forward.

GIVE ME CONTROL!

Charlie hesitated, his mind racing. The last time he let Chekonost take control, the demon had all but refused to relinquish it.

No.

WE'RE GOING TO DIE.

What if he wasn't strong enough to reclaim his body this time? Wasn't this exactly what Kar'roc had been waiting for all along? To turn him into a puppet? A hollow shell dancing to an alien will? He could already feel Chekonost probing beneath his skin; his muscles twitched involuntarily as the demon tried to force its way in.

The infernal took another step closer, the heat from its body warping the air around it.

TIME IS RUNNING OUT.

Okay!

SAY IT. SAY THAT YOU GIVE ME CONTROL.

'Yes, damn it. I give you control!'

Chapter 26

THE DEMON SURGED THROUGH Charlie's body, forcing him into the crevices of his own mind as it seized command. It was quicker this time, more fluid—as if it had already mastered the transition.

Chekonost propelled them forward in a sprint, leaping the pit infernal with inhuman speed.

No! No, don't leave Josh.

The boy is of no consequence. He will slow us down.

We're not leaving Josh here to die!

Chekonost snorted, setting off at full tilt.

No! Charlie screamed inside his own head.

An electric thrum intensified the sigil on his hand, surging pain through his flesh and shooting up his arm like he'd touched a live wire. The demon jerked to a stop, its pained hiss escaping Charlie's lips. It seemed, his bond to the dagger still granted him a measure of control over Chekonost—at least for now.

We will die down here. Let me save us.

Save the boy.

How exactly am I supposed to do that?

Fight.

A cackle burst unbidden from his lips.

Fight a pit infernal? Are you insane?

We're not leaving Josh alone with that thing.

A frustrated growl rumbled out of Charlie's throat as the demon clenched his fists. Even if I were in my own body, I would not fight a pit infernal. You will kill us both!

We have to try.

The demon spat a curse in a language Charlie didn't know. Fine.

With a bellow that ripped through Charlie's chest, they raced towards the pit infernal. The creature paused, blinking in surprise, clearly unaccustomed to its meal charging at it. Its hesitation didn't last long. The infernal lowered its huge head, lips peeling back to reveal blood-stained teeth. And then it charged.

Chekonost swerved at the last second; the intense heat pouring off the infernal washed a wave of scalding air over Charlie's skin. The beast's hooves skidded across the warped and blackened gravel, struggling for traction as it tried to correct its path.

Chekonost tightened his fist, rotating Charlie's body with the action. Driving all of his enhanced strength through his arm, the demon delivered a punch that connected with the beast's flank—the exact same spot where its dead counterpart had left a gaping wound. Charlie felt the agonising impact, his skin melting and tearing as it stuck to the creature's scalding hide. Chekonost wrenched them free. Charlie's flesh bubbled and burst, like his hand was being roasted alive.

The creature flattened its ears against its skull. It reared, its muscles tensing, as it let out a shriek of pain. But after a moment, it had regained its balance. The pit infernal snorted its contempt, sending a thick, billowing plume of black smoke outwards that curled around them.

Being this close to an infernal felt like inhaling flames. The insides of Charlie's nostrils burned as the demon drew in a hard breath.

With the skin on Charlie's hand already mending itself, Chekonost backed away, but the pit infernal lunged, forcing them to leap aside. Its movements were slower now, more rigid, yet, it did nothing to quell the intense heat as the beast came at them, its hooves leaving black tracks wherever they landed.

With stiff, faltering strides, the infernal trampled over the corpse of its fallen brethren, hooves sinking into the charred flesh of the second beast as though it were overripe fruit. If it weren't for the crack of the dead creature's ribs snapping beneath the weight, Charlie would have questioned whether it had bones at all.

Chekonost and the beast circled each other, churning up bits of the corpse as they moved. The stench of burnt meat lingered in the air like a noxious fog.

What are you doing?

What would you like me to do? Any suggestions would be most welcome.

Dread descended upon Charlie. They were going to die down here.

Josh hadn't moved a muscle, clinging desperately to the tunnel wall behind him. His body trembled as he sobbed.

Tell him to run.

Why? He clearly can't be bothered to save himself.

Just do it.

'Human Josh—'

No, just Josh!

'Just Josh,' the voice, not quite Charlie's, echoed. 'You should run.'

HE IS NOT LISTENING. HE CLEARLY WANTS TO DIE.

Again!

'Josh, run!' A bellow this time.

The lad's head whipped up. Seeing the pit infernal turned away and with an open path before him, he gave a quick nod and moved. Josh hobbled away, dragging his injured leg behind, each slow stride costing him precious time, but at least he was moving.

The infernal's ears twitched at the sound of Josh's shambling footsteps. It turned its attention to the young man.

No... Do something!

Bending low, Chekonost ripped one leg off the dead creature and launched it. The limb struck the larger creature on the side of the head. It jerked in place, momentarily forgetting about Josh.

Its nostrils flared; wide, glaring eyes fixed on Charlie as it bared its teeth in a snarl. And then it lunged, chunks of flesh and bone raining down where its hooves obliterated the remainder of the corpse.

Chekonost propelled them backwards, striking the wall with such force that it knocked the air from

Charlie's lungs. The creature hurtled towards him. At the last possible moment, Chekonost dove to the side. With its hooves slick with gore, the creature couldn't stop itself in time. It crashed into the wall with a bone-rattling *thud*. The structure—already weakened from the explosion—crumbled, sending a cascade of rubble raining down around them. Chunks narrowly missed Charlie as Chekonost manoeuvred them away.

The beast snorted in fury when part of the tunnel collapsed on its rear end. Stone hissed and cracked beneath the relentless heat, as the wall around it disintegrated. Its eyes flashed dangerously.

THERE. HAPPY?

Not really...

The pit infernal bucked and heaved wreckage from the collapsed tunnel off its back. Its front hooves pawed at the gravel, sending up a spray of orange sparks. It shuddered, muscles quivering. The smouldering veins along its body blazed brighter, distorting the air around it. Was it getting even hotter?

The rubble entombing its rear began to groan and pop.

UH OH.

Uh oh?

A fresh wall of heat slammed into Charlie, knocking them back, as chunks of concrete and twisted metal exploded with a thunderous roar. Josh shrieked in the distance.

The pit infernal staggered from the rubble, its immense chest heaving as it shook off flaming dust and grit. Charlie prayed the creature's injuries were finally taking their toll, but then it made a hollow, rumbling sound—part snarl, part growl, and all seething rage.

Oh shit.

TIME TO RUN?

Was there another choice? Clearly, they couldn't fight this thing—it just kept on coming. They could flee while they still had the chance, but there was no way the young man would make it.

We can't leave Josh.

Chekonost gave a throaty grunt of irritation.

The tunnel groaned above them ominously. If they didn't act soon, it might collapse.

Despite the terror flooding Charlie's mind, the demon grinned.

'Josh,' Chekonost said, a hint of glee in his tone. 'Listen to me. You need to run. I'll catch up.'

'Are y-you—'

A grating howl erupted from the pit infernal. Josh's eyes widened. He gulped then turned and stumbled over the misshapen tracks, his legs unsteady and his limp exaggerated. The infernal looked poised to give chase, until Chekonost seized a hunk of concrete and hurled it at the beast's head. It struck with a dull *thwack*, causing the beast to recoil violently.

Dazed by the impact, the creature swayed, shifting its weight in an effort to regain its bearings. Then, slowly, it turned and vaulted at Charlie.

Chekonost sprang to the side, narrowly avoiding being crushed as the pit infernal smashed into another section of the wall. The heat pouring off its body scorched a livid burn across Charlie's ribs as he hit the deck. Heaving himself upright, the demon dashed them both to the other side of the tunnel. The concrete above them trembled, a prolonged groan of cement grinding against cement that sent dust and loose stone scattering to the ground.

With a strained, sluggish motion, the pit infernal shook its head free from the glowing hole it had created.

Sweat dripped down Charlie's back, pooling at the base of his spine. Chekonost swiped a hand across his forehead, hissing as his skin blistered, burst apart and healed in such rapid succession, it actually rippled.

The infernal launched another attack and once again, Chekonost dodged at the last moment, sending the creature skidding into the wall. The tunnel groaned under the strain, shuddering ominously in response.

A chunk of concrete landed between them, shattering into jagged shards that ricocheted in every direction. One struck the pit infernal in the eye; it reared back, thrashing its head around with an ear-splitting roar. Chekonost darted forward, snatching a slab of rock from the rubble as he went. Charlie's muscles tensed like knotted steel as the demon, with an animal grunt, hurled it upward. The projectile slammed into the ceiling, triggering a cascade of destruction. Great sections of the tunnel collapsed, one ear-splitting crash after the other. The entire structure trembled as slabs of concrete rained down, each impact reverberating through the ground.

Chekonost sprinted, pushing Charlie's body to its limit, as debris fell in a deadly torrent, sealing the infernal beneath a mountain of rubble. The cacophony of destruction slowly faded, replaced by an eerie, suffocating silence.

Charlie's legs buckled, and he dropped to the ground, his chest heaving with each breath. Behind him, a towering wall of wreckage sealed off the passage. If the pit infernal had survived, it would take hours to claw its way free. For now, they had what they desperately needed: time.

Chekonost blew out a slow breath, swiping the sweat from Charlie's brow in a very human gesture. His lungs were on fire.

NEED TO EAT.

What?

WEAK. NEED TO EAT.

Chekonost stood, inhaling deeply. The pungent odour of sweat, piss, and cheap aftershave drifted around him. Saliva filled Charlie's mouth.

No.

Chekonost rolled Charlie's neck, listening to the soft pops of his spine.

YES.

You don't need to eat, Lily's energy—

IT IS NOT ENOUGH! IT IS TOO SLOW. I NEED MORE.

No!

The demon strained to listen. Charlie heard no sounds of footsteps, only the patter of falling detritus and the dying groan of the tunnel as its decaying insides sloughed away. Josh had stopped running.

Give me back control of my body. Now.

NO.

Chekonost, I command you! Give me back control of my body. Right now!

I THINK NOT.

Amusement rolled through the demon. It started walking towards Josh, a slow, deliberate pace that sent terror through Charlie's mind.

I command you to relinquish control of my body. Chekonost, I command you!

The demon's laughter bubbled up, a shuddering cackle that shook his frame.

Shit. Shit. Shit. Charlie pressed his will against the demon, desperately trying to force his way back into his own flesh. He didn't know what to do; words had never failed him before. But they were just words, just talk—maybe he needed something more. Maybe he needed an incantation.

Chekonost, by Kar'roc's will, I claim dominion over thee.

The demon stumbled his next step.

Chekonost, by the blood of the archdemon, I bind thee.

The sigil on his left hand ignited, sending electric heat up his arm and into his chest. The demon screamed.

No! I will not submit to a decrepit meat bag! I WILL NOT BE CONTROLLED.

Charlie pressed on, summoning all willpower to fight against the mental barriers the demon had constructed against him.

Chekonost, by my mortal soul, I compel thee. Serve me!

The sigil flared brighter, the crescent and three dots glowing orange in the dim light. Bit by bit he forced the demon back, harried it into the recesses of his mind, felt his own essence seep back into his muscles, his skin.

I HATE YOU!

Charlie staggered, drawing a deep breath in, as he flexed his hands. He traced a finger over the sigil, warm to the touch, and exhaled, his muscles quivering from the fight. Loathing poured into his mind. He sensed the demon sulking in the corners of his consciousness.

Charlie clenched his jaw. Never again. Never would he let the demon seize control of his body. It had played its hand—and lost.

The game was over.

Chapter 27

Pain. Not sharp and sudden, but slow and seeping. It spread through Sachiko's body.

It was the first thing she became aware of as her breath caught and a groan slipped from her lips. Her ribs throbbed with every shallow inhale. Slowly, it all came back to her. She jerked upright, regretting it immediately when the ache in her chest returned with a vengeance.

'Shh, shh. It's okay.'

Sachiko turned towards the voice. A woman. The woman she'd seen before she'd blacked out, was staring at her with a troubled expression. The brunette attempted a smile, but it was a small, sad thing that only lasted a second before it slipped away.

'Where am I?' Sachiko's voice trembled and her teeth chattered uncontrollably. She hugged herself, trying to use what little warmth she had left against the chill.

'The cellar of the White Stag,' the woman replied. 'It's an old, abandoned pub.'

Sachiko blinked, her eyes adjusting to the dim light. She took in her cold, damp surroundings.

Metal kegs lined the mildew-streaked walls; stacks of rusted chairs huddled in shadowy corners. A dust-coated table sat askew nearby, illuminated by the pale glow of an LED lantern—the room's sole light source. The windows were boarded up so tightly that the faint slices of light leaking through barely made a difference. Judging by the lantern's weak glow, its batteries wouldn't last much longer. Discarded tools covered the floor, their edges dulled by time and neglect. But it was the ritualistic circle carved into the concrete that stole her breath. Her jaw dropped as the gravity of the scene hit her like a wave of ice-cold water.

The woman's voice pulled her back. 'Was there anyone else with the men who brought you here?'

'Sorry?'

'The men,' she repeated. 'The ones who brought you here. Was there anyone else with them?'

'I... I don't know.'

The woman slumped against the bars of her cage. The metal rattled. She drew her knees to her chest, burying her head in her folded arms. 'Then it's true,' she murmured, her voice muffled. 'He's dead.'

Her flat tone made it impossible to know if this was a good or bad thing.

Sachiko blinked again, unsure of what to say. Her throat was parched. She adjusted her position, trying to find some relief from the hard base of the cage. Reaching forward, she worked her fingers up the bars, pushing and pulling, testing for weaknesses.

'Don't bother. We've all tried.'

Sachiko jerked in surprise. She hadn't noticed the second person slumped in the neighbouring cage, mistaking it at first for a pile of dirty clothing. The blonde sat up. Her hair was a matted knot of curls, her pale skin streaked with grime. Her clothes—tattered grey joggers and a mud-caked sweatshirt—had seen better days.

'Don't waste your time looking for your phone, either,' the blonde added. Sachiko instinctively checked her pocket. Empty. 'They took it. Along with your ID. Everything.'

A shiver crawled up Sachiko's spine, the faint flicker of hope she had guttering out. 'How long have you two been down here?'

The blonde woman gave a forlorn shrug.

Ignoring the anxious pull in her gut, Sachiko continued, 'What are your names?'

'Lydia.' She nodded at the brunette who still had her head tucked in her arms. 'And you've already met Sophie.'

'Sachiko,' she said. 'How did you end up here?'

'I was jogging,' Lydia began, her voice shaky. 'Had my earbuds in. My mum always told me to leave one out, to stay aware of my surroundings, but I didn't listen. I never thought it would happen to me. Then—' her voice cracked, '—someone hit me. Hard. I didn't even see who it was. Next thing I know, I wake up here.' Tears welled in her eyes. 'I'm going to die here, aren't I?'

'No,' Sachiko said firmly. 'We're going to get out.'

Lydia's gaze flicked to Sachiko's lab coat. 'Are you a doctor?'

'Yes.'

'Will people be looking for you?'

Sachiko opened her mouth then closed it again. Her family was in Japan. Between the time difference and her shift patterns, they'd grown accustomed to waiting hours, or even days, for her to return their calls. And given the chaos at O.O.T.I.S headquarters, it could be a while before anyone even realised she was missing.

Lydia nodded knowingly. Her expression became distant as she turned her head away.

There had to be some way out of this. Determined, Sachiko searched the pockets of her lab coat again. There had to be something she could use: a paper clip, a spring from a ballpoint pen—anything to pick the lock. She probed the fabric until she felt something hard. The vial! She'd forgotten she still had it. She smoothed down her coat, pressing the vial close to her body. A thrill of excitement bubbled up in her chest. She had the makings of a plan.

'It won't work.' Ash's voice surprised her. It came from another corner of the cellar, where a separate, reinforced cage held him. The gatekeeper's shackles clinked as he shifted, his piercing-green eyes glowing in the weak light.

'How... did you know?'

'I can smell it. The lindwurm venom. A dose that concentrated is strong enough to kill, but only one of them. There are three of them up there. And without the keys to the locks, you'll be stuck.' There was no malice in his words. It was just a statement of fact.

'Will you help us?' Sachiko asked.

He held up his arms, jangling his shackles.

Her heart sank. Without the key, there was no way to remove them. Breaking them was out of the question; they'd been forged to withstand any force, any element. Each ward meticulously imbued so that the restraints would contain a Level-11 threat.

'Then we get the keys,' she said finally, meeting his eye.

Sophie spoke up, 'They need him for the ritual. The gatekeeper. I overheard them.'

All eyes turned to her.

She crawled towards Sachiko, knotting her fingers through the bars of the cage, and continued, her sour breath clouding. 'They've been trying to summon something. Some sort of demon, but it hasn't worked and it's getting too risky for them to find more women.'

Sachiko wanted to ask her what she meant by *more women*, but Sophie stayed her tongue.

'They're waiting for Eric,' Sophie continued. 'But if he doesn't come back. If he's... dead, it's only a matter of time before they'll try it without him.'

Sachiko regarded Ash. 'If we get the keys, will you help us escape?'

He studied her in silence, his expression unreadable. Then he spoke, his voice low. 'I will, but on one condition.'

Her stomach knotted. 'What condition?'

What could a malafrax demon possibly want from her? She had nothing to offer, no magical ability, no secret power. Did he think her position within O.O.T.I.S could grant him access to an artefact or classified knowledge? If that was the case, he was out of luck. She'd never betray the Order. Never.

He sighed, like he knew exactly what she was thinking. 'I was bound to a gateway for millennia, cursed to endure an endless purgatory of isolation. I have no intention of spending the rest of my existence in yet another prison. I'll help you, but when it's done, I request that you let me go.'

'But the Order—'

'I'm fully aware of what the Order will do if they catch me. I want to return to my own realm.'

Sachiko swallowed, the weight of the situation pressing down on her. She glanced at the other two women in the cages. Their hollow eyes were fixed on her, silently pleading. If it was only her life on the line, maybe she'd refuse. Maybe she'd hold her ground, put faith in the Order to find her and do things by the book.

But it wasn't just her. And for all she knew, the Order might not even realise she was missing until it was too late.

The thought sank like a stone in her chest, scraping against the sides of everything she stood for. If they waited, all of them might die.

She forced herself to meet Ash's gaze. If his only desire was to return to his realm, surely that posed no threat to humanity. It wasn't ideal, and it definitely wasn't standard procedure, but right now, it was survival.

'Alright.'

'I want your word.' His green eyes bored into hers, unwavering, as if searching her soul.

'You have it,' Sachiko said firmly. 'I promise if you help us escape, I won't stop you from going home.'

'Home,' he echoed with a bitter smile. 'I'm not sure I'd call it that... I'll help you.'

Sachiko turned to Sophie, 'How do we get the men to come downstairs?'

Sophie cast a nervous glance at Lydia before answering, 'Usually, if we scream, someone comes down.' Her face fell. 'But... it's normally only one of them.'

'Then we wait,' Sachiko said.

'Wait for what?' Lydia asked, hysteria creeping into her words.

'The ritual.'

Lydia shook her head, her lank, blonde curls whipping her face. 'No! No, I'm not going to die like that!'

'Shh, keep your voice down,' Sophie urged, eyes flicking to the ceiling.

'No! We have to do it now. We *have* to do it now!' Lydia's voice pitched higher, almost breaking. She scrambled to her knees and, gripping the bars with white-knuckled hands, rattled them with all her strength.

'Lydia, calm down. They'll hear you...' Sophie whispered.

'It's okay for you,' Lydia spat. 'You're not the one they're going to gut. That psycho's your brother. He's not going to let them kill you. But me? I watched those girls die one by one. I don't want to be next. I'm *not* going to be next!'

'Lydia, shh,' Sophie hissed. 'You're going to ruin everything.'

'I'm not going to die down here. I'm not.' Her eyes were wild, feverish. She shook her head again. 'I'm not!'

Lydia threw her weight against the bars, crashing against them in desperation. 'Hey! Down here.' she screamed. 'Now. Something's wrong!'

Sachiko stared at her in shock. Overhead, there was a *thud*, followed by the unmistakable sound of heavy footsteps.

Sophie turned to Lydia, her mouth open in disbelief. The other girl had stopped shouting, her face now a ghostly white.

'Oh no,' Lydia whispered, her hands quivering. 'Oh no, no, no. That's Sean... That's Sean.' She curled into a ball in the corner of her cage, her whimpering breaths sharp and hard.

Sophie gasped. She flapped her hands at Sachiko, gesturing for her to get back from the bars. 'Don't do *anything*. Don't say *anything*.'

Sachiko did as instructed, her heart hammering in her chest. Just as her spine pressed against the bars, the door to the cellar slammed open, flooding the room with blinding artificial light. She shielded her eyes against it; her pulse pounded in her ears.

The wooden stairs creaked underfoot as Sean began his slow descent, the beam of his torch sweeping over the cages. Each strident squeak was matched by Lydia's quivering gasps. As he reached the bottom, his grey eyes locked on Lydia. A slow, cruel smile spread across his face.

Chapter 28

Josh ran. With every step, agony flared the injury in his leg. White-hot pulses of pain shot from his ankle to his knee. It felt like splinters of glass grinding into exposed nerve. Sweat slicked his skin. But stopping wasn't an option—not with that thing behind him.

Coward.

He'd left Charlie to die. But what choice did he have? He was no match for that monster.

Just as he began to wrestle with that guilt, a faint rustling in the darkness behind him shattered his reverie. His breath hitched with the realisation something had followed him. Josh slammed himself into the tunnel wall, eyes squeezed shut, drawing in shallow, panicked breaths. If he didn't move, if he didn't make a sound, maybe it wouldn't see him.

Something grabbed his arm.

Josh screamed.

'Josh, it's me!'

The voice was a distant murmur, lost in the chaos of his blind panic. He lashed out, struggling, but the grip held firm.

'Josh, it's me. It's Charlie.'

He opened his eyes, his vision adjusting to the dim light and the man before him.

'Charlie?' he managed, his throat so dry, he could barely choke out the words. 'W-what? How—?'

'The tunnel collapsed on the beast.' Charlie released his grip, giving Josh some much needed space.

'H-how are you s-still alive?'

'Luck, mostly.'

Luck? Josh's throat bobbed as he flicked his uncertain gaze past Charlie.

The old man followed his line of sight. 'We don't have time to stand around. That thing might not be dead. We need to move.'

Josh shuddered. The thought of that creature making a reappearance twisted his gut and sent burning bile into his throat. If they died down here, who would save Sophie? She needed him, and he wasn't going to let her down. He was going to get her out of this mess—*his* mess—if it was the last thing he did.

How Charlie had not only survived but walked away unscathed was beyond him. The only apparent casualty was his clothing. It hung in tatters, and where it hadn't been shredded was now a charred mess of melted fabric. His face was a grubby mix of dirt and ash, streaked with unidentified dark smears that Josh didn't want to think about.

Had their escape really been just luck?

What did it matter? Charlie had saved them both and what had he done? Pissed himself and ran away, that's what. A coward through and through, useless, pathetic... just like his mum had always told him.

But Charlie wasn't a coward. And Charlie was going to help him.

Realising he was staring, Josh cleared his throat and blurted the first question that came to mind. 'What happened to your arms?'

Charlie tensed, his eyes dropping to the silver scars on his exposed skin covered by a thin layer of grime. For a moment, Josh feared he'd made the older man angry. He didn't want to upset him or lose his help. He opened his mouth to apologise, but Charlie spoke first.

'My dad,' Charlie said, his voice low and rough. 'He used me as an ashtray. Some of these scars are from broken bottles. Some from his belt. He was a real piece of shit.'

Josh met his eyes, then tugged up the tattered cuff of his own suit jacket. He unbuttoned the sleeve of his shirt and rolled it up, revealing his own raised scars. 'My m-mum,' he said quietly.

Charlie's expression softened. He gave a nod. 'Let's go find your sister.'

They trudged through the tunnel. The electric hum of the lights buzzed overhead. Every now and then, Josh stole glances at Charlie in awe. Charlie was just like him—battered, bruised, broken—but he was strong, capable. If anyone could help him save Sophie, it was Charlie.

'So how did you get into this mess in the first place?' Charlie asked, his voice breaking the silence.

'I was a courier,' Josh answered. 'One day this guy asked me to deliver something for him, c-cash-in-hand.'

'Drugs?'

'N-no. I don't think so. I didn't ask. Mostly it was boxes. Like antiques and stuff. The guy was huge, s-scary, with a big bushy beard, shaved head, and tattoos. Looked like he belonged to a b-biker gang. Had a nice car, though. A burnt-orange Mustang.'

Charlie stiffened beside him. 'An orange Mustang?'

'Yeah, a real beaut.'

'Did you get his name?'

He nodded. 'Mundy Wilcoxson.' Charlie briefly closed his eyes, as if the name was familiar. Josh pulled uneasily at the hem of his suit jacket. It had been a while since he'd said the name aloud. 'Anyway, a package went missing—a book. Got s-stuck under the seat of my car. I didn't realise it until I got home. Eric found it. After that, everything started going to shit.'

'Your brother stole it?'

Josh hesitated, biting the inside of his cheek. Would Charlie still help him if he knew the truth about Eric? Finally, he gave a nod. 'Yeah, he showed it to his friends. That's when they... they started their c-cult. I never thought he'd kill anyone.'

Charlie's eyebrows shot up. 'Wait—you're saying he's actually murdered people?'

Josh threw up his hands. 'I swear I wanted to give the book back, but Mundy got so angry when he found out it was lost. I couldn't face him. For a while, things went back to normal. He never mentioned the book again.

I carried on doing his work on the side, but then he disappeared a few weeks ago.'

'Who, Eric?'

'No, Mundy. I was still making deliveries when I s-saw men in black suits outside his house. I didn't stop. A few days later, when they were gone, I went back to drop off his packages, but he wasn't there. I think he g-got arrested. Without the extra cash, I c-c-couldn't afford my bills. I'd gotten so used to the money, but with all the direct debits and stuff I still needed to pay off, I wasn't going to m-make my rent. So, I put some of his stuff up on eBay.' Heat crept up his neck; he stared at the floor as he limped along behind Charlie. 'One of the packages had this wand-looking thing inside. Quartz, with a copper wire handle and a little red gem embedded in it. I thought it might be a r-ruby or something.'

'Ruby?' Charlie's brow furrowed.

Josh nodded. 'Looked like it might be worth a few quid. Anyway, I listed it, and the next thing I know, I'm stuck in that derelict old pub. Eric has the wand and S-Sophie's locked up in a cage in the cellar.'

'This wand. Was there anything special about it?'

'Not that I could tell. It c-cut me when I first picked it up.' He lifted his hands, showing Charlie his palms. Fresh scabs mingled with reddish scars, scored deeply into his skin. The newer ones he couldn't even recall getting.

Charlie slowed, studying Josh's hands with a frown.

They walked without speaking for a while. Every so often, Charlie glanced around, his eyes narrowing, as though listening for something just beyond the edge of hearing.

Josh rubbed the base of his throat anxiously. He hoped they weren't too late. The thought of Sophie locked in that cellar, pleading with him to help her, was engraved into his mind. He needed to save her, to prove that he wasn't completely useless. But the idea that she might never want to see him again cleaved into his chest like an axe, leaving behind a hollow, aching void. He could understand it though; he'd always been weaker than Eric. It was his fault that all this had happened to her. Eric knew that Sophie was Josh's weakness, knew he'd do anything to protect her. It had been the same for Eric, too. Once.

'What else do you remember about this wand?' Charlie said, snapping Josh out of his trance.

'Erm...' He thought back to the day he'd found it. Just another box among many. The fear that Wilcoxson might come back and demand his stuff had settled like a rock in his gut, growing heavier with each package he opened. He'd known, even as he'd powered up his laptop, that there would be no coming back from it. Still, he was pretty sure the guy had been either locked up or was in hiding. He hoped it wasn't the latter.

The box had been nondescript, no address, just a name scrawled across the cardboard. Archibald Morgan. He remembered it clearly because it had struck him as funny at the time. No one was called Archibald anymore. Archie, sure. But Archibald? Was he from the eighteenth century or something?

'It was in a plain cardboard box. N-nothing special. Sometimes stuff came in fancy wooden cases or metal ones, but mostly just standard shipping boxes, like that one. There was a name on it but no address. The wand was wrapped in something... like sheep's w-wool.'

'The name, you remember it?'

'Oh, sure. It was Ar—'

A bloodcurdling scream cut him off.

Charlie's arm shot out, stopping Josh in his tracks.

'W-what was—'

'Shh.' Charlie held a finger to his lips and motioned for Josh to back up against the wall.

They sidestepped cautiously along the tunnel.

The scream rang out again, harsh and shrill. Josh clapped his hands over his ears, heart pounding. It sounded like Sophie, the way she'd screamed when their mother used to hit her. The way she'd screamed that first night Eric had locked her in the cage. It had made him sick to his stomach, hearing her. He'd wanted to help her, but Tommo had refused, physically restraining him. He'd begged, pleaded, wept, but Tommo had stood there, resolute. Josh had hated him more than anyone else in his life. But most of all, he'd hated himself. For not being strong enough to protect her.

The screams raked through his head, yet, his hands did nothing to muffle the sound. They pierced his skull, stabbed at his brain. Black dots flared across his vision. At some point, he'd stopped following Charlie and slumped down the wall, clutching his temples, willing the noise to stop.

What if he was too late? What if Sophie was already dead?

His chest constricted with each strained and shallow breath that never quite filled his lungs.

'S-s-stop,' he whispered, his voice fraying. 'Please, s-stop. S-s-stop.'

But the screams only grew louder, thickening the air around him. Like living, clawing things, they tore at his ears, entered his throat, scraped at his lungs. Shadows crowded his vision, pressing in like dark tides. Every gasp he made was engulfed by waves that washed over him, threatening to consume him.

'No… p-p-please…' It was too late. He was doing it again; being weak, being a coward.

He knew what was coming. Who was coming. But a part of him welcomed the absolute darkness. Anything to escape the screams.

Chapter 29

Sachiko flinched as Sean descended the final step, his boot landing on the cellar floor with a muted *thud*. The fear radiating from the two caged women beside her was contagious, their breathless whimpers awakening an instinctive urge within her to flee. All she could do was watch as his oily gaze slid over her, leaving a filthy residue in its wake, before settling on Lydia. A grin split his face. Lydia shook her head, muttering incoherently as her spine clattered against the bars.

'What's wrong now?' Sean drawled.

Footsteps followed him down the stairs. Damanjeet loitered just behind, unable to pass with Sean in the way.

Sachiko's chest ignited with white-hot rage at the sight of Daman. Her hands curled into tight fists at her sides, nails biting into her palms, as she forced herself to stay still. Her eyes tracked his every move, but he remained oblivious to her, his attention fixed on the man in front of him.

Two of the three. Would one of them have the keys?

Her fingers twitched, inching towards the hidden vial inside her lab coat. But just as she steeled herself to act, a sharp movement caught her eye. Ash shook his head, his warning freezing her in place.

No. He was right. One vial. One chance. She couldn't waste it.

If it was true that they were waiting for Eric, it meant she had time. Time to form a plan. She and the other captives would have to work together to have any chance of making it out. She couldn't do it alone. Patient. She had to be patient.

Sean waddled towards a quivering Lydia. She was making faint, strangled noises, almost too quiet to hear.

'Well,' Sean sneered, his smile spreading wider. 'What can I help you with?'

'I... I... didn't—' Lydia choked out between sobs.

'You didn't?' Sean's tone was mockingly sweet. 'I'm sure I heard you shouting.' He leant to the side, pulling a set of keys from his pocket.

'No... I—I...' Lydia stammered, turning to Sachiko, her eyes widening in a silent plea.

Sachiko gave the faintest shake of her head. *No, not now.*

Sean flicked through each key, taking a step closer towards the cage.

'No, no, please!' Lydia scrambled against the crate's floor, fingers clawing at the plastic, feet kicking back in desperation. But there was nowhere to go.

Sean inserted the key into the lock.

'No!' Lydia screeched, her voice raw with terror. 'No!'

A grunting Sean bent down and thrust his thick hand into the cage. Metal clattered as Lydia flailed in a futile attempt to avoid his grasp. He clamped her upper arm, and she let out a yelp.

'*No*, no!' Her cries became screams as he yanked her out of the cage, dragging her on her knees.

'I like you in this position,' Sean said, his gaze dark and hungry.

Lydia looked up through the tangle of filthy blonde hair, trying to jerk back, but his grip held her in place. He licked his lips.

Damanjeet hissed. 'What are you doing?'

Sachiko's head snapped up. Would Damanjeet stop him?

As if sensing her attention, Damanjeet's eyes flicked to hers. With one look, the faint spark of hope she'd been clinging to flickered out. His focus shifted back to Sean.

'She was making too much noise.' Sean replied, not taking his eyes off Lydia. He adjusted the front of his trousers and she recoiled in disgust.

'Put her back in,' Damanjeet said. 'We still need her. When Eric gets—'

'Eric's dead, Daman. You saw him get buried under the rubble with Tommo. No one walks away from that.'

Damanjeet scoffed, shoving a hand through his dark hair. 'Well then we're all fucked.'

'Don't be so dramatic.'

'We need Eric for this to work.'

Sean rolled his eyes. 'We don't need him. I've got everything covered.' He paused, smug. 'Cameras. Battery-operated. I installed them upstairs. I know where the book is. I know where the wand is. Hell, I even know whenever that pussy Josh rubs one out.'

Damanjeet's face twisted in disbelief. 'You did *what?*'

'It's amazing what you can buy.'

'Does Eric know?'

'Doesn't matter now. He's dead.'

Damanjeet pursed his lips but didn't push. 'I think we should wait.'

'Wait for what? Get your head out of your arse, Daman. He's not coming back.'

'And if he does?'

Sean lifted his shoulders lazily. 'Then I'll handle it.' His hard eyes slid back to Lydia. 'Now, let me deal with this one.' He hooked a meaty finger under her chin, forcing her head up. 'You and me need to have a little chat about all this noise.'

'Daman, please!' Sachiko yelled, her voice cracking. 'Don't let him do this.'

Damanjeet's head tilted slightly at her outburst. For a fleeting moment, she thought she saw hesitation as his gaze shifted to Sean. When the two men locked eyes, tension bristling between them, for a heartbeat, Sachiko was sure Damanjeet would intervene.

Instead, he raised an eyebrow, his voice cold and flat. 'As long as he doesn't kill her, he can do what he likes.'

The words hit Sachiko like a slap to the face. Her breath caught as Sean smirked, triumph curling the corners of his mouth into something twisted. He grabbed Lydia's arm, hauling her upright with a vicious tug.

Lydia staggered, her knees buckling, but Sean yanked her forward easily as if she weighed nothing.

Sachiko slumped back, utterly helpless. She looked at Damanjeet one last time, searching for any trace of the man she thought she knew. But only a stranger stared back at her.

'No!' Lydia's screams were hysterical. She writhed in Sean's grip, clawing at his hand, but her efforts were weakening with every step. She twisted, desperate, her tear-streaked face turning towards Sachiko. 'Do it! Please! Do it now!'

Sachiko's heart pounded, her hand twitching. But with Damanjeet watching her, Sean too, she couldn't use the vial. Their scrutiny pinned her in place.

When Sachiko did nothing, Sean let out a derisive snort and continued dragging Lydia towards the stairs. The woman's screams melted into desperate, wheezing sobs. Her body went limp in defeat as he hauled her upward. By the time they reached the top, she'd fallen silent and her head hung to her chest.

Damanjeet's eyes lingered on Sachiko a moment longer, and for one awful second, she caught the same predatory gleam she'd seen in Sean's. Then he frowned, muttered something inaudible, and turned away, following Sean without another word.

The door slammed shut behind them.

Silence enveloped the cellar.

Sophie exhaled, her eyes glistening.

Ash stared at the space where Lydia had been, expressionless.

Sachiko's shoulders sagged, her gaze falling to the floor.

Heavy footsteps from above dislodged dust in quivering motes from the ceiling. No one spoke. Not until the distant slam of another door and Lydia's muffled screams shattered the stillness.

'There was nothing you could've done,' Sophie whispered. 'Without Eric keeping them in check, it was only a matter of time before this happened. The way Sean stared at us... He was getting off on it.' She hugged her knees, shoulders trembling.

'This Eric—what's so special about him?' Ash said.

Sophie sniffed, wiping her cheeks with the back of her hand. 'He was never special. Not until he found the book. After that he changed. And then, when he got the wand, it was like he became someone else. Angry. Cruel. Like the world owed him something.'

'And Josh?'

Sophie's face crumpled. 'Josh is my brother—was. If what they said is true, he's also dead.' She drew in a shaky breath. 'Eric was the only reason they didn't hurt me and I knew it. I hated it. Watching him carve up those women, knowing I'd never be next... I felt relieved.' Her voice wavered, thick with guilt. 'They'd get their throats slit, and all I could think was I'm glad it's not me. That's awful, isn't it?'

Sachiko gave her a sympathetic look. 'And if Eric's not dead. What happens when he comes back?'

'Then Josh will, too.'

'That's a good thing though, right?'

Sophie's expression hardened. 'It depends which of them turns up first.'

'What do you mean?'

'You can't have one without the other. Josh has Dissociative Identity Disorder. Eric... he's his alter.'

Chapter 30

Eric's head spun with confusion. With his back pressed against something hard, he let his senses adjust. The air was stuffy, darkness pressing in from all sides. Without the faint, scattered glow from the emergency fixtures lining the walls, he'd be blind. He inhaled, catching the stale scent of oil mingled with a faint trace of burnt charcoal.

Where am I? He blinked, his brow furrowing at seeing the metal tracks stretched out in front of him. *The Underground?*

Gradually his scattered thoughts pieced themselves together. He'd been in the gatekeeper's cell, had the creature in his grasp. Then—an explosion... *Fucking Sean*! That must mean he was now beneath O.O.T.I.S headquarters, lost in some kind of subterranean tunnel network.

Then where the fuck was the gatekeeper?

'Josh?'

The male voice startled him. He snapped his eyes up to a worried old man staring at him. Eric blinked again.

He thinks I'm Josh.

He tilted his head, taking in the stranger. He had to be in his sixties at least, covered in grime, his clothes torn and streaked with black. His grey hair was flecked with grit, and sweat had carved damp tracks through the dark smudges on his forehead. His eyes were sharp, studying him with growing concern.

Concern, or suspicion?

He should probably say something.

'I'm o-o-okay,' he said, emulating Josh's stutter. Was that right? Everything he knew about Josh had come from Sophie—how the stutter worsened when Josh was nervous, how it made him self-conscious. Eric cursed himself for not paying more attention to her descriptions, for not caring enough to ask about specifics. Now, he'd just have to wing it.

The man's stare lingered for a moment before he nodded. 'We need to go.'

A piercing scream rang through the tunnel, then abruptly cut off.

Spurred into motion, Eric clambered to his feet, gasping as pain flared through his ankle. He bit back a yell.

Fuck. Was something broken? What was that scream?

His gaze flicked to the old man—who the hell was this guy?—then down to his thighs. Had Josh pissed himself?

A thousand questions raced through his mind, yet he couldn't voice a single one. Not without exposing himself. Without knowing how much Josh had told this old geezer, he couldn't take any chances.

The stranger moved through the shadows, gesturing for him to follow. Limping, Eric became increasingly aware that they were moving towards the sound of the scream. His stomach tightened, dread coiling around his insides.

The whispers began to stir at the edges of his mind, muted and unintelligible. They latched onto his thoughts, feeding his paranoia. *The old man's up to something.* His pulse quickened. *Is this a trap?*

The whispers swelled, dark and urgent, clouding his mind. Maybe he should just kill the stranger and be done with it.

As Eric began to visualise the most effective way to take him down, the man stopped abruptly, holding up a finger.

Something rumbled in the depths of the tunnel, the vibrations thrumming through the ground, the walls. Something prowling just beyond the shadows. Something big.

The fuck?

The man pointed ahead.

Eric squinted, trying to make sense of the darkened tunnel, but saw nothing. His chest tightened as the growls grew closer. The man kept pointing. *Was this a joke?* He opened his mouth to demand answers, but the stranger put his finger to his lips, silencing him.

Then, finally, Eric saw it. A faint outline, barely distinguishable from the rest of the wall in the gloom. An access door!

The stranger motioned for Eric to stay put and edged forward. He touched the door, probing it before grasping the grimy handle. He gave it a firm tug.

Nothing.

A second, harder yank followed. Still, the door didn't budge.

Eric felt a chill creep up his spine. They were trapped. Panic clawed up his insides as the growls stalked them. The man leant in to the door, muscles straining. For a split-second, Eric wasn't sure what he was doing, but then came the groan of metal under stress.

Slowly, the man pulled again. The door's hinges creaked and the sound reverberated through the tunnel, causing Eric's heart to stutter. He flicked his gaze back to the darkness, worried that whatever might be out there could lunge at any moment.

With one final, deliberate heave, the old man wrenched open the door. The frame juddered in place. It moved just enough to create a gap wide enough for them to slip through.

How the hell...

The man turned and shot Eric a sharp look, waving him through. Eric didn't hesitate. Fuelled by adrenaline, he hobbled forward, his swollen ankle protesting as he squeezed through the narrow opening.

Behind him, the door closed with a dull *thunk*, sealing them off from whatever prowled the darkness on the side they'd just been on.

After what felt like a lifetime of trudging silently across the tracks of yet another Tube line, Eric began to slow. Every step sent shooting pain up his leg until his stomach churned with nausea.

Seriously, how far do these tunnels even go? Brother Bains hadn't mentioned anything about a sprawling underground maze. Wouldn't it have been easier to reach the gatekeeper from here instead of relying on Brother Adams and his dark-web explosives?

Unless... Could Damanjeet and Sean be in on this together? It wasn't like Damanjeet had never hidden things from him before—he'd kept quiet about working for the Order until Eric had found the book. And Sean? His moral compass was so fucked up the prick couldn't tell north from south. Maybe they'd set this whole thing up to get Eric out of the picture.

No. They wouldn't dare.

Besides, he was the only one who knew where the book and wand were hidden. He was the one marked by the demon. He traced the blackened threads on his collarbone that pulsed in time with his heartbeat.

Eyeing the flickering lights ahead, Eric clenched his jaw. *Enough*. He was done with this. Done limping along after the old man, done with the sickening, throbbing effort of trying to keep up. Were they even going the right way? And where in the hell was Brother Thompson? Tommo was supposed to be keeping an eye on Josh. Had he bailed too? No, he'd been right there when the floor gave way... Oh.

Fuck.

The plan was falling apart. If Tommo was buried under a heap of rubble, did that mean the gatekeeper was, too? There were too many variables. Too many what ifs. The only logical move now was to return to the White Stag. Regroup.

Eric stifled a growl and stuffed his hands into his pockets. Something sharp jabbed his palm. He pulled it out. A business card? He glanced at the old man to make sure he wasn't paying attention and angled it towards the dim light. Charlie Haynes? Unsolved crimes?

Oh shit. It all clicked into place. Josh was leading someone who worked for the police straight to the pub. *Fucking Josh*, ruining everything. Again.

The whispers eddied in the currents of his mind, whirling through his consciousness in disorientating swells of frustration and impatience. Jaw tight, Eric resisted the urge to crumple the card and returned it to his trouser pocket.

'Charlie?' Eric ventured.

'Yeah?'

Damn it.

'How long do you think it'll take us to get out of here?' Shit, he'd forgotten the stutter. He quickly added, 'I'm w-w-worried about S-Sophie.' Was he laying it on too thick?

'I'm not sure. These tunnels should lead to a way out eventually, an emergency staircase or something. I think it's all connected to the actual Underground network. Must be how they transport the cryptids.'

So, he knows about cryptids. Was Charlie Haynes an O.O.T.I.S agent? It would be just like Josh to lead the Order straight to their doorstep.

'C-cryptids?' Eric repeated, feigning confusion. He was certain that idiot Josh knew nothing about the supernatural, never having thought to open the pages of the book. It was hard to believe Eric had once been just as ignorant until a few months ago. The book had changed everything. Now, all he needed to do was get back to the pub and figure this mess out.

'Similar to the thing that attacked us,' Charlie said.

Attacked? They were attacked and Josh was still fronting? Eric frowned.

Charlie continued, 'My point is, we should find a way out soon.'

And then what? Josh had really fucked him over this time.

No matter. He'd use Charlie to get back to the pub, then deal with him later. After all, the guy was a pensioner. How hard could it be to kill him?

Chapter 31

THEY WERE COMING UP on an exit. Charlie felt the subtle shift in temperature, the stir of a distant breeze cutting through the stale air. The promise of freedom.

They'd need a car. He couldn't risk using his own. Too dangerous. If O.O.T.I.S caught on, Charlie might lead them straight to the gatekeeper. That couldn't happen. Not yet. Not until he'd rid himself of the demon.

'How did you get here?' Charlie asked.

Josh stared at him blankly. The young man was acting weird. Maybe it was the shock of everything that had happened or the pain of his injury.

'Did you drive?' he pressed.

'Uh, y-yeah. We came in a van.'

'All of you?'

Josh nodded.

Charlie cursed. If Chekonost was right and the others had taken the gatekeeper, the van was probably gone, too. He exhaled sharply and kept walking. They'd just have to cross that bridge when they came to it.

He glanced at Josh again. The young man's expression had shifted—something off, something he couldn't quite place. Or maybe it was just him. He was on edge, justifiably so, but it was no reason to take it out on Josh. All the poor kid wanted to do was save his sister. And after nearly being buried alive, then being attacked by a pit infernal, it was a wonder he was functioning at all. Hell, it's not as if Charlie was running at a hundred percent either.

He shook off his suspicions, forcing his mind back to the task at hand. All that mattered now was getting out of these godforsaken tunnels and finding the gatekeeper. Once he was rid of Chekonost, rid of the dagger, rid of his link to the demon realm, he could put all this behind him.

Sure, the Order was going to be pissed, but what could they do? It's not like they could keep him locked in a cell when he became an ordinary person again. No, most likely they'd alter his memories and send him on his way. And he would be fine with that.

No more O.O.T.I.S, no more demons... No more Diane.

The thought hit him harder than expected. Once this was over, Diane wouldn't have any reason to stick around. Hell, would he even remember her? Maybe she wouldn't want him to. After what happened that morning—after Debbie—it was probably for the best. Still, the weight on his chest became hard to ignore.

He kept walking. No car. No plan. But at least he knew where they were headed.

Chekonost simmered at the edges of his awareness, sending waves of resentment through his skull. Ever since he'd forced the demon from his body, it had been sulking. Giving him the silent treatment. The quiet was nice. Even if it was laced with loathing.

It scared him, though, how hard it had been to regain control. He was the dagger's master, that should have been enough. But with the blade beyond his reach, maybe it wasn't. Diane had said that the Maw always returned to its master, yet inside Lily it couldn't. Without some tangible way to keep Chekonost in check, would the demon eventually take over?

How many of the dagger's previous masters had played host to the demon inside? Was he the first? Christ, what if he ended up exactly like Stephen? What if he became worse? How long until he lost himself to Kar'roc's will? Became just another tool in the archdemon's destruction?

He couldn't let that happen. Nothing else mattered. And if saving Josh's sister was part of the deal, well, then that would be a bonus. But if not... Charlie shook the thought away. Jesus, how could he even think like that? She was a person. Josh's family.

Blowing out a breath, he pressed on.

Up ahead, something caught his eye. An exit. It had to be. The engineers would need access to these tunnels, especially if they were being used to transport cryptids and artefacts, as he suspected.

'Josh, come on. It's just ahead.' Charlie jogged forward. He heard Josh's stumbling footsteps quickening behind him.

At the door, he signalled the young man to stop. Carved into the frame were wards. Not exactly

Underground standard—maybe O.O.T.I.S had lines that ran parallel to the actual Tube network. He pressed down on the handle and braced, half-expecting the symbols to glow white and launch him across the tunnel. But aside from the low thrum of energy ghosting across his skin like static, nothing happened.

The door creaked open without fanfare, stirring up a cloud of dust. He coughed. Clearly, this particular exit hadn't been used in a while.

'How are you with heights, Josh?'

Josh's lips pressed together briefly. 'O-okay, I guess.'

'Good, because it looks like we're going straight up.'

They climbed the narrow, spiral staircase without a word, each step causing the grated metal to shudder. Every tremor rattled Charlie's bones, setting his nerves on edge. Not for the first time, he imagined the rusted guardrail giving way and the whole structure collapsing under them, sending them plummeting to their deaths on the cold, hard ground below.

Wiping the sweat from his brow, he glanced at a thick tangle of cobwebs clinging stubbornly to the brickwork. Something black scuttled in the darkness. Charlie averted his gaze, focusing instead on one of the wall-mounted security cameras. Its lens sat motionless. Thank Christ for the blackout, but how long would that last? The longer they took to break ground, the riskier things got.

Josh's breathing became laboured.

'You alright?' Charlie asked.

'Y-yeah. Cardio's not my thing.'

'If you need a break—'

YOU DO NOT HAVE TIME.

Charlie jerked at the sound of the demon's voice, his shock giving way to confusion. Then he heard it; the hum of electricity, and the mechanical whir of the security camera resetting itself.

'Josh, we need to move. Now.'

'W-why?'

'The cameras. Run!'

Charlie broke into a sprint, each pounding footfall causing the metal stairs to flex alarmingly beneath him. If the black suits spotted them, it was over. They'd be dragged back, kicking and screaming, and his one chance to reach the gatekeeper—before Eric and his cult did God-knows-what with him—would go up in smoke.

Below, a sudden bloom of light burst through the dark as the power surged back on. Behind him, Josh's ragged gasps echoed, the boy struggling to keep pace.

LEAVE HIM. HE'S SLOWING YOU DOWN. YOU KNOW WHERE THE GATEKEEPER IS. YOU DON'T NEED HIM.

'Josh, hurry!' Charlie yelled, his voice tight. The rail groaned under his grip as he propelled himself forward. Another flare of light shot up from below. Christ, were they motion-activated, or was someone tracking them?

Reaching the top, Charlie slammed into the door. He tumbled out into daylight. Josh staggered through seconds later and dropped to his knees, his body convulsing with dry retches. His face was beetroot red;

sweat dripping from his temples. He looked about ready to keel over.

Charlie gave him a moment to recover, then offered a hand.

Josh squinted up at him, shielding his eyes from the glaring sun. 'You're not... not... even winded.'

Shit.

He *should* be out of breath. Too late to do anything about it now.

'I run,' he said. 'A lot.' That, at least, was true. 'Come on. We'd better get moving.'

They had emerged on the far side of O.O.T.I.S headquarters, just beyond the emergency vehicles and crowds swarming the blast site. The explosion had ripped a gaping hole in the side of the building, scattering charred bricks and shattered glass across the road like shrapnel. Thick, black plumes of smoke continued to coil into the sky from multiple points, marking the scale of devastation.

Charlie gaped. 'Jesus Christ.'

They hurried down the street, slipping unnoticed past pedestrians who were transfixed by the carnage in the distance. Only when they reached a carpark tucked down a quiet side road did they slow, briefly catching their breath.

'Is one of these y-yours?' Josh asked.

'No,' Charlie muttered. 'We're borrowing one.'

'Borrowing?'

'Temporarily.'

YOU ARE A THIEF.

Charlie scanned the vehicles. 'We need something old,' he muttered. 'No high-tech alarms.'

'How about t-that one?' Josh pointed to a black Vauxhall Corsa. 'It's the same model as m-mine. Immobilisers, but nothing fancy. They get stolen all the time.'

The car was tucked in a corner space, obscured from the main road by an overgrown bush that had been liberally decorated with empty cans and crisp packets.

'Perfect.'

A PETTY CRIMINAL. A FITTING WAY TO MARK YOUR RETIREMENT FROM THE POLICE—BY GETTING YOURSELF THROWN BEHIND BARS. HOW POETIC.

Setting his jaw, Charlie walked briskly to the car and tugged on the handle. Locked. His mouth pressed into a tight line.

'Can we break the window?' Josh asked.

Charlie glanced up at the nearby flats. 'I'd rather not if I can avoid it. They might not see it, but they'd sure as hell hear it.'

Josh huffed, kicking out at a shopping trolley that was half-stuck in the bushes. It clanged loudly against the pavement. Charlie stared at his reaction.

INTERESTING. LOOKS LIKE SOMEONE HAS ANGER ISSUES.

Granted, he hadn't known Josh for long, but the lad had seemed so spineless earlier. This sudden outburst didn't add up. He made a quick check for onlookers, then looked at Josh who was rubbing at his chest irritably. His eyes were locked on the trolley, like it had personally offended him.

The trolley!

Forgetting Josh's tantrum, Charlie crouched down and focused on the thin, silver bars. With minimal effort, he pried one free—the metal snapping clean at the joint—then bent it into a makeshift hook.

Standing up, he wiggled the tool in front of Josh. 'Must've come loose when you kicked it.'

A LIAR AND A THIEF.

With one final look around, Charlie carefully slid the hook between the car window and the doorframe, angling it towards the lock mechanism. He moved it slowly, feeling for resistance until it caught. A quick pull and the lock popped up with a satisfying *click*.

Josh's jaw dropped, clearly impressed. 'How did you—?'

'I had a life before the police.'

After tossing the piece of metal, Charlie got in and eyed the dash. No alarm, thankfully. Leaning over, he unlocked the passenger door for Josh.

'You know how to h-hotwire this thing?' The car bobbed lightly as Josh climbed in beside him and pulled the door closed.

Charlie hesitated. *Shit.*

A sigh eddied through his brain. I HAVE EATEN MORE COMPETENT CRIMINALS THAN YOU FOR BREAKFAST.

An explosion of memories detonated in his mind, disorienting and disconcertingly vivid. His hand—no, someone else's hand—yanked the panel off the steering column and pulled out a fistful of wires. With a flick of a switchblade, the plastic sheathing was sliced away, revealing the copper beneath. In one fluid motion, the battery and ignition wires were twisted together, then bridged to the starter wire.

Charlie gasped, rearing back. His white-knuckled fists locked onto the steering wheel.

YOU'RE WELCOME.

Josh stared at him. 'Are you okay?'

'Yeah.' He swallowed hard. 'I'm fine.'

With the memories still fresh in his mind, Charlie copied the steps. The engine roared into life.

Josh made an appreciative noise. 'Nice.'

Charlie grunted, pulling out of the space.

'You know the way?' Josh asked.

'Yeah, I think I can remember. If not, you can give me directions.'

'Okay.' Josh fell silent a moment, then added, 'I mean, I'll do my b-b-best. They had me blindfolded when we drove up there. But I think I can remember the t-turns.'

Charlie gave a nod of acknowledgement, barely registering the boy's words.

It was all coming together. Soon, he'd be rid of the demon for good. Finally free of the toxic presence inside his skull.

Chapter 32

LYDIA HAD BEEN BACK in her cage for a while now. Sean had practically thrown her down the cellar stairs. She hadn't fought him then, hadn't yelled, hadn't even cried—and somehow, that made it worse. She couldn't have been gone more than half an hour, but the look on her face said it had been a lifetime. The emptiness in her eyes reflected a haunted pain that words couldn't touch. She hadn't spoken since, just curled into a ball in the corner of the crate, hugging herself tightly, as if she could disappear into her own embrace.

Even now, Sachiko could hear Lydia's frantic screams replaying in her mind—the ones that had echoed through the building while she was gone. That chilling soundtrack of terror and agony had stretched every moment into an eternity.

With each second, her heart broke a little more for the woman. She should have done something. She should have at least tried. If she'd lured Sean closer, used the sedative on him, stolen the keys, maybe she could have spared Lydia her nightmare.

Sachiko sucked on her lower lip, retreating inwards. The regret of what she hadn't done pressed down on her until it became painful to breathe.

'Lydia...' Sophie's voice wavered.

What could she possibly say? What could any of them say? *Are you alright? Are you hurt?* The answers to both questions were written on the faces of everyone in the room. Even Ash looked disturbed, his expression darkening even more as he surveyed the scene.

'What do we do?' Sophie's voice trembled.

Sachiko wasn't sure who she was addressing, but the gatekeeper answered, 'We stick to the plan. Wait for them to start the ritual. They'll need to remove my shackles for me to access my power, which means they'll have the keys with them.' He turned his intense green eyes on Sachiko. 'Once they release me, you have to create a reason for them to get close to you. When they're within reach, use the toxin. I'll take out the remaining two while you create the distraction.'

'Can't you just take them all out at once?' Sophie asked.

Ash replied, tone firm, 'They won't release me without having some way to control me. I'll need the distraction to overpower them before they can.'

Sophie nodded.

The floorboards squealed above them.

'How much longer do you think it'll be?' Sophie whispered.

Ash rubbed at his jaw. 'I'm not sure. Probably soon. They don't strike me as the patient types.'

Muffled voices from above grew louder. The door to the cellar creaked open.

'This is a mistake,' a male voice grumbled.

'Well fuck off then, Ben,' Sean said. 'Go home to your beast of a wife and your brats.'

'Fuck you, Sean. Daman, reason with him, would you? When Eric gets back—'

'Eric?' Sean interrupted. 'What's your obsession with Eric all of a sudden? I thought you were still sore at him for busting your lip? Or do you like it rough?'

'Fuck off.'

'Enough,' Damanjeet barked. 'If we're going to do this, let's do it. If we wait too long, it will only be a matter of time before the Order finds us.'

Sachiko and Sophie exchanged nervous glances. All of a sudden, Sachiko's heart was in her throat, anxiety roiling through her. It was happening. She touched her lab coat, feeling the contour of the vial hidden within.

As the three men filtered into the cellar, adorned in red robes—hoods drawn back to hang down from the cowls at their shoulders—Sachiko's fear became palpable. These men were insane.

Her eyes darted to Sean, who held an aged, leather-bound book in one hand and in the other... The Bloodvein Wand. Recognition struck her like a punch to the gut. She couldn't suppress the sharp intake of breath. That's what she'd seen on Damanjeet's laptop! That's what he'd tried so desperately to hide from her.

'See I told you,' Damanjeet said to her, a sneer curling his lips. 'You could've joined us, been part of something greater—bigger than the Order, bigger than yourself. But you turned your back on me. I thought you were different, Sachiko. I thought you understood me.'

Sean watched the exchange, his brow furrowing. 'Join us? Who the fuck said this Chinky little bitch could join us?'

Damanjeet growled. 'She's Japanese, you idiot.'

'Whatever. She's not joining us, unless it's in the bedroom.'

'Touch her and I'll kill you,' Damanjeet warned, straightening to his full height. His eyes narrowed dangerously. 'She's mine.'

Sachiko recoiled. *His?* 'I'm not a possession,' she shouted, 'I'll never be yours!'

The room fell silent.

Damanjeet's expression flickered with hurt, but it quickly morphed into cold anger. 'Maybe not now, but you will be.'

Sachiko's breath caught; the fire inside was doused by a cold chill that ran through her body.

'Got a mouth on her, don't she?' Sean chuckled. 'I bet she can do all kinds of things with that mouth.'

Damanjeet took a step forward, squaring up to him. 'I'm warning you.'

'Yeah? What're you going to do, *huh?* What in the fuck do you think you can do abou—'

Damanjeet drove his fist into Sean's gut, cutting his taunts short. Sean doubled over, sending the wand and book flying from his grip. Both hit the floor.

'Fuck!' Sean wheezed, pain contorting his face. 'You bastard. You hit me!'

'I told you. She's off limits. Do you understand?'

'Fuck. Yes, I understand. This isn't some spicy romance novel, y'know. Jesus.'

Sachiko watched the power shift from Sean to Daman. She swallowed, her throat rough and dry.

'Good. Now that's sorted, can we get back to the book,' Damanjeet said, bending to retrieve it.

Sean, gasping and red-faced, glared at him for a moment longer, then snatched the wand from the concrete before dropping it again with a curse. Blood dripped from his palm. He squinted at it.

Damanjeet shook his head. 'Careful, we need that wand in one piece.' He flicked through the book, the yellowed pages whispering beneath his fingers.

The third man, Ben, stood to the side, watching uncertainly as Damanjeet tapped one page with a nod.

'Okay,' Damanjeet said. 'Sean, get the circle set up.'

'You're the one with the book. You do it.'

'Don't be a dick. I know you've read it. You know what's involved. Get to it,' Damanjeet ordered.

Grumbling, Sean gathered the hem of his robes and shuffled towards a rusted filing cabinet. It screeched in protest as he yanked open one of the dented drawers, causing the whole thing to wobble precariously. He riffled through the contents, muttering to himself as objects clinked together. Finally, he withdrew a handful of small items and slammed the drawer shut with a grunt. Waddling back to the ritualistic circle carved into the concrete, he placed each item carefully on the symbols etched around its perimeter.

Sachiko fixed her glasses and leant forward, her heart quickening. If she could get a good look at the objects, maybe she could decipher the type of demon they were trying to summon. As Sean moved, she followed, straining to see.

First, a small bird skull. She frowned, none the wiser. Without knowing the bird's species, its significance remained a mystery.

Next, a shard of mirror.

Then, a tarnished copper key.

And finally, a feather—white with a cream base, speckled with brown. Recognition flickered. A barn owl feather. That had to mean the skull belonged to the same bird.

Owls... wisdom, knowledge. The mirror shard, perhaps for insight. The key... a symbol for unlocking hidden truths?

Her mind raced. Sachiko bit her lip, trying to piece it all together. There were countless demons that traded in secrets.

Shifting position, she squinted. Sean stepped back, dusting his hands off on his robes. Her eyebrows knitted—where was the fifth item? Most demonic rituals required five offerings, representations of the demon. She scanned the circle again. What was she missing? Her gaze drifted to the cages. Her stomach twisted.

A sacrifice.

Under his robes, Sean rummaged through his jeans pockets and produced a set of keys. He flicked through them, selected one, and moved to the gatekeeper's cage.

'No funny stuff,' he muttered, inserting one key in the lock.

Ash made an amused noise, watching Sean flatly. There was no trace of fear in his face. No sign that any of this concerned him in the slightest.

He opened the door, tugging Ash forward by his shackles.

'Uh-uh-uh, wait a second,' Damanjeet said, carefully placing the book on the concrete, leaving it open on the page he'd been studying.

'What?'

'Don't undo those just yet. The moment they're off, he regains his full power. Those wards are the only thing stopping him from becoming a monster.'

Sean pulled the key back with a jerk of his wrist.

Ash smiled, giving Sean a look that said *maybe next time*.

'I need to test something first.' Damanjeet pinched the Bloodvein Wand between his thumb and forefinger like it might bite. He turned it so that the red gemstone embedded in the copper wire faced the gatekeeper, and thrust it forward. 'Kneel.'

Ash arched an eyebrow, but otherwise didn't move.

Damanjeet's frustration grew. He marched forward and grabbed Sean's hand, forcing it to close around the wand's copper hilt. Sean cried out, blood dribbling down his palm, as he attempted to wrench himself free.

'Tell it to kneel,' Damanjeet said.

Sean gritted his teeth, his face twisting in a pained scowl. 'K-kneel.'

Ash watched them with a bored expression.

'Again!'

'Kneel.'

Again, nothing happened.

Ben approached, laying his hand on Damanjeet's shoulder. 'Let's just wait for Eric, yeah?'

Damanjeet shrugged him off violently. 'Like your life depends on it, Sean!'

Sean looked at him, his expression shifting from pain to unease. He turned to the gatekeeper. 'Kneel!' he shouted, his voice catching with the effort.

The wand trembled in his grip, but still the gatekeeper didn't kneel.

'Give me that,' Damanjeet snarled, snatching the wand from Sean. It made a wet sucking noise as the copper strands slid from the man's blood-soaked palm.

'See?' Ben said, glancing nervously between them. 'There's a reason Eric always took the lead. We can't do this without him.'

'I have a backup plan.' Damanjeet spun on his heel.

Fear prickled down Sachiko's spine as he neared the cage, his gaze locked onto her. Her heart beat like a warning drum, but she forced herself to meet his stare, chin raised in silent challenge.

'I won't help you,' she said, willing him closer. The urge to rip the vial from her lab coat and plunge it into him was overwhelming, but she fought it back, waiting for the right moment.

'You don't have a choice,' Damanjeet shot back, his dark eyes becoming slits. 'I gave you a chance, but you rejected it. Just like you rejected me. This is the way it has to be now.' His tone grew hard. 'Keys!'

Sean fumbled for the bunch of keys, finally passing them over without a word. Damanjeet flipped through them one-handed, taking his time, making her watch. Making her wait.

Dread pooled in her stomach. As he picked out the correct key and slid it into the padlock, she shrieked, clambering to the back of the cage. At the same time, she pulled out the vial, clutching it tightly in her fist.

Damanjeet's hand closed around her arm. He yanked her forward. The force of the motion jarred through her body. Every ridge and every rivet of the crate's base caught at her legs, scraping and bruising her skin. Still, she kept her grip on the vial, fist clenched, as he dragged her inch by painful inch. He dug his fingers into her flesh, hauling her up and out, so that the cage bars scored against her thigh. She yelped.

Sachiko landed hard on the concrete and quickly pushed herself into a sitting position, meeting his eyes with unbridled hatred. 'You're a disgrace,' she spat. 'How could you do this? You've forgotten your humanity. Betrayed the Order.'

'Betrayed the Order?' Damanjeet laughed without humour. 'The Order betrayed me! I warned them what would happen if they kept closing all the gateways, but they wouldn't listen. I gave them all the data, but they didn't care. The Brimstone Chorus is coming, and ordinary mortals like me and you don't stand a chance against it. It's time to stack the odds a little. You'll see. When the time comes, you'll thank me. Your friend here understands what I'm talking about.' He shot a look at Ash and smirked.

'The Brimstone Chorus?' Sachiko uttered. No, that was just a legend. The worst-case scenario. It couldn't possibly be true.

Ash's expression turned solemn. He gave her a single nod—the end of the world was coming.

Damanjeet wrenched her to her feet, causing her to yelp again. She eased the vial up her palm and carefully, very carefully, hooked her nail under the cap. With a faint pop, she pried it loose and exposed the needle beneath. She would need to wait until his attention was elsewhere. She had one chance. One. If Sachiko failed, they'd all be trapped here—or worse.

'Don't just stand there, get the book,' Damanjeet barked, pivoting away from her and brandishing the wand at Sean.

This was it. Sachiko twisted, bringing her arm up and around, aiming for his throat.

But Damanjeet was faster. He jabbed her wrist with his elbow; the needle glanced uselessly off his robes. The jarring impact shot through her hand, causing her numb fingers to twitch open.

The vial fell to the floor.

Chapter 33

SACHIKO SUCKED IN A sharp, panicked breath as the vial skittered across the concrete towards the stairs. Each heart-stopping *clink* spun it further out of reach. It didn't shatter, but there was no way she could get it now. It was lost to the shadows.

Damanjeet struck her hard across the face, snapping her neck to the side. The jolt sent white flashes through her vision. She staggered, struggling to stay upright.

'You think we didn't know what you were up to?' Sean sneered, jabbing a thick finger at the far corner. 'You think I'd install cameras all over this place but miss the cellar? We heard every word.'

She blinked through the sting of tears, backing away, trying to focus.

What were they going to do now? Their one chance... She'd blown it.

Ash moved in a blur. With a snarl, he lunged at Damanjeet, slamming into his back. He looped his shackled hands around Damanjeet's throat. The metal links tightened as he heaved him back. Sean shouted something incoherent, diving into the fray, sending the three men crashing to the floor. Damanjeet gasped for air, his face darkening, as he struggled to wedge his fingers under the chains biting into his neck.

'The vial!' Ash's yell snapped Sachiko back to reality.

She threw herself towards the stairs, dropping to her hands and knees. Frantically, she scrambled in the near-darkness, her fingers scouring the cold concrete.

A body barrelled into her, driving the air from her lungs. She hit the floor. Ben pinned her down, his full weight on top of her. She twisted beneath him, managing to rake her nails across his face. He recoiled with a yelp, giving her a split second to shove him off and continue her desperate search.

He grabbed her shoulders and yanked her back. She cried out, flailing wildly as Ben forced her to the floor again and kicked her in the ribs. Pain lanced through her chest. She curled in on herself only to have her wrists jerked out in front of her. Cold metal bit into her skin as the handcuffs clicked shut around them.

'No!' Sachiko shrieked, thrashing against the restraints.

Ben wrenched her arms up, twisting her wrists so hard her bones threatened to snap. She shot her gaze to Ash, but he was on his knees now, a knife pressed against his throat. The wards on his shackles blazed white.

Damanjeet stood over him, swiping at his split lip. 'Bring her over here.'

Ben dragged Sachiko forward, hauling her up to her knees, as Damanjeet passed the blade to Sean.

Snatching up the wand, Damanjeet forced it into Sachiko's palm. She hissed as copper wire sunk into her flesh. He closed her hand around it, pressing his own over hers, squeezing more until the wand dug deeper, making her cry out.

'Now, tell him to kneel,' Damanjeet said.

Sachiko gritted her teeth. 'No.'

He backhanded her across the face; the sound cracked through the cellar. 'Tell him to kneel.'

Her mouth filled with blood. She spat it onto the floor, glaring up at him with all the hatred she could muster. 'No.'

Damanjeet smiled. It was a cruel and terrible smile, filled with the promise of violence. 'Tell him to kneel.' His gaze shifted to Lydia. Sachiko's breath caught. She tried to mask her fear, but Damanjeet had seen it. His smile became crueller. He placed a finger under her chin, tilting her head up, forcing her to meet his eyes. 'You're an intelligent woman, Sachiko. I think we both know how this will end.'

He stepped away and trailed his hand over a dusty table until his fingers closed around a rusty box cutter. Flipping the blade out with a metallic snap, he glanced back at Sachiko before striding towards Lydia's cage.

With the box cutter in hand, Damanjeet unlocked the crate and dragged Lydia out. Her body was rigid at first, like a coiled spring, but the moment his hand knotted in her hair, she seemed to go limp, as though surrendering to the inevitable. Her eyes never left the floor, as her mind retreated to a place where the horrors couldn't follow.

Damanjeet wrenched Lydia's head back, pressing the blade against her exposed throat. 'Tell him to kneel,' he growled, the steel biting into her skin. A thin line of red welled up. 'Or her blood is on your hands.'

A sob tore from Sachiko's lips. 'Kneel,' she whispered, her voice breaking.

'Like you mean it.' Damanjeet snarled, pressing the blade harder.

'Kneel!' Sachiko cried, tears pricking her eyes.

The wand pulsed. Pain exploded in her hand as its copper strands embedded deeper. She tried to pull free, to let it drop, but the wand held fast, as if compelling her to keep her grip. Her hand cramped, fingers locking around it, as red veins bloomed within the crystal. She gasped in horror.

The gemstone blazed.

Ash groaned, dropping to the floor. His arms outstretched and his head pressed against the concrete in submission.

Damanjeet laughed, victorious. 'I knew it! You're special, Sachiko, just like I said.'

The wand's hold on her weakened. She felt it—an opportunity, a sudden release of pressure. Without thinking, she ripped it free from her flesh. A gasp of relief and a sob followed. She watched the blood-red veins in the crystal fade, draining away, until nothing remained but a ghostly reminder of the agony she'd just endured.

'*No, no...*' Damanjeet cooed. 'You'll need that again. Pick it up.'

Sachiko flicked her eyes to Lydia. Reluctantly, she reached for the wand.

'That's it.'

Wincing, she closed her hand around the blood-slick shaft once more, forcing the copper shards back into her palm. Fresh pain lanced through her and she screamed.

With a casual shove, Damanjeet sent Lydia crumpling to the ground. 'Sean, unshackle the gatekeeper.'

Sean paused, uncertainty flickering across his face. 'You sure? What about the candles?'

Damanjeet gave him a withering look. 'The candles are meaningless, just Eric's flair for theatrics. The ritual will work perfectly fine without that nonsense.'

'And the sacrifice?' Sean added.

Damanjeet's jaw tightened. He frowned at the box cutter in his hand, turning it over, staring at it a fraction too long. His attention shifted to Lydia, trembling at his feet, and his scowl deepened. But Sachiko caught something else in his expression: hesitation. She knew he had no qualms about killing, not after what he'd done to Michelle, so why the reluctance now? Maybe this ritual demanded something more than just another life?

'I think we need to see whether the gatekeeper is up to the task first,' he said, before directing his focus back to Sachiko. 'Tell him not to resist.'

She flinched at the command.

'Don't resist,' she said weakly, her voice trembling. Again, the Bloodvein Wand drank from her, causing the crystal to pulse with tendrils of scarlet.

Ash's eyes fluttered and his body went slack, as the tension left him.

Sean moved quickly, unlocking the shackles with a sharp, metallic click. They clattered to the floor. Ash's green eyes flashed with brief defiance and for a second, Sachiko dared to hope. But then the ruby in the wand blazed, casting a sinister glow over her hands.

The gatekeeper quivered, his muscles betraying him, locking him in place.

'Now, tell him to open a gateway,' Damanjeet said.

Sachiko gaped, her heart racing. 'No, please! There's no way of knowing what might come through.'

'Do it.'

'Please, you know this is wrong. I know you. This isn't—'

'*Know* me? You don't know anything about me.' His voice turned venomous. 'Tell him to open a gateway or Lydia dies.'

A strangled whimper caught on Sachiko's lips. 'Open a gateway.' The gemstone flared. The wand drank. And Ash threw his arms out wide.

The air vibrated, thick with power, plunging the room into a darkness so complete, it swallowed all detail save for the green glow of Ash's eyes. His voice droned as he muttered words of an incantation. They pitched and fell in time with the electric quiver radiating out from where he stood. A rift began to form above them, a smouldering void of sulphur and choking fumes. The breach widened, casting an ominous red glow over the room. Dust spewed from the tear between realms, a foul storm of churning ash that coated the floor in a fine, gritty film.

Sachiko forced herself to breathe. The naeshin demon had been terrifying, but this... this was on another level.

Damanjeet's grin widened as he stepped forward, the eerie light casting wild shadows across his features and making him look utterly deranged.

Then the gateway spasmed, contracting in on itself. Ash, pale and sweat-soaked, staggered under the strain of keeping it open.

'What's happening?' Damanjeet shouted to Sean, his confidence wavering.

'I don't know...'

'Do something!' Damanjeet roared at no one in particular, his eyes bulging beneath the lambent red of the shrinking gateway.

'Damanjeet, this won't work,' Sachiko screamed. 'I told you.'

Ash's legs buckled. He collapsed beneath the swirling murk of the dissipating mist. The gateway winked out of existence.

'I told you we needed to wait for Eric,' Ben said.

Damanjeet bared his teeth. 'Fuck.' He marched over to Ash and booted him in the chest. 'What happened?'

'My power was already drained before your people captured me.'

'We'll try again.'

'I need rest... food... to recover my strength.'

The roar Damanjeet made was animalistic.

'What if he can't open another gateway?' Ben asked.

'Then we're fucked.' Damanjeet ran a hand through his beard. 'Get them back in the cages. We'll try again in a while. Bring *it* something to eat.'

A trembling Sachiko still knelt, her grip on the wand tight, despite the blood slicking her hands. She didn't dare move. Fear kept her rooted to the spot, every muscle in her body taut and ready to flee but unable to move her. Out of the corner of her eye, she saw Ash stir, lifting his head from the ground. He met her gaze and, despite his weakness, gave her a slow, deliberate wink.

A creak sounded from above. Then, with a violent crash, the cellar door flew open.

Chapter 34

As it turned out, Charlie didn't need Josh to direct him. The way to the White Stag came back to him easily, as if no time had passed at all. He'd eaten there often, back when things had been simpler. Before the divorce. He recalled Debbie sitting across from him at their usual table and Meggy, so small her little hands could barely hold a fork.

The food had been good. The company better.

But, after things had soured between them, the White Stag had become just another casualty of time. He'd never walked through those doors again. Funny how the happiest moments in life could twist into something thorned, snagging at his insides, reopening old wounds. So, he'd done what he always did and buried the memories deep enough that they never saw the light of day.

Yet, despite all the years, some things just refused to be forgotten.

The narrow country lane was riddled with potholes. The car slammed into each one, the suspension groaning with every bone-rattling lurch. Brambles reached out at them, scratching at the sides of the Corsa as they drove, clawing at the paintwork in a desperate attempt to drag them to a stop.

'What's the plan after this?' Charlie asked loudly over the steady hum of the engine.

Josh turned from the passenger window. 'What?'

'For you and Sophie?'

'Oh.' He drew in a breath and released it. 'Find somewhere safe. Somewhere no one can hurt us again.' His answer was slow and measured.

JOSH SEEMS DIFFERENT.

Charlie couldn't argue. Ever since they'd escaped O.O.T.I.S headquarters, something in Josh had changed. His demeanour felt... off. And then there was the smell. At first, he'd chalked it up to the lingering stench of sulphur and ash from the pit infernal, but it clung to the boy even now.

Maybe he was overthinking it. Josh had been through hell. His strange behaviour could just be a coping mechanism, a way of processing the trauma. Poor kid.

YOU ARE LETTING YOUR PAST BLIND YOU. OPEN YOUR EYES.

What would you know about it?

YOUR CHILDHOOD IS MAPPED OUT ACROSS YOUR BODY IN SCARS. IT DOESN'T TAKE A GENIUS TO CONNECT THE DOTS. YOU RELATE TO THE HUMAN JOSH. YOU SYMPATHISE WITH HIM. YOU ARE WEAK. STUPID. JUST KILL HIM.

Charlie ignored the demon's words, shifting gears and pressing down harder on the accelerator. He didn't want to admit how close to the truth Chekonost really was.

He *did* see himself in Josh. And damn it, he wanted to help the boy. No one deserved a life scarred by abuse.

If he could do just one good thing, help just one person, it might prove that he still had control. Over his mind. Over his life. Prove that he wasn't becoming the heartless monster that haunted him every time the dagger—every time Stephen—crossed his thoughts.

He wasn't just a pawn in Kar'roc's game. He refused to be.

Whatever Chekonost thought, Charlie still had a choice. He'd make sure of it.

Another pothole elicited a grunt from him. Christ, he didn't remember the drive taking this long. How much time did he have until O.O.T.I.S realised he was gone? A few hours? With Diane actively ignoring him, maybe more. Enough to find the gatekeeper. Assuming the gatekeeper would help at all.

IT IS HIS JOB.

What?

THE SOLE PURPOSE OF A GATEKEEPER IS TO MAINTAIN THE GATEWAY. TO ESCORT DEMONIC ENTITIES BETWEEN REALMS.

What? So things can just cross freely?

HOW DID YOU THINK THEY ENTERED YOUR REALM?

Charlie hadn't thought about it. Hadn't wanted to. His discovery that demons were real was still fresh. Since that day, he'd wanted nothing more than to go back to the way things had been. Before the dagger, before Kar'roc, before Chekonost.

I figured they were summoned? Like in the book, Ritualistic Sacrifice in Ancient Magical Practices.

A low, mocking laugh reverberated in his mind.

SOME ARE. IT IS HOW MY ESSENCE WAS ENSNARED IN THAT DAGGER ALMOST A CENTURY AGO. BUT OTHERS—DEMONS OF LESSER POWER—CAN SLIP THROUGH WHEN THE VEIL IS AT ITS WEAKEST.

Lesser power? Charlie tightened his grip on the steering wheel. *What about the stronger ones?*

THE MAGIC OF THE VEIL PREVENTS THEIR PASSING. THE STRONGER THE DEMON, THE GREATER THE RESISTANCE. FOR NOW, AT LEAST.

For now? His knuckles turned white.

Auntie had told him as much, when she'd spoken about the Brimstone Chorus, and how it would herald the end of days. He hadn't wanted to believe it at the time, passing her warning off as her having a screw loose. Especially after she'd spouted all that nonsense about souls. Except, it had turned out to be true.

When he'd become host to the demon, had he somehow compromised the veil? No, Auntie said that the Brimstone Chorus had already begun. But then why?

BECAUSE SOMETHING HAS DISTURBED THE BALANCE.

Disturbed the balance? Like what?

I DON'T KNOW. THAT IS WHY I SAID *SOMETHING.* IS THIS AN AGE THING? WOULD YOU LIKE ME TO SPEAK SLOWER?

Refusing to bite, Charlie exhaled and focused on the road. *This thing, whatever it is, it can't break through, right?*

AS FAR AS I'M AWARE, NOT UNLESS THE VEIL IS BREACHED FROM THE HUMAN REALM. IT IS WHY KAR'ROC BESTOWED THAT WRETCHED DAGGER ON MANKIND. IT IS A WEAPON OF IMMENSE POWER, CAPABLE OF RENDING THE VEIL SO VIOLENTLY, EVEN THE STRONGEST OF US COULD PUSH THROUGH.

But the weaker demons can get through on their own?

ONLY THROUGH A GATEWAY. USUALLY. SOMETIMES, SOMETHING BREACHES THE VEIL FIRST—A RITUAL, AN ARTEFACT, WAYWARD MAGIC. BUT AT TIMES, THE VEIL THINS ON ITS OWN.

A ritual—like the one in the book?

WHAT DO YOU THINK THE PURPOSE OF A RITUALISTIC SUMMONING IS? IT CREATES A TEMPORARY ENTRY POINT INTO YOUR REALM. WITH ENOUGH MAGIC, HUMANS CAN TEAR OPEN THE VEIL. BUT IF THEIR SPELL FAILS, IF THE PROTECTIVE CIRCLE FALLS, THE DEMON CAN CROSS UNHINDERED. SOME HUMANS HAVE EVEN EVOLVED TO ABSORB OUR ENERGY—THOSE ARE THE ONES YOU SHOULD FEAR.

Witches?

The demon laughed again. NO. WITCHES DRIVE OUT OUR ENERGY, SCORCHING IT AWAY AS THEY WEAVE THEIR SPELLS. THAT'S WHY THEY

REEK OF BURNT MATCHES AND BRIMSTONE. BUT THERE ARE OTHERS... HUMANS WHO HUNGER FOR OUR POWER, CHANNELLING IT TO FUEL THEIR MAGIC. WHEN THEY PUSH TOO FAR, WHEN THEY SIPHON MORE THAN THEY CAN HANDLE, IT TEARS AT THE VEIL. AND WHERE THE VEIL WEAKENS DEMONS WAIT, READY TO BRING BLOODY CHAOS INTO YOUR WORLD. YOU HAVE MET SUCH A HUMAN.

A muscle twitched in his jaw. *Banning.*

BANNING, the demon repeated, almost wistfully.

But you said only the lesser demons can cross over? So, as long as the dagger remains inaccessible, humanity is safe?

Mocking contempt shuddered through Charlie's body. ASTOUNDING.

Charlie bristled. *What?*

YOUR IGNORANCE. IT REALLY KNOWS NO BOUNDS. YOU TRULY UNDERSTAND NOTHING ABOUT YOUR OWN REALM, DO YOU?

Enlighten me.

IMAGINE, IF YOU WILL, WHAT WOULD HAPPEN TO YOUR PATHETIC WORLD SHOULD A DEMON COME INTO FULL POSSESSION OF ONE SUCH AS BANNING. A HUMAN WHO COULD HARNESS THE POWER OF THE REALM OF FIRE AND SHADOW?

But Banning didn't breach the veil.

BANNING'S POWER WAS STILL IN ITS INFANCY, AND THE DEMON'S HOLD ON HIM... FRACTURED. BUT THERE ARE OTHERS. THOSE WHO HAVE HAD

CENTURIES TO HONE THEIR GIFTS, TO BECOME STRONG ENOUGH TO ENDURE THE TOUCH OF AN ARCHDEMON.

So, why hasn't it happened yet?

BECAUSE THEY ARE FEW AND FAR BETWEEN. HUMANS ARE STILL HUMANS. WEAK. PATHETIC. THOSE ABLE TO WIELD OUR GIFTS USUALLY SLIP INTO INSANITY. POISONED BY THE VERY POWER THEY STEAL FROM US. THEY DIE, LONG BEFORE THEY ARE OF ANY USE. FUNNY REALLY, THAT THE HUMANS WHO CAN BREACH THE VEIL OFTEN PERISH BEFORE THEY FULFIL THEIR POTENTIAL. The demon's tone sank lower, a jagged rasp now that stabbed and twisted inside Charlie's skull. THE FALL OF MANKIND IS INEVITABLE. ALL IT NEEDS IS A SINGLE SPARK. A CATALYST TO IGNITE THE RUIN.

A branch whipped across the window to his right. Charlie straightened in his seat.

JUST THINK, IT COULD BE YOU.

He shuddered. The nightmares where the demon whispered to him. Was it trying to force him to breach the veil? Was this all part of Kar'roc's plan?

Josh's gaze on him pulled Charlie back to the present. He relaxed his grip on the steering wheel, letting his shoulders drop a little.

'What can we expect when we get to the pub?' Charlie asked.

'Sophie,' Josh said. 'Locked up with another woman.'

'And Eric's friends, how many are left?'

'Three. Assuming they all survived.' There was something oddly distant about his delivery.

Charlie stole another glance at the young man, unease gnawing at his gut.

The rest of the drive passed in silence. He still couldn't shake the feeling that something was off. Josh had been terrified, desperate, in the tunnels. But now, his voice was steadier, his posture more controlled. Was this the same kid who'd been so scared out of his mind hours ago that he'd lost control of his bladder? Maybe he was just in shock.

The pub came into view as they crested a small hill, a white blemish against the otherwise unspoiled landscape. Towering woods enveloped the area, their branches stripped bare, stark and exposed beneath the winter-grey sky. The car park remained, though it had never provided much space even in its heyday. Now, only a single vehicle was parked there—a lone, white transit van.

'Someone's here,' Josh said.

Charlie pulled the car off the road and under the cover of the trees, parking it behind a cluster of knotted stumps huddled together amidst the gnarled roots and damp, leaf-strewn earth.

'Is there a way in other than the front door?'

Josh shook his head. 'I don't know. I was b-blindfolded when they used to bring me here. And I was always watched by T-Tommo.'

Charlie's stomach churned. The feel of the eyeball's thick, gelatinous remains in his mouth replayed.

He swallowed hard and glanced at Josh, just in time to catch the flicker of emotion on his face. Had he looked... upset? Christ, why was he reading so much into everything? It was a natural human reaction to death, wasn't it?

Smothering his suspicions, Charlie unbuckled his seatbelt and stepped out of the car. 'Come on, let's go get Sophie.'

The woods pressed in around them as they ducked beneath the low-hanging branches. The chill in the air bit at Charlie's exposed skin through the torn slashes in his clothes. Every step sounded louder than it should, as the snap of twigs underfoot echoed like gunfire in the silence. Too much silence.

Where were the rustling sounds of small animals scurrying through the underbrush? The owl hoots or the distant cry of foxes?

HE IS HIDING SOMETHING, WE SHOULD KILL HIM.

Charlie gritted his teeth. *I said no.*

They moved towards the pub, keeping to the treeline. As they neared the white transit van, Charlie checked through the windows, holding his breath. Empty. He exhaled quietly, then crept towards the short set of steps leading to the entrance.

The cracked concrete crumbled at the edges, loose fragments shifting beneath his feet as he ascended. He slowed his pace. The last thing he needed was to slip and land on his arse, alerting everyone to their presence.

At the top, he reached out and tested the handle. The door clicked open. He glanced back and motioned for Josh to lead the way.

'Show me where the basement is,' Charlie said, in a hushed tone.

Josh gave a nod, and slipped inside. His footsteps were eerily light, as he carefully avoided certain floorboards. Charlie followed closely, mimicking his movements.

The bar area was a dismal shadow of its former glory. Even in the starved light seeping through the gaps around the boarded windows, Charlie could discern every detail with Chekonost's *gifts*. Empty spirit bottles lined the shelves like forgotten relics of a past life. The wooden bar counter, thick with dust and covered in scratches and stains, bore the scars of time. Barstools had been arranged in a circle nearby, their seats conspicuously clean, hinting at recent use.

Charlie caught a glimpse of his distorted reflection in the fractured mirror before he eyed the empty tables. A pang of nostalgia sliced through his chest. Taking a breath, he steeled himself and focused on the worn floorboards beneath his feet.

At last, they stopped in front of another door.

'Down here,' Josh whispered, his voice tight. He moved aside, allowing Charlie to take the lead.

Charlie pushed the door open, barely stepping forward before Josh slammed into him from behind, sending him tumbling down the stairs.

He twisted, thrusting a hand out to catch himself. His palm cracked against the old wooden handrail.

Splintered oak snapped under his weight. Charlie fell, momentum dragging him forward, as his body crashed against the steps.

SEE. I TOLD YOU SO.

The demon's voice echoed in his head, but Charlie barely registered it. He landed hard. Pain shot through his hand as something sharp bit into his palm.

He sprang to his feet but faltered; the world spun as vertigo hit him. His vision tunnelled. He looked down, heart pounding. Shards of glass jutted out from his hand; clear liquid mingled with the blood from his palm. A vinegary scent filled his nostrils, triggering a flicker of recognition. With trembling fingers, he pulled the pieces free.

Shouting echoed from above, distant and distorted.

Charlie tried to move, but the ground continued to tilt beneath him. Darkness crept in from all sides, tightening around him like a noose.

His legs gave out. He hit the cold floor, and everything went black.

Chapter 35

The old man plummeted down the stairs in a delicious series of bone-breaking thuds. Eric watched with intrigue. *This* was the man Josh had put his faith in? This washed-up pensioner? It was a joke. But then Josh was a joke. Once Eric received his ultimate gift, his alter would be a thing of the past.

The whispers slithered through Eric's mind, hissing their approval. They would help him silence Josh. Would make Eric whole. And why not? What had Josh ever done but cower and hide? Eric had been created to protect. To keep Sophie safe. And with this power, nothing would touch them. She might despise him now, but eventually, she'd see the truth—he was doing it all for her. To make sure nobody ever hurt her again.

Charlie hit the concrete.

Eric tilted his head. Was the old man dead?

No?

Against all odds, he pushed himself up, albeit unsteadily.

How? It shouldn't be possible. He didn't even seem injured. Charlie raised a quivering hand, then picked something out of his palm, his body swaying. A momentary surge of adrenaline, perhaps?

It happened. Eric had once heard about someone walking away from a car crash unscathed, only to drop dead seconds later due to a broken neck. This could be the same. And just like that, Charlie crumpled to the floor. Except that he was still breathing...

Unconscious. Good enough.

Eric took the stairs one by one, descending into the chill of the cellar. What he saw when he reached the bottom ignited a fire inside him.

'You dare?' he snarled, stepping over the old man's limp body, glaring at the disarray around the cellar.

His so-called Brothers stood gawking at him, adorned in their ceremonial robes. The blonde woman was out of her cage, lying in a shuddering heap on the concrete. But what really stoked the flames of his fury was that the book—the sacred book—lay discarded on the floor, abandoned like some worthless trinket. His pulse quickened, intensifying the pounding in his chest.

And there, trembling on her knees, her wrists cuffed, was a woman he didn't recognise. She was clutching his wand. Blood dribbled from her palm. Thin threads of crimson tainted the quartz crystal, its purity defiled. Eric clenched his jaw so tightly his teeth felt like they might crack as he forced himself to make sense of the treachery before him.

Then he saw it—*him.*

The gatekeeper. The one thing that mattered. Lying broken on the concrete like a discarded tool. *His* tool, rendered useless and weak.

His vision blurred for a moment as the rage overtook him. The whispers were no longer soothing—they were screaming now, fuelling the inferno within him. Eric's hands curled into fists. His nails dug hard into his scabbed palms until they broke the skin.

'Who. Did. This?' The words came out in a hoarse whisper, deadly quiet, but the danger they stoked was palpable, a calm before the storm. His gaze swept the room, his every breath feeling like he was dragging fire through his lungs. 'Who touched what was *mine?*'

His Brothers baulked, exchanging glances, but no one spoke. Cowards. Every last one of them.

Eric's world hazed with red as the whispers reached fever pitch. With a savage swing, he knocked the table to the ground in a deafening clatter. His scream tore through the room, primal, unstoppable.

'You dare touch what is mine!?' His voice was a bellow now, raw and untethered, shaking the very air around him. He slammed his fist into the nearest wall. The impact sent a shockwave of pain through his arm, but it only fed the rage.

'You had *one* task!' he roared, his breath coming in ragged gasps. He glared at the cowering figures. 'One task and you failed!'

Eric's chest heaved as he whirled around. His eyes landed on the gatekeeper once more. Useless. Spent. Everything was slipping through his fingers, and it was their fault. His Brothers had stolen from him. His future, his power.

The anger inside him reached boiling point, shaking his entire body with the force of it. He felt as though he could tear the world apart with his bare hands. And he would. He would make them all pay.

With another savage roar, Eric thrust a finger at the gatekeeper. 'Which one of you had the nerve to try and take this from me?'

The men in the room shook, but no one dared move. Not a word, not a breath. The tempest was coming, and there would be no mercy.

Ben cowered beneath his stare, Sean looked away, but Daman... Damanjeet met his eyes without a trace of contrition.

'You,' Eric hissed, stalking across the room. He stopped mere inches from the man, his skin prickling with heat, his teeth bared. 'You thought you could take the power for yourself?'

Damanjeet held his gaze for a moment longer, then broke eye contact, his posture sagging. 'We thought... you were dead.'

'Dead?' Eric scoffed, incredulous. 'I have a higher purpose.' He ripped off his ruined suit jacket and yanked at his shirt. The buttons popped open to reveal the black veins etched across his chest. 'I bare the demon's mark. Me! The gift was promised to me, and you dared to try and take it?'

Damanjeet shrank back. 'We—I just thought if you were gone, we should continue your work.'

Eric narrowed his eyes, studying the man. 'Who's she?' He pointed at the kneeling woman. 'And why is she holding my wand?'

'A backup plan,' Damanjeet said quickly. 'In case this failed. Her blood contains latent magic—'

'*Failed?*' The word sliced the air between them. 'We don't need her. We have the gatekeeper. What's wrong with him?'

'He says he needs food.'

'Then feed him!' Eric snapped, ripping the wand from the woman's grip. He marched to the corner of the cellar, fixing Sean with a murderous glare as he passed. 'And when I told you to install cameras—' he reached up and yanked the hidden device from its spot with a snarl, '—it wasn't so you could spy on me.' His temples pulsed. With a ferocious yell, he hurled it at the wall. The camera exploded on impact, scattering shards of plastic across the floor.

Sean's face paled. 'I... I just thought if Josh tried to escape—'

'That's what Brother Thompson was for,' Eric said.

'Where is Tommo?' Damanjeet asked.

'Dead. Apparently.' The pang of regret he felt surprised Eric. Of all the Brothers, Tommo was the one he'd been closest to. His right-hand man. The only one he'd trusted to keep an eye on Josh. But, that wouldn't be a problem for much longer.

Damanjeet pointed to Charlie. 'And him?'

Eric chuckled darkly. 'Someone Josh tried to enlist to save Sophie. Works for the police. Speaking of which, check his pockets—make sure he's got nothing useful. And get rid of his phone.'

Damanjeet crouched over the old man, pulling a smashed phone from the pocket of his singed trousers. He turned it over, showing Eric the cracked screen. 'Looks like it's bricked.'

'Get rid of it anyway,' Eric muttered, bending to retrieve the book before pacing towards Sophie's cage.

She glared at him with the same defiance he'd always known. The same defiance burning in her since they were children.

'Did anyone touch you?' he asked softly.

She didn't answer, her hatred palpable.

'Did they?'

Her lip curled in a sneer.

He took that as a no.

Despite all her bravado, Eric had always been able to read her. Always knew. It had been that way ever since they were kids. Back when their mother had been too far gone to even lift her head, and her so-called boyfriends would start sniffing around Sophie. And Josh? Well, Josh had been useless.

Eric had protected her then. He was protecting her now. Why couldn't she see that? With power, he could keep her safe forever. No one would ever hurt her again. She'd come around. She had to. He'd make her see that. Eventually.

Eric crouched in front of her cage. His voice low, he said, 'I'm doing this for you.'

Her expression shifted, and she shuffled forward. Hope flickered in his chest. Was this it? Was she finally beginning to understand?

She spat in his face.

Eric hissed, rising to his feet and wiping the glob of saliva from his cheek. Shaking his head, he turned his back on her. She would see. In time, she would see.

With the book under his arm, he stared at the wand in his hand. He traced the surface of the quartz crystal. The faintest hint of red still marbled through it. The sight made him uncomfortably possessive. The wand was his. *His*! Knowing that it bore the blood of another felt like a desecration, sullying its very essence.

With a tight-lipped frown, he headed for the stairs. As Eric moved, something sharp dug into his thigh. He put his hand in his pocket and pulled out the offending article. The old man's business card. Scowling, he crumpled it and let it drop.

'Prepare the circle. I'm going to change. Feed the gatekeeper. Once I'm done, we'll start the ritual.' He cast a backwards glance at the assembled group. 'And for heaven's sake, clean yourselves up. We want to look our best for when our guest arrives.'

He caught sight of their nervous glances, the dawning realisation that they needed him. That they couldn't do this without him. But they'd tried to take what was rightfully his. They'd crossed a line. Now, as Eric considered the demon's gifts, the choice was clear. They had to be dealt with. Once he had his power, there would be no room for weakness or mercy.

No loose ends.

Chapter 36

'Charles?' Sachiko whispered, straining through the bars to prod him. He was breathing, that was a relief. But he was out cold. Ironic, really, that her earlier plans to sedate him in the lab had come to fruition at the worst possible moment.

Ash was watching her, his eyes flicking between her and Charles with keen interest. For someone who'd practically been unconscious not long ago, he appeared surprisingly well. She was convinced that his wink had meant his failure to maintain the gateway had been a ruse, but if his powers were truly waning, he might not be the asset she'd previously assumed. And that could be a problem.

'Who is he?' Sophie said, nodding.

'He's one of my patients. Charles Haynes. A good man. Used to be a detective.'

Sophie's eyes lit up, then dimmed. 'Is he going to be okay?'

'Yes. He fell on the vial. He's just sedated.'

'For how long?'

Sachiko frowned as she made the mental calculations. Rapid onset had been her main goal when developing the sedative, to ensure it took effect before Charles could fight back. Beyond that, its duration was an educated guess. Given the unknowns of the ex-detective's connection to the dagger, there was no way to predict how long it would hold.

'It's hard to say. It could be a few hours, maybe a day.'

Sophie's face fell. 'Oh.'

Ash shifted; the empty plate from his earlier meal scraped against the iron bars. 'It won't be long before he wakes.'

'What? How do you know?' Sachiko said.

'I can smell the toxin degrading. His body's breaking it down.'

'But...' Sachiko trailed off. Had she miscalculated the dose? Or had her suspicions about Charles been valid all along?

No. She wasn't about to go down that route again. They still didn't fully understand the implications of his connection to the dagger. It had already enhanced his eyesight, his hearing, his physical capabilities. The longer that link continued, the more these abilities might manifest. It was the reason for the check-ups. And if Charles woke up sooner, that would be a blessing; they needed a way out before those maniacs completed the ritual.

Especially now, after seeing those blackened veins spread across Eric's chest.

She'd recognised the demon rot immediately. A poison. Rarely an issue for witches, but it made ordinary humans dabbling in forbidden energies vulnerable.

Everything she'd ever read about it suggested that the most common form of exposure occurred after a demon marked the summoner as part of a pact. The bearer would become stronger and faster, depending on their natural abilities. But if that person was a magic wielder... well, that was a different story.

However, it wasn't the only way to become infected. It didn't always require a demon. Sometimes, mere exposure to the realm of fire and shadow could bring about the same corruption—whether through the reckless use of dark energy, a cursed artefact, or a forbidden spell. The result was always the same; the rot would infest their body and mind, poisoning them from the inside out until madness took hold. Twisting the subjects into hateful, rage-filled shells. Only the strongest of magic wielders could fight the spread, but they were few and far between.

There was no love lost between witches and those who employed the use of the dark energies. The latter were generally considered abominations, cursed. And rightly so. They were stronger and more powerful, capable of living for centuries undetected—if they could control their abilities. Yet, when the madness took hold, the destruction they could unleash made them a very real threat. Over the centuries, witches had taken it upon themselves to eradicate these beings. A bitter twist of fate, given that hunters often mistook witches for those who dabbled in the dark currents of the realm of fire and shadow.

'Is it true?' Sachiko asked Ash, her voice a near-whisper. 'That Eric will be able to summon the demon again?'

'Yes, it's true,' he said. 'I can sense his connection to it. He made a blood oath—it was the demon's only option.'

'The *demon's* only option?'

Ash gestured to the summoning circle. 'That sigil there—it's misaligned. Just enough to stop the demon from fully manifesting. If it hadn't been, Eric could have simply broken the perimeter and let it cross over. I doubt he even realises his mistake, but the demon would have. That's why it made a pact instead—why it marked him.

'The rot isn't just a curse, it's a tether. It will push Eric to fulfil his end of the bargain, drive him mad until he does. And if he fails, he'll die a slow, agonising death.'

Sophie sat up, alert. 'What? What are you talking about?'

Ash regarded her flatly. 'Your brother made a pact with a demon in exchange for power. The demon has poisoned him. Those markings on his flesh will spread. His mind will deteriorate, and he'll die. But not before he commits terrible acts.'

'So,' Sophie choked out, tears welling in her eyes, 'everything he's done—all those women—is because of the poison inside him?'

Ash weighed his response carefully. 'Most likely.'

Sachiko could tell from his guarded expression, from the way he watched Sophie, that he was trying to soften the truth. To convince her that her brother wasn't a complete monster. Would Sachiko want to know if it were her sister who'd committed such atrocities? Or would she prefer the comfort of a lie? Probably the lie.

Sophie buried her face in her hands, sobbing violently.

Lydia remained curled on her side, unresponsive save for the rise and fall of her chest, staring into nothingness. Trauma disassociation. Sachiko had seen it before. Many agents experienced PTSD—regardless of their training—due to delayed responses to attacks or connections with magical artefacts. She'd witnessed normal people brought in for memory realignment experience it, too. She always hoped the mind weavers could manage to heal their trauma so it wouldn't resurface in other ways.

'What do we do now?' Sachiko asked.

'We wait,' Ash said, his focus back on Charles.

Sachiko frowned. 'What is it?'

'What do you mean?'

'You keep looking at him. Can you sense something?'

Ash didn't answer right away. His eyes stayed on Charles, betraying nothing. 'His link to the realm of fire and shadow was... unexpected.'

Sachiko stiffened. '*Was* unexpected? You say that like you've met him before.'

'No. A mutual friend once told me about him.'

This raised even more questions, but that wasn't what she wanted to know. 'What else can you sense?'

Ash tilted his head slightly. 'That you have magic in your blood, but you can't access it.'

Sachiko's fingers twitched and she glanced away for a moment. She fidgeted with the hem of her lab coat before clearing her throat. 'I meant about Charles. His link to the demon realm?'

Ash's unblinking gaze met hers. 'He's bound to Kar'roc's Maw.'

'Yes, he's its master.'

He nodded. 'That makes sense.'

'Anything else? Can you sense whether...' She trailed off. Did she really want to voice her suspicions to a demon? What if Ash was lying? She didn't know him, and O.O.T.I.S had detained him for a reason.

If he wasn't a threat, wouldn't they have released him or transferred him to one of the more specialised holding facilities by now? Ash was clearly being uncooperative. Still, her doubts about Charles had plagued her for weeks, and if the gatekeeper could shed some light on the truth, maybe it was worth asking. What harm could it do?

'Whether...?' he prompted.

She squared her shoulders. 'Can you tell if there's a demonic presence inside him?'

Ash blinked, his expression unreadable. 'Was he aware you'd been taken?'

The question caught her off-guard. 'Sorry?'

'Charlie, was he aware that you'd been abducted from O.O.T.I.S headquarters?'

Charlie? She opened her mouth to answer, then closed it again. She frowned at Ash. 'No. I don't believe so.'

Maybe it *was* true that Charles and the gatekeeper shared a mutual friend.

Her lips thinned. Was the ex-detective more embroiled in the world of the supernatural than she'd been led to believe?

She pressed the thought to the back of her mind, something about the gatekeeper's question nagging at her. *Had* Charles known that she was missing?

Sachiko glanced down at him. Whatever had happened, he'd been through the wringer. Dust coated his skin, streaked grey in places. He'd lost his jacket somewhere along the line, and his shirt was shredded around his arms, stained with blood. If it wasn't for the shallow rise and fall of his chest, it would have been easy to think he was dead. The young man, Eric, had been in a similar state, his clothes in tatters. And what was it he'd said? Josh had tried to enlist Charles to save Sophie. So, no, he couldn't have known that she'd been taken prisoner.

Ash still hadn't answered her original query. Now, her nerves were shot and her patience wore thin. 'Is there a demonic entity possessing Charles' body or not?'

Ash quirked an eyebrow in what seemed like amusement. 'Why don't you ask him yourself? He's waking up.'

Chapter 37

Charlie became aware of voices, muffled and distant, struggling to rise above the thick fog of his mind. It felt like he'd been hit by a bulldozer.

He opened his eyes, wincing when his skull throbbed. Christ, what happened? He'd been coming down the stairs. Then—Josh had pushed him!

I TOLD YOU HE WAS HIDING SOMETHING. YOU DON'T LISTEN. I WOULD SAY IT WAS BECAUSE YOU ARE OLD AND HARD OF HEARING, BUT WE BOTH KNOW THAT'S ONLY HALF TRUE.

With a groan, he sat up. He was in a cage of some kind. No... a crate. A fucking dog crate. Jesus.

PATHETIC. THEY THINK THIS THING CAN HOLD ME?

The room slowly sharpened into focus. He recognised it from Tommo's memories—the cellar of the White Stag. Each breath he took misted in the freezing air; the chill had seeped all the way into the marrow. Numbly, he rubbed his hands together, staring straight ahead at the ritualistic circle carved into the concrete floor. The sight of it sent a wave of unease rolling through him. The patterns cut deep into the stone dragged his thoughts unwillingly back to the pages he still kept hidden at home, filled with the same unsettling symbols.

NOW THAT IS A PROPER CIRCLE. A MASTERPIECE COMPARED TO THE CRUDE BLOOD SPLATTERS YOU'VE CREATED. IT'S CLEAR WHY YOU HIDE THOSE PAGES AWAY. YOUR COMPLETE LACK OF ARTISTIC FLAIR MUST BE ONE OF MANY EMBARRASSMENTS YOU CARRY.

Worked though, didn't they?

A seething resentment unfurled from the darkest corners of his mind.

'Charles?'

The voice was familiar. 'Sachiko?'

'Are you okay?'

'Never better.'

He massaged the bridge of his nose, willing the throb in his head to subside. The smell of ammonia did nothing to ease the churning in his gut. And there was something else too, buried deep beneath the mouldering stench of rot and the reek of sweat. A copper tang that he'd become all too familiar with over the passing months: blood. A lot of it. Although he couldn't see it, the smell was throughout the cellar, like a phantom presence whispering of violent ends, and whose suffering was soaked into the very foundations.

He inhaled again. The frigid air sliced through his sinuses, slashing at his brain like razor blades.

Christ! Can't you do something about the pain?

YES. I CAN.

Nothing happened. The throbbing continued.

Well?

I DON'T WANT TO. YOU DESERVE TO SUFFER.

Charlie clenched his jaw. He turned his head, instantly regretting it when the movement stabbed him between his eyes. 'Sachiko, what're you doing here?'

As he said it, something in her expression changed. She looked almost disappointed.

'Damanjeet betrayed us. He let them in—the men who set off the explosions. He took me as a backup plan.'

'Backup plan?'

'Because of my blood.'

Blood? His brow creased. The implication of her words sank in. 'But you told me you weren't a witch?'

'I'm not. My powers are recessive.'

STOP PRATTLING. THE GATEKEEPER IS HERE!

Charlie adjusted his position and saw the blond young man staring at him with unnerving familiarity, much like when they'd first passed each other in the corridor at O.O.T.I.S headquarters. His green eyes shone in the dim light.

'It's a pleasure to meet you, Charlie,' the gatekeeper said.

'Do we know each other?'

'We have a mutual friend.'

'A mutual friend—Nick?'

'No, Jack.'

For a moment, Charlie couldn't place the name. Then it clicked. Jacqueline Fletcher, the girl with the dark eye makeup and silver-white hair. The sole survivor from the cemetery massacre.

'Jack Fletcher,' he said quietly.

'She spoke fondly of you. Said she regrets leaving the way she did.'

That took him aback. The last memory he had was of her bolting out of his office after he'd shown her the photo of Stephen. He didn't know how to respond.

'You're different to how she described you,' the gatekeeper said, a knowing look in his eyes.

Charlie shifted uncomfortably, aware that Sachiko was watching him.

OH... HE KNOWS.

He couldn't risk his secret being revealed. Couldn't let Sachiko learn the truth. He held his breath, waiting. But the gatekeeper said nothing more, only watched him, the shackles on his slim wrists jangling lightly with each subtle movement.

Charlie cleared his throat. 'What *is* this?' He gestured vaguely at the cellar, refusing to look at the ritualistic circle. 'What's happening? Where's Josh?'

'You mean Eric,' a female said.

Charlie blinked at her, his enhanced eyesight sharpening every detail. The delicate oval shape of her face, the deep brown of her eyes, the gentle slope of her nose, the high cheekbones... it was all eerily familiar. 'Sophie?'

Sophie froze mid-breath, her body going still. 'How did you know?'

'Josh wouldn't stop talking about you. You look like him,' he said, rubbing the back of his neck. A sharp ache flared in his bruised ribs and he winced. 'I told him I'd help him save you.' He paused, frustration creeping into his voice. 'But I don't get it. Why did he push me down the stairs?'

'That wasn't Josh.'

'I don't understand.'

'That was Eric, Josh's alter.'

'His what?

'His alter. He has Dissociative Identity Disorder. Split personalities. There used to be more, but now—ever since he got those black marks on his skin—it's just Eric.' Her voice caught on the name.

'Josh and Eric... are the same person?' Charlie frowned. 'Josh said Eric locked you in here?'

She nodded. 'It's the only way he knows how to control Josh. To use me against him.'

The thought that the very person he was trying to save Sophie from had been the one to take her in the first place made his head ache.

I'M NOT SURPRISED. YOUR BRAIN IS BROKEN.

'He wants to summon a demon,' Sachiko said, still looking at him oddly.

'A demon? Christ.' They had more than enough demons in the room already. 'Why?'

'It promised him power.'

'In exchange for—?'

'Breaching the veil.'

'*What?*' Charlie sat up suddenly, hissing a curse when his head hit the top of the crate. 'But won't that set off the, y'know, the demon apocalypse?'

Sachiko's gaze sharpened. 'The Brimstone Chorus.'

Charlie kept his expression neutral, willing his voice to stay even. 'Yeah, the Brimstone Chorus. Diane told me about it.'

Before Sachiko could ask any follow-up questions, the gatekeeper said, 'The breach required for that to happen would be too great for any normal person to achieve. The demon merely wishes to enter the human realm unimpeded.'

'Still, that doesn't sound like a good thing,' Charlie uttered.

'No. You'll probably all die. Horribly.'

I LIKE HIM.

'Jesus,' he breathed. 'Have we got a plan?'

Sachiko shook her head. 'No. I was going to sedate one of them while Ash—'

'Ash?'

She pointed to the gatekeeper—who gave him a half wave—then continued, 'While Ash was unshackled, but, the vial is gone.'

'Vial?' That smell! The sharp, acidic scent that had clung to her during their appointments over the past few weeks. That's what he'd landed on. A sedative.

Charlie fixed her with an accusing stare. She looked away, avoiding his eyes.

HA! I TOLD YOU. YOU SHOULD HAVE KILLED HER WHEN YOU HAD THE CHANCE.

Taking a moment to gather his thoughts, Charlie surveyed the dimly lit cellar. 'We need a new plan.'

His gaze swept over the assortment of makeshift weapons scattered around: disused tools, rusted chairs, and dented beer kegs. With what was at their disposal, he and the gatekeeper... he and *Ash* could easily overwhelm Eric and his lackeys.

WITH THOSE SHACKLES HE IS USELESS.

Can you break them?

The demon studied the warded metal through Charlie's eyes.

NO. THEY ARE DESIGNED TO DISABLE MAGICAL ENTITIES. THEY WOULD INHIBIT MY ABILITIES. WE NEED THE KEY.

Which I'm guessing Eric and his buddies have.

Charlie nodded at the restraints. 'I assume they need to take those off in order for the ritual to work?'

Ash replied, 'Yes.'

'So, we wait for them to come down, unshackle you, and then break out of our cages.'

Sophie gave a dry, empty laugh. 'And how are we supposed to do that?' She rattled the crate door to illustrate. 'Don't you think we'd have escaped by now if we could?'

Slipping his fingers through the bars, he tugged on the lock. He exaggerated the motion, jiggling the lock as if testing it, before pressing down hard on the shackle with his thumb. It snapped under the pressure.

'It's unlocked,' he announced. 'They must not have checked it properly when they put me in here.'

MY, MY. DECEPTION IS BECOMING SECOND NATURE TO YOU. YET SOMEHOW, I AM THE DESPICABLE ONE?

Sophie and Sachiko exchanged glances, their faces brightening with the realisation that they had a chance.

Charlie directed his attention to Ash. 'Once they take those things off of you, if I subdue Josh—I mean Eric—then you'll be free to help the others escape?'

The gatekeeper nodded.

'Then we just need to wait.'

Chapter 38

THIS WAS IT. IT was finally happening.

Eric rubbed at his collarbone, the raised blackened veins warm against his fingers. He was finally about to get everything the book promised him. Finally going to be something. Someone.

He stood before the grimy mirror. A chipped bowl of cold, bottled water sat on the warped MDF sideboard in front of him. Goose bumps pricked his flesh as he studied his reflection. Scratches marred his skin, the sting sharp whenever he touched them. He'd been lucky to come away with such minor injuries, though his ankle still lanced with pain when he put too much weight on it.

With a sigh, he splashed water onto his face; he winced when the cold bit into the scrapes. The dirt smeared and thinned beneath his fingers as he rubbed. He dipped his hands back into the bowl again, turning the water a murky brown. Lastly, he snatched up a small towel and wiped away the last traces of filth.

Once he was done, Eric tossed the towel on the floor and grabbed his robes. He shrugged them on, wincing when the thick material glanced off his tender ribs. His skin was black and blue in places. How he'd survived that collapse, he had no idea. Fate, perhaps. Yes, the universe's sign that he was on the right path.

After pulling his head through the hole, he adjusted the cowl, pushing it back just enough to see clearly. His lips curled into a smile and his brown eyes gleamed back at him through the dingy glass. *Much better.* Gently, he lifted the book.

He'd studied it so many times that the spine had become permanently bent. All those hours of research had changed the shape of the book, just as the book had changed him. It practically fell open to the right spot in his hands. The worn pages sighed beneath his fingers as he found the correct ritual. His eyes scanned the symbols, each one committed to memory.

Moving to the side, he grabbed the charcoal and carefully copied the mark he needed onto his forehead. It still amused him that the first time he'd attempted this, he'd drawn it in reverse. *How far I've come.* The whispers fluttered through his mind, full of excitement, full of promise. They urged him forward, praising him for doing so well.

Setting the charcoal down, he inspected the symbol on his forehead. It was good. He dipped his fingers into the water and wiped away a fleck of black, ensuring it was flawless.

After one last look at himself, Eric rolled his shoulders and reached for the wand. The copper warmed to his touch; the coiled wire nestled against his palm. The sharp-edged fronds of metal found the grooves they had made before, brushing against his skin like the familiar caress of a lover's kiss. He smiled.

He'd made his decision. His Brothers had to die for their treason. He was their leader—the whispers tickled at the back of his mind—no, their god. To try and steal his gifts for themselves, well, that was nothing short of blasphemy. They deserved to die. And he would honour their past service with a quick death. But not before he had claimed what was rightfully his. He wasn't an idiot.

Brushing his thumb over the red gem set into the copper, he limped from the room.

The floorboards creaked and groaned beneath his weight, and the smell of damp clung thickly to his nostrils. Frigid air nipped at his ankles, the movement of his robes creating a faint breeze there.

He paid no mind to the cracks in the walls or the graffiti left by past squatters. His focus was only on the stairs leading to the bar area.

As he descended, the hush of quiet conversation reached his ears. When he entered the disused bar, the muttering died away. His Brothers awaited him, clean. At least now they were vaguely presentable. He nodded in approval.

'Are you ready Brothers?' Eric commanded.

They murmured their agreement.

Adjusting the book in his grip, Eric carefully placed the wand in the pocket of his robes. 'I'll initiate the circle and summon Vamonthir. Once the demon is here, release the shackles on the gatekeeper. I'll compel it to open a gateway inside the circle, allowing Vamonthir to pass through.'

A spark of excitement crackled in the air between them.

Good. Let the idiots have their moment of happiness.

With a sharp gesture, he signalled for them to descend into the cellar. He let them go ahead; the last thing he needed was one of them pushing *him* down the stairs.

The Brothers moved into their positions around the ritualistic circle, fanning out a little to compensate for Tommo's absence.

Eric observed them, suppressing the loathing that crawled beneath his skin. He forced a smile and placed the book down in the spot where he'd take his place. His gaze flicked to the cluster of half-melted candles near the far wall. Dragging his injured leg along, Eric crossed the cellar and retrieved them, careful not to let any stray ribbons of wax soil his robes. There hadn't been time to deal with the blood stains on his cuffs, but at least they matched his attire.

One by one, he placed the candles along the circle's edge, meticulously spacing them out to prevent any mishaps. He still remembered the chaos when one had toppled, mid-ritual, its flame singeing Ben's robes. He couldn't risk the pub going up in smoke.

He took his time, striking each match with a snap and watching the flames catch, then flicker with a hungry glow. The soft hiss of the wick mingled with the faint scent of smoke. The cellar took on a new life, the dim light sharpening the Brothers' faces into mask-like expressions.

When the last candle was lit, he inspected the circle's unbroken line of light before stepping forward to adjust the owl skull, nudging it into perfect alignment. Satisfied that the preparations were flawless, he turned to Sean. 'Brother Adams, the keys.'

Sean tossed the set to him. He caught them mid-air.

From the cages, eyes filled with rapt attention watched his every move. As they should. They would bear witness to his ascension—if they were lucky.

He studied the prisoners, pondering his choice. If the Japanese woman was who he suspected, Daman's obsession with her ran deep. Perhaps he should choose her, give him a taste of his own medicine. But no, if Damanjeet were to become difficult, it could ruin everything.

The old man then? Would Vamonthir be satisfied with the shrivelled liver of an OAP? Probably not. And he certainly wasn't willing to jeopardise another summoning attempt with an offering that was likely to disappoint the demon.

His gaze settled on the girl—Lydia. Yes, she would do. She'd already lived longer than she should have. Proved more trouble than she was worth.

He limped towards her cage, picking the right key as he went. She didn't cower or flinch as she had before. Instead, she stared through him with a hollow, broken expression.

Something had happened to her while he was gone. He shot Sean an accusatory look. The man shrank a little, but said nothing. Not that it mattered; it wouldn't make a difference to her liver.

Eric slid the key into the padlock and twisted. It clicked open.

'Josh,' the old man said. 'Don't do this.'

'I'm afraid Josh isn't here right now,' Eric replied coldly, pulling open the door. 'Out.' He commanded.

The girl remained motionless, her vacant stare fixed on nothing.

'I said out!' Still, she didn't move.

Eric reached inside, grabbing her roughly by the arm, and dragged her out. She flinched, her eyes widening as if seeing him for the first time, breaking her free from her stupor.

'No!' she shrieked, desperately trying to wrench herself away and scrabble back into the safety of the cage.

But Eric held firm, his fingers tightening. Balanced on his weakened leg, he steadied himself against the crate before slamming his full weight down on her ankle. Her bone snapping made a gut-wrenching crunch sound. She screamed, collapsing forward. Ignoring the pain radiating through his own leg, he hauled her by her broken foot across the cellar.

She screamed in agony, nails ripping as she clawed at the floor, leaving bloody streaks. She made a horrid retching noise and sprayed bile across the concrete. Her hair dragged through it as he wrenched her forward.

Eric wrinkled his nose in disgust.

Sean came to his side. The sight of him towering over her sent her into a frenzy. She thrashed violently.

'Lydia, no!' Sophie screamed. 'Eric, don't do this. Please!'

'No, stop!' The cries of the other captives exploded through the cellar, their cage doors rattling in a discordant cacophony that filled the cramped space.

'Josh, don't!' Charlie yelled.

Eric dropped the girl's leg and pointed at the old man. 'I'm not Josh.'

'Eric, please,' Charlie corrected. 'Don't do this.'

Eric rolled his eyes.

Lydia spluttered, reaching desperately for something glinting in the dim light. Eric lunged forward, snatching it from her reach—a screwdriver. He exhaled sharply, shifting his weight to pin her hand beneath his shoe, pain knifing through his ankle. Her scream pierced the silence, drilling into his skull. 'Shut up!' he snarled, raising the screwdriver high.

A harsh crash rang out behind him, freezing him mid-swing.

His gaze snapped to Charlie's cage, its door now rattling wide open. The old man was scrambling out, glaring at Eric with a fury that sent a prickle down his spine.

'Stop him!' Eric barked.

Sean charged at Charlie.

'Charlie, no!' the gatekeeper's voice thundered, shaking the air.

'I won't stand by and watch her die...' Charlie shoved Sean aside and leapt at Eric.

Eric stumbled back, gripping the hilt of the screwdriver tighter as Damanjeet and Ben tackled the old man. But he fought with unnatural strength, launching them away with a snarl.

The whispers in Eric's mind swelled into a chaotic storm of fury and agitation, each one clashing against his thoughts with relentless intensity. He could barely hear Lydia's screams over the bedlam. She was dragging herself towards the stairs. He rushed to pull her back.

The cellar had descended into madness.

Sean scrambled to his feet, tackling the old man into a row of kegs; metal clanged violently against the walls. Charlie twisted, punching Sean hard enough to send him reeling.

'Charlie, stop! This wasn't the plan,' the Japanese woman yelled.

Plan?

Breathing hard through his teeth, Eric yanked Lydia backwards. This was all going to shit. If he drove the screwdriver through her brain, the old man wouldn't have anything left to fight for. Surely Damanjeet and Sean could take him down?

Flipping Lydia onto her back, Eric let out a snarl. Despite her broken ankle, she fought like a cornered animal, fists flying wildly in his direction. He kicked her injured leg again and she howled, her body curling in on itself.

He seized the moment, straddling her chest and pinning her arms beneath his knees. His fingers tangled in her hair, yanking her head back. The blade of the screwdriver gleamed in his hand, poised to strike.

A bellow to his right gave him no time to prepare as Charlie barrelled into him, sending him sprawling. Eric crashed onto a wooden crate filled with bottles. Glass shattered under his weight, splintered edges jabbing into his ribs and slicing his arms. Somehow, he kept his hold on the weapon.

This wasn't the first time he'd been attacked. A childhood of abuse had taught him how to roll with the impact, how to fall.

Where the hell were his Brothers?

The old man was on top of him now, his eyes wild, triggering a surge of panic that detonated through Eric's veins. He thrashed beneath Charlie's crushing grip, struggling to deal with his overpowering strength. Charlie trapped his wrist, pinning the hand that clutched the screwdriver to the floor and rendering it useless. Eric screamed out his frustration, bucking uselessly against the unyielding concrete. He clawed at Charlie's arm with his free hand, desperate to break the hold. The pressure on his ribs was crushing, each breath a hopeless, painful wheeze.

He couldn't fight. Couldn't think. He had to do something. Anything.

With a twist of his body, Eric drove his knee up into Charlie's groin.

Charlie grunted, his face contorting in pain. His grip on Eric's wrist slackened just enough for Eric to switch hands with the weapon. Sean lunged in, grabbing at the old man's shoulders, but Charlie threw his head back, connecting with Sean. The wet crunch of Sean's nose breaking sent him staggering away, blood spilling down his face. Charlie turned on Eric again, growling like a feral animal.

The whispers screamed at Eric to fight, but when he tried to drive his knee up again, Charlie anticipated it, shifting to absorb the blow into his thigh. Then the old man's hand found Eric's throat, clamping down with inhuman strength.

Eric's eyes bulged, his chest spasming, as he tried to drag in air that wouldn't come. His vision blurred as the pressure built in his head, like it was being squeezed from the inside. Panic erupted inside him, blood roaring in his ears. Every nerve in his body screamed for oxygen, but his strength was fading quickly, his hands weakening, as they clawed uselessly at Charlie's grip. His pulse thundered louder, the edges of his vision darkening as his lungs burned, aching for relief. Fear took over—all-consuming. He was suffocating.

A sudden explosive weight crashed down on him. Eric looked up to see Damanjeet had thrown himself onto Charlie's back. The added burden squeezed the last remnants of air from Eric's lungs, but it also freed his throat. He writhed, his hands pinned between Charlie's chest and his own, the screwdriver infuriatingly just out of reach. He tried to move his arm, but with so much weight on him, he could do little more than wriggle his head.

Charlie reared back, using his elbow to crack Damanjeet in the face. The move unpinned Eric's arms. Ben lunged at the man next, but Charlie lashed out, grabbing his leg and flinging him to the ground. With a furious glare, he turned back to Eric.

That's when Eric plunged the screwdriver into Charlie's eye.

Chapter 39

SACHIKO WATCHED THE BLADE of the screwdriver sink into Charles' eye—saw him freeze for an instant before toppling lifelessly to the floor—and screamed his name. Blood dribbled from the wound on his face, tracing red lines down his cheek. His one remaining eye stared right through her, glassy and unseeing.

She shook her head, tremors wracking her body, dread coiling through her like barbed wire, twisting her insides. Her heart raced, each beat lurching in time with her shallow breathing. Too fast. It was too fast. Every inhale felt like a vice tightening around her chest. The realisation hit her: she was going into shock.

Eric heaved Charles' legs off him and sat up.

It was over. All of it. Without Charles to help them escape while the gatekeeper was under the influence of the Bloodvein Wand, they didn't stand a chance.

Hot tears streaked down her face. No matter how hard she tried, she couldn't keep her gaze from returning to Charles. To that one vacant hazel eye.

'Fuck,' Eric muttered, climbing to his feet and brushing the dust from his red robes.

Lydia was dragging herself up the staircase but he spotted her. With an unintelligible growl, he grabbed her by the ankle and yanked her down again. She wailed, her shrieks becoming agonised gasps, as she thudded down each step. When she hit the concrete floor, Eric grabbed a fistful of her hair and slammed her head into the bottom step—once, twice, three times—until her cries cut off and her body went limp.

Sachiko covered her mouth, her every muscle trembling.

She could hear Sophie's muffled sobs beside her.

'Help me,' Eric snapped to the men.

Under his direction, they dragged Lydia's unconscious body across the cellar.

'And sort this mess out.' Eric gestured at the disarray—the metal chairs strewn across the concrete, some overturned, others wedged at odd angles. The toppled kegs. The shattered wooden crates and broken glass bottles, their lethal shards glinting in the quivering light. Three candles had fallen in the skirmish, their smouldering wicks casting reedy tendrils into the air.

And then there was Charles, his bloodied corpse just another part of the *mess*.

Damanjeet grabbed the ex-detective by the legs and, adjusting his stance, dragged his body across the cellar. Charles' face twisted grotesquely, the flesh contorting as it scraped against the rough concrete, the screwdriver quivering in his socket. There was something so obscene about it. Despite her medical training, despite seeing death countless times, Sachiko had not grown accustomed to its unyielding finality.

'*Yasuraka ni onemurikudasai*, Charles,' she whispered, wiping at her damp eyes. *Rest in peace, Charles.*

The sound of Eric's shuffling drew her attention. He bent to retrieve the shard of mirror, which sat askew from its designated symbol within the circle. Holding it up, he squinted at his reflection and swore, before carefully returning it to its rightful place.

'I'll be right back. And for the love of God, check the padlocks this time.' Eric half-stomped, half-shambled across the cellar, snatching the book up off the floor before heading up the stairs, leaving the others to handle the clean-up.

Damanjeet approached the cages one by one, rattling the padlocks. When he reached Sachiko, he gave her a long, measured look, his eyes tracking the tears rolling down her cheeks. His mouth twitched, his brow furrowed. He glanced at Charles' body before refocusing on her.

'I remember him. From this morning,' Damanjeet said, his voice tinged with suspicion. 'Why were you seeing him?'

The hint of jealousy beneath the words was unmistakable. A shiver of revulsion slithered across her skin. Sachiko lifted her chin and held his gaze, but remained silent.

He ran a hand down his beard and, with an almost imperceptible shake of his head, rattled the padlock with a sharp, frustrated jolt.

'Should we wait down here?' Ben asked, breaking the tension.

'Probably for the best,' Damanjeet said.

'I need to pee.'

'Then go pee. What am I, your mother?'

Ben glanced around nervously before disappearing up the stairs, leaving just Damanjeet and Sean. They stood in silence, Sean fixated on Lydia. He took a forward step.

'Don't touch her,' Damanjeet said tersely.

Sean rocked back on his feet, holding up his hands. 'Wasn't gonna.'

'I mean it. You've already had your fun. He'll lose his shit if you go near her again.'

'Yeah, well, it's not me he's pissed at.'

Damanjeet's eyes narrowed. 'What's that supposed to mean?'

'He's got a serious fucking grudge, and it's your fault.'

'My fault?'

Sean flicked him a look, lips curling. 'You started the ritual without him.'

'*You* were the one who tried to start it!'

'Yeah, yeah,' Sean scoffed. 'But you're the one who actually pulled the trigger. He's gonna fuck you up, you know that, right?'

'You don't know shit.'

Sean kept going. 'Don't I? He's not the same. He's lost it, man. You can see it in his eyes. Eric doesn't give a fuck about any of us. This is all about him. Him and her.' He jerked his chin at Sophie.

'He needs us.'

'Does he?'

'What the hell are you getting at?' Damanjeet closed the distance.

Sean threw up his hands in defence. 'Whoa, whoa, easy. I'm not saying shit. Just... watch your back.'

'Since when do you give a fuck about anyone but yourself?'

A small, derisive smile tugged at Sean's lips. 'Whatever. Do what you want.'

Their conversation died away. Without a word, they drifted to opposite ends of the cellar, busying themselves with restoring some order to the upheaval around them.

'Hey,' Sophie whispered. 'That guy... was he a friend?'

Sachiko flinched. She wanted to say yes, but the truth—her suspicions against Charles—sat like a lead weight in her gut. Now he was gone. Dead. Leaving behind his daughter, granddaughter... and Diane. How on earth was she supposed to tell Diane?

She inhaled deeply, then blew out the breath through clenched teeth. 'He was my patient. We had just finished our session when they came for Ash.'

'And he came to find you?'

'I think he came with your brother to find you. I don't think he even knew I was here.'

'What are we going to do?'

They both glanced at the remaining men, then at Ash. His expression was distant, his green eyes periodically flicking over to where Charles' body lay. No doubt he was thinking what Sachiko did, what they all likely were, that without Charles, there was no way out. For all her training, all her experience—everything she'd seen—she didn't expect to go out like this. Locked in a dog crate in some filthy, abandoned cellar.

The stairs creaked. Her heart leapt into her throat, but it was just Ben returning.

'All better?' Sean sneered.

'Fuck off. What's your problem?'

Sean smirked but didn't say anything else.

An anxious silence settled over the room, brittle and taut, ready to shatter at the slightest provocation.

The floorboards creaked again, louder this time.

This was it. Time had run out.

Chapter 40

Eric descended the stairs, the symbol meticulously redrawn on his forehead, the book clutched reverently against his chest. Everything leading up to this moment had been a complete and utter shit show. But now the old man was dead. Hopefully, there'd be no more surprises.

As his feet hit the concrete, the reek of captive fear flooded his senses. He breathed it in, allowing it to ground him in the present, steel him for what came next.

The whispers in his head urged him forward. After placing the LED lantern on the table, he stopped at the perimeter of the ritualistic circle and laid the book down on the concrete.

His Brothers were staring at him. He straightened, treating them to a broad grin. 'My knife,' he said.

He hadn't always enjoyed this part of the ritual—the *sacrificial reaping*, as he liked to call it—but now it offered a twisted sort of thrill. Adding some pomp and ceremony in the beginning had made it easier to stomach what came next. Especially after the first time.

What a disaster. He'd perforated the bowel during the initial incision. The stench of waste and the sight of the seeping brown sludge mixing with blood had made him puke all over himself. But that was a lifetime ago, the embarrassment nothing but a distant memory.

Now, watching the spark of life extinguish from someone's eyes, being in complete control of someone else's fate—it was intoxicating.

Damanjeet stepped forward, presenting him with a polished wooden box. Eric flipped open the lid and lifted the ornate knife from its plush-velvet insert. It had been among the items in the van when Josh's little courier job had gone tits up. Eric had been drawn to it instantly; the sleek stainless-steel blade, adorned with intricate engravings along the spine, was both elegant and menacing. The handle, crafted from dark wood and accented with brass, felt as if it had been sculpted just for his grip. It was breathtaking. As far as he knew, there wasn't anything particularly special about it, but when he'd first shown his Brothers they'd drooled over the weapon.

He held the blade flat across both palms. 'The sacrificial blade,' he intoned, bowing his head. His Brothers echoed him, their voices a quiet murmur, as they dipped their heads in veneration.

Damanjeet took the box away.

Eric approached Lydia's unconscious form and crouched beside her, turning her onto her back. A livid gash marred her forehead where he'd struck it against the step, blood crusted around the wound. With one hand gripping the blade, he pulled her top up, exposing her midriff. He trailed his fingers along her soft flesh, stopping just below her right breast, and prodded the curve of her ribs. In one smooth motion, he pushed the knife into her skin, making a clean cut through the layers of fat and muscle. Her eyes shot open; a bloodcurdling scream ripping from her throat. She bucked but his Brother's were there to help. They pinned her in place. Damanjeet bore down on her thighs to minimise her frenzied contortions while Ben restrained her arms.

Eric pressed the blade deeper into her abdomen, feeling the elastic resistance as he dragged it through her flesh, inch by inch. Blood pumped out across her stomach in a warm torrent. She convulsed violently, her screams petering out into tiny gasps. Her eyelids fluttered, then she collapsed into stillness. Eric sliced around her ribs with deliberate precision, clearing the path to her liver. He needed to get this right. Everything needed to be perfect.

Satisfied with his work, he placed the blade down. Taking a steadying breath, he forced his hands inside her cavity. The warmth of her blood engulfed his fingers as he pushed deeper, stretching skin and muscle apart with a squelch.

Beneath the light of the flames, he could see the organ, its dark surface glistening with the faint pulse of her fading heartbeat. With one hand still inside Lydia's body, Eric reached for the knife again. With quick, precise flicks, he severed the connective tissue surrounding the liver; ligaments, blood vessels, bile ducts. It all surrendered to the keen edge of the blade. He wrinkled his nose, setting the knife down once more, as the bitter stench of the seeping yellow bile mingled with the copper tang already flooding his nostrils. It caught at the back of his throat. He swallowed, tasting Lydia's final seconds of life—savouring them.

'From life we take, for power we give.'

His Brother's repeated his words, rising to take their places at the circle's perimeter.

Plunging his hands into Lydia's abdomen once more, he secured the liver and pulled. It gave with a wet, sucking noise as he pried it from her body. Slick and yielding, the heavy organ warmed his hands.

Moving to the circle, Eric bent to lay the organ down in its designated symbol, just as he had done countless times before. At the last moment, it slipped from his grasp, landing with a splat on the floor.

He cursed. What if he'd damaged it? What if Vamonthir didn't come? *No.* It would work this time. He could feel it. The whispers told him so. Told him he was close. That they were appreciative of his work. Proud, even. The thought gave him comfort, steadied his hand.

He wiped his bloodied palms on his robes and nodded to his Brothers.

Taking a deep breath, Eric raised his arms and began to chant. His Brothers joined him, their voices becoming one, melding into a resonant drone that reverberated through the cellar. He fixed his stare on the arcane symbols at his feet, willing them to respond.

The first flicker of blue light ignited his excitement. He reached into his pocket for the wand, pulled it free and cupped it like it was an extension of himself. The wire strands bit into his skin, reopening old wounds and drinking from him eagerly. He relished the pain, welcomed the burn, as his blood flowed into the quartz crystal and brightened the red feathery threads within it. The crimson gemstone blinked into life. Heat blossomed in the copper as the chanting grew stronger, warming his palm.

One by one the sigils blazed, bathing the cellar in an otherworldly blue glow. The pungent smell of burning flesh hit him, sharp and overpowering. Eric looked down, his voice steady as the smouldering organ charred and shrank before his eyes. A *whoosh* of energy surged up from the circle's centre, creating a shimmering wall at its edges.

Yes! It's happening!

The air crackled; the space within the circle shuddered. Reality warped and wavered like a mirage on the horizon... and then it split apart. The stench of sulphur filled the cellar as a torrent of dust erupted from the rift, swirling against the magical barrier, curling in on itself in great billowing torrents.

Eric's eyes widened. He glanced at his Brothers, awe painted on their faces.

This is it...

Slowly, the breach expanded. A low, resonant wail shuddered up through Eric's feet and quivered in his chest, squeezing the air from his lungs for a heartbeat.

A clawed hand crept up from the darkness, followed by an arm.

Desperation fuelled Eric's chants. He needed the rift to remain open. He was so close. Whether or not the words made a difference at this stage, he didn't know, but he wasn't about to leave it to chance. He raised his voice, letting it carry above the distant roar of the void.

The demon pushed through the gap, nostrils flaring, as its elongated face came into view. It surveyed the scene before it, the molten slits of its eyes narrowing with a predatory hunger. The skin around its cracked jaw shifted like burnt parchment, glowing faintly, as a menacing grin stretched across its face.

Eric dropped to his knees, prostrate before the creature. 'Vamonthir, warden of secrets, guardian of forbidden knowledge, I am but your lowly servant.' He heard the rustle of robes as his Brothers followed suit.

'Rise,' the demon commanded, its voice a deep, resonating growl.

Eric stood, feeling the electric pressure of the barrier holding the demon bristle against his skin.

'I have the gatekeeper.'

The demon nodded slowly, its razor-sharp teeth catching the dim light.

Eric continued, 'I will open a gateway to this realm for you. But first—'

A low snarl escaped the demon's mouth. 'First? You dare ask of me?'

He stood firm. 'We had a pact. A deal. A gateway in exchange for power.'

'Yet, there is no gateway.'

'First, bestow your gifts upon me.'

The demon's laughter rumbled through the cellar, shaking the very foundations. 'No. I have borne witness to your previous attempts.'

So, it'd been watching him. But how?

The whispers in his mind grew louder. Eric understood what they had been—*who*. Why had he not realised before?

The demon said, 'Open the gateway, and once I have laid foot in your realm, then I shall bestow the promised gifts upon you.'

Eric exhaled, feeling the unease radiating from his Brothers. They continued the chant, their voices wavering, as they cast nervous glances his way.

Frustrated, Eric turned the wand on the gatekeeper. What choice did he have?

'Bow,' he said.

The wand pulsed violently in his grip, his blood spreading farther through the quartz crystal, its spidery-red veins deepening, thickening with each greedy pull. A quiver shot up his arm turning his fingers numb. A shuddering gasp fell from his lips when Eric noticed how pale his hand had become. The wand was drinking him dry.

The gatekeeper bowed to the command.

The low, scraping rasp of Vamonthir's laughter wiped the triumphant grin from Eric's face. Confused, Eric pressed on. With one hand, he fished out the set of keys and crossed the cellar to unlock the gatekeeper's cage.

'Up,' he commanded. The gatekeeper obeyed, climbing out of the crate and standing tall.

Vamonthir's laughter intensified. It was freaking him out. Eric glanced back at it, the hairs on his neck standing on end. He'd expected the demon to be impressed, grateful even, but not amused.

What the hell was so funny? What was he missing?

Eric said, 'I'm going to release you, and you're going to open a gateway. Understand?'

'I understand,' the gatekeeper said without emotion.

Eric reached the key towards the shackles.

Vamonthir's laughter cut off abruptly. 'Stop.'

Eric froze in place. He looked back. 'Stop?'

'The gatekeeper is not under the influence of the Bloodvein Wand.'

'What? Of course he is...'

As Eric turned the gatekeeper jerked forward, smashing his forehead into Eric's nose. Pain exploded through his face. He yelled, reeling back, both wand and key slipping from his grasp as he checked his injured face. Blood gushed through his fingers.

Vamonthir's cackling resumed.

Pressing the sleeve of his robes to his bloodied nose, Eric snatched a breath and blinked through the blur of tears.

The fucker had been faking. If it weren't for Vamonthir's warning, Eric would have unshackled the gatekeeper and lost everything.

Why the hell wasn't this working? He'd staked everything on the Bloodvein Wand. The book had promised it had the power to control demons—that the fragment of Solomon's stone would bend them to the will of its wielder. But clearly, he was missing something.

It had his blood. What more did it need?

Blood. Blood was the issue.

What had Damanjeet said about a backup plan?

'Brother Bains, get the woman!' Eric shouted, the sharp pain in his shattered nose turning his voice raw. He dabbed at his face with his cuff again, and spat crimson onto the concrete.

The Japanese woman screamed in protest, struggling against Damanjeet's grip as he wrenched her out of the cage and dragged her to her feet.

Eric bent to retrieve the wand. 'You,' he said straightening, 'You can use the wand?'

She glared at him.

'Give me your hand.'

She refused to move, but Damanjeet forced her hand up.

Eric pressed the wand into her bloodied palm. She screeched as the copper pierced her flesh. Eric closed her hand around it.

'Tell him to bow,' he demanded.

The woman stared at him. 'No.'

'Tell him to bow,' he repeated, louder this time.

'No.' Her lips twisted into a smirk. 'What are you going to do? You've butchered everyone else. The only ones left now are the gatekeeper, your sister, and me. You need us.'

Eric bit back the frustration welling inside him. She was right.

Vamonthir's gaze bore down on him, watching, judging. The whispers slithered through his brain, hissing at him to take control, to assert his strength. He couldn't look weak. Not in front of the demon, not in front of his Brothers, and certainly not in front of this smart-mouthed little bitch. Even so, he couldn't kill either of them, and he wouldn't harm Sophie. This had all been for her, after all.

Well, mostly.

'Do it,' he hissed, getting up in the woman's face.

'Fuck you.'

Damanjeet's eyes widened, clearly shocked by her language.

'I might not be able to kill you,' Eric said, venom lacing his words. 'But that doesn't mean I can't hurt you. A lot.' He sensed Damanjeet tense. Was he going to be a problem?

'Hold her other hand out, Brother Bains,' Eric ordered.

'What?' he replied, warily.

'You heard me. Do it.'

Hesitating, Damanjeet glanced at the circle. Then, shying away from Vamonthir's presence, he did as instructed.

'No, Daman!' the woman yelled, struggling against his grip, trying to tear herself free. 'Daman please! Please don't let him do this.' But Damanjeet held her firm.

'Pass me the knife,' Eric said, holding out a hand expectantly.

Sean handed him the sacrificial blade. Eric pressed its point into her fingertip, drawing blood. Then, grasping her roughly by the wrist, he dug it under her nail.

She fought in place, every effort to yank her hand away thwarted by Damanjeet's steadfast grip. With a deft flick, Eric jerked the blade upward, ripping the nail free. She bit down hard. A strangled grunt escaped her as blood oozed from the wound.

'Eric, no!' Sophie's cries echoed around the cellar. 'Don't do this.'

He gritted his teeth, ignoring her pleas.

'Why?' A sob escaped his sister's lips. 'Why are you doing this?'

How could she ask him such a ridiculous question?

'For you, Sophie,' he said, his voice cutting above the woman's shrieks. 'For you, and for me. So that nobody can hurt us again.'

'Hurt us?' She shook her head. Lank strands of hair fell across her face as she gripped the bars. Her gaze flicked uneasily to the demon then back to Eric. 'Look at what you're doing. Look at what you've become. All those women... you killed all those women. You're worse than Mum ever was, worse than any of those men she brought home.' Her eyes shot back to the demon, the fear in them plain. 'That thing's changing you. It's turned you into a monster.'

Her words ploughed through his chest, forcing the breath from his lungs. He stood, momentarily dumbfounded, his mouth gaping like a fish.

'This isn't you. Please, Eric. Don't do this.'

'Worse than Mum?' he breathed, his voice low. 'I protected you, Sophie. Protected you when that coward Josh couldn't. Do you know how many times I was beaten to within an inch of my life? By her? By those men? Sophie, I almost died saving you. I'm just trying to keep you safe.'

'Eric, you're murdering people!'

'You don't understand.' He held up a hand to silence her. 'But you will.' Eric turned back to the Japanese woman. 'Tell the gatekeeper to bow.'

'Don't do this,' the woman pleaded through a bubble of spit and tears. 'The demon is lying to you. Once you release it, it will kill you. It will kill all of us.'

'You're wrong,' Eric spat. 'We made a pact. It marked me. Gave me its promise.' He touched his collarbone and the veins.

'That's not a promise. It's poisoning you. Forcing its will upon you, using your own desires, your own fear against you. That mark is demon rot. It's infecting your brain.'

No. She was lying, the whispers told him so. She just wanted him to remain weak. She worked for the Order. They hoarded all the gifts of the realm of fire and shadow. Kept them locked away from the rest of mankind so that nobody could challenge them. Could challenge their power. He knew what she was trying to do.

'Tell him to bow,' Eric repeated, his patience wearing thin.

'No, no,' she stammered, but her resistance slipped through her fingers like sand. She was strong, he'd give her that. But everyone broke eventually. There were far worse things than having your nails ripped out, and he should know. The things some of his mother's boyfriends had done to him...

He snatched her wrist, the blade gleaming as he brought it to her thumb.

'Do it.' The knife slid easily under her skin, peeling it away in one slow, deliberate motion.

The violent screams that erupted from her throat crashed inside his skull. It was like his brain was being struck with a hammer, an assault on his senses that fractured behind his eyes like shockwaves. He despised the sound, despised the way it shattered his thoughts and darkened his vision with flashes of black. But the whispers... the whispers cut through the noise, louder and stronger in the demon's presence, grounding him.

'Bow,' she cried, her voice cracking with a sob.

Eric felt it then—the surge of power, invisible but palpable, pressing through the air, as it flowed from the wand to the gatekeeper. He watched the creature try to resist, its green eyes bulging in exertion, but its body yielded, bowing before him.

'Excellent.' He knelt, plucking the key from the cold concrete. *Fool me once...*

His eyes fixed on the gatekeeper. He needed to be certain. In a swift, brutal arc, Eric slashed the blade across the woman's chest. The fabric of her lab coat split open, the skin beneath peeling apart.

She howled in agony, yet the gatekeeper didn't so much as flinch.

Eric laughed. Vamonthir laughed. Their voices became a singular, unsettling harmony that resonated through the cellar. After a moment, the sound faded, allowing a heavy silence to settle in its wake.

Vamonthir watched him with rapt interest, its eyes fixated on the key in his hand.

Eric slid it into the shackles and turned it. The click was followed by an immediate rush of adrenaline, sending goose bumps skittering across his skin. He lifted the heavy shackles from the gatekeeper's wrists, noting the creature's blank expression as it awaited further orders.

'Now, tell him to open the gateway.'

The woman clutched at her bleeding ribs, her face ashen beneath the sheen of sweat. Blood soaked into the torn fabric of her lab coat, staining it a deep crimson.

'No,' she said through clenched teeth. Her voice was thin. 'Do what you want to me, but I won't help you.'

The dark hum in Eric's mind urged him forward, urged him to make her suffer. Make her scream.

'Oh, you'll help me,' he cooed, his lips twisting into a cruel smile.

He brushed her cheek with the tip of the blade, just beneath her glasses. 'You'll do exactly what I say... or I'll ruin that pretty little face of yours. Bit. By. Bit.'

Chapter 41

WAKEY, WAKEY.

Charlie forced one eye open. The other was a searing inferno of pain.

YOU MIGHT WANT TO PULL THAT OUT.

Confused, he blinked. A stab of raw, burning agony exploded from his left eye socket.

I TOLD YOU.

What the hell happened?

YOU GOT STABBED IN THE EYE. WITH A SCREWDRIVER.

Am I dead?

HA! I WISH.

Charlie raised a shaky hand to his face, fingers brushing the screwdriver's handle. A torturous jolt shot through him, coursing fire through his body.

IF I WERE YOU, I'D USE ONE HAND TO PULL AND ONE HAND TO SECURE YOUR EYE IN PLACE. THERE'S NO WAY YOU COULD PULL OFF AN EYE PATCH.

Nausea churned in his gut as he gingerly pressed down either side of the screwdriver. Taking a breath, he yanked. The sensation of it sliding out was unbearable;

he barely kept from retching. As the screwdriver dropped to the ground, his eye began to heal—the tissue crawling and prickling, knitting itself back together. Light danced and flickered as his vision began to sharpen. Slowly, the pain subsided, his sight returning to full clarity.

Sachiko's scream echoed through the cellar, snapping him back to the chaos at hand.

Charlie pushed himself to his feet, taking in the scene—shadows, blood, and the unmistakable presence of a demon. For a moment he froze, locked in place by a paralysing sense of déjà vu. But this wasn't the creature from his nightmares, this was something much worse, something real. *Shit...*

They'd performed the summoning ritual.

Tearing his eyes from the wall of energy containing the demon, Charlie snarled. His gaze fell on Josh—Eric, whoever the hell he was. He sprinted forward, launching himself at the boy, sending them both pitching to the concrete. Sachiko's screech rang out as something flew from her hands and clattered against the floor. But the sound didn't register above the rage roaring in Charlie's veins as he began to pummel Eric, raining down blow after blow, each punch harder than the last. Every strike filled him with euphoria. Christ, but he wanted to kill him.

Ash unleashed a guttural bellow, breaking Charlie's obsession. The gatekeeper's body convulsed, muscles writhing and distorting, as he threw open his arms. His skin rippled, taking on a greenish hue, splitting apart only to reform into what looked like scales. His form became monstrous, huge, his skull warping and elongating, until he didn't resemble anything even remotely human. Christ, but the boy looked just like a...

DRAGON.

Charlie gaped, rage forgotten, his hand frozen inches from Eric's battered face.

Ash lashed out with savage force, his clawed hand sinking into one of the robed men's skulls, crushing it like rotten fruit. Clumps of brain matter and splintered shards of bone sprayed across the floor before the man's body crumpled in a heap. The others scrambled, but Ash's tail swept them off their feet, scattering them like ragdolls.

With its blood-slicked claws, the gatekeeper traced a series of complex symbols in the air, growling in a harsh, ancient language. A deep, vibrating hum shook the cellar walls, dislodging plaster and dust from above. Metal rattled violently as the cages quaked, the turmoil punctuated by the clatter and crash of objects toppling and smashing around them.

Within the circle the demon howled, thrashing violently, raking its talons against the invisible barrier in a spray of white sparks. A churning mass of shadow coiled around the creature's feet, rolling up the confines of its translucent prison like thick, choking smog. It seeped inwards, engulfing the demon in a dark, suffocating shroud. The blue symbols around the circle's perimeter guttered out, shattering the wall of energy. Smoke billowed across the concrete, snuffing out the candles. Near-darkness blanketed the cellar as silence fell. The dim, artificial glow of the lanterns barely cut through the gloom.

The demon was gone.

Ash, human once more, sank to his knees.

With a surge of strength, Eric twisted, throwing Charlie off with a frantic scream. Charlie scrambled to his feet, his breaths coming in ragged bursts as the boy tried to push himself up. Eric's screams were unintelligible, his bulging eyes locked on the space where the demon had been.

In one swift motion, Charlie grabbed a dented keg from the ground and swung it with brutal force, catching Eric in the side and knocking him back down. The cold metal quivered with the impact, sending satisfying shudders up his arms.

WHAT ARE YOU DOING? DON'T JUST STAND THERE! KILL HIM! The demon urged. PULVERISE HIM!

The sudden surge of unbridled anger flooded Charlie's senses. Distantly, he registered the robed men's shrieks, the gatekeeper's savage bellows, but they were nothing more than background noise—lost beneath the thunder of his pulse. Charlie glared at Eric who clutched at his ribs with a groan, unable to stand. He took a step closer to the young man, lifting the keg high above his head.

'*No*, Charles, stop!' Sachiko grabbed at his arms, pressing something hard against his skin. Her voice was desperate. 'Don't kill him.'

He shrugged her off, Chekonost's influence burning in his veins, but her words pierced through the haze of red, making him pause.

KILL HIM.

'No, Charles.'

HE DESERVES IT!

'He deserves it,' Charlie repeated, the words scraping through his insides and up his throat.

'Yes, but *you* don't.' She snatched at his arms again.

The keg remained in the air.

Chekonost's fury rode through him, eddying with his own. His muscles quivered with anticipation, aching to release, to feel Eric's skull resist as it caved beneath the weight of the steel in his hands. The boy had lied to him, betrayed him, just like everyone else. He was so fed up with being let down. His whole life he'd been hurt by those closest to him. Wasn't it his turn to finally get his own back?

The thought shocked him. *No. No, this isn't me...*

'If you kill him, there's no going back,' Sachiko pressed.

Charlie hesitated. Something caught at his flesh. His gaze flicked to the wand in her hands. Its jagged copper strands had cut his arm, causing a thin trail of red to appear. Realising that he was bleeding, Sachiko jerked the wand back. And that's when he noticed it, the red glint of a gemstone. It looked just like the fragment of Solomon's stone set into the pommel of Kar'roc's Maw... but smaller.

The sigil on his hand pulsed, a low, rhythmic thrum beneath his skin.

'Charles, if you kill him, you'll be a murderer.' Sachiko's words kept coming, her voice steady, tethering him to his humanity. 'Everything you've ever done, everything you've ever worked towards, everything you've taught Meghan, Evelyn—the difference between right and wrong—it'll all be gone. Don't become the monster you fear. Don't become like Stephen.'

Charlie's grip faltered, the weight suddenly too much to bear. The keg fell to the floor with a crash.

NO! WHAT ARE YOU DOING?

I'm not Stephen. I'm not a monster. I won't become what you want me to be. I refuse.

The demon bellowed inside his head, its prize slipping out of reach. YOU'LL BECOME WHAT YOU'RE DESTINED TO BE. YOU DON'T HAVE A CHOICE!

There's always a choice.

Straightening, Charlie turned to Sachiko, who looked him in his now-healed eye. She took a step back. He'd expected some kind of reaction, a gasp, a scream—anything but the sombre, almost sad expression she now wore on her bleeding face. Christ, her cheek...

Unsure of what to say, he broke eye contact.

Around them, the cellar was a bloodied mess. Ash stood naked, drenched in gore. Limbs and bodies lay scattered around him, their ceremonial robes shredded and stained wet with the aftermath of a violent end.

OOOH, A BUFFET. Charlie's stomach grumbled, making him feel instantly sick.

WELL, WHAT ARE YOU WAITING FOR? THIS IS OUR CHANCE.

Ash's piercing green eyes were on him, scrutinising. 'You appear to have a problem.'

Charlie traced the sigil. 'I do.'

'I can help,' Ash said, his voice calm. 'Our mutual friend Jack would want me to. But once the presence is gone, you'll return to how you were before. Any previous ailments, any illnesses, will come back.'

'You know about—?'

'I sense the demon inside you. Your link to the realm of fire and shadow is strong. Without a way to contain it, it *will* consume you.' He glanced at Charlie's sigil. 'Solomon's stone should've been enough to subdue it. Where is the Maw?'

'It got eaten.'

'Eaten?'

'By a hellhound.'

'Ah. That would explain it.' A small sigh escaped the gatekeeper's lips. 'There's another fragment here. Luckily for you.' Charlie's gaze found the wand again and Ash gave him a knowing smile.

'I'm going to open a gateway,' Ash said. 'If you want to rid yourself of the entity, now's the time. After that, I'm going home.' He looked pointedly at Sachiko.

Charlie frowned at her, unable to mask his surprise. 'You're just letting him go?'

Every appointment they'd had, Sachiko had followed protocol to the letter, never deviating from their routine. At first, he'd thought she was making allowances for his OCD, easing him into a sense of security so he'd comply without fuss. But over time, he'd realised it hadn't been entirely for him—she was simply a stickler for the rules. And the way she'd hounded him over her suspicions about Chekonost, setting endless little tests to catch him out...

Yet here she was, letting the gatekeeper walk away without a second thought. It didn't compute.

'What sense is there in keeping him here?' Sachiko said, her voice slightly breathless as she pressed her palm to her bloodied ribs. 'The Order contains and neutralises supernatural threats. If Ash returns to the realm of fire and shadow, he will no longer be a threat.'

'What about me?' Charlie said quietly. 'I lied to you.'

HURRY UP!

A small crease appeared between Sachiko's eyebrows. 'I know.'

'But if the gatekeeper... if Ash, can get rid of the demon's essence, then I'll be back to normal. There'll be no reason for the Order to keep harassing me.'

'Harassing?'

He gave her a flat look.

'I suppose they have been quite persistent,' she conceded. 'But after Stephen... It's not just the threat of you becoming a killer. It's what happens if you lose yourself, if you give in to Kar'roc's will. You have to understand why it was so vital for us to monitor you.

That thing—' She pointed to the smouldering outlines of the ritualistic circle. 'That was most likely a lesser demon. Too powerful to cross into our realm without help, but strong enough to cause some serious damage. But an archdemon? A whole realm of demons? They'd destroy us. Even the Order isn't equipped to deal with an invasion of that magnitude.'

Charlie gulped. His curse wasn't just his burden; it could wipe out the world. He'd been so concerned about Chekonost's effect on him, on becoming like Stephen, he'd never given any real thought to what his link to the realm of fire and shadow *really* meant. Christ, the demon had even told him as much.

HMPH.

He met Sachiko's eyes. 'But if I get rid of it...'

She nodded. 'Like Ash said, if you get rid of it, you'll be just a normal person again. We'll still need to check in on you occasionally, but other than that, you can live your life. Enjoy your retirement.'

He smiled despite himself.

URGH, CAN WE JUST GET ON WITH IT? I'm not exactly having the time of my life, either.

Ash gave him a nod, and for a second, Charlie wondered whether it was meant for him or for Chekonost.

'Why are you helping me?' Charlie asked the gatekeeper, suspicion edging into his voice.

'Believe it or not, I like your realm. I've spent millennia here. I've watched humanity thrive, watched you at your worst, your best. I have friends here.'

'Like Jack.'

'Yes, like Jack. I don't want to see this world destroyed. The demon realm is a harsh, volatile place. Only the strongest, the smartest, survive. If the veil were to fall, it'd be a bloodbath. It's happened before. Not with your realm, but with others.'

'But you want to leave?'

'It's not that I want to, it's that I have to. I can't remain a prisoner here any longer. There's nothing I can do this side of the veil, but on the other side, I might have a chance. Here, the Order will cage me. I'll always be a threat to them. I'll never be free. I'd rather fight day and night for my existence than live trapped within the walls of a cell.'

'I'll help you, for Jack, for your realm. But I only have enough energy to open one more gateway, so whether you choose to keep the presence within you is up to you, but this will be your only chance to rid yourself of it.'

Charlie scoffed, 'Why the hell would I want to keep it?'

RUDE.

When Ash let out a pained chuckle, Charlie saw what bad shape he was truly in.

'Give me your hand,' Ash said.

Charlie quirked an eyebrow.

'I need physical contact to draw out the entity.'

That made sense. He offered it. Ash clasped it firmly, pressing his thumb against the sigil.

'You'll feel some... discomfort. Whatever you do, don't break contact.'

Charlie nodded, but his nerves prickled at the word *discomfort*.

The gatekeeper rose to his full height, rolling his shoulders back with a low crack. His eyes blazed with an unnatural green glow, bathing his face in a sickly pallor. Then—his eyebrows drew together in confusion.

'What?' Charlie asked.

'It's your mind...' Ash hesitated.

'My mind?'

I KEEP TELLING YOU, YOUR MIND IS BROKEN.

'It's nothing to worry about. It seems you're slightly less susceptible to magic than most—nothing that would buy you more than a couple of seconds against a mental attack, but still unexpected.' He adjusted his stance, focus sharpening, and tightened his grip on Charlie's hand. 'Remember, don't break contact.'

Charlie felt it then—the surge of power—more potent than anything he'd ever experienced. It was like the time he'd touched one of the runes at O.O.T.I.S headquarters. But this was magnified tenfold, as though he'd stepped into a storm of raw, crackling electricity.

His whole body reacted to it, the sharp, static pressure making the hairs on his arms stand on end. His breath hitched; his muscles contorted in torturous spasms. The sigil on his hand flared with an intense burn. Charlie tried to cry out, but his throat constricted around the sound. With teeth gritted against the searing heat, he glanced down at his hand to see the raised scars glowing a vivid orange—the three dots to the left of the convex line pulsing like embers embedded into his flesh. The heat of it was unbearable, as though he was igniting from within.

Charlie swallowed back the pain, refusing to give in.

YES. YES! THIS IS FINALLY IT. I WOULD SAY IT HAS BEEN A PLEASURE, BUT IT HAS NOT. I WILL BE GLAD TO BE RID OF YOU, YOU DECREPIT, OLD MEAT SACK. MAY YOU DIE A SLOW AND AGONISING DEATH.

With the pain in his hand so excruciating, Charlie couldn't process the demon's taunts. The air around him pulsed, pressing down on his senses, thrumming in his ears. A steady *whoomph whoomph* beating in time with his pulse. Then, with a sound like tearing fabric, the air split open.

He jerked back, but the gatekeeper held him in place, eyes blazing with fierce green light. Sweat coated the young man's body, the ritual clearly taking a physical toll.

As Charlie glanced into the gaping void, a sulphuric stench hit him, thick and suffocating. Dust swirled out of the gateway, blanketing him and the gatekeeper in a fine layer of gritty brown. Though he couldn't see what existed in the depths, he shuddered. Somehow, in his bones, he *knew* what was on the other side—the sprawling, red landscape from his nightmares, and Kar'roc, waiting to rise up from the yawning earth like he did night after night.

Anxiety coiled tighter in his chest, forcing his hand into a trembling fist.

'It's okay, Charlie. Just don't let go.' Ash's words were strained, forced through gritted teeth.

THIS ISN'T RIGHT. WHY IS HE SO WEAK? IT SHOULD BE DONE BY NOW.

Charlie ignored the demon, trying to focus.

'This next part's going to smart a bit,' Ash added.

'Don't tell me—I'm going to feel a slight pinch?' Charlie chuckled, his voice a little too high-pitched.

The gatekeeper's smile was thin. 'Something like that. Ready?'

Charlie nodded, steeling himself. 'Ready.'

This was it—the moment he would get his life back. He could finally be free. Free of Chekonost; free of the dagger; free of the nightmares. Free to rebuild his life. The thought filled him with a sudden, euphoric hope. He could patch things up with his family... maybe even Diane. Find himself a little part-time job. The anticipation swelled in his chest, almost dizzyingly so.

Ash began to chant, each ancient syllable creating a deep, rhythmic hum in the air. The burn of the sigil amplified with brutal intensity, searing through Charlie's hand like molten metal, branding his skin from the inside out. He ground his teeth, biting down on the scream clawing at his throat.

The pain escalated, radiating up his arms and through his veins. He squeezed his eyes shut, jaw clenched tight, as the pressure coursed through his bones. It felt like he was caught in a vice that tightened with every beat of his heart. His body was on the verge of tearing itself apart. Every fibre of his being screamed for release, but he clung on, muscles spasming, forcing himself to hold firm.

DO NOT LET GO!

This was for his family—for Meggy, for Evie. This was to keep them safe. This was for everyone. He leant into the torment, refusing to give in.

The crushing pressure was in his head now. He could feel it squeezing his skull.

YES! YES!

The gatekeeper's chanting grew louder, a harsh mix of sounds that grated unnaturally against his ears.

Charlie opened his eyes.

The young man was in bad shape; beads of sweat dripped from his ashen brow, and his body had slumped. But his eyes still flared with that eerie, green light, burning with relentless focus as he forced the words from quivering lips.

THIS IS...

Chekonost's voice thinned, each word fading. The unbearable agony in Charlie's head began to ease, bit by bit.

It was working. By Christ, it was actually working!

Then, a shrill scream pierced the air.

Chapter 42

CHARLIE CRANED HIS NECK in time to see Eric on his feet, an elaborate blade glinting in his hand. The boy lunged for Sachiko, his eyes wide and wild, yanking her close. She thrashed, lashing out and clawing at his grip, but Eric held fast. Her shouts filled the cellar as she fought against him to no avail. Time slowed when Eric's gaze met Charlie's.

He raised the knife, its razor-sharp edge catching the light. Eric smiled, then brought it down in a swift arc.

Charlie was moving before his mind could catch up, his hand slipping from the gatekeeper's grip. As soon as the contact was broken, it was like he was plunged into a sea of sudden clarity. Everything became sharper; the world brighter, the sounds crisper.

NO! Chekonost bellowed. NO. NO. WHAT ARE YOU DOING?

But Charlie was already launching himself at Eric. He collided with the boy, sending all three of them crashing to the ground in a tangled heap. The blade never met its target, skittering harmlessly across the concrete.

Charlie didn't hesitate. He slammed his fist into Eric's head, knocking him out cold.

NO... WHAT HAVE YOU DONE? GET BACK TO THE GATEKEEPER!

Leaping to his feet, Charlie sprinted towards Ash. But it was too late. The young man gave him a pained expression before stepping through the gateway. It rippled, shimmering—and then, with a soft hiss, collapsed in on itself, vanishing into nothingness.

NOOO! Chekonost's roar thundered in his mind, shaking Charlie to his core.

Desperation overtook him. He launched at the spot where the gateway had been, grasping at the empty air, as if sheer force of will could rip it open again.

'No! No...' Charlie dropped to his knees, disbelief crashing into him like a fist to the gut. 'Please... no...'

His voice broke, trailing off into a shattered whisper. He'd acted on instinct, all else forgotten in that single, reckless moment. Sacrificed everything. And for what? For an O.O.T.I.S agent? A woman who cared more about a demonic artefact than she did him?

His chest tightened, the hopelessness giving way to something darker. Whether the emotion was his or Chekonost's, it didn't matter. It heaved within him, swelling and pitching like the rolling tide, drowning everything else.

Sachiko knew now. Knew about the demon. Knew about the powers he'd been trying to keep hidden. She'd lock him in a cell. He'd spend the rest of his life being prodded and poked like an animal. A prisoner.

No. She owed him. He'd saved her goddamned life.

His whole body quaked from the storm raging inside him. He turned slowly.

'Charles?' Sachiko's voice wavered.

He stepped forward, eyes locked on her.

SHE RUINED EVERYTHING. KILL THE BITCH!

He clenched his fists, knuckles white, breathing through his teeth.

It would be so easy to just wrap his hands around her throat and squeeze.

What did he have left now? Nothing. His one shot, gone. He'd thrown it all away. For her. For Sachiko. She was the only one who knew the truth. The only one who could still ruin him. The only loose end between him and freedom.

'Charles?' she whispered again, her voice pleading. When he didn't respond, she shuffled back, clutching her ribs. 'Are you okay?'

RIP HER APART!

He took another menacing step. His foot landed on something solid, freezing him. The wand lay beneath his shoe, red shards of light from the gemstone embedded in its copper hilt scattering across the floor.

'Josh, please. Please, no!' Sophie's wails pierced through the haze of his thoughts as she huddled over her brother, sobbing uncontrollably.

Charlie's gaze shifted, drawn to her. When had she escaped her cage?

It struck him as distantly odd that she would still care for him. After everything he'd done—keeping her prisoner, putting her through hell—here she was, weeping for him. She could've run. She should've run. But no... he was her brother. Her family.

His rage ebbed. He sank to his knees, the guilt of what he had almost done crashing down on him.

'Charles?' Sachiko's voice trembled.

He couldn't answer. Couldn't look at her. How close he'd come to killing her. The shame, the disgust. It made him sick. He covered his face with his hands, choking on a sob.

'I'm so sorry,' he whispered, his voice rough.

Sachiko placed a gentle hand on his back. They stayed like that for a moment while he collected himself, Sophie's muffled cries the only sounds breaking the silence.

Charlie inhaled deeply, then, squaring his shoulders, exhaled and looked up at Sachiko. 'What happens now?'

'I'm sorry, Charles, but I have to tell them. You're too much of a threat.'

'Please don't,' he said weakly.

'You heard what Ash said. We can't risk the demon's hold on you growing. What if you hurt someone?'

Like he'd almost hurt her; she may as well have said it aloud. The words cut through him, twisting in his chest, lodging between his ribs like a thousand blades.

'Please, I—I can't—' The sentence shrivelled on his lips. He knew she was right. What if he hurt his daughter? His granddaughter? Or worse... It didn't bear thinking about. His cheeks burned as tears welled in his eyes. 'Just—Please, let me say goodbye. Let me get things in order and say goodbye to Meggy and Evie. Just give me a week, Sachiko. Please.'

She shook her head, pain flickering across her face. 'Charles, I can't.'

'Please,' he whispered. 'I'm never going to see them again, am I?'

Her expression was stricken, but she stayed silent.

'Will you erase me from their memories?'

'No, no that's not—'

'Then what?' Bitterness sharpened his words. 'You'll tell them I went away? That I died? It makes the most sense, doesn't it? Nobody goes looking for a dead man.'

'Charles...'

'Just one week. One week and I'll turn myself in. I just want to see them one last time. Make sure they're looked after before I—' His voice cracked. 'Before they think I'm gone. Please Sachiko, I'm never going to see my granddaughter grow up. Give me this at least.'

Sachiko's eyes glistened with unshed tears. Her lips parted, then pressed into a thin line, as if she were fighting some unseen battle within herself. He could see the war play out in the tight set of her jaw, and the flicker of doubt creasing her brow. This went against everything she stood for—her work, her principles.

Her gaze dropped to the wand. She stared at it for a long moment, tension coiled tight in her frame. Then, finally, she exhaled, shoulders sinking ever so slightly. 'I can give you three days.'

His heart sank. 'That's not enough—'

'And that's only if you take the fragment of Solomon's stone with you. It will help you maintain control over the entity.' Her voice softened, 'I'm sorry, Charles. It's all I can offer. If you don't report back to headquarters in three days, O.O.T.I.S will find you. It will be worse for you if that happens.'

Part of him wanted to argue, to tell her he could disappear, slip through the cracks where no one could follow. The Order had no way of tracking him. But if he ran, it would be a life on the move, an endless purgatory. What would that be worth—trading one type of prison for another? Either way, he'd lose the chance to see his family again. If he turned himself in, maybe, just maybe, Jasmin might visit him, bring him a photo of Meggy or Evie. Maybe it wouldn't be so bad.

I WILL MAKE YOU SUFFER. YOU STOLE MY LIFE—NOW I'LL TEAR YOURS APART, PIECE BY PIECE. I WILL DESTROY EVERYTHING YOU LOVE. POISON EVERY THOUGHT, TAINT EVERY MEMORY, TURN EVERY MOMENT OF PEACE INTO AGONY. YOU WILL NEVER BE FREE OF ME. I WILL DRIVE YOU TO THE EDGE, UNTIL YOUR ONLY ESCAPE IS TO END YOUR WRETCHED EXISTENCE. AND AFTER, I WILL DRAG YOU BACK, JUST TO BREAK YOU ALL OVER AGAIN.

The demon's loathing surged through Charlie like a noxious, black tide, coursing through every fissure of his mind. He bent, retrieving the wand.

'Careful with it,' Sachiko warned, flinching as she curled her injured hand into a protective fist.

He gave her a nod of acknowledgement, tracing his thumb over the ruby-red gemstone. Immediately, Chekonost's presence recoiled, slithering back into the recesses of his consciousness. It lingered there, seething. With deliberate care, he pried the stone from its setting, the copper wires twisting and bending beneath his fingers.

YOU WILL RUE THE DAY—

I command you to be silent.

The demon's voice snuffed out like a candle.

Red light scattered across his palm as he turned the stone over. The sigil between his thumb and forefinger began to itch.

'It's in your head, isn't it?' Sachiko said. It wasn't really a question.

'Yes.'

'Since the dockyard?'

He nodded.

'All this time... Why didn't you just tell me?'

'Isn't it obvious?'

'But the danger...'

'I thought I could control it.' He raised a hand, forestalling her next question. 'I'm not Stephen. He was just its host. I'm it's master.'

'But without Kar'roc's Maw, without the magic bound to the stone itself, how have you managed for so long?'

'It's hard,' he admitted, his voice low. 'But now, with this,'—he closed his fist around the fragment of Solomon's stone—'it'll be easier.'

'Does it... talk to you?'

'It doesn't shut up.'

'Does—'

Charlie cut her off with a shake of his head. There was no time. In three days, she could interrogate him to her heart's desire. Right now, he just wanted to be back with his family. While he still had the chance.

'I promise, I'll answer all your questions, but I have to see them first—Meggy and Evie.'

She nodded, casting a wary glance at his clenched fist. 'Okay, Charles.'

He discarded the rest of the wand, wanting nothing more than to leave this godforsaken pub for good, but something nagged at the back of his mind.

'What about them?' He gestured at Sophie and... Josh? Yes, it had to be Josh. The boy was sitting now, clutching at his head, while his sister spoke to him in hushed tones. If Charlie had wanted to, he could have listened in on their conversation. Heard every word. But it felt like an intrusion. And he was tired. He just wanted to go home.

'I can't keep them here, not in my condition.' Sachiko moved her hand from her ribs, revealing the red bloom across her clothes. Between that and her face, she was a sorry state; her hands, her lab coat, nearly every part of her was smeared with stains of red, and a sickly sheen of sweat beaded on her skin. 'I'll do my best to convince them, but if they run, they run. At worst, they'll be picked up in a few days.'

'Won't the Order read your memories, find out what happened? Find out about me?'

Sachiko shook her head. 'My record is clean. They'll ask questions, but if Josh and Sophie cooperate, things should go smoothly. If they don't... They might resort to other methods to uncover the truth. But by then, you'll already be back in custody. If the full truth comes out, I might lose my job.' Her voice caught, and she met his eyes. 'But we'll see.'

'And what about Josh?'

'That's not up to me but he'll most likely be imprisoned, indefinitely. Especially given that his body has been infected.'

'But it was Eric who murdered those people. Him and his cult. The explosions—'

'I'm not saying it won't be complicated... Look, Charles, right now, if you want to go, go. With everything going on at headquarters—search and rescue, containment—it'll take time for them to deal with this. But not much. That's why I can only give you three days.'

Charlie nodded. 'What will you do?'

'I'll rest for a moment. Then I'll try to find a phone.' She glanced at the wreckage around them. 'The energy from the ritual may have fried all the electronics anyway. If nothing works, I'll walk until I find someone.'

He nodded at her stab wound. 'Are you sure you'll make it?'

She gave a short, breathy laugh, then winced. 'I knew you had a soft spot in there somewhere. I'll be fine for now. If the knife had hit anything vital, I wouldn't be standing here talking to you. It's nothing a few stitches and a course of antibiotics can't cure.'

'Sachiko... thank you.'

She gave a small, sad smile. 'Three days.'

'Three days,' he agreed.

As he turned to leave, the fragment of Solomon's stone gripped tightly in his hand, Sachiko called after him.

'Charles, keep it safe—not just for your own sake. We can't let it fall into the wrong hands again.'

He paused, glancing back. 'Don't worry, I won't let it out of my sight. Besides,' he said with a lopsided grin, 'after becoming master of the dagger and host to the demon, I'm pretty sure I couldn't mess things up any more, right?'

Sachiko's returning smile, as he made his way to the stairs, was faint. 'Goodbye, Charles.'

The rotten wood groaned beneath his weight. When he got to the top, he cast a final, concerned glance at Sachiko, but she just mouthed the word, *Go*. His gaze drifted to Sophie and Josh next, still huddled together. Josh gave a shy wave, dipping his head in what Charlie could only assume was thanks. He returned the gesture and walked through the door.

Three days. That's all he had.

Chapter 43

THE CELLAR DOOR SWUNG shut, rattling against its warped and splintered frame. Sachiko stared at it as Charles' footsteps faded. Blowing out an uneven breath through chattering teeth, she straightened. The motion pulled at the gash in her chest. She pressed her palm firmly against her ribs and winced, which sent a searing pain through her cheek.

'Sachiko?'

She turned at the sound of Sophie's voice. 'Yes?'

'Are you going to be alright?'

'I think so.'

Sophie and Josh shared a doubtful glance.

'W-what now?' Josh said, grimacing as he adjusted his stained robes. He was a mess. His nose was badly broken, the bridge misshapen and already swollen to nearly twice its normal size. The skin was stretched taut and shiny, and an angry purple-black bruise had spread beneath both eyes. Cuts marred his cheekbones, some shallow, others deeper, raw and glistening where the scabs had split open. A puffy and inflamed gash near his temple had produced a drying trail of reddish-brown down to his jaw.

Sachiko stiffened. She knew it wasn't fair—knew that Josh wasn't Eric, that he had no memory of what had happened. But knowing didn't change the way her stomach clenched when she looked at him. Same face. Same voice. Same eyes that had watched her writhe in agony while Eric had carved into her flesh. She forced herself to breathe, to push past it, but the memories clung to her—still too fresh to ignore.

'I'm going to look for a phone.' Avoiding his gaze, she flexed her numb fingers, willing some warmth into them.

'We'll come with you.'

Josh crossed the cellar, stopping to grab one of the lanterns as he went. Shadows writhed and twisted as the light swung in his grip, drawing Sachiko's attention to the bodies strewn across the concrete floor. Damanjeet's lifeless eyes stared through her, his mouth slightly agape, as if on the verge of speaking. But his final words, whatever they had been, were held in place forever by the cold grip of death.

'They weren't good people,' Josh said quietly, following her gaze.

It was true. Damanjeet hadn't been a good person. Everything she thought she knew about him had turned out to be a lie. The realisation left her feeling violated. They'd shared countless conversations, cups of coffee, and yet he'd blindsided her.

How could she have been so stupid? So naive? She'd been so fixated on exposing Charles that she hadn't seen the real threat bringing her lattes.

She brushed her fingers over the swollen cut on her cheek, flinching at the sharp sting the move elicited. She'd trusted Damanjeet, and it had nearly cost her her life. Now, she was trusting Charles. Regardless of what she'd promised him, could she really risk the fate of the world just so he could have a few days with his family? He'd lied to her. Lied about the demon with such conviction that she'd questioned her own instincts, doubted what she knew to be true. Could she afford to believe him again?

Setting her jaw, she gave Josh a sharp nod. 'Let's go. Maybe we can find some coats while we're at it.'

Josh hesitated, glancing at his sister. 'Soph?'

Sophie stood frozen, staring at Lydia's mutilated body. 'It's not right,' she whispered. 'It's not right, leaving her like this.'

Sachiko stepped beside her. 'No, it's not. But there's nothing we can do except leave everything to the authorities.'

'Can't we... bury her or something?'

Sachiko shook her head sadly. None of them were in any condition to dig a grave, and O.O.T.I.S wouldn't thank her for disturbing the bodies. 'When the authorities come, they'll be able to identify her, inform her family. At least they'll get some closure.'

Sophie sniffed, giving a reluctant nod. 'Yeah, that makes sense. It's just... sad. Her last moments were so awful.' She sobbed quietly. Josh put his arm around her shoulder and gave her a comforting squeeze. 'And the other women… I don't know what the men did with their bodies. They're probably out in the woods somewhere.'

'Don't worry, they'll be found,' Sachiko said.

'Shouldn't we cover her, at least?'

Josh held the lantern higher. Then, murmuring something under his breath, he limped over to one of the few tables that hadn't been overturned, grabbed a white sheet, and shuffled back to Lydia's body. Sophie stifled a gasp as Josh draped the sheet over the dead woman. The three of them stood in heavy silence, words feeling inadequate. After a few minutes, Josh cleared his throat, breaking the stillness. It was time to go.

Sachiko followed the pair up the creaking stairs, gripping a torch in one hand, and clutching what remained of the handrail with the other as if her life depended on it. She kept her footsteps slow and deliberate.

When they reached the ground floor, Sophie volunteered to search for coats and a phone.

Damp with sweat, Sachiko cast the torchlight around the bar area and shuffled over to one of the stools. She dropped onto the seat. The impact sent a fresh wave of pain through her body, and she groaned.

Josh sat beside her, folding in on himself. 'I d-didn't mean for any of this to happen,' he said, his voice barely above a whisper.

Sachiko glanced at him.

'I just wanted s-s-some extra cash. I didn't know what Eric was planning to do.'

Unsure of what to say, she let Josh speak. He fidgeted with his sleeve.

'It's my fault,' he continued, his voice breaking. 'All of it.' A single tear rolled down his cheek.

Before she could reply, the loud creak of footsteps interrupted them. Both of them turned towards the sound, Josh quickly wiped his face with his sleeve. Sophie appeared in the doorway, lantern light spilling around her, a bundle of coats in her arms.

'Found these,' she said with a frown, dropping the pile onto a nearby chair. 'No phones though.'

Sachiko forced a smile, grateful for the interruption. Slowly, she got up off the stool. Sophie handed her the thickest coat and helped her ease into it. Sachiko nodded gratefully, doing up the buttons and sliding her hands into the pockets. The layer was a big help against the biting cold.

'There are a few houses a c-couple of miles away,' Josh said, pulling his robes off and tossing them aside with disgust. He grabbed a padded black jacket and eased his arms into it. He visibly shook as he fumbled with the zip.

Sachiko weighed the odds. 'You'll both come with me?'

Sophie shot Josh a sharp look, her eyes bulging, but he didn't seem to notice as he replied, 'Yes.'

'Josh,' Sophie said, stepping forward, her gaze darting between her brother and Sachiko. 'That wasn't what we agreed.'

'I c-can't do it, Soph. I can't run.'

'But we—'

'You were right. There's s-something wrong with Eric. I didn't want to believe it, didn't want to believe that he could ever hurt you...'

'Josh, it's okay. We can start over. We can—'

'No, Soph.' He stepped forward and brushed a tear from her cheek. 'All I ever wanted was to keep you s-safe. I thought that's what he wanted, too. But after everything he's done... I can't risk it happening again. It should have been me protecting you, Sophie. I was always too w-weak. Too weak to stop you from getting hurt. I can help you now. I'm going to turn myself in. At the very least, it will keep you safe from him.'

Sophie's breath hitched, her fingers curling into fists at her sides. 'Josh, you don't have to do this.'

'Yes, I do.'

A strangled sob tore from her throat. 'Josh...'

'You knew you'd have to l-leave me behind eventually. At least this w-way you get to keep everything else.'

'I didn't mean it. I was scared. Those things I said... I don't want to leave you behind, Josh. I don't.'

'It's okay.' He reached for her hands and squeezed them tight. 'Let me do this for you, Soph. Let me k-keep you safe.'

A sobbing Sophie clung to Josh's hands, her grip desperate, as though letting go might shatter her completely. The fight drained from her in slow, shuddering breaths, her resistance crumbling before Sachiko's eyes.

Sachiko swallowed against the tightness in her throat. She gave them a few more minutes, then inhaled deeply and released it. 'We need to move.' She glanced at the door. The howling wind rattled the boarded-up glass panes. 'The sooner we get out of here, the better.'

A glacial breeze buffeted them as they stepped outside, whipping Sachiko's hair across her face. She shivered, inhaling the cold night air. The sharpness of it stung at her nostrils and raked down her lungs, but it was a welcome relief from the rancid stench of the pub.

Just beyond the carpark, the woods loomed. The skeletal branches swayed, their outlines sharp against the sky. They scratched at one another, knocking together like old bones, as the wind stirred through them. Moonlight pooled through the gaps, illuminating the ground with its dappled, silver sheen.

A narrow winding country road led away from the carpark. Sachiko was immensely grateful for it. The idea of navigating through the trees, where every shadow could hide a twisted root or concealed hole, filled her with a visceral dread. If she tripped and fell, she might never get up again.

Sophie shuffled where she stood, her breath pluming in the chill. 'Can you both manage the walk?'

'Yeah, I'll be okay.' Josh said. 'You?' He turned to Sachiko, holding up the lantern, blinding her. She shielded her eyes and he quickly lowered it again. 'S-sorry.'

'Yes, I should be fine. Which way?'

'We just have to follow the road that way,' Josh said, pointing. 'Keep going s-straight, and in a couple of miles, we'll come across some houses.'

Sachiko took a deep, quivering breath. Two miles. Just another two miles. She could do that. 'Lead the way.'

The two siblings went ahead of her, the light of Josh's lantern bobbing unevenly with each stumbling step, as they trudged down the road. Sachiko started walking, the torchlight cutting a narrow path in front of her, guiding her step by step into the night.

❧

'Oh my God! Chris, quickly, call an ambulance. Come in, come in!'

The woman ushered Sachiko into the house after Josh and Sophie. The wall of heat that hit her as she stepped over the threshold was a Godsend. She had no idea how long it had taken them to get there. It felt like hours. With all their injuries, they'd had to stop several times. At some point, the wound on her chest had opened up again, the blood soaking through the front of her coat. Every frigid gust made it feel like she was being stabbed all over again. By the time the house had come into view, she was shivering so violently, she could barely speak. Her fingers were so numb she couldn't feel them anymore.

Sachiko's teeth rattled as she tried to thank the stranger.

She couldn't even remember sitting, but at some point, a hot mug of tea had been pushed into her hands. She'd drained the contents to thaw her body.

'May I—' The pain cut her off and she hissed. She slumped into the seat. 'May I use your phone, please?'

'Of course! Of course you can.' The woman—Jess—took the empty mug from her and bustled out of the room. She returned a moment later with a cordless handset and passed it to Sachiko, who took it with quiet thanks. 'We'll give you all some privacy, won't we, Chris?'

'Oh, yep.'

As the man started to rise, Sachiko cleared her throat, catching Josh and Sophie's attention. She gave a subtle nod towards the door. No words were needed—the message was clear.

'I... uh, need the b-bathroom,' Josh mumbled, making an awkward attempt to stand.

Jess turned to her husband. 'Chris, love, why don't you show him where it is?' Then, offering Sophie a reassuring smile, she added, 'Come on, sweetheart. Let's go put the kettle on again and see if we can find some biscuits while we wait for the ambulance, yeah?'

Sophie hesitated for a second, her eyes flicking to Sachiko, but then she nodded and followed Jess into the kitchen.

The door clicked softly shut behind them, leaving Sachiko alone. She waited a second longer, then dialled.

After three rings a male answered, 'Good evening, you've reached the British Institute of Archives and Research. How can I assist you?'

'It's Doctor Sachiko Nakamura, IS-5642-23. I have a time-sensitive update on a particular collection.'

There was a brief silence, followed by a single beep. The male's tone subtly shifted. 'Good evening, Doctor Nakamura. Can you confirm if this collection requires immediate attention?'

Sachiko paused, her eyes flicking to the door. Her mind filled with images of the dead bodies they'd left behind. 'Yes. I've uncovered four... important documents regarding the White Stag file, with some additional materials that need immediate archival.'

'Understood.' There was a slight rustle on the other end of the line. 'Can you confirm if any of the items were compromised or exposed to third parties?'

'Yes, there was third party exposure.'

'I see.' The operative cleared his throat lightly. 'For our records, could you confirm the number of individuals present at the time of discovery, excluding yourself?'

Sachiko bit her lip. Three. Josh, Sophie and Charles.

Charles was a threat. She'd seen the unbridled hatred in his eyes, and how close he'd come to losing himself to the demon's will. But he'd pulled back from the brink, regained control—and with the fragment of Solomon's stone in his possession, he now had a means to keep it. He was about to lose everything, his family, his freedom. He deserved the chance to say goodbye.

'Two,' she said finally. 'A brother and sister in their early to mid-twenties, Josh and Sophie.'

'We'll dispatch a team for retrieval.'

'Thank you.'

'Is there anything else?'

'No, nothing else.'

'Very well. Stay safe, Doctor Nakamura. We'll take it from here.'

The line clicked off.

Three days. She could give Charles that.

Chapter 44

CHARLIE GRIPPED THE STEERING wheel, headlights cutting through the narrow, dark country lane, as memories of the White Stag churned in his head. He couldn't help but think of the last time he'd been there, with Debbie and Meghan. Back when things had made sense, before everything had gone wrong. The pub, like his life, was falling apart, its last days spent inhabited by psychos. He could relate.

Everything had gone to shit.

But he had three days. Sachiko had promised him that.

He kept a wary eye on the rear-view mirror. He needed to be careful; if the Corsa he drove had been reported stolen, he didn't want to spend his last days of freedom rotting in a police cell. The thought of DI Clarke strolling in to see him disgraced and behind bars was almost unbearable. One day into retirement and locked up? He'd never live it down.

For the umpteenth time, he pressed his fingers to his pocket, checking for the fragment of Solomon's stone. He'd need to find something secure to keep it in. It was his lifeline, the only barrier between him and the demon's corrosive influence.

There was so much to sort out. What would happen to his house? Who would take care of his fish, his plants? But beneath all the trivial worries lurked the real nightmare: how in the hell was he going to explain this to Meggy and Evie? Tell them he was moving? Travelling the world? No, they wouldn't buy it. He'd only just got the place put back together again, and he never travelled. *Christ.* Maybe he'd let O.O.T.I.S spin the lies. They were experts at that, after all.

The car shuddered and jerked as he drove. He shifted down a gear. He couldn't see Meggy and Evie like this—filthy, caked in dirt, blood, and God knew what else. No, he'd have to go home first, get cleaned up. Then maybe stop off at a supermarket, grab some of their favourite snacks and a Blu-ray for them to watch. He had to make the most of his time with them—assuming that Meggy would even let him through the front door. The memory of Evie's little face crumpling, the shock, the confusion, the fear, it still haunted him. And the damage he'd done to the kitchen. He wouldn't blame them if they never wanted to speak to him again.

He shook his doubts off, sitting a little taller. That was before; now, with the shard of Solomon's stone, he didn't have to worry about Chekonost getting out of hand.

IT IS NOT ME YOU SHOULD BE WORRYING ABOUT. JUST BECAUSE YOU'VE GOT THE STONE

DOESN'T MEAN YOUR LINK TO THE DEMON REALM HAS LESSENED.

Charlie flinched, just about keeping the steering wheel straight.

Quiet, he growled inwardly.

It was settled: home, supermarket, Meggy's house. He thought about the people he'd be leaving behind; his girls, his friends. The probability was, he might get to see Jasmin again, but Nick... Charlie should try and see him before turning himself in. Try to apologise, while he still could. He owed him that much.

Nick had taken a chance on him, and in return, he had torn his world apart. He knew he couldn't make things right, that no amount of sorrys would bring Nick's husband back, or return things to the way they'd been. But now that Nick was aware of the supernatural world, maybe Charlie could try and explain what had happened. Sure, his friend might hate him for it, but at least he'd know the truth.

Maybe if he'd told the truth from the start, he wouldn't be in this mess right now.

Rain speckled the windscreen as Charlie drove on.

Charlie shifted his grip on the shopping bags and knocked on the door of the small yellow-bricked terrace. His hand trembled slightly as he pulled it back. The knot in his gut tightened, nausea creeping in with every passing second.

What if they didn't answer? What if Meghan had already decided that she was done with him—that he'd ruined the last moment he'd ever have with them? The thought closed in around him, heavy and suffocating. His mouth went dry as he stared at the door, willing it to open, terrified of what he'd face if it did.

The door swung inwards, and there she was. Meghan, his little girl, eyes red-rimmed and swollen. His heart sank. Jesus, this was it, wasn't it? The moment she'd tell him to leave, that she couldn't trust him anymore.

But instead, his daughter crumpled, her face twisting with emotion. Before he could even speak, she burst into tears and threw herself into his arms.

The shopping tumbled to the ground as Charlie returned her hug. This wasn't the reaction he'd prepared for. He'd been ready for screaming, for the door slamming in his face, but this?

'Meggy?' He gently pulled back, searching her tear-streaked face, his voice uncertain. 'Meggy, what's wrong?'

'I thought—you were—dead,' she sobbed, her words choking out between gasps.

'*Dead*? Why would you think I was dead?'

'Charlie?' Jasmin appeared in the hallway, her expression shifting from shock to elation, then swiftly to guilt.

He barely had time to process her reaction before Evie came charging out of the door, her tiny frame slamming into him with enough force to almost knock him over.

'Grandad!' she cried, clinging on to him with her good arm.

Charlie blinked in confusion. 'What's going on?'

'The Archives,' Jasmin said. 'They were bombed today.'

He frowned. *Archives?* It dawned on him then: O.O.T.I.S headquarters.

'It's all over the news,' she added, a look of disbelief clouding her face.

'Grandad!' Evie tugged at his jacket. 'Where have you been? We couldn't find you.'

'I was at home,' he lied, the words thick on his tongue.

'No, you weren't,' Jasmin shot back, her voice tight. 'We checked.'

Shit.

'I *was* at the Archives,' he said, tracing the black ring on his little finger. 'But then I went home, pottered about for a bit, went for a run... to clear my head. Then I came straight here.' He gestured to the shopping on the ground. 'I did go to the shops first.'

Jasmin's eyes narrowed. 'We tried calling.'

'I, uh, I dropped my phone.' Charlie gave a helpless shrug. 'At the petrol station. Someone ran it over before I realised.'

Evie's eyes, full of worry, remained locked on him, but Meghan's became sceptical. 'Jas said your car was still in the Archives car park.'

Double shit.

'Nope, must've been someone else's,' he muttered, bending down to grab the shopping bags. He gestured for Evie to step inside, then quickly shut the door behind them, and slipped out of his shoes. The last thing he wanted was for them to start searching for his Audi.

Meghan followed him into the kitchen as he placed the bags on the counter. 'But it's all over the news. Come and see.'

He gave her a hesitant smile, then followed her into the living room.

Grabbing the remote, Meghan switched on the TV.

Sure enough, there was O.O.T.I.S headquarters. The building still mostly intact, surrounded by emergency service vehicles and cordoned off to the public. It was obviously a replay from earlier, given the daylight. The footage panned across to where the damage was most extensive. Thick black columns of smoke billowed out from gaping craters in the roof. A reporter was interviewing a young woman in a barista's apron. Charlie recognised the Déjà Brew logo partially obscured by the breaking-news banner scrolling across the bottom of the screen.

Meghan jabbed at the remote, turning up the volume.

'There was just this massive explosion,' the barista said, *'It shook the whole shop. We didn't know what had happened. Some of us went to see what was going on, and then there was another explosion.'*

Meghan shook her head, and turned off the screen. 'We thought...' her voice caught, 'We...'

'We thought you were there,' Jasmin finished for her.

'Look,' he said, turning his hands this way and that. 'I'm fine. See? Not a scratch.'

Evie flung herself at him again, her bottom lip quivering. 'I'm so glad you're okay. I'm sorry I made you angry.'

'Oh, Evie, no,' Charlie said softly, his chest constricting. 'It's me who's sorry. I never meant to scare you. What I did was wrong, so wrong. I lost my temper. But I wasn't angry at you, I could never be angry at you. I love you. I love you and your mum so very much.'

He gave her another quick hug, then glanced at Meghan feeling self-conscious and exposed. But before his daughter could respond, Jasmin cut in.

'We're glad you're okay, Charlie. But when I couldn't find you, couldn't reach you, I had to tell Meghan and Evie that you'd gone to the Archives to... research something.' Her eyes widened slightly.

'Yeah, I did.' He nodded, trying to keep up with the narrative. 'But like I said, I didn't stay long. Just... lucky, I guess.' He squeezed his fists together, the tension in the room pressing in on him. 'Let me just go sort the shopping.'

'I can help,' Evie said.

'No, no. I've got a couple of surprises for you and your mum and I don't want you to see. You just wait here and I'll be back in a minute. Jasmin can help.'

Jasmin followed him into the kitchen. He could feel her eyes boring into his back. She had questions. What he needed to decide now was just how many he would answer.

They emptied the contents of the bags in fragile silence.

'Tea?' Jasmin called out. When both Meghan and Evie responded in the affirmative, she flicked on the kettle, pressed the kitchen door shut, and rounded on Charlie. She grabbed him by the arm as if he might try and escape.

'Where in the hell were you, Charlie?'

'I told you—'

'Don't give me that bullshit. You were supposed to meet Sachiko for a check-up.'

Charlie looked down at her hand, then met her gaze. She released her grip.

'I did. I was there, okay? I was visiting Lily when the black alert sounded. I went...' He licked his lips, struggling to say his next words. It was now or never. Hell, it's not like she wouldn't find out soon anyway. 'I went to find the gatekeeper.'

'The gatekeeper? Why the fuck would you need to see him?'

'Because I needed his help.'

'*Help*? Charlie, what in God's name are you talking about?'

He flicked his eyes to the sigil marking his skin. Jasmin followed his gaze, her brow creasing. She opened her mouth to speak, her confusion plain, then clicked her jaw shut. Slowly, she turned to stare at the hole in the tiles where the whisky bottle had shattered, then faced him again. She paled.

'Oh God!' she whispered. 'No, Charlie, no...'

'Yes.'

'All this time?'

He hung his head.

'Charlie, what the fuck?' Her expression hardened. 'That thing's been inside you all this time?'

He nodded.

'Shit.' She stepped away from him. 'It explains everything—the mood swings, the erratic behaviour, your OCD getting worse, retirement... Debbie.'

'I—' He cleared his throat, forcing the words past the lump lodged there, 'I came back to say goodbye.'

'Goodbye? You're not planning to run, are you?'

'No!'

Relief flickered across her face. He wasn't sure how he felt about that.

'Charlie, after what that thing did to Stephen—'

'I'm not Stephen,' he said quietly.

'Charlie, that thing changes people. It chews them up and spits them out, leaving behind a fucking mess.'

'I'm not Stephen,' he repeated, more firmly this time. 'And I've got this.' He pulled the fragment of Solomon's stone from his pocket.

'What the fuck, Charlie? Where did you get that?'

'I'll explain everything, but not now.' He nodded at the door.

Jasmin's jaw ticked as she folded her arms across her chest. It was obvious she wasn't happy about his revelation, but she didn't push. 'Fine. Later.'

'I've got three days. Three days to get everything sorted.'

'What?' She paused. 'The Order knows?'

'Not yet.'

'You're turning yourself in?'

He nodded again. 'You're right, Jasmin. I can't stay like this forever. This thing's toxic. It's poisoning my brain. All it cares about is killing and mayhem. I missed my one shot to get rid of it, and now... now it's pissed. The stone helps, but it's not enough. I need the dagger. I need to banish this thing before it gets worse.'

The kettle's rumble died down as it clicked off. Jasmin gave him a stricken look. She knew there was more, but they couldn't hide in the kitchen forever.

'I... I... Jesus, Charlie. I'm so sorry.'

'Yeah. Tell me about it. I'm glad you're here.' He gave her a pointed look. 'To look after Meggy and Evie.'

Her face fell, tears glistening in the corner of her blue eyes.

'Right,' he said, turning back to the last few items of shopping still on the worktop. 'I said I have a surprise for my girls, so I'd better get it sorted. You okay to make the tea?'

She let out a quiet murmur of agreement. He didn't want to look at her, couldn't bear to see that scared, sad expression etched on her face anymore. Maybe he should've lied. Let her spend the next few days in blissful ignorance. But she would have found out soon enough. At least this way, she could be on guard. If things got worse, she could do something about it. About him. Chekonost had been a nightmare before, but now the thing was livid. It blamed him for being trapped inside his head. He blamed himself, too.

'I need a new mobile,' he said, trying to sound casual. 'I want to phone Alnus House, see if I can catch up with Nick before I go.'

He gazed out of the window at the uniform grey sky. He'd been so close. So close to having everything he wanted. Now he was on borrowed time.

Epilogue

THE CAR ROLLED TO a stop amongst the woodland. Archibald Morgan frowned at the derelict pub and extended out his senses. He detected no life within, save for the few rodents and insects scuttling about.

'Thank you, Oliver.'

The driver regarded him in the rear-view mirror and dipped his head respectfully before stepping out. The back door clicked open a moment later, and Archibald climbed from the vehicle, twigs snapping under foot. He pulled his overcoat tighter against the chill. Master Barrow had always instilled upon him that one should never deplete their central core of power. And given that he knew not what awaited him, squandering any amount of energy—even the trivial quantity required to stave off the cold—would be reckless.

A disturbance pulsed in the air around the building. A stirring of dark energies seeping into the world, reminiscent of the disruptions caused by summoning circles, but distinctly different. No, this was more than just a summoning circle; it was a gateway. A gatekeeper had been here—*had* being the crucial word. Long gone, if the eddies and ripples of the currents were any indication. He had seen this sort of thing before.

Archibald pressed down the unease rising within him.

It had taken him far too long to track down the Bloodvein Wand. Mundy Wilcoxson had let him down, allowing himself to be apprehended by the Order. Worse still, he had let the wand slip from his possession. Yet Archibald could still sense it in the pub, an artefact of immense power. The thought gave him hope.

'Wait here, Oliver.'

The aged driver nodded. Long ago, he would have insisted on accompanying Archibald, as was his duty. But the years had taken much from the man, not least the colour from his hair and the strength from his muscles. Without much in the way of protection, Oliver simply bowed and said, 'Very good, sir.'

Archibald smiled. 'Please, sit in the car, Oliver. The weather is inclement. Keep the engine running so that the warmth remains for my return.'

They both knew it was more for Oliver's benefit than his own, but dignity was worth preserving, especially when it was all one had left.

Archibald continued alone. The sounds of the woods closed in around him. The rustle of the bare branches scratched at the sky, and the brittle whisper of dead leaves and frost-crisped debris shifted underfoot. His pace quickened, excitement spurring his muscles into a near-jog.

The building was in disrepair; dingy white walls, cracked and peeling, with weather-worn patches of exposed brick crumbling from its broken façade as time slowly reclaimed it. The windows were boarded, the door too, though it hung ajar, bumping lightly against the frame where the breeze caught it.

Archibald seized the door in one gloved hand before it rebounded with another dull *thunk*. Inside, the darkness was absolute, and with the sun already lost beneath the horizon, no light filtered in from outside. He extended his senses again, pushing them deeper into the woods, picking up just Oliver's presence. Satisfied, he opened his palm, willing energy from his core, until a blue orb blazed into life. He stepped inside, allowing the door to continue its slow, uneven knocking.

A nauseating smell of decay greeted him, mingled with the dampness of the place. He wrinkled his nose.

The orb in his palm cast a blue glow across the walls, shadows stretching around him, as he navigated the building. He moved through the bar area, stepping over discarded bottles and litter scattered across the warped wooden floorboards, scanning for an access route below. He spotted a door at the back and made his way towards it.

Yes, he could have sent one of his employees to retrieve the wand, but with recent disasters—Banning's reckless blunder that cost him Kar'roc's Maw, and Mundy's utter incompetence that nearly lost him the Bloodvein Wand—he wasn't leaving anything to chance. With one segment of Solomon's stone within reach and another in his possession, he was edging ever closer to his goal of attaining all three pieces. He wouldn't let another mistake derail his plans. Not this time.

As he pushed open the door, he was immediately assaulted by the raw stench of human waste. Grimacing, he yanked a handkerchief from his pocket, pressed it to his nose, and descended the creaking stairs into the cellar. He stopped as his shoes met the concrete, pausing to survey the scene.

It was a bloody mess, literally. Three bodies dressed in red ceremonial robes lay bent and broken, amid pooling stains that looked almost black in the ethereal glow. One appeared to be missing a head, the others various limbs. A fourth lay concealed beneath a dingy white sheet.

Archibald raised his hand, drawing upon his power and feeding it out towards the mangled corpses. He read their state. Based on the lingering warmth, they couldn't have been killed more than a couple of hours ago. Withdrawing the energy inside, he walked over to the crude circle carved into the concrete.

He rolled his eyes. It was all wrong—the symbols, the structure. This circle had been crafted to summon a single, specific demon. It was inefficient. Novice work. Summoning beings from the realm of fire and shadow didn't require such a rigid, single-use design. It could never be repurposed for anything else. A wasted effort. Whoever had created it would have been better off using a crayon; at least then, the misaligned sigil could have been rectified.

Amateurs. Ordinary mortals caused so much destruction. They had no idea what they were doing.

His gaze landed on an old, tattered leather-bound book lying next to the circle, its cover splattered with gore. He crouched down to pick it up, noting the brittle binding as he straightened. Archibald released the sphere of light so it hovered above him. Under its glow, he wiped the spine clean.

Squinting at the faded Latin script, he read aloud with disdain, 'The Grimoire of Unholy Contracts and Spirits,' then flicked through the fragile, yellowed pages. They were filled with incantations and detailed illustrations, all of them worthless. With a sneer, he tossed the book back to the floor, where it landed with a heavy thud.

Vamonthir, warden of secrets.

He scoffed. Vamonthir was a liar, a fraud. Mistakenly documented as having the capacity to grant magical abilities in return for favours.

Folly. The demon had no more power to bestow such gifts than he did. And even if it had, the chances of it acting of its own volition to do so were almost zero. Demons didn't give anything unless they had to. He touched his neck where the blackened veins beneath his skin throbbed faintly.

He would know.

Enough distractions.

Following the rhythmic throb of the wand, he moved on from the circle, briefly taking in the empty cages lining the mouldering walls, and picked his way through the chaos. With the tip of his Oxford shoe, he nudged bits and pieces out of the way until something glinted amongst the wreckage.

He bent, pushing aside the final pieces of debris. The wand!

Cautiously, he grasped it by the hilt—positioning his fingers to avoid the copper strands that threatened to pierce his gloves—and turned it over in his hands.

The stone was gone! His jaw clenched, frustration boiling within him.

Did the Order have it? *No.* Taking a deep breath, he allowed his thoughts to clear. It was evident that O.O.T.I.S hadn't been here yet; the bodies, the book, the wand and the circle would all be gone by now. All traces of their presence scrubbed away as though they'd never existed in the first place.

The stone fragment must be hidden amongst the wreckage. He channelled more energy into the orb above him, illuminating the dim room.

Archibald searched for what felt like hours, but to no avail. The stone was gone. Lost. Examining the wand again, he changed his mind. The copper had been bent and warped, the stone forcibly removed. Someone had stolen it.

With a snarl, he hurled the useless artefact at the wall. It struck the brick with a loud clatter, chipping fragments of quartz off the wand before it fell into the shadows.

Why was this happening? It seemed like no matter what he did, no matter how meticulously he planned, something always went awry. For almost two centuries he had pursued the fragments of Solomon's stone. He couldn't afford to let them slip from his grasp again, not with the Brimstone Chorus already in motion. Time was running out.

He kicked the floor with a barely restrained growl. The action sent a crumpled piece of white card skittering in front of him. Narrowing his eyes, Archibald picked it up and smoothed it against his palm.

'Charlie Haynes.'

A laugh clawed its way up from the depths of his frustration. Charlie Haynes, master of Kar'roc's Maw, in the picture yet again.

Was it possible that the retired detective had taken the stone? But to what end? There were too many unanswered questions. Too many variables at play. What he needed was answers, and quickly. He tucked the creased business card into his pocket.

It was time to pay Mr Haynes a visit.

Thank You

Readers are the most powerful and effective tool when it comes to independent authors such as myself. So firstly, I would like to thank you for taking the time to read my book. Secondly, if you enjoyed it, I would be very grateful if you could leave a review (just a few words would do) on whichever platform you prefer.

Don't forget!
If you haven't already, you can get your **FREE** Brimstone Chorus starter story at elizabethjbrown.com

Acknowledgements

My Heartfelt Thanks:

To my husband and son, thank you for enabling me to pursue my dreams. Your unwavering support and endless patience mean more to me than words can say.

To the family and friends who listen to all my unhinged ideas and still haven't disowned me, you're the best.

To my amazing cover artist, Ben Baldwin, and my eagle-eyed editor, Kate Gallagher, your talents have helped shape this book into the best possible version of itself.

To my author friends—there are too many to name—but M. L. Rayner, Leigh Kenny, Daniel J. Barnes, Lee Mountford, Sammy Scott, and Andrew Van Wey are just a few of the people who have offered me guidance, support, friendship, and an endless supply of glitter (which, by the way, I'm still finding in my office).

To Kirsty Mills, who always agrees to lend me her

eyes. Don't worry, I won't let Chekonost anywhere near them.

To Carl Thompson, who let me use his father's name, Tommo, for one of my characters, even knowing his fate.

And finally, to my Advance Readers, thank you for all your time and effort. I appreciate it more than you know.

Thank you all for encouraging me.

Author Note

Please note that I am a British author and use UK English spelling and grammar throughout my books.

About the author

Elizabeth was born in Kent, England. This probably explains her obsession with tea and cake. She currently writes the Brimstone Chorus series, dark fantasy horror featuring demons, witches and a whole host of things that go bump in the night.

For more information about Elizabeth J. Brown and her books, please visit elizabethjbrown.com

Readers' group:
www.facebook.com/groups/1361685394266696
Facebook: @ElizabethJBrownAuthor
Twitter: @EJBrownAuthor
Instagram: @elizabethjbrownauthor

Books by Elizabeth J. Brown

www.ingramcontent.com/pod-product-compliance
Lightning Source LLC
Chambersburg PA
CBHW030919120726
47906CB00002B/402